THE
MEMOIRS OF A PHYSICIAN

THE ELIXIR OF LIFE

Dumas, Vol. Seven

ALEXANDRE DUMAS

THE MEMOIRS OF A PHYSICIAN

ILLUSTRATED WITH DRAWINGS ON WOOD BY
EMINENT FRENCH AND AMERICAN ARTISTS

Fredonia Books
Amsterdam, The Netherlands

The Memoirs of a Physician

by
Alexandre Dumas

ISBN 1-58963-213-3

Reprinted from the 1902 edition

Fredonia Books
Amsterdam, The Netherlands
http://www.fredoniabooks.com

MEMOIRS OF A PHYSICIAN.

CHAPTER I.

THE FIELD OF THE DEAD.

GREAT storms are always succeeded by calms, fearful in their very stillness, but bearing healing on their wings.

It was about two o'clock in the morning. The moon, wading between large white clouds which hovered over Paris, showed in strong relief, by her wan and sickly light, the inequalities of this sad spot, and the pits and holes in which so many of the fleeting crowd had found an untimely grave.

Here and there in the moonlight, which was obscured from time to time by the large white floating clouds we have mentioned, might be seen, on the margin of the slopes and in the ditches, heaps of corpses with disordered attire, stiffened limbs, livid and discolored faces, and hands stretched out in an attitude of terror or of prayer.

In the center of this place, a heavy, tainted smoke, emitted from the burning embers of the timber, contributed to give to the Place Louis XV. the appearance of a battle-field.

Over this bloody and desolate plain, flitted, with rapid and mysterious steps, shadowy figures, who stopped, looked stealthily round, bent down, and then fled. They were the robbers of the slain, attracted to their prey like vultures to the decaying carrion. They had not been able to rob the living, and they came to despoil the dead. Surprised at seeing themselves anticipated by their fellow-robbers, they might be seen escaping sullenly and fearfully at the sight of the tardy bayonets which menaced

them.   But the robber and the lazy watchman were not
the only persons moving among the long ranks of the
dead.

There were some there, with lanterns, who might have
been taken for curious lookers-on.   Sad lookers-on, alas !
for they were parents and anxious friends, whose children,
brothers, friends, or lovers had not returned home.   They
had come from great distances, for the dreadful news
had already spread over Paris like a hurricane, scattering
dismay and horror, and their anxiety had been quickly
changed into active search.   It was a sight perhaps more
dreadful to behold than the catastrophe itself.   Every expression was portrayed on these pale faces, from the
despair of those who discovered the corpse of the beloved
being, to the gloomy uncertainty of those who had
found nothing, and who cast an anxious and longing
glance toward the river, which flowed onward with a
monotonous murmur.

It was reported that many corpses had already been
thrown into the river by the provostry of Paris, who
wished to conceal the fearful number of deaths their
guilty imprudence had occasioned.

Then, when they had satiated their eyes with this fruitless spectacle, and standing ankle deep in the Seine, had
watched with anguished hearts its dark waters flow past
unburdened with the loved bodies of those whom they
sought, they proceeded, lantern in hand, to explore the
neighboring streets, where it was said many of the wounded
had dragged themselves, to seek for help, or at least to
flee from the scene of their sufferings.

When, unfortunately, they found among the dead the
object of their search—the lost and wept-for friend—then
cries succeeded to their heart-rending surprise, and their
sobs, rising from some new point of the bloody scene,
were responded to by other and distant sobs.

At times the place resounded with noises of a different
kind.   All at once a lantern falls and is broken—the living has fallen senseless on the dead, to embrace him for
the last time.

There are yet other noises in this vast cemetery. Some of the wounded, whose limbs have been broken by the fall, whose breast has been pierced by the sword, or crushed by the weight of the crowd, utters a hoarse cry, or groans forth a prayer, and then those who hope to find in the sufferer a friend, hastily approach, but retire when they do not recognize him.

In the meantime, at the extremity of the place, near the garden, a field-hospital is formed by the kindness and charity of the people. A young surgeon, known as such by the profusion of instruments which surround him, has the wounded men and women brought to him ; he bandages their wounds, and while he attends them, he speaks to them in words which rather express hatred for the cause than pity for the effect.

To his two robust assistants, who pass the sufferers in bloody review before him, he cries incessantly :

"The women of the people, the men of the people, first ! They can be easily recognized ; they are almost always more severely wounded, certainly always less richly dressed."

At these words, repeated after each dressing with a shrill monotony, a young man, torch in hand, is seeking among the dead, has twice already raised his head. From a large wound which furrows his forehead, a few drops of crimson blood are falling. One of his arms is supported by his coat, which he has buttoned over it ; and his countenance, covered with perspiration, betrays deep and absorbing emotion.

At these words of the surgeon, which he has heard as we have said for the second time, he raises his head, and looking sadly on the mutilated limbs which the operator seems almost to gloat over.

"Oh, sir," said he, " why do you make a choice among the victims ? "

"Because," replied the surgeon, raising his head at this interruption," because no one will care for the poor if I do not think of them, and the rich are always well looked after. Lower your lantern, and search upon the

ground : you will find a hundred poor people for one rich
or noble.   In this catastrophe, with a good fortune which
will in the end weary even Providence, the noble and the
rich have paid the tribute they generally pay—one in a
thousand."

The young man raised his torch to a level with his bleeding forehead.

"Then I am that one," said he, without the least anger ;
"I, a gentleman, lost among so many others in the crowd,
wounded in the forehead by a horse's hoof, and my left
arm broken by falling into a pit.   You say that the noble
and the rich are sought after and cared for ; you see
plainly, however, that my wounds are not yet dressed."

"You have your hotel—your physician.   Return home,
since you can walk."

"I do not ask for your cares, sir ; I seek my sister, a
beautiful young girl of sixteen—killed, probably, alas !
though she is not of the people.   She wore a white dress,
and a chain with a cross round her neck.   Though she has
her hotel and her physician, answer me, for pity's sake,
sir, have you seen her whom I seek ? "

"Sir," said the young surgeon, with a feverish vehemence which showed that the ideas he expressed had long
boiled within his breast, "sir, Humanity is my guide.   It
is to her service I devote myself ; and when I leave the
noble on their bed of death to assist the suffering people,
I obey the true laws of Humanity, who is my goddess.   All
this day's misfortunes have been caused by you.   They arose
from your abuses, from your usurpations.   Therefore,
bear the consequences.   No, sir, I have not seen your sister."

And after this harsh apostrophe, the operator returned
to his task.   A poor woman had just been brought to him,
whose two legs were fractured by a carriage.

"See !" he exclaimed, calling after Philip, who was
rushing away, "see ! do the poor bring their carriages to
the public festivals to break the legs of the rich ? "

Philip, who belonged to that class of the young nobility
from which sprung the Lafayettes and Lameths, had often
professed the same maxims which terrified him in the

mouth of this young man, and their application recoiled upon him like a judgment.   His heart bursting with grief, he left the neighborhood of the hospital and continued his sad search.   He had not proceeded many steps, when, carried away by his grief, he could not repress a heartrending cry of :

"Andrée ! Andrée ! "

At that moment there passed by him, walking with hasty steps, a man already advanced in years, dressed in a gray cloth coat and milled stockings, his right hand resting on a stick, while with the left he held one of those lanterns made of a candle inclosed in oiled paper.

Hearing Philip's cry of grief, he guessed what he must be suffering, and murmured :

" Poor young man ! "

But as he seemed to have come for the same purpose as himself, he passed on.   Then all at once, as if he reproached himself for having passed unheeding by so much suffering, without attempting to console it :

"Sir," said he, " pardon me for mingling my grief with yours ; but those who are struck by the same blow should lean on each other for support.   Besides, you may be useful to me.   You have already sought for a considerable time, I see, as your light is nearly extinguished, and you must, therefore, be acquainted with the most fatal localities of the place."

" Oh, yes, sir, I know them."

" Well, I also seek some one."

" Then look first in the great ditch ; you will find more than fifty corpses there."

" Fifty !   Just Heaven !   So many victims killed at a fête ! "

" So many !   Sir, I have already looked at a thousand faces, and have not yet found my sister."

" Your sister ? "

" It was yonder, in that direction, that she was.   I lost her near the bench.   I have found the place since, but no trace of her was visible.   I am about to recommence the search, beginning with the bastion."

"To which side did the crowd rush, sir?"

"Toward the new buildings, in the Rue de la Madeleine."

"Then it must have been toward this side?"

"Yes, and I therefore searched on this side first; but there were dreadful scenes here. Besides, although the tide flowed in that direction, a poor, bewildered woman soon loses her senses in such a scene; she knows not whither she goes, and endeavors to escape in the first direction that presents itself."

"Sir, it is not probable that she would struggle against the current. I am about to search the street on this side; come with me, and, both together, we may perhaps find——"

"And whom do you seek? Your son?" asked Philip, timidly.

"No, sir; but a child whom I had almost adopted."

"And you allowed him to come alone?"

"Oh! he is a young man of eighteen or nineteen. He is master of his own actions; and as he wished to come, I could not hinder him. Besides, we were far from expecting this horrible catastrophe! But your light is going out."

"Yes, sir; I see it."

"Come with me; I will light you."

"Thank you—you are very good; but I fear I shall incommode you."

"Oh, do not fear, since I must have searched for myself. The poor child generally came home very punctually," continued the old man, proceeding in the direction of the streets, "but this evening I felt a sort of foreboding, I waited up for him; it was already eleven o'clock, when my wife heard of the misfortunes of this fête from a neighbor. I waited for two hours longer, still hoping that he would return. Then, as he did not appear, I thought it would be base and cowardly in me to sleep without having news of him."

"Then we are going toward the houses?" asked the young man.

" Yes ; you said the crowd must have rushed to this side, and it certainly has done so. The unfortunate boy had doubtless been carried this way also. He is from the provinces, and he is alike ignorant of the usages and the localities of this great town. Probably this was the first time he had ever been in the Place Louis XV."

"Alas ! my sister is also from the provinces, sir."

" What a fearful sight," said the old man, turning away from a group of corpses clasped together in death.

"Yet it is there we must look," replied the young man, resolutely holding his light over the heap of dead.

" Oh ! I shudder to look at it, for I am a simple and unsophisticated man, and the sight of destruction causes in me an unconquerable horror."

"I had this same horror ; but this evening I have served my apprenticeship to butchery and death ! Hold, here is a young man of about eighteen ; he has been suffocated, for I see no wounds. Is it he whom you seek ?"

The old man made an effort, and held his lantern close to the body.

"No, sir," said he, "no ; my child is younger, has black hair, and pale complexion."

" Alas ! all are pale to-night," replied Philip.

"Oh, see !" said the old man, "here we are, at the foot of the Garde Meuble. Look at these tokens of the struggle. The blood upon the walls, these shreds of garments upon the iron bars, these torn dresses on the points of the railing."

"It was here—it was certainly here," murmured Philip.

" What sufferings !"

" Oh, heavens !"

" What ?"

" Something white under these corpses ! My sister had a white dress on. Lend me your lamp, sir, I beseech you."

In fact, Philip had seen and snatched a shred of white cloth. He let go his hold, having but one hand to take the lamp.

"It is a fragment of a woman's dress, held firmly in a
young man's hand," cried he—"of a white dress like my
sister's. Oh! Andrée! Andrée!" And the young man
uttered heartrending sobs. The old man now approached.

"It is he!" exclaimed he, opening his arms.

This exclamation attracted the young man's attention.

"Gilbert!" exclaimed Philip in his turn.

"You know Gilbert, sir?"

"Is it Gilbert whom you seek?"

These two questions were uttered simultaneously. The
old man seized Gilbert's hand; it was as cold as death.
Philip opened the young man's dress, pushed aside the
shirt, and placed his hand upon his heart.

"Poor Gilbert!" said he.

"My dear child!" sobbed the old man.

"He breathes, he lives! He lives, I tell you!" exclaimed Philip.

"Oh! do you think so?"

"I am certain of it—his heart beats."

"It is true," replied the old man. "Help! help!
There is a surgeon yonder."

"Oh, let us succor him ourselves, sir ;-just now I asked
that man for help, and he refused me."

"He must help my child!" cried the old man, indignantly. "He must. Assist me, sir, to carry Gilbert
to him."

"I have only one arm, but it is at your service, sir,"
replied Philip.

"And I, old as I am, feel strong again! Come!"

The old man seized Gilbert by the shoulders ; the young
man took his two feet under his right arm, and in this
manner they advanced toward the group in the midst of
which the surgeon was operating.

"Help! help!" cried the old man.

"The men of the people first! The men of the people
first!" replied the surgeon, faithful to his maxim, and
sure each time he replied thus of exciting a murmur of
applause among the group which surrounded him.

"It is a man of the people whom I am bringing," replied the old man, with vehemence, but beginning to share in the general admiration which the firm and resolute tone of the young operator excited.

"After the women, then," said the surgeon; "men have more strength to support pain than women."

"A simple bleeding will suffice, sir," replied the old man.

"Oh! it is you again, my young nobleman?" said the surgeon, perceiving Philip before he saw the old man.

Philip did not reply. The old man thought that these words were addressed to him.

"I am not a nobleman," said he; "I am a man of the people; my name is Jean Jacques Rousseau."

The doctor gave a cry of astonishment, and making an imperative gesture.

"Give place," said he, "to the man of nature! Make room for the emancipator of the human race! Place for the citizen of Geneva!"

"Thanks, sir," said Rousseau, "thanks!"

"Has any accident happened to you?" asked the young doctor.

"Not to me, but to this poor child. See."

"Ah! you too," cried the physician, "you, too, like myself, represent the cause of humanity."

Rousseau, deeply moved by this unexpected triumph, could only stammer forth some almost unintelligible words. Philip, dumb with astonishment at finding himself in the presence of the philosopher whom he admired so highly, remained standing apart. Those who stood around assisted Rousseau to lay the fainting Gilbert upon the table. It was at this moment that the old man glanced at the person whose assistance he was imploring. He was a young man about Gilbert's age, but his features presented no appearance of youth. His sallow complexion was withered like that of an old man; his heavy and drooping eyelids covered an eye like that a serpent's, and his mouth was distorted as if in an epileptic fit.

His sleeves turned back to the elbow, his arms covered

with blood, surrounded by lifeless and bleeding limbs, he seemed more like an executioner at work, and glorying in his task, than a physician accomplishing his sad and holy mission.

Nevertheless, Rousseau's name seemed to have had so much influence over him as to cause him to lay aside for an instant his usual brutality ; he gently opened Gilbert's sleeve, tied a band of linen round his arm, and opened the vein.

The blood flowed at first drop by drop, but after some moments the pure and generous current of youth spouted forth freely.

" Ha ! we shall save him," said the operator. " But he will require great care ; his chest has been rudely pressed."

" I have now to thank you, sir," said Rousseau, " and praise you, not for the exclusive preference you show for the poor, but for your care and kindness toward them. All men are brothers."

" Even the noble, even the aristocrats, even the rich ? " asked the surgeon, his piercing eyes flashing from beneath his heavy eyelid.

" Even the noble, the aristocrats, the rich, when they suffer," said Rousseau.

" Sir," said the operator, " excuse me. I am from Baudry, near Neufchatel ; I am a Switzer like yourself, and therefore a democrat."

" A countryman ! " cried Rousseau, " a native of Switzerland ! Your name, sir, if you please ? "

" An obscure name, sir ; the name of a retiring man who devotes his life to study, waiting till he may, like yourself, devote it to the good of humanity. My name is Jean Paul Marat."

" Thanks, Monsieur Marat," said Rousseau. " But while enlightening the people as to their rights, do not excite them to vengeance ; for if they should ever revenge themselves, you will perhaps be terrified at their reprisals."

Marat smiled a fearful smile.

" Oh ! if that day should happen during my life ! " said he ; " if I could only have the happiness to witness it."

Rousseau heard these words, and, alarmed at the tone in which they were uttered, as a traveler trembles at the first mutterings of the far distant thunder, he took Gilbert in his arms and attempted to carry him away.

" Two volunteers to help Monsieur Rousseau ! Two men of the people ! " cried the surgeon.

" Here ! here ! here ! " cried twenty voices simultaneously.

Rousseau had only to choose ; he pointed to the two strongest, who took the youth up in their arms.

As he was leaving the place he passed Philip.

" Here, sir," said he, " I have no more use for the lantern ; take it."

" Thank you, sir," said Philip ; " many thanks."

He seized the lantern, and while Rousseau once more took the way to the Rue Plastrière, he continued his search.

" Poor young man ! " murmured Rousseau, turning back, and seeing Philip disappear in the blocked-up and encumbered streets. He proceeded on his way shuddering, for he still heard the shrill voice of the surgeon echoing over the field of blood, and crying :

" The men of the people ! None but the men of the people ! Woe to the noble, to the rich, to the aristocrats ! "

CHAPTER II.

THE RETURN.

WHILE the countless catastrophes we have mentioned were rapidly succeeding each other, M. de Taverney escaped all these dangers as if by a miracle.

Unable to oppose any physical resistance to the devouring force which swept away everything in its passage, but at the same time calm and collected, he had succeeded in maintaining his position in the center of a group which was rolling onward toward the Rue de la Madeleine. This group crushed against the parapet walls of the place, ground against the angles of the Garde Meuble, had left a long trail of wounded and dead in its path ; but, decimated as it was, it had yet succeeded in conducting the remnant of its number to a place of safety. When this was accomplished, the handful of men and women who had been left dispersed themselves over the boulevards with cries of joy, and M. de Taverney found himself, like his companions, completely out of danger.

What we are about to say would be difficult to believe, had we not already so frankly sketched the character of the baron. During the whole of this fearful passage, M. de Taverney—may God forgive him !—had absolutely thought only of himself. Besides that, he was not of a very affectionate disposition, he was a man of action ; and, in the great crises of life, such characters always put the adage of Cæsar's *age quod agis,* in practise. We shall not say, therefore, that M. de Taverney was utterly selfish, we shall merely admit that he was absent. But once upon the pavement of the boulevards, once more master of his actions, sensible of having escaped from death to life, satisfied, in short, of his safety, the baron gave a deep sigh of satisfaction, followed by a cry—feeble and wailing—a cry of grief.

" My daughter !" said he, " my daughter !" and he remained motionless, his hands fell by his side, his eyes were fixed and glassy, while he searched his memory for all the particulars of their separation.

" Poor dear man !" murmured some compassionate women.

A group had collected around the baron, ready to pity, but above all to question. But M. de Taverney had no popular instincts ; he felt ill at ease in the center of this compassionate group, and making a successful effort he broke through them, and, we say it to his praise, made a few steps toward the place.

But these few steps were the unreflecting movement of

paternal love, which is never entirely extinguished in the heart of man. Reason immediately came to the baron's aid and arrested his steps. We will follow, with the reader's permission, the course of his reasoning. First, the impossibility of returning to the Place Louis XV. occurred to him. In it there was only confusion and death, and the crowds which were still rushing from it would have rendered any attempt to pass through them as futile as for the swimmer to seek to ascend the fall of the Rhine at Schaffhausen. Besides, even if a Divine arm enabled him to reach the place, how could he hope to find one woman among a hundred thousand women ? And why should he expose himself again, and fruitlessly, to a death from which he had so miraculously escaped ?

Then came hope, that light which ever gilds the clouds of the darkest night. Was not Andrée near Philip, resting on his arm, protected by his manly arm and his brother's heart ?

That he, the baron, a feeble and tottering old man, should have been carried away, was very natural ; but that Philip, with his ardent, vigorous, hopeful nature—Philip with his arm of iron—Philip responsible for his sister's safety—should be so, was impossible. Philip had struggled, and must have conquered.

The baron, like all selfish men, endowed Philip with those qualities which his selfishness denied to himself, but which nevertheless he sought in others—strength, generosity and valor. For one selfish man regards all other selfish men as rivals and enemies, who rob him of those advantages which he believes he has the right of reaping from society.

M. de Taverney, being thus reassured by the force of his own arguments, concluded that Philip had naturally saved his sister ; that he had perhaps lost some time in seeking his father to save him also, but that probably, nay, certainly, he had taken the way to the Rue Coq Heron, to conduct Andrée, who must be a little alarmed by all the scene, home.

He therefore wheeled round, and descending the Rue

des Capucines, he gained the Place des Conquetes, or Louis le Grand, now called the Place des Victoires.

But scarcely had the baron arrived within twenty paces of the hotel when Nicole, placed as a sentinel on the threshold where she was chattering with some companions, exclaimed : "And Monsieur Philip ? and Mademoiselle Andrée ? What has become of them ? " For all Paris was already informed by the earliest fugitives of the catastrophe, which their terror had even exaggerated.

"Oh ! heavens !" cried the baron, a little agitated, "have they not returned, Nicole ? "

" No, no, sir, they have not been seen."

" They must probably have been obliged to make a detour," replied the baron, trembling more and more in proportion as the calculations of his logic were demolished ; and he remained standing in the street waiting in his turn along with Nicole, who was sobbing, and La Brie, who raised his clasped hands to heaven.

" Ah ! here is Monsieur Philip ! " exclaimed Nicole, in a tone of indescribable terror, for Philip was alone.

And in the darkness of the night, Philip was seen running toward them, breathless and despairing.

" Is my sister here ? " cried he, while yet at a distance, as soon as he could see the group assembled at the door of the hotel.

"Oh, my God ! " exclaimed the baron, pale and trembling.

"Andrée ! Andrée !" cried the young man, approaching nearer and nearer ; " where is Andrée ? "

"We have not seen her ; she is not here, Monsieur Philip. Oh ! heavens ! my dear young lady ! " cried Nicole, bursting into tears.

" And yet you have returned ! " said the baron, in a tone of anger, which must seem to the reader the more unjust, that we have already made him acquainted with the secrets of his logic.

Philip, instead of replying, approached and showed his bleeding face, and his arm, broken and hanging at his side like a withered branch.

" Alas ! alas ! " sighed the old man, " Andrée ! my poor
Andrée ! " and he sank back upon the stone bench beside
the door.

"I will find her, living or dead ! " exclaimed Philip,
gloomily. And he again started off with feverish activity.
Without slackening his pace, he secured his left arm in
the opening of his vest, for this useless limb would have
fettered his movements in the crowd, and if he had had a
hatchet at that moment he would have struck it off.   It
was then that he met on that fatal field of the dead,
Rousseau, Gilbert, and the fierce and gloomy operator who,
covered with blood, seemed rather an infernal demon presiding over the massacre, than a beneficent genius appearing
to succor and to help.   During a greater portion of the
night, Philip wandered over the Place Louis XV., unable
to tear himself away from the walls of the Garde Meuble,
near which Gilbert had been found, and incessantly
gazing at the piece of white muslin which the young man
had held firmly grasped in his hand.

But when the first light of day appeared, worn-out,
ready to sink among the heaps of corpses scarcely paler
than himself, seized with a strange giddiness, and hoping,
as his father had hoped, that Andrée might have returned
or been carried back to the house, Philip bent his steps
once more toward the Rue Coq Heron.   While still at a
distance he saw the same group he had left there, and
guessing at once that Andrée had not returned, he stopped.
The baron, on his side, had recognized his son.

" Well ? " cried he.

" What ! has my sister not returned ? " asked the young
man.

"Alas ! " cried with one voice, the baron, Nicole, and
La Brie.

" Nothing—no news—no information—no hope ? "

" Nothing ! "

Philip fell upon the stone bench of the hotel ; the baron
uttered a savage exclamation.

At this very moment a hackney coach appeared at the
end of the street ; it approached slowly, and stopped in

front of the hotel. A woman's head was seen through the door, resting on her shoulders as if she had fainted. Philip, roused by this sight, hastened toward the vehicle. The door of the coach opened, and a man alighted, bearing the senseless form of Andrée in his arms.

"Dead! dead! They bring us a corpse!" cried Philip, falling on his knees.

"Dead!" stammered the baron, "oh, sir, is she indeed dead?"

"I think not, gentlemen," calmly replied the man who carried Andrée; "Mademoiselle de Taverney, I hope, is only in a swoon."

"Oh! the sorcerer, the sorcerer!" cried the baron.

"The Count de Balsamo!" murmured Philip.

"The same, sir, and truly happy to have recognized Mademoiselle de Taverney in this frightful mêlée."

"In what part of it, sir?" asked Philip.

"Near the Garde Meuble."

"Yes," said Philip. Then, his expression of joy changing suddenly to one of gloomy distrust:

"You bring her back very late, count," said he.

"Sir," replied Balsamo, without seeming in the least surprised, "you may easily comprehend my embarrassing situation. I did not know your sister's address, and I had no resource but to take her to the Marchioness de Sévigny's, a friend of mine who lives near the royal stables. Then this honest fellow whom you see, and who assisted me to rescue the young lady—come hither, Courtois." Balsamo accompanied these last words by a sign, and a man in the royal livery appeared from the coach. "Then," continued Balsamo, "this worthy fellow, who belongs to the royal stables, recognized the young lady as having one evening drove her from Muette to your hotel. Mademoiselle de Taverney owes this lucky recognition to her marvelous beauty. I made him accompany me in the coach, and I have the honor to restore Mademoiselle de Taverney to you, with all the respect due to her, and less injured than you think." And as he concluded he gave the young girl into the care of her father and Nicole.

For the first time, the baron felt a tear trembling on his eyelids, and though, no doubt, inwardly surprised at this mark of feeling, he permitted it to roll unheeded down his wrinkled cheeks. Philip held out the only hand he had at liberty to Balsamo.

" Sir," he said, " you know my name and address. Give me an opportunity of showing my gratitude for the service you have rendered us."

" I have only fulfilled a duty," replied Balsamo. " Do I not owe you a hospitality ? " And, bowing low, he made a few steps to retire, without replying to the baron's invitation to enter. But returning :

" Excuse me," said he, " but I omitted to give you the exact address of the Marchioness de Sévigny. She lives in the Rue St. Honore, near the Fueillants. I thought it necessary to give you this information, in case Mademoiselle de Taverney should think proper to call on her."

There was in this precision of details, in this accumulation of proofs, a delicacy which touched Philip deeply, and affected even the baron.

" Sir," said the baron, " my daughter owes her life to you."

" I know it, sir, and I feel proud and happy at the thought," replied Balsamo.

And this time, followed by Courtois, who refused Philip's proffered purse, he entered the fiacre, which drove off rapidly.

Almost at the same moment, and as if Balsamo's departure had put an end to her swoon, Andrée opened her eyes, but she remained for some minutes mute, bewildered, and with a wild and staring look.

" Oh, heavens ! " murmured Philip ; " has Providence only half restored her to us ? Has her reason fled ? "

Andrée seemed to comprehend these words, and shook her head ; but she remained silent and as if under the influence of a sort of ecstasy. She was still standing, and one of her arms was extended in the direction of the street by which Balsamo had disappeared.

"Come, come," said the baron ; "it is time to end all this. Assist your sister into the house, Philip."

The young man supported Andrée with his uninjured arm. Nicole sustained her on the other side ; and, walking on, but after the manner of a sleeping person, she entered the hotel and gained her apartments. There, for the first time, the power of speech returned.

"Philip ! My father !" said she.

"She recognizes us ! she knows us again !" exclaimed Philip.

"Of course I know you again ; but, oh, heavens ! what has happened ?"

And Andrée closed her eyes, but this time not in a swoon, but in a calm and peaceful slumber.

Nicole, left alone with her young mistress, undressed her and put her in bed.

When Philip returned to his apartments, he found there a physician whom the thoughtful La Brie had run to summon, as soon as the anxiety on Andrée's account had subsided.

The doctor examined Philip's arm. It was not broken, but only dislocated, and a skilful compression replaced the shoulder in the socket from which it had been removed. After the operation, Philip, who was still uneasy on his sister's account, conducted the doctor to her bedside.

The doctor felt her pulse, listened to her breathing, and smiled.

"Your sister sleeps as calmly as an infant," said he. "Let her sleep, chevalier ; there is nothing else necessary to be done."

As for the baron, sufficiently reassured on his children's account, he had long been sound asleep.

CHAPTER III.

M. DE JUSSIEU.

WE must again transport the reader to the house in the Rue Plastrière, where M. de Sartines had sent his agent, and there, on the morning of the thirty-first of May, we shall once more find Gilbert stretched upon a mattress in Therese's room, and, standing around him, Therese and Rousseau with several of their neighbors, contemplating this specimen of the dreadful event at the remembrance of which all Paris still shuddered.

Gilbert, pale and bleeding, opened his eyes; and as soon as he regained his consciousness, he endeavored to raise himself and look round, as if he were still in the Place Louis XV. An expression of profound anxiety, followed by one of triumphant joy, was pictured in his features; then a second cloud flitted across his countenance, which resumed its somber hue.

" Are you suffering, my dear child ? " inquired Rousseau, taking his hand affectionately.

" Oh ! who has saved me ? " asked Gilbert. " Who thought of me, lonely and friendless being that I am ? "

" What saved you, my child, was the happy chance that you were not yet dead. He who thought of you was the same Almighty Being who thinks of all."

" No matter; it is very imprudent," grumbled Therese, " to go among such a crowd."

" Yes, yes, it is very imprudent," repeated all the neighbors, with one voice.

" Why, ladies," interrupted Rousseau, " there is no imprudence when there is no manifest danger, and there is no manifest danger in going to see fire-works. When danger arrives under such circumstances, you do not call the sufferer imprudent, but unfortunate. Any of us present would have done the same."

Gilbert looked round, and seeing himself in Rousseau's

apartment, endeavored to speak, but the effort was too
much for him ; the blood gushed from his mouth and
nostrils, and he sank back insensible. Rousseau had been
warned by the surgeon of the Place Louis XV., and therefore was not alarmed. In expectation of a similar event,
he had placed the invalid on a temporary mattress without sheets.

"In the meantime," said he to Therese, "you may put
the poor lad to bed."

"Where ?"

"Why here, in my bed."

Gilbert heard these words. Extreme weakness alone
prevented his replying immediately, but he made a violent
effort, and, opening his eyes, said, slowly and painfully,
"No, no ; up-stairs."

"You wish to return to your own room ?"

"Yes, yes, if you please ;" and he completed with his
eyes, rather than with his tongue, this wish, dictated by
a recollection still more powerful than pain, and which
with him seemed to survive even his consciousness.

Rousseau, whose own sensibility was so extreme, doubtless understood him, for he added :

"It is well, my child ; we will carry you up. He does
not wish to inconvenience us," said he to Therese, who
had warmly applauded the resolution. It was therefore
decided that Gilbert should be instantly installed in the
attic he preferred.

Toward the middle of the day, Rousseau came to pass
the hours he usually spent in collecting his favorite plants,
by the bedside of his disciple ; and the young man, feeling
a little better, related to him, in a low and almost inaudible voice, the details of the catastrophe. But he did not
mention the real cause why he went to see the fire-works.
Curiosity alone, he said, led him to the Place Louis XV.
Rousseau could not suspect anything further, unless he
had been a sorcerer, and he therefore expressed no surprise at Gilbert's story, but contented himself with the
questions he had already put, and only recommended patience. He did not speak either of the fragment of mus-

lin which had been found in Gilbert's hand, and of which Philip had taken possession.

Nevertheless, this conversation, which, on both sides, bordered so narrowly on the real feelings of each, was no less attractive on that account ; and they were still deeply absorbed in it, when, all at once, Therese's step was heard upon the landing.

"Jacques !" said she, "Jacques."

"Well, what is it ? "

"Some prince coming to visit me in my turn," said Gilbert, with a feeble smile.

"Jacques !" cried Therese, advancing, and still calling.

" Well ! What do you want with me ? "

Therese entered.

" Monsieur de Jussieu is below," said she ; " he heard that you were in the crowd during that night, and he has come to see if you have been hurt."

" The good Jussieu !" said Rousseau. " Excellent man, like all those who, from taste or from necessity, commune with nature, the source of all good ! Be calm, do not move. Gilbert, I will return."

" Yes, thank you," said the young man.

Rousseau left the room.

But scarcely had he gone when Gilbert, raising himself as well as he could, dragged himself toward the skylight, from which Andrée's window could be seen.

It was a most painful effort for a young man without strength, almost without the power of thought, to raise himself upon the stool, lift the sash of the skylight, and prop himself upon the edge of the roof. Gilbert, nevertheless, succeeded in effecting this. But once there, his eyes swam, his hand shook, the blood rushed to his lips, and he fell heavily to the floor.

At that moment the door of the garret opened, and Rousseau entered, followed by Jussieu, to whom he was paying great civility.

"Take care, my dear philosopher, stoop a little here," said Rousseau. " There is a step there—we are not entering a palace."

"Thank you; I have good eyes and stout limbs," replied the learned botanist.

"Here is some one come to visit you, my little Gilbert," said Rousseau, looking toward the bed. "Oh! good heavens! where is he? He has got up, the unfortunate lad!"

And Rousseau, seeing the window open, commenced to vent his displeasure in affectionate grumblings. Gilbert raised himself with difficulty, and said, in an almost inaudible voice, "I wanted air."

It was impossible to scold him, for suffering was plainly depicted in his pale and altered features.

"In fact," interrupted M. de Jussieu, "it is dreadfully warm here. Come, young man, let me feel your pulse; I am also a doctor."

"And better than many regular physicians," said Rousseau, "for you are a healer of the mind as well as of the body."

"It is too much honor," murmured Gilbert, feebly, endeavoring to shroud himself from view in his humble pallet.

"Monsieur de Jussieu insisted on visiting you," said Rousseau, "and I accepted his offer. Well, dear doctor, what do you think of his chest?"

The skilful anatomist felt the bones, and sounded the cavity by an attentive auscultation.

"The vital parts are uninjured," said he. "But who has pressed you in his arms with so much force?"

"Alas! sir, it was death!" said Gilbert.

Rousseau looked at the young man with astonishment.

"Oh! you are bruised, my child, greatly bruised; but tonics, air, leisure, will make all that disappear."

"No leisure—I cannot afford it," said the young man, looking at Rousseau.

"What does he mean?" asked Jussieu.

"Gilbert is a determined worker, my dear sir," replied Rousseau.

"Agreed; but he cannot possibly work for a day or two yet."

" To obtain a livelihood," said Gilbert, " one must work every day ; for every day one eats."

" Oh ! you will not consume much food for a short time, and your medicines will not cost much."

" However little they cost, sir," said Gilbert, " I never receive alms."

" You are mad," said Rousseau, " and you exaggerate. I tell you that you must be governed by Monsieur de Jussieu's orders, who will be your doctor in spite of yourself. Would you believe it," continued he, addressing M. de Jussieu, " he had begged me not to send for one ? "

" Why not ? "

" Because it would have cost me money, and he is proud."

" But," replied M. de Jussieu, gazing at Gilbert's fine expressive features with growing interest, " no matter how proud he is, he cannot accomplish impossibilities. Do you think yourself capable of working when you fell down with the mere exertion of going to the window ? "

" It is true," sighed Gilbert, " I am weak ; I know it."

" Well, then, take repose, and above all, mentally. You are the guest of a man whom all men obey, except his guest."

Rousseau, delighted at this delicate compliment from so great a man, took his hand and pressed it.

" And then," continued M. de Jussieu, " you will become an object of particular care to the king and the princes."

" I ! " exclaimed Gilbert.

" You, a poor victim of that unfortunate evening. The dauphin, when he heard the news, uttered cries of grief ; and the dauphiness, who was going to Marly, remained at Trianon, to be more within reach of the unfortunate sufferers."

" Oh, indeed ! " said Rousseau.

" Yes, my dear philosopher, and nothing is spoken of but the letter written by the dauphin to Monsieur de Sartines."

" I have not heard of it."

"It is at once simple and touching. The dauphin receives a monthly pension of two thousand crowns. This morning his month's income had not been paid. The prince walked to and fro quite alarmed, asked for the treasurer several times, and as soon as the latter brought him the money, sent it instantly to Paris, with two charming lines to Monsieur de Sartines, who has just shown them to me."

"Ah, then you have seen Monsieur de Sartines to-day?" said Rousseau, with a kind of uneasiness, or rather distrust.

"Yes, I have just left him," replied M. Jussieu, rather embarrassed. "I had to ask him for some seeds. So that," added he, quickly, "the dauphiness remained at Versailles to tend her sick and wounded."

"Her sick snd wounded?" asked Rousseau.

"Yes; Monsieur Gilbert is not the only one who has suffered. This time the lower classes have only paid a partial quota to the accident; it is said that there are many noble persons among the wounded.

Gilbert listened with inexpressible eagerness and anxiety, It seemed to him that every moment the name of Andrée would be pronounced by the illustrious naturalist. But M. de Jussieu rose.

"So our consultation is over?" said Rousseau.

"And henceforward our science will be useless with regard to this young invalid; air, moderate exercise, the woods—ah! by the by, I was forgetting——"

"What?"

"Next Sunday I am to make a botanical excursion to the forest of Marly; will you accompany me, my illustrious fellow-laborer?"

"Oh!" replied Rousseau, "say, rather, your unworthy admirer."

"Parbleu! that will be a fine opportunity for giving our invalid a walk. Bring him."

"So far?"

"The distance is nothing; besides, my carriage takes me as far as Bougival, and I can give you a seat. We will go by the Princess's Road to Luciennes, and from thence proceed to Marly. Botanists stop every moment, our invalid will carry our camp-stools; you and I will gather samples, he will gather health."

"What an amiable man you are, my dear Jussieu!" said Rousseau.

"Never mind; it is for my own interest. You have, I know, a great work ready upon mosses, and as I am feeling my way a little on the same subject, you will guide me."

"Oh!" exclaimed Rousseau, whose satisfaction was apparent in spite of himself.

"And when there," added the botanist, "we shall have a little breakfast in the open air, and shall enjoy the shade and the beautiful flowers. It is settled?"

"Oh, certainly."

"For Sunday, then?"

"Delightful. It seems to me as if I were fifteen again. I revel beforehand in all the pleasure I have in prospect," replied Rousseau, with almost childish satisfaction.

"And you, my young friend, must get stronger on your legs in the meantime."

Gilbert stammered out some words of thanks, which M. Jussieu did not hear, and the two botantists left Gilbert alone with his thoughts, and above all with his fears.

CHAPTER IV.

LIFE RETURNS.

IN the meantime, while Rousseau believed his invalid to be on the high-road to health, and while Therese informed all her neighbors that, thanks to the prescriptions of the learned doctor, M. de Jussieu, Gilbert was entirely out of danger—during this period of general confidence the young man incurred the worst danger he had yet run, by his obstinacy and his perpetual reveries. Rousseau could not be so confident, but that he entertained in his

inmost thoughts a distrust solidly founded on philosophical reasonings.

Knowing Gilbert to be in love, and having caught him
in open rebellion to medical authority, he judged that he
would again commit the same faults if he gave him too
much liberty. Therefore, like a good father, he had
closed the padlock of Gilbert's attic more carefully than
ever, tacitly permitting him meanwhile to go to the window, but carefully preventing his crossing the threshold.
It may easily be imagined what rage this solicitude, which
changed his garret into a prison, aroused in Gilbert's
breast, and what hosts of projects crowded his teeming
brain. To many minds constraint is fruitful in inventions.
Gilbert now thought only of Andrée, of the happiness of
seeing and watching over the progress of her convalescence,
even from afar; but Andrée did not appear at the windows of the pavilion, and Gilbert, when he fixed his
ardent and searching looks on the opposite apartments, or
surveyed every nook and corner of the building, could
only see Nicole carrying the invalid's draught on a porcelain plate, or M. de Taverney surveying the garden and
vigorously taking snuff as if to clear and refresh his
intellect. Still these details tranquilized him, for they
betokened illness but not death.

"There," thought he, "beyond that door, behind that
blind, breathes, sighs, and suffers she whom I adore, whom
I idolize—she whose very sight would cause the perspiration to stand upon my forehead and make my limbs tremble—she to whose existence mine is forever riveted—she
for whom alone I breathe and live!"

And then, leaning forward out of his window—so that
the inquisitive Chon thought, twenty times in an hour,
that he would throw himself out—Gilbert with his
practised eye took the measure of the partitions of the
floors, of the depth of the pavilion, and constructed an
exact plan of them in his brain. There M. de Taverney
slept; there must be the kitchen; there Philip's apartments; there the cabinet occupied by Nicole; and, last
of all, there must be Andrée's chamber—the sanctuary at

the door of which he would have given his life to remain for one day kneeling.

This sanctuary, according to Gilbert's plan, was a large apartment on the ground floor, guarded by an ante-chamber, from which opened a small cabinet with a glass door, which, agreeably to Gilbert's arrangement, served as Nicole's sleeping-chamber.

"Oh !" exclaimed the excited youth in his fits of jealous fury, "how happy are the beings who are privileged to walk in the garden on which my window and those of the staircase look. How happy those thoughtless mortals who tread the gravel of the parterre ! for there, during the silence of night, may be heard Mademoiselle Andrée's plaints and sighs."

Between the formation of a wish and its accomplishment there is a wide gulf ; but fertile imaginations can throw a bridge across. They can find the real in the impossible—they know how to cross the broadest rivers and scale the highest mountains, by a plan peculiarly their own.

For the first few days Gilbert contented himself with wishing. Then he reflected that these much-envied, happy beings were simple mortals, endowed as he was, with limbs to tread the soil of the garden, and with arms to open the doors. Then, by degrees, he pictured to himself the happiness there would be in secretly gliding into this forbidden house—in pressing his ears against the Venetian blinds through which the sounds from the interior were, as it were, filtered. With Gilbert wishing did not long suffice ; the fulfilment must be immediate.

Besides, his strength returned rapidly ; youth is fruitful and rich. At the end of three days, his veins still throbbing with feverish excitement, Gilbert felt himself as strong as he had ever been in his life.

He calculated that, as Rousseau had locked him in, one of the greatest difficulties—that of obtaining an entrance into the hotel of the Taverneys by the street-door—was placed out of the question ; for, as the entrance-door opened upon the Rue Coq Heron, and as Gilbert was

locked up in the Rue Plastrière, he could not of course
reach any street, and had therefore no need to open any
doors. There remained the windows. That of his garret
looked down upon a perpendicular wall of forty-eight feet
in depth.

No one, unless he were drunk or mad, would venture to
descend it. " Oh ! those doors are happy inventions
after all," thought he, clinching his hands, "and yet
Monsieur Rousseau, a philosopher, locks them ! "

To break the padlock ! That would be easily done ;
but if so, adieu to the hospitable roof which had sheltered
him.

To escape from Luciennes, from the Rue Plastrière,
from Taverney—always to escape, would be to render himself unable to look a single creature in the face without
fearing to meet the reproach of ingratitude.

" No !" thought he, " Monsieur Rousseau shall know
nothing of it."

Leaning out of his window, Gilbert continued :

" With my hands and my legs, those instruments
granted to free men by nature, I will creep along the tiles,
and, keeping in the spout—which is narrow indeed, but
straight, and therefore the direct road from one end to the
other—I shall arrive, if I get on so far, at the skylight
parallel to this. Now, this skylight belongs to the stairs.
If I do not reach so far, I shall fall into the garden ; that
will make a noise, people will hasten from the pavilion,
will raise me up, will recognize me, and I die nobly, poetically, pitied ! That would be glorious !

" If I arrive, as everything leads me to believe I shall, I
will creep in under the skylight over the stairs, and descend barefooted to the first story, the window of which
also opens in the garden, at fifteen feet from the ground.
I jump. Alas, my strength, my activity are gone ! It is
true that there is an espalier to assist me. Yes, but this
espalier with its rotten frame-work will break ; I shall
tumble down, not killed nobly and poetically, but whitened
with plaster, my clothes torn, ashamed, and looking as if
I had come to rob the orchard ! Odious thought ! Mon-

sieur de Taverney will order the porter to flog me, or La Brie to pull my ears.

" No ! 1 have here twenty pack-threads, which, twisted together, will make a rope—according to Monsieur Rousseau's definition that many straws make a sheaf. I shall borrow all these pack-threads from Madame Therese for one night. I shall knot them together, and when I have reached the window on the first floor, I shall let the rope to the little balcony, or even to the lead, and slip down into the garden."

When Gilbert had inspected the spout, attached and measured the cords, and calculated the height by his eye, he felt himself strong and determined.

He twisted the pieces of twine together, and made a tolerably strong rope of them, then tried his strength by hanging to a beam in his garret, and, happy to find that he had only spat blood once during his efforts, he decided upon the nocturnal expedition.

The better to hoodwink M. Jacques and Therese, he counterfeited illness, and kept his bed until two o'clock, at which time Rousseau went out for his dinner walk and did not return till the evening. When Rousseau paid a visit to his attic, before setting out, Gilbert announced to him his wish of sleeping until the next morning ; to which Rousseau replied that as he had made an engagement to sup from home that evening he was happy to find Gilbert inclined to rest.

With these mutual explanations they separated. When Rousseau was gone, Gilbert brought out his pack-threads again, and this time he twisted them permanently.

He again examined the spout and the tiles ; then placed himself at the window to keep watch on the garden until evening.

CHAPTER V.

THE AERIAL TRIP.

GILBERT was now prepared for his entrance into the enemy's camp, for thus he mentally termed M. de Taverney's ground, and from his window he explored the garden with the care and attention of a skilful strategist, who is about to give battle, when in his calm and motionless mansion, an incident occurred which attracted the philosopher's attention.

A stone flew over the garden wall and struck against the angle of the house. Gilbert, who had already learned that there can be no effect without a cause, determined to discover the cause, having seen the effect.

But although he leaned out as far as possible, he could not discover the person in the street who had thrown the stone. However, he immediately comprehended that this maneuver had reference to an event which just then took place; one of the outside shutters of the ground floor opened cautiously, and through the opening appeared Nicole's head.

On seeing Nicole Gilbert made a plunge back in his garret, but without losing sight of the nimble young girl. The latter, after throwing a stealthy glance at all the windows, particularly at those of the pavilion, emerged from her hiding-place and ran toward the garden, as if going to the espalier where some lace was drying in the sun. It was on the path which led toward the espalier that the stone had fallen, and neither Nicole nor Gilbert lost sight of it. Gilbert saw her kick this stone—which, for the moment, became of such great importance—before her several times, and she continued this maneuver until she reached the flower border, in which the espalier stood. Once there, Nicole raised her hands to take down the lace, let fall some of it, and, in picking it up again, seized the stone.

As yet Gilbert could understand nothing of this movement, but seeing Nicole pick up the stone as a greedy schoolboy picks up a nut, and unroll a slip of paper which was tied round it, he at once guessed the degree of importance which was attached to the aerolite.

It was, in fact, nothing more or less than a note which Nicole had found rolled round the stone. The cunning girl quickly unfolded it, read it, and put it into her pocket, and then immediately discovered that there was no more occasion for looking at the lace—it was dry.

Meanwhile, Gilbert shook his head, saying to himself, with the blind selfishness of men who entertain a bad opinion of women, that Nicole was in reality a viciously inclined person, and that he, Gilbert, had performed an act of sound and moral policy in breaking off so suddenly and so boldly with a girl who had letters thrown to her over the wall.

Nicole ran back to the house, and soon reappeared, this time holding her hand in her pocket. She drew from it a key, which Gilbert saw glitter in her hand for a moment, and then the young girl slipped this key under a little door which served to admit the gardener, and which was situated at the extremity of the wall opposite the street, and parallel to the great door which was generally used.

"Good!" said Gilbert. "I understand—a love letter and a rendezvous. Nicole loses no time ; she has already a new lover."

And he frowned, with the disappointment of a man who thinks that his loss should cause an irreparable void in the heart of the woman he abandons, and who finds this void completely filled.

"This may spoil all my projects," he continued, seeking a factitious cause for his ill-humor. "No matter," resumed he, after a moment's silence, "I shall not be sorry to know the happy mortal who succeeds me in Mademoiselle Nicole's good graces."

But Gilbert, on certain subjects, had a very discerning judgment. He calculated that the discovery which he had made, and which Nicole was far from suspecting, would

give him an advantage over her which might be of use to
him ; since he knew her secret, with such details as she
could not deny, while she scarcely suspected his, and, even
if she did, there existed no facts which could give a color
to her suspicions.   During all these goings and comings,
the anxiously expected night had come on.

The only thing which Gilbert now feared was the return
of Rousseau, who might surprise him on the roof or on
the staircase, or might come up and find his room empty.
In the latter case, the anger of the philosopher of Geneva
would be terrible, but Gilbert hoped to avert the blow by
means of the following note, which he left upon his little
table, addressed to the philosopher :

"MY DEAR AND ILLUSTRIOUS PROTECTOR,—Do not think
ill of me, if, notwithstanding your recommendations, and
even against your order, I have dared to leave my apartment.   I shall soon return, unless some accident, similar to
that which has already happened to me, should again take
place ; but at the risk of a similar, or even worse accident, I
must leave my room for two hours."

"I do not know what I shall say when I return," thought
Gilbert, "but at least Monsieur Rousseau will not be uneasy
or angry."

The evening was dark.   A suffocating heat prevailed, as
it often does during the first warmth of spring.   The sky
was cloudy, and at half-past eight the most practised eye
could have distinguished nothing at the bottom of the dark
gulf into which Gilbert peered.

It was then, for the first time, that the young man perceived that he breathed with difficulty, and that sudden
perspirations bedewed his forehead and breast—unmistak-
able signs of a weak and unhinged system.   Prudence
counseled him not to undertake, in his present condition,
an expedition for which strength and steadiness in all his
members were peculiarly necessary, not only to insure success, but even for the preservation of his life ; but Gilbert
did not listen to what his physical instincts counseled.

His moral will spoke more loudly ; and to it, as ever, the young man vowed obedience.

The moment had come. Gilbert rolled his rope several times round his neck, and commenced, with beating heart, to scale the skylight ; then, firmly grasping the casement, he made the first step in the spout toward the skylight on the right, which was, as we have said, that of the staircase and about two fathoms distant from his own.

His feet in a groove of lead, at the utmost eight inches wide, which groove, though it was supported here and there by holdfasts of iron, yet, from the pliability of the lead, yielded to his steps ; his hands resting against the tiles, which could only be a point of support for his equilibrium, but no help in case of falling, since the fingers could take no hold of them ; this was Gilbert's position during this aerial passage which lasted two minutes, but which seemed to Gilbert to occupy two centuries.

But Gilbert determined not to be afraid ; and such was the power of will in this young man, that he proceeded. He recollected to have heard a rope dancer say, that, to walk safely on narrow ways one ought never to look downward, but about ten feet in advance, and never think of the abyss beneath, but as an eagle might, that is, with the conviction of being able to float over it at pleasure. Besides, Gilbert had already put these precepts in practise in several visits he had paid to Nicole—that Nicole who was now so bold that she made use of keys and doors instead of roofs and chimneys.

In this manner he had often passed the sluices of the mill at Taverney, and the naked beams of the roof of an old barn. He arrived, therefore, at the goal without a shudder, and once arrived there, he glided beneath the skylight, and with a thrill of joy alighted on the staircase. But on reaching the landing-place he stopped short. Voices were heard on the lower stories ; they were those of Therese and certain neighbors of hers, who were speaking of Rousseau's genius, of the merit of his books, and of the harmony of his music.

The neighbors had read " La Nouvelle Héloise," and

confessed frankly that they found the book obscure. In
reply to this criticism, Mme. Therese observed that they
did not understand the philosophical part of this delightful
book.   To this the neighbors had nothing to reply, except
to confess their incompetence to give an opinion on such a
subject.

This edifying conversation was held from one landing-
place to another ; and the fire of discussion, ardent as it was,
was less so than that of the stoves on which the savory
suppers of these ladies were cooking.   Gilbert was listening to the arguments, therefore, and snuffing the smell of
the viands, when his name, pronounced in the midst of the
tumult, caused him to start rather unpleasantly.

" After my supper, " said Therese," I must go and see if
that dear child does not want something in his attic."

This " dear child " gave Gilbert less pleasure than the
promise of the visit gave him alarm.   Luckily, he remembered that Therese, when she supped alone, chatted a long
time with her bottle, that the meat seemed savory, and
that after supper meant—ten o'clock.   It was now only a
quarter to nine.   Besides, it was probable that, after supper,
the course of ideas in Therese's brain would take a change,
and that she would then think of anything else rather than
of the " dear child."

But time was slipping past, to the great vexation of
Gilbert, when all at once one of the joints of the allied
dames to burn.

The cry of the alarmed cook was heard, which put an
end to all conversation, for every one hurried to the theater
of the catastrophe.   Gilbert profited by this culinary
panic among the ladies, to glide down the stairs like a
shadow.

Arrived at the first story, he found the leading of the
window well adapted to hold his rope, and, attaching it by
a slip-knot, he mounted the window-sill and began rapidly
to descend.

He was still suspended between the window and the
ground, when a rapid step sounded in the garden beneath
him.   He had sufficient time, before the step reached him,

to return, and holding fast by the knots, he watched to see who this untimely visitor was.

It was a man, and as he proceeded from the direction of the little door, Gilbert did not doubt for an instant but that it was the happy mortal whom Nicole was expecting.

He fixed all his attention, therefore, upon this second intruder, who had thus arrested him in the midst of his perilous descent. By his walk, by a glance at his profile seen from beneath his three-cornered hat, and by the particular mode in which this hat was placed over the corner of his attentive ear, Gilbert fancied he recognized the famous Beausire, that exempt whose acquaintance Nicole had made in Taverney.

Almost immediately he saw Nicole open the door of the pavilion, hasten into the garden, leaving the door open, and, light and active as a bird, direct her steps toward the greenhouse—that is to say, in the direction in which M. Beausire was already advancing.

This was most certainly not the first rendezvous which had taken place, since neither one nor the other betrayed the least hesitation as to their place of meeting.

" Now I can finish my descent," thought Gilbert ; " for if Nicole has appointed this hour for meeting her lover, it must be because she is certain of being undisturbed. Andrèe must be alone then—oh, heavens ! alone."

In fact, no noise was heard in the house, and only a faint light gleamed from the windows of the ground floor. Gilbert alighted upon the ground without any accident, and, unwilling to cross the garden, he glided gently along the wall until he came to a clump of trees, crossed it in a stooping posture, and arrived at the door which Nicole had left open, without having been discovered. There, sheltered by an immense aristolochia, which was trained over the door and hung down in large festoons, he observed that the outer apartment, which was a spacious ante-chamber, was, as he had guessed, perfectly empty. This ante-chamber communicated with the interior of the house by means of two doors, one opened, the other closed ; Gilbert guessed that the open one was that belonging to

Nicole's chamber. He softly entered this room, stretching out his hands before him for fear of accident, for the room was entirely without light; but at the end of a sort of corridor was seen a glass door whose frame-work was clearly discerned against the light of the adjoining apartment. On the inner side of this glass door was drawn a muslin curtain.

As Gilbert advanced along the corridor, he heard a feeble voice speaking in the lighted apartment; it was Andrée's, and every drop of Gilbert's blood rushed to his heart. Another voice replied to hers; it was Philip's. The young man was anxiously inquiring after his sister's health.

Gilbert, now on his guard, proceeded a few steps further, and placed himself behind one of those truncated columns surmounted by a bust, which at that period, formed the usual ornament of double doors. Thus concealed, he strained his eyes and ears to the utmost stretch; so happy, that his heart melted with joy; so fearful, that the same heart shrunk together till it seemed to become only a minute point in his breast.

He listened and gazed.

APTER VI.

THE BROTHER AND SISTER.

GILBERT, as we have said, gazed and listened. He saw Andrée stretched on a reclining-chair, her face turned toward the glass door, that is to say, directly toward him. This door was slightly ajar.

A small lamp with a deep shade was placed upon an adjoining table, which was covered with books, indicating the only species of recreation permitted to the invalid, and lighted only the lower part of Mlle. de Taverney's face. Sometimes, however, when she leaned back, so as to rest against the pillow of the inclining-chair, the light overspread her marble forehead, which was veiled in a lace cap.

Philip was sitting at the foot of her chair with his back toward Gilbert ; his arm was still in a sling, and all exercise of it was forbidden.

It was the first time that Andrée had been up, and the first time also that Philip had left his room.   The young people, therefore, had not seen each other since that terrible night, but each knew that the other was recovering and hastening toward convalescence.   They had only been together for a few moments, and were conversing without restraint, for they knew that even if any one should interrupt them, they would be warned by the noise of the bell attached to the door which Nicole had left open.   But of course they were not aware of the circumstances of the door having been left open, and they calculated upon the bell.

Gilbert saw and heard all, therefore ; for, through this open door, he could seize every word of their conversation.

" So now," Philip was saying, just as Gilbert took his place behind a curtain hung loosely before the door of a dressing-room, " so now you breathe more easily, my poor sister ? "

" Yes, more easily, but still with a slight pain."

" And your strength ? "

" Returns but slowly ; nevertheless, I have been able to walk to the window two or three times to-day.   How sweet the fresh air is ! how lovely the flowers !   It seems to me that, surrounded with air and flowers, it is impossible to die."

" But still you are very weak ; are you not, Andrée ? "

" Oh, yes, for the shock was a terrible one.   Therefore," continued the young girl, smiling and shaking her head, " I repeat that I walk with difficulty, and am obliged to lean on the tables and the projecting points of the wainscoting.   Without this support my limbs bend under me, and I feel as if I should every moment fall."

" Courage, Andrée !   The fresh air and the beautiful flowers you spoke of just now, will cure you, and in a week you will be able to pay a visit to the dauphiness, who, I am informed, sends to inquire so kindly for you."

"Yes, I hope so, Philip ; for the dauphiness, in truth, seems most kind to me."

And Andrée, leaning back, put her hand upon her chest and closed her lovely eyes.

Gilbert made a step forward with outstretched arms.

"You are in pain, my sister ? " asked Philip, taking her hand.

"Yes ; at times I have slight spasms, and sometimes the blood mounts to my head, and my temples throb ; sometimes again I feel quite giddy, and my heart sinks within me."

"Oh," said Philip, dreamily, "That is not surprising ; you have met with a dreadful trial, and your escape was almost miraculous."

"Miraculous is, in truth, the proper term, brother."

"But, speaking of your miraculous escape, Andrée," said Philip, approaching closer to his sister, to give more emphasis to the question, "do you know I have never yet had an opportunity of speaking to you of this catastrophe ? "

Andrée blushed and seemed uneasy, but Philip did not remark this change of color, or, at least, did not appear to remark it.

"I thought, however," said the young girl, "that the person who restored me to you gave all the explanations you could wish ; my father, at least, told me he was quite satisfied."

"Of course, my dear Andrée ; and this man, so far as I could judge, behaved with extreme delicacy in the whole affair ; but still some parts of his tale seemed to me, not suspicious, indeed, but obscure—that is the proper term."

"How so, and what do you mean, brother ? " asked Andrée, with the frankness of innocence.

"For instance," said Philip, "there is one point which did not at first strike me, but which has since seemed to me to bear a very strange aspect."

"Which ? " asked Andrée.

"Why, the very manner in which you were saved. Can you describe it to me ? "

The young girl seemed to make an effort over herself.

"Oh, Philip," said she, "I have almost forgotten—I was so much terrified."

"No matter, my sweetest Andrée ; tell me all you remember."

"Well, you know, brother, we were separated about twenty paces from the Garde Meuble. I saw you dragged away toward the garden of the Tuileries, while I was drawn toward the Rue Royale. For an instant I could distinguish you making fruitless attempts to rejoin me. I stretched out my arms toward you, crying, ' Philip ! Philip !' when, all at once, I was, as it were, seized by a whirlwind, which raised me aloft and bore me in the direction of the railings. I felt the living tide carrying me toward the wall, where it must be dashed to atoms ; I heard the cries of those who were crushed against the railings ; I felt that my turn would come to be crushed and mangled ; I could almost calculate the number of seconds I had yet to live, when, half dead and almost frantic, raising my hands and eyes to heaven in a last prayer, I met the burning glance of a man who seemed to govern the crowd, and whom the crowd seemed to obey."

"And this man was the Count Joseph Balsamo?"

"Yes ; the same whom I had already seen at Taverney —the same who, even there, inspired me with such a strange terror ; he, in short, who seems to be endowed with some supernatural power, who has fascinated my sight with his eyes, my ears with his voice ; who has made my whole being tremble by the mere touch of his finger on my shoulder."

"Proceed, proceed, Andrée," said Philip, his features and voice becoming gloomier as she spoke.

"Well, this man seemed to tower aloft above the catastrophe, as if human suffering could not reach him. I read in his eyes that he wished to save me—that he had the power to do so. Then something extraordinary took place in me and around me. Bruised, powerless, half dead as I was, I felt myself raised toward this man as if some unknown, mysterious, invincible power drew me to him. I

felt as if some strong arm, by a mighty effort, was lifting
me out of the gulf of mangled flesh in which so many unhappy victims were suffocating, and was restoring me to
air, to life.   Oh, Philip," continued Andrée, with a sort
of feverish vehemence, "I feel certain it was that man's
look which attracted me to him.   I reached his hand, I
was saved!"

"Alas!" murmured Gilbert, "she had eyes only for
him; and I—I—who was dying at her feet—she saw me
not!"

He wiped his brow, bathed in perspiration.

"That is how the affair happened, then?" asked
Philip.

"Yes, up to the moment when I felt myself out of
danger.   Then, whether all my force had been exhausted
in the last effort I had made, or whether the terror I had
experienced had outstripped the measure of my strength,
I do not know, but I fainted."

"And at what time do you think you fainted?"

"About ten minutes after we were separated, brother."

"Yes," pursued Philip, "that was about midnight.
How, then, did it happen that you did not return till
three o'clock?   Forgive me this catechizing, which may
seem ridiculous to you, dear Andrée, but I have a good
reason for it."

"Thanks, Philip," said Andrée, pressing her brother's
hand.   "Three days ago I could not have replied to you
as I have now done; but to-day—it may seem strange to
you what I am about to say—but to-day my mental vision
is stronger; it seems to me as if some will stronger than
my own ordered me to remember, and I do remember."

"Then tell me, dear Andrée, for I am all impatience to
know, did this man carry you away in his arms?"

"In his arms?" said Andrée, blushing; "I do not
well recollect.   All I know is, that he extricated me out
of the crowd.   But the touch of his hand caused me the
same feeling as at Taverney, and scarcely had he touched
me when I fainted again, or, rather, I sunk to sleep; for
fainting is generally preceded by a painful feeling, and on

this occasion I only felt the pleasing sensation attendant on sleep."

"In truth, Andrée, what you tell me seems so strange that if any other related these things I should not believe them. But proceed," continued he, in a voice which betrayed more emotion than he was willing to let appeâr.

As for Gilbert he devoured Andrée's every word, for he knew that so far, at least, each word was true.

"When I regained my consciousness," continued the young girl, "I was in a splendidly furnished saloon. A *femme de chambre* and a lady were standing beside me, but they did not seem at all uneasy, for when I awoke they were smiling benevolently."

"Do you know what time this was, Andrée ?"

"The half hour after midnight was just striking."

"Oh !" said the young man, breathing freely, "that is well. Proceed, Andrée, with your narrative.

"I thanked the ladies for the attentions they lavished on me ; but knowing how uneasy you would be, I begged them to send me home immediately. Then they told me that the count had returned to the scene of the accident to assist the wounded, but that he would return with a carriage and convey me back himself to our hotel. In fact, about two o'clock I heard a carriage roll along the street ; then the same sensation which I had formerly felt on the approach of that man overpowered me ; I fell back trembling and almost senseless upon a sofa. The door opened. In the midst of my confusion I could still recognize the man who had saved me ; then for a second time I lost all consciousness. They must then have carried me down, placed me in the carriage, and brought me here. That is all I can remember, brother."

Philip calculated the time, and saw that his sister must have been brought direct from the Rue des Ecuries du Louvre to the Rue Coq Heron, as she had been from the Place Louis XV. to the Rue des Ecuries du Louvre ; and, joyfully pressing her hand, he said, in a frank, cheerful voice :

"Thanks, my dear sister, thanks ; all the calculations

correspond exactly. I will call upon the Marchioness **de**
Sévigny, and thank her in person. In the meantime, one
word more, upon a subject of secondary importance."

" Speak."

" Do you remember seeing among the crowd any face
with which you were acquainted ? "

" No, none."

" The little Gilbert's, for example ? "

" In fact," said Andrée, endeavoring to recall her
thoughts. " I do remember to have seen him. At the moment when we were separated he was about ten paces from
me."

" She saw me ! " murmured Gilbert.

" Because, while searching for you, Andrée, I discovered
the poor lad."

" Among the dead ? " asked Andrée with that peculiar
shade of interest which the great testify for their de-
pendents.

" No, he was only wounded ; he was saved, and I hope
he will recover."

" Oh, I am glad to hear it," said Andrée , " and what
injury had he received ? "

" His chest was greatly bruised."

" Yes, yes, against thine, Andrée ! " murmured Gilbert.

" But," continued Philip, " the strangest circumstance
of all, and the one which induced me to speak of the lad,
was, that I found in his hand, clinched and stiffened by
pain, a fragment of your dress."

" That is strange, indeed."

" Did you not see him at the last moment ? "

" At the last moment, Philip, I saw so many fearful
forms of terror, pain, selfishness, love, pity, avarice, and
indifference, that I felt as if I had passed a year in the
realms of torment, and as if these figures were those **of**
the damned passing in review before me. I may, therefore, have seen the young man, but I do not remember
him."

" And yet the piece of stuff torn from your dress ? and
it was your dress, Andrée, for Nicole has examined it."

" Did you tell the girl for what purpose you questioned her ? " asked Andrée ; for she remembered the singular explanation she had had at Taverney with her waiting-maid on the subject of this same Gilbert.

" Oh, no ! However, the fragment was in his hand. How can you explain that ? "

" Oh, very easily," said Andrée, with a calmness which presented a strange contrast to the fearful beating of Gilbert's heart ; " if he was near me when I felt myself raised aloft, as it were, by this man's look, he has probably clung to me to profit by the help I was receiving, in the same manner as a drowning man clings to the belt of the swimmer."

" Oh ! " said Gilbert, with a feeling of angry contempt at this explanation of the young girl ; " oh, what an ignoble interpretation of my devotion ! How these nobles judge us sons of the people ! Monsieur Rousseau is right ; we are worth more than they ; our hearts are purer and our arms stronger."

As he once more settled himself to listen to the conversation of the brother and sister, which he had for a moment lost during this aside, he heard a noise behind him.

" Oh, heavens ! " murmured he, " some one in the anteroom ? "

And hearing the step approach the corridor, Gilbert drew back into the dressing-room, letting the curtain fall before him.

" Well, is that madcap Nicole not here ? " said the Baron de Taverney's voice, as he entered his daughter's apartment, touching Gilbert with the flaps of his coat as he passed.

" I dare say she is in the garden," said Andrée, with a tranquillity which showed that she had no suspicion of the presence of a third person ; " good evening, my dear father."

Philip rose respectfully ; the baron motioned him to remain where he was, and taking an armchair, sat down near his children.

" Ah, my children," said the baron, " it is a long journey from the Rue Coq Heron to Versailles, when, instead of going in a good court carriage, you have only a fiacre drawn by one horse. However, I saw the dauphiness, neverthelesss."

"Ah," said Andrée, "then you have just arrived from Versailles, my dear father ? "

"Yes ; the princess did me the honor to send for me, having heard of the accident which had happened to my daughter."

"Andrée is much better, father," said Philip

"I am perfectly aware of it, and I told her royal highness so, who was kind enough to promise that as soon as your sister is completely restored she will summon her to Petit Trianon, which she has fixed upon for her residence, and which she is now having decorated according to her taste."

"I—I at court !" said Andrée, timidly.

"It is not the court, my child. The dauphiness has quiet and unobtrusive habits, and the dauphin hates show and noise. They will live in complete retirement at Trianon. However, from what I know of her highness the dauphiness's disposition, her little family parties will turn out, in the end, much better than Beds of Justice and meetings of states-general. The princess has a decided character, and the dauphin, I am told, is learned."

"Oh, it will always be the court. Do not deceive yourself, sister," said Philip, mournfully.

"The court !" said Gilbert to himself, with an emotion of concentrated rage and despair. "The court ! that is, a summit which I cannot reach, or a gulf into which I cannot dash myself. In that case, farewell, Andrée ! Lost —lost to me forever !"

"But, my father," replied Andrée, "we have neither the fortune which would warrant our choosing such a residence, nor the education necessary for those who move in its lofty circle. What shall I, a poor girl, do among those brilliant ladies, whose dazzling splendor I on one occasion witnessed, whose minds I thought so empty, but at the same time so sparkling ? Alas ! my brother, we are too obscure to mingle among so many dazzling lights !"

The baron knit his brow.

"Still the same absurd ideas," said he. "In truth, I cannot understand the pains which my family take to depreciate everything which they inherit from me, or which relates to me. Obscure! Really, mademoiselle, you are mad. Obscure! a Taverney Maison Rouge obscure? And who will shine, pray, if you do not? Fortune—pardieu! we know what the fortunes of the court are. The sun of royalty fills them, the same sun makes them blow —it is the great vivifier of court nature. I have ruined myself at court, and now I shall grow rich again at court, that's all. Has the king no more money to bestow upon his faithful servants? And do you really think I would blush at a regiment being offered to my eldest son, at a dowry being granted to you, Andrée, at a nice little appanage conferred on myself, or at finding a handsome pension under my napkin some day at dinner? No, no; fools alone have prejudices; I have none; besides, it is only my own property which is given back to me. Do not, therefore, entertain these foolish scruples. There remains only one of your objections—your education, of which you spoke just now. But, mademoiselle, remember that no young lady of the court has been educated as you have been. Nay, more, you have, besides the education usually given to the daughters of the noblesse, the solid acquirements more generally confined to the families of lawyers or financiers. You are a musician, and you draw landscapes, with sheep and cows, which Berghem need not disclaim. Now, the dauphiness absolutely dotes on cows, on sheep, and on Berghem. You are beautiful; the king cannot fail to notice it. You can converse; that will charm the Count d'Artois and the Count de Provençe; you will not only be well received, therefore, but adored. Yes, yes," continued the baron, rubbing his hands, and chuckling in so strange a manner, that Philip gazed at his father to see if the laugh was really produced by a human mouth. "Adored! I have said the word."

Andrée cast down her eyes, and Philip, taking her hand, said:

"Our father is right, Andrée, you are everything he described. None can be more worthy to enter Versailles than you."

"But I shall be separated from you," replied Andrée.

"By no means, by no means," interrupted the baron ; "Versailles is large, my dear."

"Yes, but Trianon is little," replied Andrée, haughty and rather unmanageable when she was opposed.

"Trianon will always be large enough to provide a chamber for Monsieur de Taverney. A man such as I am always finds room," added he, with a modesty which meant—always knows how to make room for himself.

Andrée, not much comforted by this promised proximity of her father, turned to Philip.

"My sister," said the latter, "you will certainly not belong to what is called the court. Instead of placing you in a convent and paying your dowry, the dauphiness, who wishes to distinguish you, will keep you near herself in some employment. Etiquette is not so rigid now as in the time of Louis XIV. Offices are more easily fused together and separated. You can occupy the post of reader or companion to the dauphiness ; she will draw with you, she will always keep you near her ; probably you will never appear in public, but you will enjoy her immediate protection, and consequently, will inspire envy. That is what you fear, is it not ?"

"Yes, my brother."

"However," said the baron, "we shall not grieve for such a trifle as one or two envious persons. Get better quickly, therefore, Andrée, and I shall have the pleasure of taking you to Trianon myself ; it is the dauphiness's commands."

"Very well, father, I shall go."

"Apropos, Philip, have you any money ?" asked the baron.

"If you want some, sir," replied the young man, "I have not enough to offer you ; if you wish to give me some, I shall answer you, on the contrary, that I have enough for myself."

"True ; you are a philosopher," said the baron, laughing sarcastically. "Are you a philosopher, also, Andrée, who has nothing to ask from me, or is there anything you wish for ? "

"I am afraid of embarrassing you, father."

"Oh, we are not at Taverney now. The king has sent me five hundred louis-d'ors ; on account, his majesty said. Think of your wardrobe, Andrée."

"Thank you, my dear father," said the young girl, joyously.

"There, there," said the baron, "see the extremes ; only a minute ago she wanted nothing, now she would ruin the Emperor of China. But no matter, ask ; fine dresses will become you well, Andrée."

Then, giving her a very affectionate kiss, the baron opened the door of an apartment which separated his own from his daughter's chamber, and left the room, saying :

"That cursed Nicole is not here to show me light."

"Shall I ring for her, father ? "

"No ; I have La Brie, who is sleeping in some armchair or other. Good night, my children."

Philip now rose in his turn.

"Good night, brother," said Andrée. "I am dreadfully tired. It is the first time I have spoken so much since my accident. Good night, dear Philip."

And she gave her hand to the young man, who kissed it with brotherly affection, but at the same time with a sort of respect with which his sister always inspired him, and retired, touching, as he passed, the door behind which Gilbert was concealed.

"Shall I call Nicole ? " asked he, as he left the room.

"No, no," said Andrée ; "I can undress alone ; adieu, Philip."

CHAPTER VII.

WHAT GILBERT HAD FORESEEN.

WHEN André was alone, she rose from the chair, and a shudder passed through Gilbert's frame.

The young girl stood upright, and with her hands, white as alabaster, she took the hair-pins one by one from her head-dress, while the light shawl in which she was wrapped slipped from her shoulders, and showed her snowy graceful neck, and her arms, which, raised carelessly above her head, displayed to advantage the muscles of her exquisite throat and bosom, palpitating under the cambric.

Gilbert, on his knees, breathless, intoxicated, felt the blood rush furiously to his heart and forehead. Fiery waves circulated in his veins, a cloud of flame descended over his sight, and strange, feverish noises boiled in his ears. His state of mind bordered on madness. He was on the point of crossing the threshold of Andrée's door, and crying:

"Yes, thou art beautiful, thou art indeed beautiful. But be not so proud of thy beauty, for thou owest it to me—I saved thy life!"

All at once, a knot in her waist-band embarrassed the young girl; she became impatient, stamped with her foot, and sat down, weak and trembling, on her bed, as if this slight obstacle had overcome her strength. Then, bending toward the cord of the bell, she pulled it impatiently.

This noise recalled Gilbert to his senses. Nicole had left the door open to hear, therefore she would come.

"Farewell, my dream!" murmured he. "Farewell, happiness! henceforth only a baseless vision—henceforth only a remembrance, ever burning in my imagination, ever present to my heart!"

Gilbert endeavored to rush from the pavilion, but the baron, on entering, had closed the doors of the corridor after him. Not calculating on this interruption, he was some moments before he could open them.

Just as he entered Nicole's apartment, Nicole reached the pavilion. The young man heard the gravel of the garden walk grinding under her steps. He had only time to conceal himself in the shade, in order to let the young girl pass him ; for, after crossing the ante-chamber, the door of which she locked, she flew along the corridor as light as a bird.

Gilbert gained the ante-chamber and attempted to escape into the garden, but Nicole, while running on and crying, " I am coming, mademoiselle ! I am coming ! I am just closing the door !" had closed it indeed, and not only closed it and double-locked it, but in her confusion had put the key into her pocket.

Gilbert tried in vain to open the door. Then he had recourse to the windows, but they were barred, and after five minutes' investigation, he saw that it was impossible to escape.

The young man crouched into a corner, fortifying himself with the firm resolve to make Nicole open the door for him.

As for the latter, when she had given the plausible excuse for her absence, that she had gone to close the windows of the greenhouse lest the night air might injure her young lady's flowers, she finished undressing Andrée, and assisted her to bed.

There was a tremulousness in Nicole's voice, an unsteadiness in her hands, and an eagerness in all her attentions, which were very unusual, and indicated some extraordinary emotion. But from the calm and lofty sphere in which Andrée's thoughts revolved, she rarely looked down upon the lower earth, and when she did so, the inferior beings whom she saw seemed like atoms in her eyes. She, therefore, perceived nothing. Meanwhile, Gilbert was boiling with impatience, since he found the retreat thus cut off. He now longed only for liberty.

Andrée dismissed Nicole after a short chat, in which the latter exhibited all the wheedling manner of a remorseful waiting-maid.

Before retiring, she turned back her mistress's coverlet, lowered the lamp, sweetened the warm drink which was standing in a silver goblet upon an alabaster night-lamp, wished her mistress good night in her sweetest voice, and left the room on tiptoe. As she came out she closed the glass door. Then, humming gaily as if her mind was perfectly tranquil, she crossed the ante-chamber and advanced toward the door leading into the garden.

Gilbert guessed Nicole's intention, and for a moment he asked himself if he should not, in place of making himself known, slip out suddenly, taking advantage of the opportunity to escape when the door should be opened. But in that case he would be seen without being recognized, and he would be taken for a robber. Nicole would cry for help, he would not have time to reach the cord, and even if he should reach it he would be seen in his aerial flight, his retreat discovered, and himself made the object of the Taverneys' displeasure, which could not fail to be deep and lasting, considering the feeling toward him by the head of the family.

True, he might expose Nicole, and procure her dismissal ; but of what use would that be to him ? He would, in that case, have done evil without reaping any corresponding advantage ; in short, from pure revenge ; and Gilbert was not so feeble-minded as to feel satisfied when he was revenged. Useless revenge was to him worse than a bad action, it was folly.

As Nicole approached the door where Gilbert was in waiting, he suddenly emerged from the shadow in which he was concealed, and appeared to the young girl in the full rays of the moonlight, which was streaming through the window. Nicole was on the point of .crying out, but she took Gilbert for another, and said, after the first emotion of terror was past :

"You here ! What imprudence !"

"Yes, it is I," replied Gilbert, in a whisper, "but do not cry out for me more than you would do for another."

This time Nicole recognized her interlocutor.

NICOLE'S TWENTY-FIVE LOUIS D'ORS

"Gilbert !" she exclaimed, "oh, Heaven !"

"I requested you not to cry out," said the young man, coldly.

"But what are you doing here, sir ?" exclaimed Nicole, angrily.

"Come," said Gilbert, as coolly as before, "a moment ago you called me imprudent, and now you are more imprudent than I."

"I think I am only too to kind you in asking what you are doing here," said Nicole ; "for I know very well."

"What am I doing, then ?"

"You came to see Mademoiselle Andrée."

"Mademoiselle Andrée ?" said Gilbert, as calmly as before.

"Yes, you are in love with her ; but, fortunately, she does not love you."

"Indeed ?"

"But take care, Monsieur Gilbert," said Nicole, threateningly.

"Oh, I must take care ?"

"Yes."

"Of what ?"

"Take care that I do not inform on you."

"You, Nicole ?"

"Yes, I ; take care I don't get you dismissed from the house."

"Try," said Gilbert, smiling.

"You defy me ?"

"Yes, absolutely defy you."

"What will happen then, if I tell mademoiselle, Monsieur Philip, and the baron that I met you here ?"

"It will happen as you have said—not that I shall be dismissed—I am, thank God, dismissed already—but that I shall be tracked and hunted like a wild beast. But she who will be dismissed will be Nicole."

"How Nicole ?"

"Certainly ; Nicole, who has stones thrown to her over the walls."

"Take care, Monsieur Gilbert," said Nicole, in a

threatening tone, "a piece of mademoiselle's dress was found in your hand upon the Place Louis XV."

"You think so?"

"Monsieur Philip told his father so. He suspects nothing as yet, but if he gets a hint or two, perhaps he will suspect in the end."

"And who will give him the hint?"

"I shall."

"Take care, Nicole! One might suspect, also, that when you seem to be drying lace, you are picking up the stones that are thrown over the wall."

"It is false!" cried Nicole. Then, retracting her denial, she continued, "At all events, it is not a crime to receive a letter—not like stealing in here while mademoiselle is undressing. Ah! what will you say to that, Monsieur Gilbert?"

"I shall say, Mademoiselle Nicole, that it is also a crime for such a well-conducted young lady as you are to slip keys under the doors of gardens."

Nicole trembled.

"I shall say," continued Gilbert, "that if I, who am known to Monsieur de Taverney, to Monsieur Philip, to Mademoiselle Andrée, have committed a crime in entering here, in my anxiety to know how the family I so long served were, and particularly Mademoiselle Andrée, whom I endeavored so strenuously to save on the evening of the fire-works, that a piece of her dress remained in my hand —I shall say, that if I have committed this pardonable crime, you have committed the unpardonable one of introducing a stranger into your master's house, and are now going to meet him a second time, in the greenhouse, where you have already spent an hour in his company——"

"Gilbert! Gilbert!"

"Oh! how virtuous we are all of a sudden, Mademoiselle Nicole! You deem it very wicked that I should be found here, while——"

"Gilbert!"

"Yes, go and tell mademoiselle that I love her. I shall say that it is you whom I love, and she will believe me, for you were foolish enough to tell her so at Taverney.

"Gilbert, my friend!"

"And you will be dismissed, Nicole; and in place of going to Trianon, and entering the household of the dauphiness with mademoiselle—instead of coquetting with the fine lords and rich gentlemen, as you will not fail to do if you remain with the family—instead of all this, you will be sent to enjoy the society of your admirer, Monsieur Beausire, an exempt, a soldier! Oh, what a direful fall! What a noble ambition Mademoiselle Nicole's is—to be the favored fair one of a guardsman!"

And Gilbert began to hum, in a low voice, with a most malicious accent:

> "In the Garde Française
> I had a faithful lover."

"In mercy, Monsieur Gilbert," said Nicole, "do not look at me in that ill-natured manner. Your eyes pierce me, even in the darkness. Do not laugh, either—your laugh terrifies me."

"Then open the door," said Gilbert, imperatively; "open the door for me, Nicole, and not another word of all this."

Nicole opened the door with so violent a nervous trembling, that her shoulders and head shook like those of an old woman.

Gilbert tranquilly stepped out first, and seeing that the young girl was leading him toward the door of the garden, he said:

"No, no; you have your means for admitting people here, I have my means for leaving it. Go to the greenhouse, to Monsieur Beausire, who must be waiting impatiently for you, and remain with him ten minutes longer than you intended to do. I will grant you this recompense for your discretion."

"Ten minutes, and why ten minutes?" asked Nicole, trembling.

"Because I require ten minutes to disappear. Go,
Nicole, go ; and like Lot's wife, whose story I told you at
Taverney, when you gave me a rendezvous among the hay-
stacks, do not turn round, else something worse will
happen to you than to be changed into a statue of salt.
Go, beautiful siren, go ; I have nothing else to say to
you."

Nicole, subdued, alarmed, conquered, by the coolness
and presence of mind shown by Gilbert, who held her
future destiny in his hands, turned with drooping head
toward the greenhouse, where Beausire was already uneasy
at her prolonged absence.

Gilbert, on his side, observing the same precautions as
before to avoid discovery, once more reached the wall,
seized his rope, and, assisted by the vine and trellis-work,
gained the first story in safety, and quickly ascended the
stairs.   As luck would have it, he met no one on his way
up ; the neighbors were already in bed, and Therese was
still at supper.

Gilbert was too much excited by his victory over Nicole
to entertain the least fear of missing his footing in the
leaden gutter.   He felt as if he could have walked on the
edge of a sharpened razor, had the razor been a league
long.   He regained his attic in safety therefore, closed the
window, seized the note which no one had touched, and
tore it in pieces.   Then he stretched himself with a delicious feeling of languor upon his bed.

Half an hour afterward Therese kept her word, and
came to the door to inquire how he was.   Gilbert thanked
her, in a voice interrupted by terrific yawns, as if he were
dying of sleep.   He was eager to be alone, quite alone, in
darkness and silence, to collect his thoughts, and analyze
the varied emotions of this ever-memorable day.

Soon, indeed, everything faded from his mind's eye ;
the baron, Philip, Nicole, Beausire, disappeared from
view, to give place to the vision of Andrée at her toilet,
her arms raised above her head, and detaching pins from
her long and flowing hair.

CHAPTER VIII.

THE BOTANISTS.

THE events which we have just related happened on Friday evening ; so that it was the second day after that the excursion which Rousseau looked forward to with so much pleasure was to take place.

Gilbert, indifferent to everything since he had heard that Andrée was soon to depart for Trianon, had spent the entire day leaning on his window-sill. During this day the window of Andrée's room remained open, and once or twice the young girl had approached it as if to breathe the fresh air. She was pale and weak ; but it seemed to Gilbert as if he would wish for nothing more than that Andrée should always inhabit that pavilion, that he should always have his attic, and that, once or twice every day, Andrée should come to the window as he had seen her that day.

The long, looked-for Sunday at last arrived. Rousseau had already made his preparations the day before ; his shoes were carefully blackened, and his gray coat, at once light and warm, was taken from the chest, to the great annoyance of Thérèse, who thought a blouse or a linen frock quite good enough for such a purpose. But Rousseau had completed his toilet without replying. Not only his own clothes, but Gilbert's also, had been passed in review with the greatest care, and the latter's had even been augmented by a pair of irreproachable stockings and new shoes, which Rousseau had presented him with as an agreeable surprise.

The herbal was also put in the nicest trim. Rousseau had not forgotten his collection of mosses which was to play a part in the proceedings of the day. Impatient as a child, he hastened more than twenty times to the window to see if the carriage that was passing was not M. de Jussieu's. At last he perceived a highly varnished chariot, a pair of splendid horses with rich harness, and an immense powdered footman standing at his door.   He ran instantly to Thérèse, exclaiming :

"Here it is ! here it is !"

And crying to Gilbert :

"Quick, quick, the carriage is waiting."

"Well," said Thérèse, sharply, "if you are so fond of riding in a coach, why did you not work in order to have one of your own, like Monsieur de Voltaire ? "

"Be quiet !" grumbled Rousseau.

"Dame ! you always say you have as much talent as he."

"I do not say so, hark you !" cried Rousseau, in a rage ; "I say—I say nothing !"

And all his joy fled, as it invariably did at the mention of that hated name.   Luckily, M. de Jussieu entered.

He was pomatumed, powdered, fresh as the spring. His dress consisted of a splendid coat of ribbed Indian satin, of a light gray color, a vest of pale lilac silk, white silk stockings of extraordinary fineness, and bright gold buckles.

On entering Rousseau's apartment he filled the room with a delightful perfume, which Thérèse inhaled without concealing her admiration.

"How handsome you are !" said Rousseau, looking askance at Thérèse, and comparing his modest dress and clumsy equipment with the elegant toilet of M. de Jussieu.

"Oh, I am afraid of the heat," said the elegant botanist.

"But the wood is damp !   If we botanize in the marshes, your silken stockings——"

"Oh, we can choose the driest places."

"And the aquatic mosses ?   Must we give them up for to-day ? "

"Do not be uneasy about that, my dear colleague."

"One would think you were going to a ball, or to pay your respects to ladies."

"Why should we not honor Dame Nature with a pair of silk stockings ? " replied M. de Jussieu, rather embar-

rassed ; " does she not deserve that we should dress ourselves for her ? "

Rousseau said no more from the moment that M. de
Jussieu invoked nature, he agreed with him, that it was
impossible to honor her too highly.

As for Gilbert, notwithstanding his stoicism, he gazed
at M. de Jussieu with envious eyes. Since he had observed so many young exquisites enhance their natural
advantages with dress, he had seen the utility, in a frivo-
lous point of view, of elegance, and whispered to himself
that this silk, this lace, this linen, would add a charm to
his youth ; and that if Andrée saw him dressed like M.
Jussieu instead of as he was, she would then deign to look
at him.

The carriage rolled off at the utmost speed of two fine
Danish horses, and an hour after their departure the botanists alighted at Bougival, and turned to the left by the
chestnut walk.

This walk, which at present is so surpassingly beautiful, was then at least quite as much so ; for the portion of
the rising ground which our explorers had to traverse,
already planted by Louis XIV., had been the object of
constant care since the king had taken a fancy to Marly.

The chestnut trees with their ruddy bark, their gigantic branches, and their fantastic forms—sometimes presenting in their knotty circumvolutions the appearance of
a huge boa twining itself round the trunk—sometimes that
of a bull prostrate upon the butcher's block and vomiting
a stream of black and clotted blood—the moss-covered
apple-trees and the colossal walnuts, whose foliage was
already assuming the dark-blue shade of summer—the
solitude, the picturesque simplicity and grandeur of the
landscape, which, with its old shadowy trees, stood out in
bold relief against the clear blue sky ; all this, clothed
with that simple and touching charm which nature ever
lends to her productions, plunged Rousseau in a state of
ecstasy impossible to be described.

Gilbert was calm, but moody ; his whole being was absorbed in this one thought :

" Andrée leaves the garden pavilion and goes to Trianon."

Upon the summit of the little hill, which the three botanists were climbing on foot, was seen the square tower of Luciennes.

The sight of this building from which he had fled, changed the current of Gilbert's thoughts, and recalled rather unpleasant recollections, unmingled, however, with fear. From his position in the rear of the party he saw two protectors before him ; and, feeling himself in safety, he gazed at Luciennes as a shipwrecked sailor from the shore looks upon the sand-bank upon which his vessel has struck.

Rousseau, spade in hand, began to fix his looks on the ground, M. de Jussieu did the same, but with this difference, that the former was searching for plants, while the latter was only endeavoring to keep his stockings from the damp.

" What a splendid Lepopodium ! " exclaimed Rousseau.

" Charming," replied M. de Jussieu ; " but let us pass on, if you have no objection."

" Ah ! the Lysimachia Fenella ! it is ready for culling —look ! "

" Pluck it, then, if it gives you pleasure."

" Oh ! just as you please. But are we not botanizing, then ? "

" Yes, yes ; but I think we shall find better upon that height yonder."

" As you please—let us go, then."

" What hour is it ? " asked M. de Jussieu ; " in my hurry I forgot my watch."

Rousseau pulled a very large silver watch from his pocket.

" Nine o'clock," said he.

" Have you any objection that we should rest a little ? " continued M. de Jussieu.

" Oh ! what a wretched walker you are," said Rousseau. " You see what it is to botanize in fine shoes and silk stockings."

" Perhaps I am hungry."

" Well, then, let us breakfast ; the village is about a quarter of a league from this."

" Oh, no ; we need not go so far."

" How so ? Have you our breakfast in your carriage ? "

" Look yonder—into that thicket ! " said M. de Jussieu, pointing with his hand toward the part of the horizon he indicated.

Rousseau stood upon tiptoe, and shaded his eyes with his hand.

" I can see nothing," said he.

" What ! Do you not see that little rustic roof ? "

" No."

" Surmounted by a weather-cock, and the walls thatched with red and white straw—a sort of rustic cottage, in short ? "

" Yes, I think I see it now ; a little building seemingly erected."

" A kiosk, that is it ? "

" Well ? "

" Well ! we shall find there the little luncheon I promised you."

" Very good," said Rousseau. " Are you hungry, Gilbert ? "

Gilbert, who had not paid any attention to this debate, and was employed in mechanically knocking off the heads of the wild flowers, replied :

" Whatever you please, sir."

" Come, then, if you please," said M. de Jussieu, " besides, nothing need prevent our gathering simples on the way."

" Oh," said Rousseau, " your nephew is a more ardent naturalist than you. I spent a day with him botanizing in the woods of Montmorency along with a select party. He finds well, he gathers well, he explains well."

" Oh, he is young ; he has his name to make yet."

" Has he not yours already made ? Oh ! comrade, comrade, you botanize like an amateur."

" Come, do not be angry, my dear philosopher. Hold !

here is the beautiful Plantago Monanthos. Did you find anything like that at your Montmorency ? "

" No, indeed," said Rousseau, quite delighted ; " I have often searched for it in vain. Upon the faith of a naturalist, it is magnificent."

" Oh, the beautiful pavilion ! " said Gilbert, who had passed from the rear-guard of the party into the van.

" Gilbert is hungry," replied M. de Jussieu.

" Oh, sir, I beg your pardon ; I can wait patiently until you are ready."

" Let us continue our task a little longer," said Rousseau, " inasmuch as botanizing after a meal is bad for digestion ; and besides the eye is then heavy and the back stiff. But what is this pavilion called ? "

" The mouse-trap," answered M. de Jussieu, remembering the name invented by M. de Sartines.

" What a singular name ! "

" Oh ! the country, you know, is the place for indulging all sorts of caprices."

" To whom do those beautiful grounds belong ? "

" I do not exactly know."

" You must know the proprietor, however, since you are going to breakfast there," said Rousseau, pricking up his ears with a slight shade of suspicion.

" Not at all—or, rather, I know every one here, including the gamekeepers, who have often seen me in their inclosures, and who always touch their hats, and sometimes offer me a hare or a string of woodcocks as a present from their masters. The people on this and the neighboring estates let me do here just as if I were on my own grounds. I do not know exactly whether this summer-house belongs to the Madame de Mirepoix or Madame d'Egmont, or—in short, I do not know to whom it belongs. But the most important point, my dear philosopher, I am sure you will agree with me, is, that we shall find there bread, fruit, and pastry."

The good-natured tone in which M. de Jussieu spoke dispelled the cloud of suspicion which had already begun to darken Rousseau's brow. The philosopher wiped his feet on the grass, rubbed the mold off his hands, and, preceded by M. de Jussieu, entered the mossy walk which wound gracefully beneath the chestnut-trees leading up to the hermitage.

Gilbert, who had again taken up his position in the rear, closed the march, dreaming of Andrée, and of the means of seeing her when she should be at Trianon.

CHAPTER IX.

THE PHILOSOPHERS IN THE TRAP.

On the summit of the hill, which the three botanists were ascending with some difficulty, stood one of those little rustic retreats, with gnarled and knotty pillars, pointed gables and windows festooned with ivy and clematis, which are the genuine offspring of English architecture, or, to speak more correctly, of English gardening, which imitates nature, or rather invents a species of nature for itself, thus giving a certain air of originality to its creations.

This summer-house, which was large enough to contain a table and six chairs, was floored with tiles and carpeted with handsome matting. The walls were covered with little mosaics of flint, the product of the river's beach, mingled with foreign shells of the most delicate tints, gathered from the shores of the Indian Ocean.

The ceiling was in relief and was composed of fir-cones and knotty excrescences of bark, arranged so as to imitate hideous profiles of fauns or savage animals, who seemed suspended over the heads of the visitors. The windows were each stained with some different shade, so that, according as the spectator looked out of the violet, the red, or the blue, glass, the woods of Vesinet seemed tinted by a stormy sky bathed in the burning rays of an August sun, or sleeping beneath the cold and frosty atmosphere of December. The visitor had only to consult his taste, that is to say, choose his window, and look out.

This sight pleased Gilbert greatly, and he amused himself with looking through the different tinted windows at the rich valley which lies stretched beneath the feet of a spectator situated on the hill of Luciennes, and at the noble Seine winding in the midst.

A sight nearly as interesting, however, at least in M. de Jussieu's opinion, was the tempting breakfast spread in the center of the summer-house, upon a table formed of gnarled and fantastic woodwork on which the bark had been allowed to remain.

There was the exquisite cream for which Marly is celebrated, the luscious apricots and plums of Luciennes, the crisp sausages of Nanterre smoking upon a porcelain dish, without the least trace being seen of any one who could have brought them thither; strawberries peeping from a graceful little basket lined with vine leaves, and beside the fresh and glistening pats of butter were rolls of homely peasant bread, with its rich brown crust, so dear to the pampered appetite of the inhabitants of towns. This sight drew an exclamation of admiration from Rousseau, who, philosopher as he was, was not the less an unaffected gourmand, for his appetite was as keen as his taste was simple.

"What folly!" said he to M. de Jussieu; "bread and fruits would have been sufficient, and even then, as true botanists and industrious explorers, we ought to have eaten the bread and munched the plums without ceasing our search among the grass or along the hedge-rows. Do you remember, Gilbert, our luncheon at Plessis Piquet?"

"Yes, sir, the bread and cherries which appeared to me so delicious?"

"Yes, that is how true lovers of nature should breakfast."

"But, my dear master," interrupted M. de Jussieu, "if you reproach me with extravagance, you are wrong; a more modest meal was never——"

"Oh!" cried the philosopher, "you do your table injustice, my Lord Lucullus."

"My table—by no means," said Jussieu.

" Who are our hosts, then ? " resumed Rousseau, with a smile which evinced at once good-humor and constraint, " Sprites ? "

" Or fairies ! " said M. de Jussieu, rising and glancing stealthily toward the door.

" Fairies ? " exclaimed Rousseau, gaily ; " a thousand blessings on them for their hospitality ! I am excessively hungry. Come, Gilbert, fall to."

And he cut a very respectable slice from the brown loaf, passing the bread and the knife to his disciple. Then, while taking a huge bite, he chose out some plums from the dish.

Gilbert hesitated.

" Come, come ! " said Rousseau. " The fairies will be offended by your stiffness, and will imagine you are dissatisfied with their banquet."

" Or that it is unworthy of you, gentlemen," uttered a silvery voice from the door of the pavilion where two young and lovely women appeared arm in arm, smiling, and making signs to M. de Jussieu to moderate his obeisances.

Rousseau turned, holding the half-tasted bread in his right hand and the remains of a plum in his left, and beholding these two goddesses, at least such they seemed to him by their youth and beauty, he remained stupefied with astonishment, bowing mechanically, and retreating toward the wall of the summer-house.

" Oh, countess," said M. de Jussieu, " you here ? What a delightful surprise ! "

" Good day, my dear botanist," said one of the ladies, with a grace and familiarity perfectly regal.

" Allow me to present Monsieur Rousseau to you," said Jussieu, taking the philosopher by the hand which held the brown bread.

Gilbert also had seen and recognized the ladies. He opened his eyes to their utmost width, and, pale as death, looked out of the window of the summer-house, with the idea of throwing himself from it.

" Good day, my little philosopher," said the other lady

to the almost lifeless Gilbert, patting his cheek with her rosy fingers.

Rousseau saw and heard—he was almost choking with rage. His disciple knew these goddesses, and was known to them. Gilbert was almost fainting.

" Do you not know her ladyship, the countess, Monsieur Rousseau ? " asked Jussieu.

" No," replied he, thunder-struck ; " it is the first time, I think——"

" Madame Dubarry," continued M. de Jussieu.

Rousseau started up, as if he stood on a red-hot plowshare.

" Madame Dubarry ! " he exclaimed.

"The same, sir," said the young lady, with surpassing grace, " who is most happy to have received in her house and to have been favored with a nearer view of the most illustrious thinker of the age."

" Madame Dubarry ! " continued Rousseau, without remarking that his astonishment was becoming a grave offense against good breeding. " She ! and doubtless this pavilion is hers, and doubtless it is she who has provided this breakfast."

" You have guessed rightly, my dear philosopher, she and her sister," continued Jussieu, ill at ease in the presence of this threatening storm.

" Her sister, who knows Gilbert."

" Intimately," replied Chon, with that saucy boldness which respected neither royal whims nor philosophers' fancies.

Gilbert looked as if he wished the earth would open and swallow him, so fiercely did Rousseau's eye rest upon him.

" Intimately ? " repeated Rousseau ; " Gilbert knew madame intimately, and I was not told of it ? But in that case I was betrayed, I was sported with."

Chon and her sister looked at each other with a malicious smile.

M. de Jussieu, in his agitation, tore a Malines ruffle worth forty louis-d'ors.

Gilbert clasped his hands as if to entreat Chon to be

silent, or M. Rousseau to speak more graciously to him. But, on the contrary, it was Rousseau who was silent and Chon who spoke.

" Yes," said she, " Gilbert and I are old friends ; he was a guest of mine. Were you not, little one ? What ! are you already ungrateful for the sweetmeats of Luciennes and Versailles ? "

This was the final blow. Rousseau's arms fell stiff and motionless.

" Oh ! " said he, looking askance at the young man, " that was the way, was it, you little scoundrel ? "

" Monsieur Rousseau ! " murmured Gilbert.

" Why, one would think you were weeping for the little tap I gave your cheek," continued Chon. " Well, I always feared you were ungrateful."

" Mademoiselle ! " entreated Gilbert.

" Little one," said Mme. Dubarry, " return to Luciennes ; your bonbons and Zamore await you, and though you left it in rather a strange manner, you shall be well received."

" Thank you, madame," said Gilbert, drily ; " when I leave a place, it is because I do not like it."

" And why refuse the favor that is offered to you ? " interrupted Rousseau, bitterly. " You have tasted of wealth, my dear Monsieur Gilbert, and you had better return to it."

" But, sir, when I swear to you——"

" Go ! go ! I do not like those who blow hot and cold with the same breath."

" But you will not listen to me, Monsieur Rousseau. "

" Well ? "

" I ran away from Luciennes, where I was kept locked up."

" A trap ! I know the malice of men."

" But, since I preferred you to them, since I accepted you as my host, my protecter, my master——"

" Hypocrisy ! "

" But, Monsieur Rousseau, if I wished for ricehs, I should accept the offer these ladies have made me."

"Monsieur Gilbert, I have been often deceived, but never twice by the same person ; you are free, go where you please."

"But where ? Good heavens !" cried Gilbert, plunged in an abyss of despair, for he saw his window, and the neighborhood of Andrée, and his love, lost to him forever —for his pride was hurt at being suspected of treachery ; and the idea that his self-denial, his long and arduous struggle against the indolence and the passions natural to his age, was misconstrued and despised, stung him to the quick.

"Where ? " said Rousseau. "Why, in the first place, to this lady, of course ; where could you meet a lovelier or more worthy protector ? "

"Oh ! my God ! my God ! " cried Gilbert, burying his head in his hands.

"Do not be afraid," said M. de Jussieu, deeply wounded, as a man of the world, by Rousseau's strange sally against the ladies ; "you will be taken care of, and whatever you may lose in one way, you will be amply compensated for."

"You see," said Rousseau, bitterly, "there is Monsieur de Jussieu, a learned man, a lover of nature, one of your accomplices," added he, with a grin which was meant for a smile, "who promises you assistance and fortune, and you may be sure, that what Monsieur de Jussieu promises he can perform."

As he spoke, Rousseau, no longer master of himself, bowed to the ladies with a most majestic air, did the same to M. de Jussieu, and then, without even looking at Gilbert, he calmly left the pavilion.

"Oh ! what an ugly animal a philosopher is ! " said Chon, coolly, looking after the Genevese, who walked, or rather stumbled, down the path.

"Ask what you wish," said M. de Jussieu to Gilbert, who still kept his face buried in his hands.

"Yes, ask, Monsieur Gilbert," added the countess, smiling on the abandoned disciple.

The latter raised his pale face, pushed back the hair

which perspiration and tears had matted over his forehead, and said with a firm voice :

"Since you are kind enough to offer me employment, I would wish to be assistant gardener at Trianon."

Chon and the countess looked at each other, and the former, with her tiny little foot, touched her sister's with a triumphant glance. The countess made a sign with her head that she understood perfectly.

"Is that practicable, Monsieur de Jussieu ?" asked the countess ; "I should wish it very much."

"If you wish it, madame," replied he, "it is done."

Gilbert bowed, and put his hand upon his heart, which now bounded with joy as a few moments before it had been overwhelmed with grief.

CHAPTER X.

THE APOLOGUE.

IN that little cabinet at Luciennes, where we have seen the Count Jean Dubarry imbibe so much chocolate, to the great annoyance of the countess, the Marshal de Richelieu was lunching with Mme. Dubarry, who, while amusing herself with pulling Zamore's ears, carelessly reclined at full length upon a couch of brocaded satin, while the old courtier uttered sighs of admiration at each new position the charming creature assumed.

"Oh, countess !" said he, smirking like an old woman, "your hair is falling down; look, there is a ringlet drooping on your neck. Ah ! your slipper is falling off, countess."

"Bah ! my dear duke, never mind," said she, absently ; and pulling a handful of hair from Zamore's head while she took a fresh position on the couch, more lovely and fascinating than that of Venus in her shell.

Zamore, entirely insensible to these graceful attitudes, bellowed with anger. The countess endeavored to quiet him by taking a handful of sugar-plums from the table, and filling his pockets with them. But Zamore was sulky, turned his pockets inside out, and emptied his sugar-plums upon the carpet.

" Oh, the little scoundrel ! " continued the countess, stretching out her tiny foot till it came in contact with the fantastic hose of the little negro.

" Oh, have mercy," cried the old marshal ; " upon my faith, you will kill him."

" Why cannot I kill everything which angers me to-day ! " said the countess ; " I feel merciless ! "

" Oh !" said the duke, " then, perhaps, I displease you."

" Oh, no ! quite the contrary ; you are an old friend, and I perfectly adore you ; but the fact is, I believe I am going mad."

" Can it be that those whom you have made mad have smitten you with their complaint ? "

" Take care ; you provoke me dreadfully with your gallant speeches, of which you do not believe one word."

" Countess ; countess ! I begin to think you are not mad but ungrateful."

" No, I am neither mad nor ungrateful ; I am——"

" Well ! confess.   What are you ? "

" I am angry, duke."

" Indeed ? "

" Are you surprised at that ? "

" Not in the least, countess ; and, upon my honor, you have reason to be so."

" Ah ! that is what annoys me in you, marshal."

Then there is something in my conduct which annoys you, countess ? "

"Yes."

" And what is this something, pray ?   I am rather old to begin to correct my faults, and yet there is no effort I would not make for you."

" Well, it is that you do not even know what is the cause of my anger, marshal."

" Oh, is that all ? "

" Then you know what vexes me ? "

" Of course ! Zamore has broken the Chinese fountain."

An imperceptible smile played around the young countess's mouth ; but Zamore, who felt himself guilty, dropped his head numbly, as if the skies were pregnant with clouds of blows and kicks.

" Oh, yes ! " said the countess, with a sigh ; " yes, duke, you are right, that is it, and in truth you are a very deep politician."

" I have always been told so," replied M. de Richelieu, with an air of profound modesty.

" Oh, I can see that without being told, duke. Have you not guessed the cause of my annoyance immediately, without looking to the right or left ? It is superb."

" Superb, indeed ; but still that is not all."

" Indeed ? "

" No, I can guess something else."

" And what can you guess ? "

" That you expected his majesty yesterday evening."

" Where ? "

" Here."

" Well ; what then ? "

" And that his majesty did not come."

" Well ; what then ? "

The countess reddened, and raised herself slightly upon her elbow.

" Oh ! " said she.

" And yet," said the duke, " I have just arrived from Paris."

" Well, what does that prove ? "

" Pardieu ! that I could not of course know what passed at Versailles ; and yet——"

" My dear duke, you are full of mystery to-day. When a person begins he should finish, or else not have commenced."

" You speak quite at your ease, countess. Allow me, at least, to take breath. Where was I ? "

" You were at : ' and yet.' "

" Oh, yes ! true : and yet I not only know that his majesty did not come, but also why he did not come."

"Duke, I have always thought you a sorcerer, and only wanted proof to be certain of the fact."

"Well ! that proof I will now give you."

The countess, who attached much more interest to this conversation than she wished to let appear, relinquished her hold on Zamore's head, in whose hair her long taper fingers had been carelessly playing.

"Give it, duke, give it," said she.

"Before my lord governor ? " asked the duke.

"Vanish, Zamore," said the countess to the negro boy, who, mad with delight, made only one bound from the boudoir to the ante-chamber

"An excellent step," murmured Richelieu ; "then I must tell you all, countess ? "

"What ! did that monkey Zamore embarrass you, duke ? "

"To tell the truth, countess, any one can embarrass me."

"Yes, I can understand that. But is Zamore any one ? "

"Zamore is neither blind, deaf, nor dumb ; therefore, he is some one. I distinguish by the title of some one, every person who is my equal in the hearing, seeing, and speaking faculties ; every person who can see what I do, hear and repeat what I say ; every person, in short, who might betray me. This theory explained, I proceed."

"Yes, yes, duke, proceed ; you will gratify me exceedingly."

"Gratify ! I think not, countess ; but no matter, I must go on. Well, the king was at Trianon yesterday."

"The little or the great Trianon ? "

"The little. The dauphiness was leaning on his arm."

"Ah ! "

"And the dauphiness, who is charming, as you know——"

"Alas ! "

"Coaxed him so much, with dear papa here, and dear papa there, that his majesty, who has a heart of gold, could not resist her. So after the walk came supper, and after supper, amusing games ; so that, in short——"

"In short," said Mme. Dubarry, pale with impatience, "in short, the king did not come to Luciennes—that is what you would say ? "

" Exactly."

" Oh, it is perfectly easily explained ; his majesty found there all that he loves."

" Ah ! by no means, and you are far from believing one word of what you say ; all that pleases him, he found, no doubt."

" Take care, duke, that is much worse ; to sup, chat, and play is all that he wants. And with whom did he play ? "

" With Monsieur de Choiseul."

The countess made an angry gesture.

" Shall I not pursue the subject further, countess ? " asked Richelieu.

" On the contrary, sir speak on."

" You are as courageous, madame, as you are witty ; let me therefore take the bull by the horns, as the Spaniards say."

" Madame de Choiseul would not forgive you for that proverb, duke."

" Yet it is not applicable. I told you then, madame, that Monsieur de Choiseul, since I must name him, held the cards ; and with so much good fortune——"

" That he won."

" By no means ; that he lost, and that his majesty won a thousand louis-d'ors at piquet, a game on which his majesty piques himself very much, seeing that he plays it very badly."

" Oh ! that Choiseul ! that Choiseul ! " murmured Mme. Dubarry. " But Madame de Grammont was of the party also, was she not ? "

" That is to say, countess, she was paying her respects before her departure."

" The duchess ! "

" Yes, she is very foolish, I think."

" Why so ? "

" Finding that no one persecutes her, she pouts ; finding that no one exiles her, she exiles herself."

" Where to ? "

" To the provinces."

" She is going to plot."

" Parbleu, what else would you expect her to do ?   Well, as she is about to set out, she very naturally wished to take leave of the dauphiness, who, naturally, is very fond of her.   That is why she was at Trianon."

" The great ? "

" Of course.   The little Trianon is not yet furnished."

" Ah ! her highness the dauphiness, by surrounding herself with all these Choiseuls, shows plainly which party she intends to embrace."

" No, countess, do not let us exaggerate ; to-morrow the duchess will be gone."

" And the king was amused where I was absent ! " cried the countess, with indignation not unmixed with terror.

" Yes, it is perfectly incredible, countess, but still it is so.   Well, what do you conclude from it ? "

" That you are well informed, duke."

" Is that all ? "

" No."

" Finish, then."

" I gather from it that we shall all be lost if we do not rescue the king from the clutches of these Choiseuls, either with his consent or without it."

" Alas ! "

" I say we," resumed the countess, " but, do not fear, duke ; I speak only of our own family."

" And your friends, countess ; permit me to claim that title.   So then——"

" Then you are one of my friends ? "

" I think I have said so, madame."

" That is not enough."

" I think I have proved it."

" That is better.   And you will assist me ? "

" With all my power, countess ; but——"

" But what ? "

" I cannot conceal from you that the task is difficult."

" Are these Choiseuls positively not to be rooted out, then ? "

" They are firmly planted at least."

" Then, whatever our friend La Fontaine may say, neither wind nor storm can prevail against this oak ? "

" The minister is a lofty genius."

" Bah ! you speak like an encyclopedist ! "

" Am I not a member of the academy ? "

" Oh, you are so slightly so."

" True, you are right ; my secretary is the member, not I. But, nevertheless, I maintain my opinion."

" But may I ask in what does this mighty genius shine ? "

" In this, madame, that he has made such a piece of work with the parliament and the English, that the king cannot do without him."

" The parliament ! Why, he excites it against his majesty."

" Of course ; therein lies his cleverness."

" He provokes the English to war."

" Of course. Peace would ruin him."

" That is not genius, duke."

" What is it then, countess ? "

" It is high treason."

" When high treason is successful, countess, it is genius, and a lofty description of genius, too."

" Then, by that mode of reasoning, I know some one who is as great a genius as Monsieur de Choiseul."

" Bah ! "

" Why, he has at least caused the parliament to revolt."

" You puzzle me exceedingly, countess."

" Do you not know him, duke ? He belongs to your own family."

" Can I have a man of genius in my family ? Do you speak of my uncle, the cardinal duke, madame ? "

" No, I mean the Duke d'Aiguillon, your nephew."

" Ah, Monsieur d'Aiguillon. Yes, true, it was he who set that affair of La Chalotais moving. 'Pon honor, he is a brave youth. Yes, true ; that was a tough piece of work. Countess, there is a man whom a woman of spirit should gain over to her cause."

" Are you aware, duke," said the countess," that I do not know your nephew ? "

" Indeed, madame ?   You don't know him ? "

" No, I have never seen him."

" Poor fellow ! In fact ; I now remember that since you came to court he has always been at Brittany.   Let him look to himself when he first sees you ; he has not latterly been accustomed to the sun."

" What does he do among all those black gowns—a nobleman of spirit like him ? "

" He revolutionizes them, not being able to do better. You understand, countess, every one takes pleasure where they can find it, and there is not much to be had in Brittany. Ah ! he is an active man.   Peste ! what a servant the king might have in him, if he wished.   Parliament would not be insolent to him.   Oh ! he is a true Richelieu.   Permit me, therefore, count-ess——"

" What ? "

" To present him to you on his first appearance."

" Does he intend to visit Paris soon? "

" Oh ! madame, who knows ?   Perhaps he will have to remain another luster in Brittany, as that scoundrel, Voltaire, says ; perhaps he is on his way hither ; perhaps two hundred leagues off ; or perhaps at the barrier."

And while he spoke, the marshal studied the lady's features to see what effect his words produced.   But after having reflected for a moment, she said :

" Let us return to the point where we left off."

" Wherever you please, countess."

" Where were we ? "

" At the moment when his majesty was enjoying himself so much at Trianon in the company of Monsieur de Choiseul."

" And when we were speaking of getting rid of this Choiseul, duke."

" That is to say, when you were speaking of getting rid of him, countess."

" Oh ! I am so anxious that he should go," said the favorite, " that I think I shall die if he remains.   Will you not assist me a little, my dear duke ? "

"Oh !" said Richelieu, bridling, "in politics, that is called an overture."

"Take it as you will, call it what you please, but answer categorically."

"Oh ! what a long, ugly adverb, in such a pretty little mouth."

"Do you call that answering, duke ?"

"No, not exactly ; I call that preparing my answer."

"Is it prepared ?"

"Wait a little."

"You hesitate, duke ?"

"Oh, no !"

"Well, I am listening."

"What do you think of apologues, countess ?"

'Why, that they are very antiquated."

"Bah ! the sun is antiquated also, and yet we have not invented any better means of seeing."

"Well, let me hear your apologue, then ; but let it be clear."

"As crystal, fair lady. Let us suppose, then, countess— you know one always supposes something in an apologue."

"How tiresome you are, duke."

"You do not believe one word of what you say, countess, for you never listened to me more attentively."

"I was wrong, then ; go on."

"Suppose, then, that you were walking in your beautiful garden at Luciennes, and that you saw a magnificent plum, one of those Queen Claudes which you are so fond of because their vermilion and purple tints resemble your own."

"Go on, flatterer."

"Well, I was saying, suppose you saw one of these plums at the extremity of one of the loftiest branches of the tree, what would you do, countess ?"

"I would shake the tree, to be sure."

"Yes, but in vain, for the tree is large and massive, and not to be rooted out, as you said just now ; and you would soon perceive that without even succeeding in shaking it, you would tear your charming little hands against its rough bark. And then you would say, reclining your head to one side, in that adorable manner which belongs only to you and the flowers : ' Oh ! how I wish I had this plum upon the ground !' and then you would get angry."

" That is all very natural, duke."

" I shall certainly not be the person to contradict you."

" Go on, my dear duke, your apologue is exceedingly interesting."

" All at once, when turning your little head from side to side, you perceive your friend, the Duke de Richelieu, who is walking behind you, thinking."

" Of what ? "

" What a question ! Pardieu ! of you ; and you say, to him, with your heavenly voice : ' Oh ! duke ! duke !'"

" Well ? "

" ' You are a man ; you are strong, you look Mahon ; shake this devil of a plum-tree for me, that I may pluck this provoking plum ? ' Is not that it, countess ? "

" Exactly, duke ; I repeated that to myself while you were saying it aloud. But what did you reply ? "

" Reply ? Oh ! I replied : ' How you run on, countess ! Certainly nothing could give me greater pleasure ; but only look how firm the tree is, how knotty the branches. I have a sort of affection for my hands as well as you, though they are fifty years older than yours.' "

" Ah ! " said the countess, suddenly, " yes, yes, I comprehend."

" Then finish the apologue. What did you say to me ? "

" I said, ' My little marshal, do not look with indifferent eyes upon this plum, which you look at indifferently only because it is not for you. Wish for it along with me, my dear marshal ; covet it along with me, and if you shake the tree properly, if the plum falls, then we will eat it together.' "

" Bravo ! " exclaimed the duke, clapping his hands.

" Is that it ? "

" Faith, countess, there is none like you for finishing an apologue. By mine honor, as my deceased father used to say, it is right well tricked out."

" You will shake the tree, duke ? "

" With two hands and three hearts, countess."

" And the plum was really a Queen Claude ? "

" I am not quite sure of that, countess."

" What was it, then ? "

" Do you know it seemed much more like a portfolio dangling from a tree."

" Then we will divide the portfolio."

" Oh, no ! for me alone. Do not envy me the morocco, countess. There will fall so many beautiful things from the tree along with the portfolio when I shake it, that you will not know how to choose."

" Then, marshal, it is a settled affair ? "

" I am to have Monsieur de Choiseul's place ? "

" If the king consents."

" Does not the king do all you wish ? "

" You see plainly he does not, since he will not send this Choiseul away."

" Oh ! I trust the king will gladly recall his old companion."

" And you ask nothing for the Duke d'Aiguillon ? "

" No, faith. The rascal can ask for himself."

" Besides, you will be there. And now it is my turn to ask."

" That is but just."

" What will you give me ? "

" Whatever you wish."

" I want everything."

" That is reasonable."

" And shall I have it ? "

" What a question ! But will you be satisfied, at least, and ask me for nothing further ? "

" Except the merest trifle. You know Monsieur de Taverney ? "

" He is a friend of forty years' standing."

" He has a son ? "

" And a daughter. Well ? "

" That is all."

" How, all ? "

" Yes ; the other demand I have to make shall be made in proper time and place.   In the meantime, we understand each other, duke ? "

" Yes, countess."

" Our compact is signed."

" Nay, more—it is sworn."

" Then shake the tree for me."

" Oh, rest satisfied ; I have the means."

" What are they ? "

" My nephew."

" What else ? "

" The Jesuits."

" Oh, ho ! "

" I have a very nice little plan cut and dry.

" May I know it ? "

" Alas ! countess——"

" Well, you are right."

" You know, secrecy——"

" Is half the battle.   I complete your thought for you."

" You are charming."

" But I wish to shake the tree also."

" Oh, very well, shake away, countess ; it can do no harm."

" But when will you begin to undermine, duke ? " asked the countess.

" To-morrow.   And when do you commence to shake ? "

A loud noise of carriages was heard in the courtyard, and almost immediately cries of " Long live the king ! " rose on the air.

" I ? " said the countess, glancing at the window, "I shall commence directly."

" Bravo ! "

"Retire by the little staircase, duke, and wait in the courtyard.   You shall have my answer in an hour."

CHAPTER XI.

THE MAKE-SHIFT OF HIS MAJESTY LOUIS XV.

LOUIS XV. was not so easy-tempered that one could talk politics with him every day ; for in truth politics were his aversion, and when he was in a bad temper he always escaped from them with this argument, which admitted of no reply :

"Bah ! the machine will last out my time."

When circumstances were favorable it was necessary to take advantage of them ; but it rarely happened that the king did not retain the advantage which a moment of good humor had caused him to lose.

Mme. Dubarry knew her king so well that, like fishermen well skilled in the dangers of the sea, she never attempted to start in bad weather.

Now, the present visit of his majesty to Luciennes was one of the best opportunities possible. The king had done wrong the previous day, and knew beforehand that he should receive a scolding ; he would therefore be an easy prey.

But however confiding the game which the hunter lies in wait for in his lurking-place, it has always a certain instinct which must be guarded against. But this instinct is set at naught if the sportsman knows how to manage it.

The countess managed the royal game she had in view, and which she wished to capture, in the following manner.

We have said that she was in a most becoming morning-dress, like those in which Boucher represents his shepherdesses. Only she had no rouge on, for Louis XV. had a perfect antipathy to rouge.

The moment his majesty was announced, the countess seized her pot of rouge and began to rub her cheeks with it vigorously.

The king saw what the countess was doing from the anteroom.

"Fie !" said he, as he entered, "how she daubs herself !"

"Ah ! good day, sire," said the countess, without interrupting her occupation even when the king kissed her on the neck.

"You did not expect me, it seems, countess ?" asked the king.

"Why do you think so, sire ?"

"Because you soil your face in that manner."

"On the contrary, sire, I was certain that I should have the honor of receiving your majesty in the course of the day."

"How you say that, countess."

"Indeed ?"

"Yes, you are as serious as Monsieur Rousseau when he is listening to his own music."

"That is because I have serious things to say to your majesty."

"Oh ! I see what is coming, countess—reproaches."

"I reproach you, sire ? And why, pray ?"

"Because I did not come yesterday."

"Oh, sire, do me the justice not to imagine that I pretend to monopolize your majesty."

"My little Jeanne, you are getting angry."

"Oh ! no, sire, I am angry already."

"But hear me, countess ; I assure you I never ceased thinking of you the whole time."

"Pshaw !"

"And the evening seemed interminable to me."

"But once more, sire, I was not speaking of that at all. Your majesty may spend your evenings where you please without consulting any one."

"Quite a family party, madame ; only my own family."

"Sire, I did not even inquire."

"Why not ?"

"Dame ! you know it would be very unbecoming for me to do so."

"Well," said the king, "if that is not what you are displeased with me, for, what is it, then ? We must be just in this world."

" I have no complaint to make against you, sire."

" But since you are angry——"

" Yes, I am angry, sire ; that is true, but it is at being made a make-shift."

" You a make-shift ? Good heavens ! "

" Yes, I ! The Countess Dubarry ! The beautiful Jeanne, the charming Jeannette, the fascinating Jeanneton, as your majesty calls me ; I am a make-shift."

" But how ? "

" Because I have my king, my lover, only when Madame de Choiseul and Madame de Grammont do not want him."

" Oh ! oh ! countess——"

" Oh, I give you my honor, sire, I say what I think. But what can you expect from me ? I am an uneducated woman. I am the mistress of Blaise—the beautiful Bourbonnaise, you know."

" Countess, the Choiseuls will be revenged."

" What matter, if they revenge themselves with my vengeance ? "

" They will despise us."

" You are right. Well, I have an excellent plan which I shall carry into execution at once."

" And that is ? " asked the anxious king.

" Simply to go at once."

The king shrugged his shoulders.

" Ah ! you do not believe me, sire ? "

" No, indeed ! "

" That is because you do not take the trouble to reason —you confound me with others."

" How so ? "

" Madame de Chateauroux wanted to be a goddess. Madame de Pompadour aimed at being a queen. Others wished to be rich, powerful, or to humiliate the ladies of the court by the weight of their favors. I have none of these defects."

" That is true."

" But yet I have many good qualities."

" That is also true."

" Mere words, of course."

" Oh, countess! no one knows your worth better than I do."

" Well, but listen. What I am going to say will not alter your conviction."

"Speak."

" In the first place, I am rich and independent of every one."

" Do you wish to make me regret that, countess ? "

Then I have not the least ambition for all that flatters these ladies, the least desire for what they aim at ; my only wish is to love sincerely him whom I have chosen, whether he be soldier or a king.   When I love him no longer, I care for nothing else."

" Let me trust you care a little for me yet, countess."

" I have not finished, sire."

" Proceed, madame."

" I am pretty, I am young, and may reasonably hope for ten years more of beauty ; and the moment I cease to be your majesty's favorite, I shall be the happiest and most honored woman in the world.   You smile, sire—I am sorry to tell you it is because you do not reflect.   When you had had enough, and your people too much, of your other favorites, you sent them away, and your people blessed you and execrated the disgraced favorite more than ever ; but I shall not wait until I am sent away.   I shall leave the place, and make it known publicly that I have left it.   I shall give a hundred thousand livres to the poor, I shall retire to a convent for a week, and in less than a month my portrait will be hung up in all the churches as that of a converted sinner."

" Oh ! countess, you do not speak seriously ? " said the king.

" Look at me, sire, and see if I am serious or not. I swear to you that I never was more serious in my life."

" Then you will commit this folly, Jeanne ?   But do you not see that by so doing you place yourself at the mercy of my whim, my lady the countess ? "

" No, sire ; to do so would be to say, ' choose between this and that ; ' whereas I say, ' adieu, sire ! ' nothing more."

The king turned pale, but this time with anger.

" If you forget yourself so far, madame, take care."

" Of what, sire ? "

" I shall send you to the Bastile, and you will find the Bastile rather more tiresome than a convent."

" Oh, sire ! " said the countess, clasping her hands. " if you would but do me that favor it would delight me ! "

" Delight you ? How so ? "

" Yes, indeed. My secret ambition has always been to be popular like Monsieur de la Chalotais or Monsieur de Voltaire. I only want the Bastile for that. A little of the Bastile, and I shall be the happiest of women. I can then write memoirs of myself, of your ministers, of your daughters, of yourself and transmit the virtues of Louis the Well-beloved to the remotest posterity. Give me the lettre de cachet, sire. Here, I will provide the pen and ink."

And she pushed a pen and inkstand which were upon the work-table toward the king.

The king, thus braved, reflected a moment ; then, rising :

" Very well, madame," said he. " Adieu."

" My horses," cried the countess. " Adieu, sire."

The king made a step toward the door.

" Chon ! " said the countess.

Chon entered.

" My trunks, my traveling equipage, and post-horses," said she, " quick ! lose no time ! "

" Post-horses ! " said Chon, startled. " Good heavens ! what is the matter ? "

" We must leave this as quickly as possible, my dear, else the king will send us to the Bastile. There is no time to be lost. Make haste, Chon, make haste."

This reproach stung Louis to the heart. He approached the countess and took her hand.

" Forgive my warmth, countess," said he.

" In truth, sire, I am surprised you did not threaten me with the gibbet."

" Oh ! countess ! "

" Of course.   Thieves are always hung."

" Thieves ? "

" Yes ; do I not steal the Countess de Grammont's place ? "

" Countess ! "

" Dame ! that is my crime, sire.

" Be just, countess, you irritated me."

" And how ? "

The king took her hands.

" We were both wrong.   Let us forgive each other."

" Are you serious in your wish for a reconciliation, sire ? "

" On my honor."

" Go, Chon."

" Without ordering anything ? " asked Chon.

" No ; order what I told you."

" Countess ! "

" But let them wait for fresh orders."

" Ah ! "

Chon left the room.

" Then you wish me to remain ? " said the countess.

" Above all things."

" Reflect on what you say, sire."

The king reflected, but he could not retract ; besides, she wanted to see how far the requirements of the victor would go.

" Go," said he.

" Immediately.   Mark, sire ! I go without saying any-thing."

" I observed it."

" But if I remain, I shall ask for something."

" Well, what is it ?   I merely ask for information."

" Ah ! you know very well."

" No."

" Yes, for you make a grimace."

"Monsieur de Choiseul's dismissal, is it?"

"Exactly."

"It is impossible, countess."

"My horses, then."

"But, ill-natured creature that you are——"

"Sign my lettre-de-cachet for the Bastile, or the letter which dismisses the minister."

"There is an alternative," said the king.

"Thanks for your clemency, sire; it seems I shall be permitted to go without being arrested."

"Countess, you are a woman."

"Fortunately I am."

"And you talk politics like an angry, rebellious woman. I have no grounds for dismissing Monsieur de Choiseul."

"I understand he is the idol of the parliament; he encourages them in their revolt."

"But there must be some pretext."

"A pretext is the reason of the weak."

"Countess, Monsieur de Choiseul is an honest man, and honest men are rare."

"Honest! he sells you to the gentlemen of the black robe, who swallow up all the gold in the kingdom."

"No exaggeration, countess."

"Half, then."

"Good heavens!" cried Louis XV.

"But I am talking folly. What are parliaments, Choiseuls, governments, to me? What is the king to me, when I am only his make-shift?"

"Once more that word."

"Always."

"Give me two hours to consider, countess."

"Ten minutes, sire. I will retire into my apartment; slip your answer under the door—there are pen, ink, and paper. If in ten minutes you have not replied, and replied as I wish, adieu. Think no more of me—I shall be gone. If not——"

"If not?"

"Then you have once more your Jeanne."

Louis XV. kissed the hands of the countess, who, like

the Parthian, threw back her most fascinating smile on him as she left the room.

The king made no opposition, and the countess locked herself into the next apartment.

Five minutes afterward a folded paper grazed the silken mat and the rich carpet beneath the door.

The countess eagerly devoured the contents of the letter, hastily wrote some words with a pencil on a scrap of paper, and, opening the window, threw the paper to M. de Richelieu, who was walking in the little courtyard under an awning, in great trepidation lest he should be seen, and therefore keeping himself out of view as much as possible.

The marshal unfolded the paper, read it, and, in spite of his five and sixty years, hastily ran to the large courtyard, and jumped into his carriage.

"Coachman," said he, " to Versailles, as quick as possible ! "

The paper which was thrown to M. de Richelieu from the window merely contained these words, " I have shaken the tree—the portfolio has fallen."

CHAPTER XII

HOW KING LOUIS XV. TRANSACTED BUSINESS.

THE next day there was a great commotion at Versailles. Whenever two courtiers met there, there was nothing but mysterious signs and significant shakes of the hand, or else folded arms, and looks upward, expressive of their grief and surprise.

M. de Richelieu, with a number of his partisans, was in the king's ante-chamber at Trianon, about ten o'clock.

The count Jean, all bedizened with lace and perfectly dazzling, conversed with the old marshal and conversed gaily, if his joyous face could be taken as testimony of the fact.

About eleven o'clock the king passed quickly through the gallery and entered the council-chamber without speaking to any one.

At about five minutes past eleven M. de Choiseul alighted from his carriage and crossed the gallery with his portfolio under his arm.

As he passed through the throng, there was a hurried movement among the courtiers, who all turned round as if talking among themselves, in order to avoid bowing to the minister.

The duke paid no attention to this maneuver ; he entered the closet where the king was turning over some papers while sipping some chocolate.

" Good morning, duke," said the king, familiarly ; " are we charmingly this morning ? "

" Sire, Monsieur de Choiseul is quite well, but the minister is very ill, and comes to request that your majesty, since you have not yet spoken, will accept his resignation. I thank the king for permitting me to take the initiative in this matter ; it is a last favor, for which I am deeply grateful."

" How, duke ? Your resignation ? what does all that mean ? "

" Sire, your majesty yesterday signed for Madame Dubarry an order which deposes me. This news is already spread all over Paris and Versailles. The evil is done ; nevertheless, I was unwilling to leave your majesty's service without receiving a formal order with the permission. For, nominated officially, I can consider myself only dismissed by an official act."

" What, duke," exclaimed the king, laughing, for the severe and lofty attitude of M. de Choiseul made him almost tremble, " did you, a man of genius and skilled in official forms, did you believe that ? "

" But, sire," said the surprised minister, " you have signed."

" What ? "

" A letter in the possession of Madame Dubarry."

" Ah ! duke, have you never felt the want of peace ? You are most fortunate. Madame de Choiseul must indeed be a model."

The duke, offended by the comparison, frowned.

" Your majesty," said he, " has too much firmness of character, and above all, too much tact and discretion, to mix up affairs of state with what you deign to call household matters."

" Choiseul, I must tell you how that affair happened ; it is very amusing. You are aware that you are very much feared in that quarter."

" Rather say hated, sire."

" Hated, if you will. Well, this mad-cap countess left me no alternative but to send her to the Bastile, or to thank you for your services."

" Well ! sire ? "

" Well, duke, you must confess that it would have been a pity to lose the sight which Versailles presents this morning. I have been amused since yesterday with seeing the couriers depart in all directions, and watching the faces brighten up or lengthen. Since yesterday Cotillion III. is Queen of France. It is exceedingly amusing."

" But the end of all this, sire ? "

" The end, my dear duke," said the king, seriously, " the end will always remain the same. You know me ; I always seem to yield, but I never yield in reality. Let the women swallow the honeyed morsel I throw them now and then, as to another Cerberus ; but let us live quietly, uninterruptedly, always together. And since we are on the chapter of explanations, keep this one for yourself. Whatever report you may hear, whatever letter you may receive from me, do not absent yourself from Versailles. As long as I continue to say to you what I do now, duke, we shall be good friends."

The king extended his hand to his minister, who bowed over it, without gratitude and without anger.

" And now, my dear duke, let us to business."

" At your majesty's pleasure," replied the minister, opening his portfolio.

" Well, tell me something of these fireworks, to begin with."

" Ah, that was a great disaster, sire."

" Whose fault was it ? "

" Monsieur Bignon's, the provost of the merchants."

" Did the people cry out very much ? "

" Oh ! very much."

" Then perhaps we had better dismiss this Monsieur Bignon."

" One of the members of parliament was nearly killed in the mélée, and his colleagues therefore took the matter up warmly. But the advocate general, Seguier, made a very eloquent speech to prove that this misfortune was the work of fate alone. His speech was applauded, and so the affair is over for the present."

" So much the better ! Let us pass to the parliament, duke. Ah ! we are reproached for that."

" I am blamed, sire, for not supporting Monsieur d'Aiguillon against Monsieur de la Chalotais. But who blames me ? The very people who carried your majesty's letter about with all the demonstrations of joy. Remember, sire, that Monsieur d'Aiguillon overstepped the bounds of his authority in Brittany, that the Jesuits were really exiled, and that Monsieur de la Chalotais was right. Your majesty has publicly acknowleged the innocence of the attorney-general. The king cannot thus be made to stultify himself. To his minister that is nothing, but in presence of his people——"

" In the meantime the parliament feels itself strong."

" And it is strong. How can it be otherwise ? The members are reprimanded, imprisoned, persecuted, and then declared innocent. I do not accuse Monsieur d'Aiguillon of having commenced this affair of La Chalotais, but I can never forgive him for having been in the wrong in it."

" Oh ! come, duke, the evil is done, think of the remedy. How can we bridle these insolent minions ? "

" Let the intrigues of the chancellor cease—let Monsieur d'Aiguillon have no more support, and the anger of the parliament will at once subside."

" But that would be to yield, duke."

" Then your majesty is represented by Monsieur d'Aiguillon, and not by me ? "

This was a home thrust, and the king felt it.

" You know," said he, " I do not like to affront my
servants, even when they have been in the wrong. But
no more of this unfortunate business ; time will decide
who is right. Let us speak of foreign affairs. I am told
we shall have a war."

" Sire, if there be war, it will be a just and necessary
war."

" With the English."

" Does your majesty fear the English ? "

" Oh ! upon the sea."

" Your majesty may rest tranquil. My cousin, the Duke
de Praslin, your minister of marine, will tell you that he
has sixty-four men-of-war, not including those which are
on the stocks. Besides, there are materials sufficient
to construct twelve more in a year. Then there are fifty
first-rate frigates—a respectable force with which to meet
a naval war. For a continental war we have more than
all that, we have the remembrance of Fontenoy."

" Very well ; but why must I fight the English, my
dear duke ? A much less skilful minister than you, the
Abbé Dubois, always avoided war with England."

" I dare say, sire. The Abbé Dubois received six
hundred thousand pounds sterling per month from the
English."

" Oh ! duke."

" I have the proof, sire."

" Well, be it so. But where are the grounds for
war ? "

" England covets all the Indies ; I have been obliged to
give the most stringent and hostile orders to your officers
there. The first collision will call forth demands for redress
from England ; my official advice is that we do not listen
to them. Your majesty's government must make itself
respected by force, as it used to do by corruption."

" Oh, let us pocket the affront. Who will know what
happens in India ? It is so far from here."

The duke bit his lips.

" There is a *casus belli* nearer home, sire," said he.

" Another ? What is that ? "

" The Spaniards claim the Malouine and Falkland Islands.. The port of Egmont was arbitrarily occupied by the English ; the Spaniards drove them from it by main force. The English are enraged ; they threaten the Spaniards with instant war if they do not give them satisfaction."

" Well ! but if the Spainards are in the wrong, let them unravel the knot themselves."

" And the family compact, sire ? ? Why did you insist on the signing of this compact, which allies so closely all the Bourbons of Europe against English encroachments ? "

The king hung his head.

" Do not be uneasy, sire," said Choiseul ; " you have a formidable army, an imposing fleet, and sufficient money. I can raise enough without making the people cry out. If we have a war, it will be an additional glory to your majesty's reign, and it will furnish the pretext and excuse for several aggrandizements which I have in the project."

" But in that case, duke, we must have peace in the interior ; let there not be war everywhere."

" But the interior is quiet, sire," replied the duke, affecting not to understand.

" No ! no ! you see plainly it is not. You love me, and serve me well. Others say they love me, and their con· duct does not at all resemble yours. Let there be concord between all shades of opinion ; let me live happily, my dear duke."

" It is not my fault, sire, if your happiness is not complete."

" That is the way to speak. Well, come, then, and dine with me to-day."

" At Versailles, sire ? "

" No ; at Luciennes."

" I regret exceedingly, sire, that I cannot ; but my family is in great alarm on account of the reports which were spread yesterday. They think I am in disgrace with your majesty, and I cannot let so many loving hearts suffer."

" And do those of whom I speak not suffer, duke ?

Remember how happily we three used to live together in the time of the poor marchioness."

The duke dropped his head, his eyes dimmed, and he uttered a half-suppressed sigh.

"Madame de Pompadour was extremely jealous of your majesty's glory, and had lofty political ideas, sire. I confess that her character sympathized strongly with my own. I often emulated and strove along with her in the great enterprises she undertook ; yes, we understood each other."

"But she meddled with politics, duke, and every one blamed her for it."

"True."

"The present one, on the contrary, is mild as a lamb ; she has never yet asked me for a single lettre-de-cachet, even against the pamphleteers and sonnet writers. Well, they reproach her as if she followed in the other's footsteps. Oh, duke ! it is enough to disgust one with progress. Come, will you make your peace at Luciennes ?"

"Sire, deign to assure the Countess Dubarry that I esteem her as a charming woman, and well worthy of the king's love, but——"

"Ah ! a but, duke——"

"But," continued M. de Choiseul, "that my conviction is, that if your majesty is necessary for the welcome of France, a good minister is of more importance to your majesty in the present juncture than a charming mistress."

"Let us speak no more of it, duke, and let us remain good friends. But calm Madame de Grammont, and let her not lay any more plots against the countess ; the women will imbroil us."

"Madame de Grammont, sire, is too anxious to please your majesty ; that is her failing."

"But she displeases me by annoying the countess, duke."

"Well, Madame de Grammont is going, sire ; we shall see her no more. That will be an enemy less."

"I did not mean that ; you go too far. But my head burns, duke ; we have worked this morning like Louis XIV. and Colbert—quite in the style of the ' Grand

Siècle,' as the philosophers say. Apropos, duke, are you a philosopher ? "

" I am your majesty's humble servant," replied M. de Choiseul.

" You charm me ; you are an invaluable man. Give me your arm, I am quite giddy."

The duke hastened to offer his arm to his majesty.

He guessed that the folding-doors would be thrown open, that the whole court was in the gallery, and that he should be seen in this triumphant position. After having suffered so much, he was not sorry to make his enemies suffer in their turn.

The usher, in fact, now opened the doors, and announced the king in the gallery.

Louis XV. crossed the gallery, leaning heavily on M. de Choiseul's arm, talking and smiling, without remarking, or seeming to remark, how pale Jean Dubarry was and how red M. de Richelieu.

But M. de Choiseul saw these shades of expression very well. With elastic step, lofty head, and sparkling eyes, he passed before the courtiers, who now approached as eagerly as they had before kept away.

" There," said the king, at the end of the gallery, " wait for me, I will take you with me to Trianon. Remember what I have told you."

" I have treasured it up in my heart," replied the minister, well knowing what a sting this cutting sentence would inflict on his enemies.

The king once more entered his apartments.

M. de Richelieu broke the file, and hastened to press the minister's hand between his meager fingers, exclaiming : " It is long since I knew that a Choiseul bears a charmed life."

" Thank you," said the duke, who knew how the land lay.

" But this absurd report," continued the marshal.

" The report made his majesty laugh very heartily," said Choiseul.

" I heard something of a letter———"

" A little mystification of the king's," replied the minister, glancing while he spoke at Jean, who lost countenance.

" Wonderful ! wonderful ! " repeated the marshal, turning to the viscount as soon as the Duke de Choiseul was out
of sight.

" The king ascended the staircase, calling the duke, who
eagerly followed him.

" We have been played upon," said the marshal to Jean.

" Where are they going ? "

" To the little Trianon, to amuse themselves at our
expense."

" Hell and furies ! " exclaimed Jean.   "Ah ! excuse
me, marshal."

" It is now my turn," said the latter.   " We shall see if
my plans are more successful than those of the countess."

CHAPTER XIII.

THE LITTLE TRIANON.

WHEN Louis XIV. had built Versailles, and had felt the
inconvenience of grandeur, when he saw the immense
saloons full of guards, the anterooms thronged with courtiers, the corridors and entresols crowded with footmen,
pages, and officers, he said to himself that Versailles was indeed what Louis XIV. had planned, and what Mansard, Le
Brun, and Le Notre had executed—the dwelling of a deity,
but not of a man.   Then the Grand Monarque, who deigned
to be a man in his leisure moments, built Trianon, that he
might breathe more freely and enjoy a little retirement.
But the sword of Achilles, which had fatigued even Achilles
himself, was an insupportable burden to his puny successor.

Trianon, the miniature of Versailles, seemed yet too
pompous to Louis XV., who caused the little Trianon, a
pavilion of sixty feet square, to be built by the architect,
Gabriel.

To the left of this building was erected an oblong square,
without character and without ornament ; this was the
dwelling of the servants and officers of the household.   It

contained about ten lodgings for masters, and had accommodations for fifty servants.

This building still remains entire, and is composed of a ground floor, a first story, and attics. This ground floor is protected by a paved moat which separates it from the planting, and all the windows in it, as well as those of the first floor, are grated. On the side next Trianon, the windows are those of a long corridor, like that of a convent.

Eight or nine doors opening from the corridor, gave admittance to the different suites of apartments, each consisting of an anteroom and two closets, one to the left, the other to the right, and of one, and sometimes two, underground apartments, looking upon the inner court of the building. The upper story contains the kitchens, and the attics, the chambers of the domestics. Such is the little Trianon.

Add to this a chapel about six or seven perches from the château, which we shall not describe, because there is no necessity for our doing so, and because it is too small to deserve our notice.

The topography of the establishment is therefore as follows : a château, looking with its large eyes upon the park and a wood in front ; and, on the left, looking toward the officers, which present to its gaze only the barred windows of the corridor, and the thickly trellised ones of the kitchen above.

The path leading from the great Trianon, the pompous residence of Louis XIV., to the little, was through a kitchen garden which connected the two residences by means of a wooden bridge.

It was through this kitchen and fruit garden, which La Quintinie had designed and planted, that Louis XV. conducted M. de Choiseul to the little Trianon, after the laborious council we have just mentioned. He wished to show him the improvements he had made in the new abode of the dauphin and the dauphiness.

M. de Choiseul admired everything, and commented upon everything with the sagacity of a courtier. He listened while the king told him that the little Trianon became every day more beautiful, more charming to live in ; and the minister added that it would serve as his majesty's private residence.

" The dauphiness," said he, "' is rather wild yet, like all young Germans ; she speaks French well, but she is afraid of a slight accent, which to French ears betrays the Austrian. At Trianon she will see only friends and will speak only when she wishes. The result will be that she will speak well."

" I have already had the honor to remark, " said M. de Choiseul, " that her royal highness is accomplished, and requires nothing to make her perfect."

On the way the two travelers found the dauphin standing motionless upon a lawn measuring the sun's altitude.

M. de Choiseul bent low, but as the dauphin did not speak to him, he did not speak either.

The king said, loud enough to be heard by his grandson :

" Louis is a finished scholar, but he is wrong thus to run his head against the sciences ; his wife will have reason to complain of such conduct."

" By no means, sire," replied a low, soft voice issuing from a thicket.

And the king saw the dauphiness running toward him. She had been talking to a man furnished with papers, compasses, and chalks.

" Sire," said, the princess, " Monsieur Mique, my architect."

" Ah ! " exclaimed the king ; " then you too are bitten by that mania, madame ? "

" Sire, it runs in the family."

" You are going to build ? "

" I am going to improve this great park in which every one gets wearied."

" Oh ! oh ! my dear daughter, you speak too loud ; the dauphin might hear you."

" It is a matter agreed upon between us, my father," replied the princess.

" To be wearied ? "

" No, but to try to amuse ourselves."

" And so your highness is going to build ? " asked M. de Choiseul.

" I intend making a garden of this park, my lord duke."

" Ah ! Poor Le Notre ? " said the king.

" Le Notre was a great man, sire, for what was in vogue then, but for what I love——"

" What do you love, madame ? "

" Nature."

" Ah ! like the philosophers."

" Or like the English."

" Good ! Say that before Choiseul, and you will have a declaration of war immediately. He will let loose upon you the sixty-four ships and forty frigates of his cousin, Monsieur de Praslin."

" Sire," said the dauphiness, " I am going to have a natural garden laid out here by Monsieur Robert, who is the cleverest man in the world in that particular branch of horticulture."

" And what do you call a natural garden ? " asked the king. " I thought that trees, and flowers, and even fruit, such as I gathered as I came along, were natural objects."

" Sire, you may walk a hundred yards in your grounds, and you will see nothing but straight alleys, or thickets cut off at an angle of forty-five degrees, as the dauphin says, or pieces of water wedded to lawns, which in their turn are wedded to perspectives, parterres, or terraces."

" Well, that is ugly, is it ? "

" It is not natural."

" There is a little girl who loves nature ! " said the king, with a jovial rather than a joyous air. " Well, come ; what will you make of my Trianon ? "

" Rivers, cascades, bridges, grottoes, rocks, woods, ravines, houses, mountains, fields."

" For dolls ? " said the king.

" Alas ! sire, for such kings as we shall be," replied the princess, without remarking the blush which overspread her grandfather's face, and without perceiving that she foretold a sad truth for herself.

" Then you will destroy ; but what will you build ? "

"I shall preserve the present buildings."

"Ah! your people may consider themselves fortunate that you do not intend to lodge them in these woods and rivers you speak of, like Hurons, Esquimaux, and Greenlanders. They would live a natural life there, and Monsieur Rousseau would call them children of nature. Do that, my child, and the encylopedists will adore you."

"Sire, my servants would be too cold in such lodgings."

"Where will you lodge them, then, if you destroy all? Not in the palace; there is scarcely room for you two there."

"Sire, I shall keep the officers as they are."

And the dauphiness pointed to the windows of the corridor which we have described.

"What do I see there?" said the king, shading his eyes with his hand.

"A woman, sire," said M. de Choiseul.

"A young lady whom I have taken into my household," replied the dauphiness.

"Mademoiselle de Taverney," said Choiseul, with his piercing glance.

"Ah!" said the king; "so you have the Taverneys here?"

"Only Mademoiselle de Taverney, sire."

"A charming girl! What do you make of her?"

"My reader."

"Very good," said the king, without taking his eye from the window through which Mlle. de Taverney, still pale from her illness, was looking very innocently, and without in the least suspecting that she was observed.

"How pale she is," said M. de Choiseul.

"She was nearly killed on the thirty-first of May, my lord duke."

"Indeed? Poor girl!" said the king. "That Monsieur Bignon deserves to be disgraced."

"She is quite convalescent again," said M. de Choiseul, hastily.

"Thanks to the goodness of Providence, my lord."

"Ah!" said the king, "she has fled."

"She has perhaps recognized your majesty; she is very timid."

"Has she been with you long?"

"Since yesterday, sire; I sent for her when I installed myself here."

"What a melancholy abode for a young girl," said Louis. "That Gabriel was a clumsy rogue. He did not remember that the trees, as they grew, would conceal and darken this whole building."

"But I assure you, sire, that the apartments are very tolerable."

"That is impossible," said Louis XV.

"Will your majesty deign to convince yourself," said the dauphiness, anxious to do the honors of her palace.

"Very well. Will you come, Choiseul?"

"Sire, it is two o'clock. I have a parliamentary meeting at half-past two. I have only time to return to Versailles."

"Well, duke, go; and give those black gowns a shake for me. Dauphiness, show me these little apartments, if you please; I perfectly dote upon interiors."

"Come, Monsieur Mique," said the dauphiness to her architect; "you will have an opportunity of profiting by the opinion of his majesty, who understands everything so well."

The king walked first, the dauphiness followed.

They mounted the little flight of steps which led to the chapel, avoiding the entrance of the courtyard which was at one side. The door of the chapel is to the left, the staircase, narrow and unpretending, which leads to the corridor, on the right.

"Who lives here?" asked Louis XV.

"No one yet, sire."

"There is a key in the door of the first suite of apartments."

"Ah, yes; true. Mademoiselle de Taverney enters it to-day."

"Here?" said the king, pointing to the door.

"Yes, sire."

"And is she there at present? If so, let us not enter."

"Sire, she has just gone down ; I saw her walking under the veranda of the court."

"Then show me her apartments as a specimen."

"As you please," replied the dauphiness.

And she introduced the king into the principal apartment, which was preceded by an anteroom and two closets.

Some articles of furniture which were already arranged,
several books, a pianoforte, and, above all, an enormous
bouquet of the most beautiful flowers, which Mlle. de
Taverney had placed in a Chinese vase, attracted the king's
attention.

"Ah!" said he, "what beautiful flowers! And yet
you wish to change the garden. Who supplies your people
with such splendid flowers ? Do they keep some for you ?"

"It is in truth a beautiful bouquet."

"The gardener takes good care of Mademoiselle de
Taverney. Who is your gardener here ?"

"I do not know, sire. Monsieur de Jussieu undertook
to procure him for me."

The king gave a curious glance around the apartments,
looked again at the exterior, peeped into the courtyard,
and went away. His majesty crossed the park, and
returned to the great Trianon, where his equipages
were already in waiting, for a hunt which was to take
place after dinner, in carriages, from three till six
o'clock.

The dauphin was still measuring the sun's altitude.

<hr>

CHAPTER XIV.

THE CONSPIRACY IS RENEWED.

WHILE the king, in order to reassure M. de Choiseul,
and not to lose any time himself, was walking in Trianon
till the chase should commence, Luciennes was the center
of a reunion of frightened conspirators, who had flown
swiftly to Mme. Dubarry, like birds who have smelled
the sportsman's powder.

Jean and Marshal Richelieu, after having looked at each

other ill-humoredly for some time, were the first to take flight. The others were the usual herd of favorites, whom the certain disgrace of the Choiseuls had allured, whom his return to favor had alarmed, and who, no longer finding the minister there to fawn upon, had returned mechanically to Luciennes, to see if the tree was yet strong enough for them to cling to as before.

Mme. Dubarry was taking a siesta after the fatigues of her diplomacy and deceptive triumph which had crowned it, when Richelieu's carriage rolled into the court with the noise and swiftness of a whirlwind.

"Mistress Dubarry is asleep," said Zamore, without moving.

Jean sent Zamore rolling on the carpet with a scientific kick inflicted upon the most highly ornamented portion of his governor's uniform.

Zamore screamed, and Chon hastened to inquire the cause.

"You are beating that little fellow again, you brute!" said she.

"And I shall exterminate you, too," continued Jean, with kindling eyes, "if you do not immediately awaken the countess."

But there was no need to awaken the countess; at Zamore's cries, at the growling tones of Jean's voice, she had suspected some misfortune, and hastened into the room, wrapped in a dressing-gown.

"What is the matter?" exclaimed she, alarmed at seeing Jean stretched at full length upon the sofa to calm the agitation of his bile, and at finding that the marshal did not even kiss her hand.

"The matter! the matter!" said Jean. "Parbleu! what is always the matter—the Choiseuls!"

"How"

"Yes! *mille tonnerres!* firmer than ever."

"What do you mean?"

"The Count Dubarry is right," continued Richelieu; "Monsieur the Duke de Choiseul is firmer than ever."

The countess drew the king's letter from her bosom.

" And this ? " said she, smiling.

" Have you read it aright, countess ? " asked the marshal.

" Why, I fancy I can read, duke," replied Mme. Dubarry.

" I do not doubt it, madame. Will you allow me to read it also ? "

" Oh ! certainly ; read."

The duke took the paper, unfolded it slowly, and read :

" To-morrow I shall thank Monsieur de Choiseul for his services. I promise it positively.   LOUIS."

" Is that clear ? " said the countess.

" Perfectly clear," replied the marshal, with a grimace.

" Well ! what ? " said Jean.

" Well ! It is to-morrow that we shall be victorious, and nothing is lost as yet."

" How ! To-morrow ? The king signed that yesterday ; therefore to-morrow is to-day."

" Pardon me, madame," said the duke ; " as there is no date to the note, to-morrow will always be the day after you wish to see Monsieur de Choiseul dismissed. In the Rue de la Grange Batelière, about one hundred paces from my house, there is a tavern, on the sign-board of which is written in red characters, ' Credit given to-morrow.' To-morrow—that is, never."

" The king mocks us ! " said Jean, furiously.

" Impossible," said the alarmed countess, " impossible ! Such a trick would be unworthy——"

" Ah, madame, his majesty is so merry," said Richelieu.

" He shall pay for this, duke," said the countess, in a tone of anger.

" After all, countess, we must not be angry with the king ; we cannot accuse his majesty of cheating or tricking us, for the king has performed what he promised."

" Oh ! " said Jean, with a more than vulgar shrug of his shoulders.

" What did he promise ? " cried the countess. " To thank Choiseul for his services."

"And that is precisely what he has done, madame. I heard his majesty myself thank the duke for his services. The word has two meanings ; in diplomacy, each takes the one he prefers. You have chosen yours, the king has chosen his. Therefore, there is no more question of to-morrow. It is to-day, according to your opinion, that the king should have kept his promise, and he has done so. I who speak to you heard him thank Choiseul."

"Duke, this is no time for jesting, I think."

"Do you think I am jesting, countess ? Ask Count Jean."

"No, by Heaven ! We were in no humor for laughing this morning when Choiseul was embraced, flattered, feasted by the king, and even now he is walking arm in arm with him in Trianon."

"Arm in arm ! " exclaimed Chon, who had slipped into the room, and who raised her snowy arms like a second Niobe in despair.

"Yes, I have been tricked," said the countess, " but we shall see. Chon, countermand my carriage for the chase. I shall not go."

"Good ! " said Jean.

"One moment," cried Richelieu. " No hurry, no pouting. Ah ! forgive me, countess, for daring to advise you ; I entreat you to pardon me."

"Go on, duke, do not apologize. I think I am losing my senses. See how I am placed ; I did not wish to meddle with politics, and the first time I touch upon them, self-love launches me so deeply. You were saying——"

"That pouting would not be wise now. The position is difficult, countess. If the king is so decidedly in favor of these Choiseuls, if the dauphiness has so much influence over him, if he thus openly breaks a lance with you, you must——"

"Well, what ? "

"You must be even more amiable than you are at present, countess. I know it is impossible ; but in a position like ours the impossible becomes necessary. Attempt the impossible, then."

The countess reflected.

" For, in short," said the duke, " if the king should adopt German manners——"

" If he should become virtuous ! " exclaimed Jean, horrified.

" Who knows, countess ? " said Richelieu ; " novelty is such an attractive thing."

" Oh ! as for that," replied the countess, with a nod of incredulity, " I do not believe it."

" More extraordinary things have happened, countess. You know the proverb of the devil turning hermit. So you must not pout."

" But I am suffocating with rage."

" Parbleu ! countess, I can believe you ; but suffocate before us, breathe freely before the enemy. Do not let the king, that is to say, Monsieur de Choiseul, perceive your anger."

" And shall I go to the chase ? "

" It would be most politic."

" And you, duke ? "

Oh, I ? If I should have to crawl on all fours, I shall go."

" Come in my carriage, then ! " cried the countess, to see what face her ally would put on.

" Oh, countess," replied the duke, smirking to hide his vexation, " it is such an honor——"

" That you refuse ? "

" I ? Heaven forbid. But, take care ; you will compromise yourself."

" He confesses it—he dares to confess it," cried Mme. Dubarry.

" Countess ! countess ! Monsieur de Choiseul will never forgive me."

" Are you already on such good terms with Monsieur de Choiseul ? "

" Countess, I shall get into disgrace with the dauphiness."

" Would you rather we should each continue the war separately, without sharing the spoil ? It is still time.

You are not compromised, and you may yet withdraw from the association."

" You misunderstood me, countess," said the duke, kissing her hands. " Did I hesitate on the day of your presentation to send you a dress, a hair-dresser, and a carriage ? Well, I shall not hesitate any more to-day. I am bolder than you imagine, countess."

" Then it is agreed. We will go to this hunt together, and that will serve me as a pretext for not seeing or speaking to any one."

" Not even to the king ? "

" Oh ! on the contrary, I shall give him such sweet words that he will be in despair."

" Bravo ! that is good tactics."

" But you, Jean, what are you doing there ? Do endeavor to rise from these cushions ; you are burying yourself alive, my good friend."

" You want to know what I am doing, do you ? Well, I am thinking——"

" Of what ? "

" I am thinking that all the ballad-writers of the town and the parliament are setting us to all possible tunes ; that the ' Nouvelles à la main ' is cutting us up like meat for pies ; that the ' Gazetier Cuirassé ' is piercing us for want of a cuirass ; that the ' Journal des Observateurs ' observes us even to the marrow of our bones ; that, in short, to-morrow we shall be in so pitiable a state that even a Choiseul might pity us."

" And what is the result of your reflections ? " asked the duke.

" Why, that I must hasten to Paris to buy a little lint and no inconsiderable quantity of ointment to put upon our wounds. Give me some money, my little sister."

" How much ? " asked the countess.

" A trifle ; two or three hundred louis."

" You see, duke," said the countess, turning to Richelieu, " that I am already paying the expenses of the war."

" That is only the beginning of the campaign, countess ; sow to day ; to-morrow you will reap."

The countess shrugged her shoulders slightly, rose, went to her chiffonier, and, opening it, took out a handful of bank-notes, which, without counting them, she handed to Jean, who, also without counting them, pocketed them with a deep sigh.

Then rising, yawning, and stretching himself like a man overwhelmed with fatigue, he took a few steps across the room.

"See," said he, pointing to the duke and the countess, "these people are going to amuse themselves at the chase, while I have to gallop to Paris. They will see gay cavaliers and lovely women, and I shall see nothing but hideous faces and scribbling drudges. Certainly I am the turnspit of the establishment."

"Mark me, duke," said the countess, "he will never bestow a thought on us. Half my bank-notes will be squandered on some opera girl and the rest will disappear in a gambling-house. That is his errand to Paris, and yet he bemoans himself, the wretch! Leave my sight, Jean, you disgust me."

Jean emptied three plates of bonbons, stuffed the contents into his pocket, stole a Chinese figure with diamond eyes from the landing, and stalked off with a most majestic strut, pursued by the exclamations of the countess.

"What a delightful youth!" said Richelieu, in the tone of a parasite who praises a spoiled brat, while all the time he is inwardly devoting him to the infernal regions; "he is very dear to you, I suppose, countess?"

"As you say, duke, he has fixed all his happiness in me, and the speculation brings him three or four hundred thousand livres a year."

The clock struck.

"Half-past twelve, countess," said the duke. "Luckily you are almost dressed. Show yourself a little to your courtiers, who might otherwise think there was an eclipse, and then let us to our carriages. You know how the chase is ordered?"

"His majesty and I arranged it yesterday; they were to proceed to the forest of Marly and take me up in passing."

"Oh! I am very sure the king has not changed the program."

"In the meantime, duke, let me hear your plan ; it is your turn now."

"Madame, I wrote yesterday to my nephew, who, if I may believe my presentiments, is already on his way hither."

"Monsieur d'Aiguillon ? "

"I should not be surprised if he crosses my letter on the road, and if he were here to-morrow or the day after at the latest."

"Then you calculate upon him? "

"Oh! madame, he does not want for sense."

"No matter who it is, for we are at the last extremity. The king might perhaps submit, but he has such a dreadful antipathy to business."

"So that——"

"So that I fear he will never consent to give up Monsieur de Choiseul."

"Shall I speak frankly to you, countess ? "

"Certainly."

"Well, I think so too. The king will find a hundred stratagems like that of yesterday. His majesty has so much wit ! And then, on your side, countess, you will never risk losing his love for the sake of an unaccountable whim."

And while he spoke the marshal fixed a searching glance on Mme. Dubarry.

"Dame ! I must reflect upon that."

"You see, countess, Monsieur de Choiseul is there for an eternity ; nothing but a miracle can dislodge him."

"Yes, a miracle," repeated Jeanne.

"And, unfortunately, we are not now in the age of miracles."

"Oh !" said Mme. Dubarry, "I know some one who can work miracles yet."

"You know a man who can work miracles, and yet you did not tell me so before ? "

"I only thought of it this moment, duke."

"Do you think he could assist us in this affair ? "

"I think he can do everything."

"Oh ! indeed ?   And what miracle has he worked ?
Tell me, that I may judge of his skill by the specimen."

"Duke," said Mme. Dubarry, approaching Richelieu,
and involuntarily lowering her voice, "he is a man who,
ten years ago, met me upon the Place Louis XV. and told
me I should be Queen of France."

"Indeed ! that is in truth miraculous ; and could he tell
me, think you, if I shall die prime minister ? "

"Don't you think so ? "

"Oh, I don't doubt it in the least.   What is his name ?"

"His name will tell you nothing."

"Where is he ? "

"Ah ! that I don't know."

"He did not give you his address ? "

"No ; he was to come to me for his recompense."

"What did you promise him ? "

"Whatever he should ask."

"And he has not come ? "

"No ! "

"Countess, that is even more miraculous than his prediction.   We must certainly have this man."

"But how shall we proceed ? "

"His name, countess—his name ? "

"He has two."

"Proceed according to order—the first ? "

"The Count de Fenix."

"What ! the man you pointed out to me on the day of
your presentation ? "

"Yes ; the Prussian officer."

"Oh ! I have no longer any faith in him.   All the sorcerers I have ever known had names ending in *i* or *o*."

"That exactly suits, duke ; for his second name is
Joseph Balsamo."

"But have you no means of finding him out ? "

"I shall task my brain, duke.   I think I know some
one who knows him."

"Good !   But make haste, countess.   It is now a quarter to one."

"I am ready. My carriage, there!"

Ten minutes afterward Mme. Dubarry and M. de Richelieu were seated side by side, and driving rapidly on their way to the hunting-party.

CHAPTER XV.

THE SORCERER CHASE.

A LONG train of carriages filled the avenues of the forest of Marly where the king was hunting. It was what was called the afternoon chase.

In the latter part of his life, Louis XV. neither shot at nor rode after the game ; he was content with watching the progress of the chase.

Those of our readers who have read Plutarch, will perhaps remember that cook of Mark Antony who put a boar on the spit every hour, so that among the six or seven boars which were roasting there might always be one ready whenever Mark Antony wished to dine.

The reason of this was that Mark Antony, as governor of Asia Minor, was overwhelmed with business ; he was the dispenser of justice, and as the Sicilians are great thieves (the fact is confirmed by Juvenal), Mark Antony had abundance of work on his hands. He had therefore always five or six roasts in various degrees of progress on the spit, waiting for the moment when his functions as judge would permit him to snatch a hasty morsel.

Louis XV. acted in a similar manner. For the afternoon chase there were three or four stags started at different hours, and accordingly as the king felt disposed he chose a nearer or more distant view halloo.

On this day his majesty had signified his intention of hunting until four o'clock. A stag was therefore chosen which had been started at twelve, and which might consequently be expected to run until that hour.

Mme. Dubarry, on her side, intended to follow the king as faithfully as the king intended to follow the stag. But hunters propose and fate disposes. A combination of circumstances frustrated this happy project of Mme. Dubarry, and the countess found in fate an adversary almost as capricious as herself.

While the countess, talking politics with M. de Richelieu, drove rapidly after the king, who in his turn drove rapidly after the stag, and while the duke and she returned in part the bows which greeted them as they passed, they all at once perceived, about fifty paces from the road, beneath a magnificent canopy of verdure, an unfortunate calèche revolving its wheels in the air, while the two black horses which should have drawn it were peaceably munching, the one the bark of a beech-tree, the other the moss growing at his feet.

Mme. Dubarry's horses, a magnificent pair presented to her by the king, had outstripped all the other carriages, and were the first to arrive in sight of the broken carriage.

" Ha ! an accident ! " said the countess, calmly.

" Faith, yes ! " said the Duke de Richelieu, with equal coolness, for sensibility is little in fashion at court ; " the carriage is broken in pieces."

" Is that a corpse upon the grass ? " asked the countess. " Look, duke."

" I think not ; it moves."

" Is it a man or a woman ? "

" I don't know. I cannot see well."

" Ha ! it bows to us."

" Then it cannot be dead."

And Richelieu at all hazards took off his hat.

" But, countess," said he, " it seems to me——"

" And to me also——"

" That it is his eminence, Prince Louis."

" The Cardinal de Rohan in person."

" What the deuce is he doing there ? " asked the duke.

" Let us go and see," replied the countess. " Champagne, drive on to the broken carriage."

The coachman immediately left the high-road and dashed in among the lofty trees.

" Faith, yes, it is my lord cardinal," said Richelieu.

It was in truth his eminence who was lying stretched upon the grass waiting until some of his friends should pass.

Seeing Mme. Dubarry approach, he rose.

" A thousand compliments to the countess ! " said he.

" How ! Cardinal, is it you ? "

" Myself, madame."

" On foot ? "

" No, sitting."

" Are you wounded ? "

" Not in the least."

" And how in all the world do you happen to be in this position ? "

" Do not speak of it, madame ; that brute of a coachman, a man whom I sent for to England, when I told him to cut across the wood in order to join the chase, turned so suddenly that he upset me and broke my best carriage."

" You must not complain, cardinal," said the countess ; " a French coachman would have broken your neck, or at least your ribs."

" Very possibly."

" Therefore, be consoled."

" Oh ! I am a little of a philosopher, countess ; only I shall have to wait, and that is fatal."

" How ! Prince, to wait ? A Rohan wait ? "

" There is no resource."

" Oh, no ! I would rather alight and leave you my carriage."

" In truth, madame, your kindness makes me blush."

" Come, jump in, prince—jump in."

" No, thank you, madame, I am waiting for Soubise, who is at the chase, and who cannot fail to pass in a few minutes."

" But if he should have taken another road ? "

" Oh ! it is of no consequence."

" My lord, I entreat you will."

" No, thank you."

" But why not ? "

" I am unwilling to incommode you."

" Cardinal, if you refuse to enter, I shall order one of

my footmen to carry my train, and I shall roam through the woods like a Dryad."

The cardinal smiled, and thinking that a longer resistance might be interpreted unfavorably by the countess, he consented to enter the carriage. The duke had already given up his place, and taken a seat upon the bench in front. The cardinal entreated him to resume his former position, but the duke was inflexible.

The countess's splendid horses soon made up for the time which had thus been lost.

"Excuse me, my lord," said the countess, addressing the cardinal, "has your eminence been reconciled to the chase ?"

"How so ?"

"Because this is the first time I have had the pleasure of seeing you join in that amusement."

"By no means, countess. I had come to Versailles to have the honor of paying my respects to his majesty, when I was told he was at the chase. I had to speak to him on some important business, and therefore followed, hoping to overtake him ; but thanks to this cursed coachman, I shall not only lose his majesty's ear, but also my assignation in town."

"You see, madame," said the duke, laughing, "monseigneur makes a free confession—he has an assignation."

"In which I shall fail, I repeat," replied the cardinal.

"Does a Rohan, a prince, a cardinal, ever fail in anything ?" said the countess.

"Dame ! " said the prince, "unless a miracle comes to my assistance."

The duke and the countess looked at each other ; this word recalled their recent conversation.

"Faith ! prince," said the countess, "speaking of miracles, I will confess frankly that I am very happy to meet a dignitary of the church, to know if he believes in them."

"In what, madame ?"

"Parbleu ! in miracles," said the duke.

"The Scriptures give them as an article of faith, madame," said the cardinal, trying to look devout.

"Oh! I do not mean those miracles," replied the countess.

"And of what other miracles do you speak, madame?"

"Of modern miracles."

"Those indeed, I confess, are rather more rare," said the cardinal. "But still——"

"But still, what?"

"Faith! I have seen things, which if they were not miraculous, were at least very incredible."

"You have seen such things, prince?"

"On my honor."

"But you know, madame," said Richelieu, laughing, "that his eminence is said to be in communication with spirits, which, perhaps, is not very orthodox."

"No, but which must be very convenient," said the countess. "And what have you seen, prince?"

"I have sworn not to reveal it."

"Oh! that begins to look serious."

"It is a fact, madame."

"But if you have promised to observe secrecy respecting the sorcery, perhaps you have not done so as regards the sorcerer?"

"No."

"Well, then, prince, I must tell you that the duke and myself came out to-day with the intention of seeking some magician."

"Indeed?"

"Upon my honor."

"Take mine."

"I desire no better."

"He is at your disposal, countess."

"And at mine also, prince?"

"And at yours also, duke."

"What is his name?"

"The Count de Fenix."

The countess and the duke looked at each other and turned.

"That is strange," said they both together.

"Do you know him?" asked the prince.

" No.   And you think him a sorcerer ? "

"I am positive of it."

" You have spoken to him, then ? "

" Of course."

" And you found him——"

" Perfect."

" On what occasion, may I ask ? "

The cardinal hesitated.

" On the occasion of his foretelling my fortune."

" Correctly ? "

" He told me things of the other world."

" Has he no other name then the Count de Fenix ? "

" I think I have heard him called——"

" Speak, sir," said the countess, impatiently.

" Joseph Balsamo, madame."

" Is the devil very black ? " asked Mme. Dubarry all at once.

" The devil, countess ?   I have not seen him."

" What are you thinking of, countess ? " cried Richelieu. " Pardieu ! that would be respectable company for the cardinal."

" And did he tell you your fortune without showing you the devil ? "

" Oh ! certainly," said the cardinal, " they only show the devil to people of no consideration ; we can dispense with him."

" But say what you will, prince," continued Mme. Dubarry, " there must be a little deviltry at the bottom of it."

" Dame ! I think so."

" Blue fire, specters, infernal caldrons, which smell horribly while they burn, eh ? "

" Oh, no ! my sorcerer is most polite and well-bred ; he is a very gallant man, and receives his visitors in good style."

" Will you not have your horoscope drawn by this man, countess ? " said Richelieu.

" I long to do so, I confess."

" Do so, then, madame."

" But where is all this accomplished ? " asked Mme.

Dubarry, hoping that the cardinal would give her the wished-for address.

"In a very handsome room, fashionably furnished."

The countess could scarcely conceal her impatience.

"Very well," said she, "but the house?"

"A very fine house, though in a singular style of architecture."

The countess stamped with rage at being so ill understood. Richelieu came to her assistance.

"But do you not see, my lord," said he, "that madame is dying to know where your sorcerer lives?"

"Where he lives, you say? Oh! well," replied the cardinal, "eh! faith—wait a moment—no—yes—no. It is in the Marais, near the corner of the boulevard Rue St. François—St. Anastasie—no. However, it is the name of some saint."

"But what saint? You must surely know them all?"

"No, faith. I know very little about them," said the cardinal; "but stay—my fool of a footman must remember."

"Oh! very fortunately he got up behind," said the duke. "Stop, Champagne, stop."

And the duke pulled the cord which was attached to the coachman's little finger, who suddenly reigned in the foaming horses, throwing them on their sinewy haunches.

"Olive," said the cardinal, "are you there, you scoundrel?"

"Yes, my lord."

"Where did I stop one evening in the Marais—a long way off?"

The lackey had overheard the whole conversation, but took care not to appear as if he had done so.

"In the Marais?" said he, seeming to search his memory.

"Yes, near the boulevards."

"What day, my lord?"

"One day when I was returning from St. Denis. The carriage, I think, waited for me in the boulevards."

"Oh, yes, my lord," said Olive, "I remember now. A

man came and threw a very heavy parcel into the carriage ; I remember it perfectly."

"Very possibly," replied the cardinal. "But who asked you about that, you scoundrel ? "

"What does your eminence wish, then ? "

"To know the name of the street."

"Rue St. Claude, my lord."

"Claude, that is it ! " cried the cardinal. "I would have laid any wager it was the name of a saint."

"Rue St. Claude ! " repeated the countess, darting such an expressive glance at Richelieu, that the marshal, fearing to let any one guess his secrets, above all when it concerned a conspiracy, interrupted Mme. Dubarry by these words :

"Ha ! countess—the king ! "

"Where ? "

"Yonder."

"The king ! the king ! " exclaimed the countess. "To the left, Champagne, to the left, that his majesty may not see us."

"And why, countess ? " asked the astonished cardinal. "I thought that, on the contrary, you were taking me to his majesty."

"Oh ! true, you wish to see the king, do you not ? "

"I came for that alone, madame."

"Very well ! you shall be taken to the king——"

"But you ? "

"Oh ! we shall remain here."

"But, countess——"

"No apologies, prince, I entreat ; every one to his own business. The king is yonder, under those chestnut-trees ; you have business with the king ; very well, the affair is easily arranged. Champagne ! "

Champagne pulled up.

"Champagne, let us alight here and take his eminence to the king."

"What ! alone, countess ? "

"You wished to have an audience of his majesty, cardinal."

"It is true."

"Well! you shall have his ear entirely to yourself."

"Ah! this kindness absolutely overwhelms me." And the prelate gallantly kissed Mme. Dubarry's hand.

"But where will you remain yourself, madame?" inquired he.

"Here under these trees."

"The king will be looking for you."

"So much the better."

"He will be uneasy at not seeing you."

"And that will torment him—just what I wish."

"Countess, you are positively adorable."

"That is precisely what the king says when I have tormented him. Champagne, when you have taken his eminence to the king, you will return at full gallop."

"Yes, my lady."

"Adieu, duke," said the cardinal.

"Au revoir, my lord," replied the duke.

And the valet having let down the step, the duke alighted and handed out the countess, who leaped to the ground as lightly as a nun escaping from her convent, while the carriage rapidly bore his eminence to the hillock from which his most Christian majesty was seeking, with his short-sighted eyes, the naughty countess whom every one had seen but himself.

Mme. Dubarry lost no time. She took the duke's arm and drawing him into the thicket:

"Do you know," said she, "that it must have been Providence who sent us that dear cardinal, to put us on the trace of our man."

"Then we are positively to go to him?"

"I think so; but——"

"What, countess?"

"I am afraid, I confess it."

"Of whom?"

"Of the sorcerer. Oh, I am very credulous."

"The deuce!"

"And you, do you believe in sorcerers?"

"Dame! I can't say no, countess."

" My history of the prediction——"

" Is a startling fact. And I myself," said the old marshal, scratching his ear, " once met a certain sorcerer."

" Bah ! "

" Who rendered me a very important service."

" What service, duke ? "

" He resuscitated me."

" He resuscitated you ? "

" Certainly ; I was dead, no less."

" Oh ! tell me the whole affair, duke."

" Let us conceal ourselves, then."

" Duke, you are a dreadful coward."

" Oh, no, I am only prudent."

" Are we well placed here ? "

" Yes, I think so."

" Well ! the story ! the story ! "

" Well, I was at Vienna—it was the time when I was ambassador there—when one evening, while I was standing under a lamp, I received a sword thrust through my body. It was a rival's sword, and a very unwholesome sort of thing it is, I assure you. I fell—I was taken up—I was dead."

" What ! you were dead ? "

" Yes, or close upon it. A sorercer passes, who asks who is the man whom they are carrying ? He is told it is I ; he stops the litter, pours three drops of some unknown liquid into the wound, three more between my lips, and the bleeding stops, respiration returns, my eyes open, and am cured."

" It is a miracle from Heaven, duke."

" That is just what frightens me ; for, on the contrary, I believe it is a miracle from the devil."

" True, marshal, Providence would not have saved a dissipated rake like you. Honor to whom honor is due. And does your sorcerer still live ? "

" I doubt it, unless he has found the elixir of life."

" Like you, marshal ? "

" Do you believe those stories, then ? "

" I believe everything. He was old ? "

" Methuselah in person."

" And his name ? "

" Ah ! a magnificent Greek name—Althotas."

" What a terrible name, marshal."

" Is it not, madame ? "

" Duke, there is the carriage returning. Are we decided ? Shall we go to Paris and visit the Rue St. Claude ? "

" If you like. But the king is waiting for you."

" That would determine me, duke, if I had not already determined. He has tormented me. Now, France, it is your turn to suffer ! "

" But he may think you are lost—carried off."

" And so much the more that I have been seen with you, marshal."

" Stay, countess, I will be frank with you ; I am afraid."

" Of what ? "

" I am afraid that you will tell all this to some one, and that I shall be laughed at."

" Then we shall both be laughed at together, since I go with you."

" That decides, me, countess. However, if you betray me, I shall——"

" What will you say ? "

" I shall say that you come with me *tête-à-tête.*

" No one will believe you, duke."

" Ah ! countess, if the king were not there ! "

" Champagne ! Champagne ! Here, behind this thicket, that we may not be seen. Germain, the door. That will do. Now to Paris. Rue St. Claude, in the Marais, and let the pavement smoke for it."

CHAPTER XVI.

THE COURIER.

It was six o'clock in the evening. In that chamber of the Rue St. Claude into which we have already introduced our readers, Balsamo was seated beside Lorenza, now awake, and was endeavoring by persuasion to soften her rebellious spirit, which refused to listen to all his prayers.

But the young girl looked askance at him, as Dido looked at Æneas when he was about to leave her, spoke only to reproach him, and moved her hand only to repulse his.

She complained that she was a prisoner, a slave ; that she could no longer breathe the fresh air, nor see the sun. She envied the fate of the poorest creatures, of the birds, of the flowers. She called Balsamo her tyrant.

Then passing from reproaches to rage, she tore into shreds the rich stuff which her husband had given her, in order by this semblance of gaiety and show to cheer the solitude he imposed on her.

Balsamo, on the other hand, spoke gently to her, and looked at her lovingly. It was evident that this weak, irritable creature filled an immense place in his heart, if not in his life.

" Lorenza," said he to her, " my beloved, why do you display this spirit of resistance and hostility ? Why will you not live with me, who love you inexpressibly, as a gentle and devoted companion ? You would then have nothing to wish for ; you would be free to bloom in the sun like the flowers of which you spoke just now ; to stretch your wings like the birds whose fate you envy. We would go everywhere together. You would not only see the sun which delights you so much, but the factitious sun of splendor and fashion—those assemblies to which the women of this country resort. You would be happy according to your tastes, while rendering me happy, in mine. Why will you refuse this happiness, Lorenza—you, who with your beauty and riches, would make so many women envious ? "

" Because I abhor you," said the haughty young girl.

Balsamo cast on Lorenza a glance expressive at once of anger and pity.

" Live, then, as you condemn yourself to live," said he ; " and since you are so proud, do not complain."

" I should not complain, if you would leave me alone. I should not complain, if you did not force me to speak to you. Do not come into my presence, or when you do enter my prison, do not speak to me, and I shall do as the poor birds from the south do when they are imprisoned in cages—they die, but do not sing."

Balsamo made an effort to appear calm.

" Come, Lorenza," said he, " a little more gentleness and resignation. Look into a heart which loves you above all things. Do you wish for books ? "

" No."

" Why not ? Books would amuse you."

" I wish to weary myself until I die."

Balsamo smiled, or rather endeavored to smile.

" You are mad," said he ; " you know very well that you cannot die while I am here to take care of you, and to cure you when you fall ill."

" Oh !" cried Lorenza, " you will not cure me when you find me strangled with this scarf against the bars of my window."

Balsamo shuddered.

" Or when," continued she, furiously, " I have opened this knife and stabbed myself to the heart ! "

Balsamo, pale as death and bathed in cold perspiration, gazed at Lorenza, and with a threatening voice :

" No, Lorenza," said he, " you are right ; I shall not cure you then ; I shall bring you back to life."

Lorenza gave a cry of terror. She knew no bounds to Balsamo's power, and believed his threat. Balsamo was saved. While she was plunged in this fresh abyss of suffering which she had not foreseen, and while her vacillating reason saw itself encircled by a never-ceasing round of torture, the sound of the signal-bell, pulled by Fritz, reached Balsamo's ear. It struck three times quickly, and at regular intervals.

" A courier," said he.

Then, after a pause, another ring was heard.

" And in haste," he said.

" Ah ! " said Lorenza, " you are about to leave me, then ! "

He took the young girl's cold hand in his. " Once more, and for the last time, Lorenza," said he, " let us live on good terms with each other, like brother and sister. Since destiny unites us to each other, let us make it a friend and not an executioner."

Lorenza did not reply. Her eyes, motionless and fixed in a sort of dreamy melancholy, seemed to seek some thought which was ever flying from her into infinite space, and which perhaps she could not find, because she had sought it too long and too earnestly, like those who, after having lived in darkness, gaze too ardently on the sun, and are blinded by excess of light. Balsamo took her hand and kissed it, without her giving any sign of life. Then he advanced toward the chimney. Immediately Lorenza started from her torpor, and eagerly fixed her gaze upon him.

" Oh ! " said he, " you wish to know how I leave this, in order to leave it one day after me and flee from me, as you threatened. And therefore you awake—therefore you look at me."

Then passing his hand over his forehead, as if he imposed a painful task on himself, he stretched his hand toward the young girl, and said, in a commanding voice, looking at her as if he were darting a javelin against her head and breast :

" Sleep ! "

The word was scarcely uttered when Lorenza bent like a flower upon its stem ; her head, for a single moment unsteady, drooped and rested against the cushion of the sofa ; her hands, of an opaque and waxen whiteness, glided down her side, rustling her silken dress.

Balsamo, seeing her so beautiful, approached her and pressed his lips upon her lovely forehead.

Then Lorenza's features brightened, as if a breath from the God of Love himself had swept away the cloud which rested on her brow. Her lips opened tremulously, her eyes swam in voluptuous tears, and she sighed as the angels must have sighed, when in earth's youthful prime they stooped to love the children of men.

Balsamo looked upon her for a moment, as if unable to withdraw his gaze ; then, as the bell sounded anew, he turned toward the chimney, touched a spring, and disappeared behind the flowers.

Fritz was waiting for him in the saloon, with a man dressed in the closely fitting jacket of a courier, and wearing, thick boots armed with long spurs.

The commonplace and inexpressive features of this man showed him to be one of the people ; but his eye had in it a spark of sacred fire, which seemed to have been breathed into him by some superior intelligence.

His left hand grasped a short and knotty whip. while with his right hand he made some signs to Balsamo, which the latter instantly recognized, and to which, without speaking he replied by touching his forehead with his forefinger.

The postilion's hand moved upward to his breast, where it traced another sign, which an indifferent observer would not have remarked, so closely did it resemble the movement made in fastening a button.

To this sign the master replied by showing a ring which he wore upon his finger.

Before this powerful signet the messenger bent his knee.

" Whence come you ? " asked Balsamo.

" From Rouen, master."

" What is your profession ? "

" I am a courier in the service of the Duchess de Grammont."

" Who placed you there ? "

" The will of the great Copht."

" What orders did you receive when you entered the service ? "

" To have no secret from the master."

" Whither are you going ? "

" To Versailles."

" What are you carrying ? "

" A letter."

" For whom ? "

" For the minister."

" Give it me."

The courier took a letter from a leathern bag fastened upon his shoulders behind, and give it to Balsamo.

" Shall I wait ? " asked he.

" Yes."

" Very well."

" Fritz ! "

The German appeared.

" Keep Sebastian concealed in the offices."

" He knows my name," murmured the adept, with superstitious fear.

" He knows everything," said Fritz, drawing him away.

When Balsamo was once more alone, he looked at the unbroken, deeply cut seal of the letter, which the imploring glance of the messenger had entreated him to respect as much as possible.   Then slowly and pensively he once more mounted toward Lorenza's apartment, and opened the door of communication.

Lorenza was still sleeping, but seemingly tired and enervated by inaction.   He took her hand, which she closed convulsively, and then he placed the letter, sealed as it was, upon her heart.

" Do you see ? " he asked.

" Yes, I see," replied Lorenza.

" What is the object which I hold in my hand ? "

" A letter."

" Can you read it ? "

" I can."

" Do so, then."

With closed eyes, and palpitating bosom, Lorenza repeated, word for word, the following lines which Balsamo wrote down as she spoke :

"Dear Brother,—As I had foreseen, my exile will be at least of some service to us. I have this morning seen the president of Rouen ; he is for us, but timid. I urged him in your name ; he has at last decided, and the remonstrance of his division will be in Versailles within a week. I am just about setting off for Rennes to rouse Karaduc and La Chalotais, who are sleeping on their post. Our agent from Caudebec was in Rouen. I have seen him. England will not stop midway ; she is preparing a sharp notification for the cabinet of Versailles. X——asked me if he should produce it, and I authorized him to do so. You will receive the last pamphlets of Morando and Delille against the Dubarry. They are petards which might blow up a town. A sad report reached me, that there was disgrace in the air ; but as you have not written to me, I laugh at it. Do not leave me in doubt, however, and reply, courier for courier. Your message will find me at Caen, where I have some of our gentlemen riding quarantine. Adieu I salute you.

"Duchess de Grammont."

After reading thus far, Lorenza stopped.

"You see nothing more ?" asked Balsamo.

"I see nothing."

"No postscript ?"

"No."

Balsamo, whose brow had gradually smoothed as Lorenza read the letter, now took it from her.

"A curious document," said he, "and one for which I would be well paid. Oh ! how can any one write such things ?" he continued. "Yes, it is always women who are the ruin of great men. This Choiseul could not have been overthrown by an army of enemies, by a world of intrigues, and now the breath of a woman crushes while it caresses him. Yes, we all perish by the treachery or the weakness of women. If we have a heart, and in that heart a sensitive chord, we are lost."

And as he spoke, Balsamo gazed with inexpressible tenderness at Lorenza, who palpitated under his glance.

"Is it true, what I think?" said he.

"No, no, it is not true!" she replied, eagerly; "you see plainly that I love you too dearly to do you any hurt, like those women you spoke of without sense and without heart."

Balsamo allowed himself to be caressed by the arms of his enchantress. All at once a double ring of Fritz's bell was repeated twice.

"Two visits," said Balsamo.

A single violent ring completed the telegraphic message.

"Important ones," continued the master; and disengaging himself from Lorenza's arms, he hastened from the apartment, leaving the young girl asleep. On his way he met the courier, who was waiting for orders.

"Here is your letter," said he.

"What must I do with it?"

"Deliver it as addressed."

"Is that all?"

"Yes."

The adept looked at the envelope and at the seal, and seeing them as intact as when he had brought them, expressed his satisfaction, and disappeared in the darkness.

"What a pity not to keep such an autograph," said Balsamo, "and, above all, what a pity not to be able to forward it by a safe hand to the king."

Fritz now appeared.

"Who is there?" he asked.

"A man and a woman."

"Have they been here before?"

"No."

"Do you know them?"

"No."

"Is the woman young?"

"Young and handsome."

"The man?"

"From sixty to sixty-five years of age."

"Where are they?"

"In the saloon."

Balsamo entered.

CHAPTER XVII.

THE EVOCATION.

THE countess had completely concealed her face in a hood. As she had found time in passing to call at the family residence, she had assumed the dress of a citizen's wife. She had come in a hackney-coach with the marshal, who, even more timid than she, had donned a gray dress, like that of a superior servant in a respectable household.

" Do you recognize me, count ? " said Mme. Dubarry.

" Perfectly, Madame la Comtesse."

Richelieu had remained in the background.

" Deign to be seated, madame, and you also, monsieur."

" This is my steward," said the countess.

" You err, madame," said Balsamo, bowing; " the gentleman is the Marshal Duke de Richelieu, whom I recognize easily, and who would be very ungrateful if he did-not recognize me."

" How so ? " asked the duke, quite confounded, as Tallemant des Reaux would say.

" My lord duke, a man owes a little gratitude, I think, to those who have saved his life."

" Ah ! ha ! duke," said the countess, laughing ; " do you hear, duke ? "

" What ! you have saved my life, count ? " asked Richelieu, quite astounded.

" Yes, my lord ; at Vienna, in the year 1725, when you were ambassador there."

" In 1725 ! But you were not born then, my dear sir."

Balsamo smiled.

" It seems to me that I was, my lord duke," said he, " since I met you, dying, or rather dead, upon a litter ; you had just received a sword thrust right through your body, and I poured three drops of my elixir upon the wound. There, hold—the place where you are ruffling your Alençon lace—rather fine, I must say, for a steward."

" But," interrupted the marshal, " you are scarcely thirty-five years of age, count."

" There, duke," cried the countess, laughing heartily, " there, you are before the sorcerer ; do you believe now ? "

" I am stupefied, countess. But at that period," continued the duke, addressing Balsamo, " you called yourself——"

" Oh ! duke, we sorcerers change our name in each generation. Now, in 1725, names ending in *us*, *os*, or *as*, were the fashion ; and I should not be surprised if at that time I had been seized with the whim of bartering my name for some Latin or Greek one. This being premised, I wait your commands, countess, and yours also, my lord."

" Count, the marshal and I have come to consult you."

" You do me too much honor, madame, especially if this idea arose naturally in your minds."

" Oh ! in the most natural manner in the world, count ; your prediction still haunts my thoughts, only I fear it will not be realized."

" Never doubt the dictates of science, madame."

" Oh ! oh !" said Richelieu ; " but our crown is a hazardous game, count. It is not here an affair of the wound which three drops of elixir can cure."

" No, but of a minister whom three words can ruin," replied Balsamo. " Well, have I guessed rightly ? Tell me."

"Perfectly," said the trembling countess. " Tell me in truth what think you of all this, duke ?"

" Oh ! do not let such a trifle astonish you, madame," said Balsamo ; " whoever sees Madame Dubarry and Richelieu uneasy, may guess the cause without magic."

" But," added the marshal, " if you can give us the remedy, I will perfectly adore you."

" The remedy for your complaint ? "

" Yes ; we are ill of the Choiseul."

" And you wish to be cured ? "

" Yes ; great magician."

" Count, you will not leave us in our embarrassment ? " said the countess ; " your honor is engaged."

" My best services are at your command, madame ; but I first wish to know if the duke had not some definite plan formed when he came here ? "

" I confess it, count. Really, it is delightful to have a count for a sorcerer ; we do not need to change our modes of speech."

Balsamo smiled.

" Come, " said he, " let us be frank."

": 'Pon honor, I wish for nothing else," replied the duke.

" You had some consultation to hold with me ? "

" That is true."

" Ah, deceiver ! " said the countess, " you never spoke of that to me."

" I could only speak of it to the count, and that in the most secret corner of his ear," replied the marshal.

" Why, duke ? "

" Because you would have blushed, countess, to the whites of your eyes."

" Oh ! tell it now, marshal, just to satisfy my curiosity. I am rouged, so you shall see nothing."

" Well," said Richelieu, " this is what I thought. Take care, countess, I am going to take a most extravagant flight."

" Fly as high as you will, duke, I am prepared."

" Oh, but I fear you will beat me the moment you hear what I am about to say."

" You are not accustomed to be beaten, my lord duke ? " said Balsamo to the old marshal, enchanted with the compliment.

" Well," continued he, " here it is. Saving the displeasure of madame, his maj--.How am I to express it ? "

" How tiresome he is," cried the countess.

" You will have it, then ? "

" Yes, yes ; a hundred times, yes."

" Then I will venture. It is a sad thing to say, count ; but his majesty is no longer amusable. The word is not of my originating, countess, it is Madame de Maintenon's."

" There is nothing in that which hurts me, duke," said Mme. Dubarry.

"So much the better; then I shall feel at my ease. Well, the count, who discovers such precious elixirs, must——"

"Find one which shall restore to the king the faculty of being amused."

"Exactly."

"Oh! duke, that is mere child's play—the *a b c* of our craft. Any charlatan can furnish you with a philter——"

"Whose virtue," continued the duke, "would be put to the account of madame's merit."

"Duke!" exclaimed the countess.

"Oh! I knew you would be angry; but you would have it."

"My lord duke," replied Balsamo, "you were right; look! the countess blushes. But just now we are agreed hat neither wounds nor love were to be treated of at present. A philter will not rid France of Monsieur de Choiseul. In fact, if the king loved madame ten times more than he does, and that is impossible, Monsieur de Choiseul would still retain the same influence over his mind which madame exerts over his heart."

"Very true," said the marshal; "but it was our only resource."

"You think so?"

"Dame! find another."

"Oh! that would be easy."

"Easy! do you hear, countess? These sorcerers stop at nothing."

"Why should I stop, where the only thing necessary is simply to prove to the king that Monsieur de Choiseul alone betrays him—that is to say, what the king would think betraying; for, of course, Monsieur de Chciseul does not think he betrays him in acting as he does."

"And what does he do?"

"You know as well as I do, countess; he supports the parliament in their revolt against the royal authority."

"Certainly; but we must know by what means."

"By the means of agents who encourage them by promising them immunity."

" Who are the agents ?　We must know that."

" Do you believe, for example, that Madame de Grammont is gone for any other purpose than to sustain the ardent and warm the timid ? "

" Certainly ; she left for no other reason," exclaimed the countess.

" Yes ; but the king thinks it a simple exile."

" It is true."

" How can you prove to him that in this departure there is anything more than he supposes ? "

" By accusing Madame de Grammont."

" Ah ! if there were nothing necessary but to accuse her, count ! " said the marshal.

" But, unfortunately, the accusation must be proved," added the countess.

" And if this accusation were proved, incontrovertibly proved, do you think Monsieur de Choiseul would still be minister ? "

" Certainly not," said the countess.

" Nothing is necessary, then, but to discover the treachery of Monsieur de Choiseul," pursued Balsamo, with assurance ; " and to display it clearly, precisely and palpably before the eyes of his majesty."

The marshal threw himself back upon an armchair, and laughed loud and long.

" Charming ! " he exclaimed ; " he stops at nothing ! Discover Monsieur de Choiseul in the act of committing treason—that is all, nothing more ! "

Balsamo remained calm and unmoved, waiting until the marshal's mirth had subsided.

" Come," said Balsamo, " let us speak seriously, and recapitulate."

" So be it."

" Is not Monsieur de Choiseul suspected of encouraging the revolt of the parliament ? "

" Granted ; but the proof ? "

" Is not Monsieur de Choiseul supposed," continued Balsamo, " to be attempting to bring about a war with England, in order that he may become indispensable ? "

" It is so believed ; but the proof ? "

" Is not Monsieur de Choiseul the declared enemy of the countess, and does he not seek, by all possible means, to drag her from the throne I promised her ? "

" Ah ! all this is very true," said the countess ; "but once more I repeat, it must be proved.   Oh ! that I could prove it."

" What is necessary for that ?   A mere trifle."

The marshal gave a low whistle.

" Yes, a mere trifle," said he, sarcastically.

" A confidential letter, for example," said Balsamo.

" Yes ; that is all—a mere nothing."

" A letter from Madame de Grammont would do, would it not marshal ? "   continued the count.

"Sorcerer, my good sorcerer, find me such a one ! " cried Mme. Dubarry.

" I have been trying for five years ; I have spent a hundred thousand livres per annum, and have never succeeded."

" Because you never applied to me, madame," said Balsamo.

" How so ? " said the countess.

" Without doubt, if you had applied to me, I could have assisted you."

" Could you ?   Count, is it yet too late ? "

The count smiled.

" It is never too late," said he.

" Oh, my dear count ! " said Mme. Dubarry clasping her hands.

" You want a letter, then ? "

" Yes."

" From Madame de Grammont ?

" If it is possible."

" Which shall compromise Monsieur de Choiseul on the three points which I have mentioned ? "

" I would give one of my eyes to see it."

" Oh ! countess, that would be too dear ; inasmuch as this letter—I will give it you for nothing."

And Balsamo drew a folded paper from his pocket.

"What is that ?" asked the countess, devouring the paper with her eyes.

"Yes, what is that ?" repeated the duke.

"The letter you wished for."

And the count, amid the most profound silence, read the letter, with which our readers are already acquainted, to his two astonished auditors.

As he read, the countess opened her eyes to their utmost width, and began to lose countenance.

"It is a forgery," said Richelieu, when the letter had been read. "Diable ! we must take care."

"Monsieur, it is the simple and literal copy of a letter from the Duchess de Grammont, which a courier, despatched this morning from Rouen, is now carrying to the Duke de Choiseul at Versailles."

"Oh, heavens !" cried the marshal, "do you speak truly, Count Balsamo ?"

"I always speak the truth, marshal."

"The duchess has written such a letter ?"

"Yes, marshal."

"She could not be so imprudent."

"It is incredible, I confess ; but so it is."

The old duke looked at the countess, who had not the power to utter a single word.

"Well," said she, at last, "I am like the duke, I can scarcely believe—excuse me, count—that Madame de Grammont, a woman of sense, should compromise her own position, and that of her brother, by a letter so strongly expressed. Besides, to know of such a letter, one must have read it——"

"And then," said the marshal, quickly, "if the count had read this letter, he would have kept it ; it is a precious treasure."

Balsamo gently shook his head.

"Oh," said he, "such a plan might suit those who have to break open letters in order to ascertain their contents ; but not those who, like myself, can read through the envelopes. Fie upon you ! Besides, what interest could I have in ruining Monsieur de Choiseul and Madame de

Grammont ? You come to consult me as friends, I presume, and I answer you in the same manner. You wish
me to render you a service ; I do so. You do not mean,
I suppose, to ask me the price of my consultation, as you
would the fortune-tellers of the Quai de la Ferraille ? ”

"Oh, count ! ” said Mme. Dubarry.

"Well, I give you this advice, and you seem not to
comprehend it. You express a wish to overthrow Monsieur de Choiseul, and you seek the means. I tell you one.
You approve of it, I put it into your hands, and—you do
not believe it.”

" Because—because—count—I——”

"The letter exists, I tell you, for I have the copy.”

" But who told you of its existence, count ? ” cried
Richelieu.

" Ah ! that is a great word—who told me ! You wish
to know, in one moment, as much as I know—I, the
worker, the adept, who has lived three thousand seven
hundred years.”

"Oh ! oh !” said Richelieu, discouraged ; " you are going to alter the good opinion I had formed of you, count.”

" I do not ask you to believe me, my lord duke ; it is
not I who brought you hither from the chase.”

" Duke, he is right,” said the countess.   " Monsieur
de Balsamo, pray do not be hasty.”

"He who has time never gets impatient, madame.”

" Will you be so good as to add another favor to those
you have already conferred upon me, and tell me how these
secrets are revealed to you ? ”

" I shall not hesitate, madame,” said Balsamo, speaking
as if he was searching for each word separately.   " The
revelation is made to me by a voice.”

" By a voice ! ” cried the duke and the countess simultaneously, " a voice tells you all ? ”

" Everything I wish to know.”

" Was it a voice that told you what Madame de Grammont has written to her brother ? ”

" I repeat, madame, it is a voice which tells me.”

" Miraculous ! ”

" Why, do you not believe it ? "

" Well ; no, count," said the duke ; " how do you imagine I can believe such things ? "

" Would you believe it if I told you what the courier who carries the letter to Monsieur de Choiseul is doing at this moment ? "

" Dame ! " exclaimed the countess.

" I would believe it," cried the duke, " if I heard the voice ; but messieurs, the necromancers and magicians have the sole privilege of seeing and hearing the supernatural."

Balsamo looked at Richelieu with a singular expression, which made a shudder pass though the veins of the countess, and even sent a slight chill to the heart of the selfish skeptic, called the Duke de Richelieu.

" Yes," said he, after a long silence, " I alone see and hear supernatural objects and sounds, but when I am in the society of people of rank—of your talent, duke, and of your beauty, countess, I display my treasures, and share them. Would you wish greatly to hear the mysterious voice which speaks to me ? "

" Yes," said the duke, clinching his hands tightly that he might not tremble.

" Yes," stammered the countess, trembling.

" Well, duke—well, countess, you shall hear it. What language shall it speak ? "

" French, if you please," said the countess. " I know no other—any other would frighten me."

" And you, duke ? "

" As madame said, French ; for then, I shall be able to repeat what the devil says, and to discover if he speak the the language of my friend, Monsieur de Voltaire, correctly. "

Balsamo, his head drooping on his breast, crossed over to the door leading into the little saloon, which opened, as we are aware, on the stairs.

" Permit me," said he, " to conceal you here, in order not to expose you to the risk of discovery."

The countess turned pale, approached the duke, and took his arm.

Balsamo, almost touching the door leading to the stairs, made a step toward that part of the house in which Lorenza was, and pronounced in a low voice the following words, in the Arabic tongue, which we translate :

" My friend—do you hear me ?   If so, pull the cord of the bell twice."

Balsamo waited to see the effect of these words, and looked at the duke and countess, who opened their eyes and ears, and the more so that they could understand what the count said.

The bell sounded twice distinctly.

The countess started from her sofa, and the duke wiped his forehead with his handkerchief.

" Since you hear me," continued Balsamo, in the same language, " press the marble button which forms the right eye of the sculptured figure on the chimney-piece ; the back will open ; pass out by this opening, cross my room, descend the stairs, and enter the apartment adjoining the one in which I am."

Immediately a faint noise, like a scarcely audible breath, told Balsamo that his order had been understood and obeyed.

" What language is that ? " asked the duke, pretending assurance.   " The cabalistic language ? "

" Yes, duke ; the language used for the summoning of spirits."

" You said we should understand it."

" What the voice said, but not what I say."

" Has the devil appeared yet ? "

" Who spoke of the devil, duke ? "

" Whom do you evoke but the devil ? "

" Every superior spirit, every supernatural being can be evoked."

" And the superior spirit, the supernatural being——"

Balsamo extended his hand toward the tapestry, which closed the door of the next apartment.

" Is in direct communication with me, my lord."

" I am afraid," said the countess ; " are you, duke ? "

" Faith ! countess, I confess to you that I would almost as soon be at Mahon or at Phillipsbourg."

" Madame la Comtesse, and you, my lord duke, listen, since you wish to hear," said Balsamo, severely, and he turned toward the door.

CHAPTER XVIII.

THE VOICE.

THERE was a moment of solemn silence ; then Balsamo asked in French :

" Are you there ? "

" I am," replied a clear, silvery voice, which, penetrating through the hangings and the doors, seemed to those present rather like a metallic sound than a human voice.

" Peste ! it is becoming interesting," said the duke ; " and all without torches, magic, or Bengal lights."

" It is fearful," whispered the countess.

" Listen attentively to my questions," continued Balsamo.

" I listen with my whole being."

" First tell me how many persons are with me at this moment ? "

" Two."

" Of what sex ? "

" A man and a woman."

" Read the man's name in my thoughts."

" The Duke de Richelieu."

" And the woman's."

" Madame the Countess Dubarry."

" Ha ! " said the duke, " this is becoming serious."

" I never saw anything like it," murmured the trembling countess.

" Good ! " said Balsamo.   " Now read the first sentence of the letter I hold in my hand."

The voice obeyed.

The duke and the countess looked at each other with astonishment bordering upon admiration.

" What has become of the letter I wrote at your dictation ? "

" It is hastening on."

" In what direction ? "

" Toward the east."

" Is it far."

" Yes, very far."

" Who is carrying it ? "

" A man dressed in a green vest, leathern cap, and large boots."

" On foot or on horseback ? "

" On horseback."

" What kind of a horse ? "

" A piebald horse."

" Where do you see him ? "

There was a moment's silence.

" Look," said Balsamo, imperatively.

" On a wide road, planted with trees."

" But on which road ? "

" I do not know ; all the roads are alike."

" What ! does nothing indicate what road it is—no post, no inscription ? "

" Stay ! stay ! A carriage is passing near the man on horseback ; it crosses his course, coming toward me."

" What kind of a carriage ? "

" A heavy carriage, full of abbés and soldiers."

" A stage-coach," said Richelieu.

" Is there no inscription upon the carriage ? " asked Balsamo.

" Yes," said the voice.

" Read it."

" Versailles is written in yellow letters upon the carriage, but the word is nearly effaced."

" Leave the carriage and follow the courier."

" I do not see him now."

" Why do you not see him ? "

" Because the road turns."

" Turn the corner, and follow him."

" Oh ! he gallops as quickly as his horse can fly ; he looks at his watch."

" What do you see in front of the horse ? "

" A long avenue, splendid buildings, a large town."

" Follow him still."

" I follow."

" Well ? "

" The courier redoubles his blows, the animal is bathed in perspiration ; its iron-shod hoofs strike the pavement so loudly that all the passers-by look round. Ah ! the courier dashes into a long street which descends. He turns to the right. He slackens his horse's speed. He stops at the door of a large hotel."

" Now you must follow him attentively, do you hear ? " The voice heaved a sigh.

" You are tired. I understand."

" Oh ! crushed with weariness."

" Cease to be fatigued, I will it."

" Ah ! Thanks."

" Are you still fatigued ? "

" No."

" Do you still see the courier ? "

" Yes, yes ; he ascends a large stone staircase. He is preceded by a valet in blue and gold livery. He crosses large saloons full of splendid gilt ornaments. He stops at a small lighted closet. The valet opens the door, and retires."

" What do you see ? "

" The courier bows."

" To whom does he bow ? "

" He bows to a man seated at a desk with his back toward the door."

" How is the man dressed? "

" Oh, in full dress, as if he were going to a ball."

" Has he any decoration ? "

" He wears a broad blue ribbon crosswise on his breast."

" His face ? "

" I cannot see it—ah——"

" What ? "

" He turns."

" What sort of features has he ? "

" A keen glance, irregular features, beautiful teeth."

" What age ? "

" From fifty-five to fifty-eight years of age."

" The duke," whispered the countess to the marshal ; " it is the duke."

The marshal made a sign as if to say, " Yes, it is he— but listen."

" Well ? " asked Balsamo.

" The courier gives a letter to the man with the blue ribbon——"

" You may say to the duke ; he is a duke."

" The courier," repeated the obedient voice, " takes a letter from the leathern bag behind him, and gives it to the duke. The duke breaks the seal, and reads it attentively."

" Well ? "

" He takes a pen and a sheet of paper and writes."

" He writes," said Richelieu ; " Diable ! if we could only know what he writes."

" Tell me what he writes,"commanded Balsamo.

" I cannot."

" Because you are too far. Enter the room. Are you there ? "

" Yes."

" Look over his shoulder."

" I am doing so."

" Now read."

" The writing is bad, small, irregular."

" Read it—I will it."

The countess and Richelieu held their breath.

" Read," repeated Balsamo, more imperatively still.

" My sister," said the voice, trembling and hesitating.

" It is the reply," said the duchess and Richelieu in the same breath.

" My sister," continued the voice, " do not be uneasy. The crisis took place, it is true ; it was a dangerous one; that is true also ; but it is over. I am anxiously awaiting to-morrow, for to-morrow it will be my turn to act on the offensive, and everything leads me to expect a decisive triumph. The parliament of Rouen, Milord X——, the petards, are all satisfactory. To morrow, after my interview with the king, I shall add a *post scriptum* to my letter, and send it to you by the same courier."

Balsamo, with his left hand extended, seemed to drag each word painfully from the voice ; while with the right hand he hastily took down those lines, which M. de Choiseul was at the same time writing in his closet at Versailles.

" Is that all ? " asked Balsamo.

" That is all."

" What is the duke doing now ? "

" He folds the paper on which he has just written, and puts it into a small portfolio which he takes from the pocket in the left side of his coat."

" You hear," said Balsamo to the almost stupefied countess.

" Well ? "

" Then he sends away the courier."

" What does he say to him ? "

" I only heard the end of the sentence."

" What was it ? "

" ' At one o'clock at the postern-gate of Trianon.' The courier bows and retires."

" Yes," said Richelieu, " he makes an appointment to meet the courier when his audience is over, as he says in his letter."

Balsamo made a sign with his hand to command silence.

" What is the duke doing now ? " he asked.

" He rises. He holds the letter he has received in his hand. He goes straight toward his bed, enters the passage between it and the wall, and presses a spring which opens an iron box. He throws the letter into the box and closes it."

" Oh ! " cried the countess and the duke, turning pale, "this is in truth magical."

" Do you know now what you wish to know, madame ? " asked Balsamo.

" Count," said Mme. Dubarry, approaching him with terror, " you have rendered me a service which I would pay with ten years of my life, or rather which I can never pay. Ask what you wish."

" Oh ! madame, you know we have already an account."

" Speak, say what you wish."

" The time has not yet come."

" Well, when it comes, if it were a million——"

Balsamo smiled.

" Oh, countess ! " exclaimed the marshal, " you should rather ask the count for a million. Cannot a man who knows what he knows, and who sees what he sees, discover diamonds and gold in the bosom of the earth as easily as he discovers the thoughts in the heart of man ? "

" Then, count," said the countess, " I bow myself before you in my weakness."

" No, countess ; one day you will acquit your debt toward me. I shall give you the opportunity."

" Count," said Richelieu to Balsamo, " I am conquered —crushed. I believe."

" As St. Thomas believed, duke. I do not call that believing, but seeing."

" Call it what you will, I will make the *amende honorable,* and in future, if I am asked about sorcerers, I shall know what to say."

Balsamo smiled.

" Madame," said he to the countess, " will you permit me to do one thing now ? "

" Speak."

" My spirit is wearied. Let me restore it to liberty by a magic formula."

" Do so, sir."

" Lorenza," said Balsamo, in Arabic, " thanks ; I love you ; return to your apartment by the same way you came, and wait for me. Go, my beloved."

" I am very tired," replied, in Italian, the voice, softer still than even during the evocation. " Hasten, Acharat."

" I come," and the footsteps died away in the distance with the same rustling noise with which they had approached.

Then Balsamo, after a few moments' interval, during which he convinced himself of Lorenza's departure, bowed profoundly, but with that majestic dignity to his visitors, who returned to their fiacre more like intoxicated persons than human beings gifted with reason, so much were they staggered and absorbed by the crowd of tumultuous ideas which assailed them.

CHAPTER XIX.

DISGRACE.

THE next morning, as the great clock of Versailles struck eleven, King Louis XV. issued from his apartment, and crossing the adjoining gallery, called in a loud and stern voice :

"Monsieur de la Vrillière ! "

The king was pale, and seemed agitated. The more he endeavored to hide his emotion, the more evident it became from the embarrassment of his looks, and the rigid tension of his usually impassible features.

A death-like stillness pervaded the long ranks of courtiers, among whom the Duke de Richelieu and Count Jean Dubarry might be seen, both seemingly calm, and affecting indifference or ignorance as to what was going on.

The Duke de la Vrillière approached, and took a lettre-de-cachet from the king's hand.

" Is the Duke de Choiseul at Versailles ? " asked the king.

" Yes, sire. He returned from Paris yesterday, at two o'clock in the afternoon."

" Is he in his hotel, or in the château ? "

" In the château, sire."

" Carry this order to him, duke," said the king.

A shudder ran through the whole file of spectators, who bent down whispering, like ears of corn under the blast of a tornado.

The king frowning, as if he wished to add terror to the scene, haughtily entered his closet, followed by the captain of the guard and the commandant of the light horse.

All eyes followed M. de Vrillière, who slowly crossed the courtyard and entered M. de Choiseul's apartments, rather uneasy at the commission with which he was charged.

During this time, loud and eager conversations, some threatening, some timid, burst forth on all sides around the old marshal, who pretended to be even more surprised than the others, but who, thanks to his cunning smile, duped no one.

M. de la Vrillière returned, and was immediately surrounded.

" Well ? " cried every one.

" Well ?   It was an order of banishment."

" Of banishment ? "

" Yes, in due form."

" Then you read it, duke ? "

" I have."

"Positively."

Judge for yourselves."

And the Duke de la Vrillière repeated the following lines, which he had treasured up with the retentive memory which marks the true courtier :

" MY COUSIN,—The displeasure which your conduct causes me, obliges me to exile you to Chanteloup, whither you must repair in twenty-four hours from this time.   I should have sent you further, had it not been for the particular esteem I feel for Madame de Choiseul, whose health is exceedingly interesting to me.   Take care that your conduct does not force me to proceed to ulterior measures."

" A long murmur ran through the group which surrounded M. de la Vrillière.

" And what did he reply to you, Monsieur de St. Florentin ? "asked Richelieu, affecting not to give to the duke either his new name or his new title.

" He replied, ' Duke, I feel convinced of the great pleasure you feel in being the bearer of this letter,"

" That was harsh, my poor duke," said Jean.

" What could you expect, count ?   A man does not receive such a tile thrown upon his head without crying out a little."

"Do you know what he will do?" asked Richelieu.

"Most probably obey."

"Hum!" said the marshal.

"Here is the duke coming," said Jean, who stood as sentinel at the window.

"Coming here!" exclaimed the Duke de la Vrillière.

"I told you so, Monsieur de St. Florentin."

"He is crossing the courtyard," continued Jean.

"Alone?"

"Quite alone—his portfolio under his arm."

"Oh! good heavens!" said Richelieu, "if yesterday's scene should be repeated!"

"Do not speak of it; I shudder at the thought," replied Jean.

He had scarcely spoken, when the Duke de Choiseul appeared at the entrance of the gallery, with head erect and confident look, alarming his enemies, or those who would declare themselves such on his disgrace, by this calm and piercing glance.

As no one expected this step after what had happened, no one opposed his progress.

"Are you sure you read correctly, duke?" asked Jean.

"Parbleu!"

"And he returns after such a letter as you have described?"

"Upon my honor, I cannot understand it."

"The king will send him to the Bastile."

"That would cause a fearful commotion."

"I should almost pity him."

"Look; he is going to the king! It is incredible!"

In fact, without paying attention to the show of resistance which the astounded usher offered, M. de Choiseul entered the king's closet. Louis, on seeing him, uttered an exclamation of astonishment.

The duke held his lettre-de-cachet in his hand, and showed it to the king almost smilingly.

"Sire," said he, "as your majesty had the goodness to forewarn me yesterday, I have indeed received a letter to-day."

"Yes, sir," replied the king.

"And as your majesty had the goodness yesterday to tell me not to look upon any letter as serious which was not ratified by the express words of the king, I have come to request an explanation."

"It will be very short, my lord duke," replied the king. "To-day the letter is valid."

"Valid!" said the duke. "So offensive a letter to so devoted a servant?"

"A devoted servant, sir, does not make his master play a ridiculous part."

"Sire," replied the minister, haughtily, "I was born near the throne, that I might comprehend its majesty."

"Sir," replied the king, in a severe voice, "I will not keep you in suspense. Yesterday evening you received a courier from Madame de Grammont in your closet at Versailles."

"It is true, sire."

"He brought you a letter?"

"Are a brother and sister forbidden to correspond?"

"Wait a moment, if you please. I know the contents of that letter."

"Oh, sire!"

"Here it is. I took the trouble to copy it with my own hand."

And the king handed to the duke an exact copy of the letter he had received.

"Sire!"

"Do not deny it, duke; you placed the letter in an iron coffer standing at your bedside."

The duke became pale as a specter.

"That is not all," continued the king, pitilessly; "you have replied to Madame de Grammont's letter. I know the contents of that also. It is there in your portfolio, and only wants the *post scriptum*, which you are to add when you leave me. You see I am well informed, am I not?"

The duke wiped his forehead, on which the large drops of perspiration were standing, bowed without uttering a word, and left the closet, tottering as if he had been struck with apoplexy. Had it not been for the fresh air which fanned his face, he must have fallen.

But he was a man of strong will. When he reached the gallery he had regained his strength, and with erect forehead passed the hedge of courtiers, and entered his apartments in order to burn and lock up several papers.

A quarter of an hour afterward, he left the château in his carriage.

M. de Choiseul's disgrace was a thunderbolt which set all France in flames.

The parliament, sustained in reality by the tolerance of the minister, proclaimed that the state had lost its firmest pillar. The nobility supported him as being one of themselves. The clergy felt themselves soothed by this man, whose personal dignity, often carried even to the extent of pride, gave almost an appearance of sanctity to his ministerial functions.

The encyclopedist or the philosophical party, who were very numerous, and also very strong, because they were re-enforced by all the enlightened, clever, and caviling spirits of the age, cried out loudly when the Government was taken from the hands of a minister who admired Voltaire, pensioned the " Encyclopedia " and preserved, by developing them into more useful manner, the traditions of Mme. de Pompadour, the female Mecænas of the writers of the " Mercure," and of philosophy in general.

The people had far better grounds for complaint than any of the other malcontents. They also complained, but without reasoning, and, as they always do, they hit the truth and laid bare the bleeding wound.

M. de Choiseul, absolutely speaking, was a bad minister, and a bad citizen ; but relatively he was a paragon of virtue, of morality, and of patriotism. When the people, dying of hunger, in the fields, heard of his majesty's prodigality, and of Mme. Dubarry's ruinous whims, when open warnings were sent him, such as "L'homme aux quarante écus," or advices like "Le Contrat Social," and secret revelations like the "Nouvelles à la main," and

the " Idées singulières d'un bon citoyen," they were terrified at the prospect of falling back into the impure hands
of the favorite, less respectable than a collier's wife, as
Bauveau said, and into the hands of the favorite's favorites ; and, wearied with so much suffering, they were
alarmed to behold the future looking even blacker than
ever.

It was not that the people, who had strong antipathies,
had also strong sympathies.   They did not like the parliament, because they who ought to have been their natural
protectors, had always abandoned them for idle inquiries,
questions of precedence, or selfish interests ; and because,
dazzled by the borrowed light of the royal omnipotence,
they imagined themselves something like an aristocracy,
occupying an intermediate place between the nobility and
the people.

They disliked the nobility from instinct and from memory.   They feared the sword as much as they hated the
church.   Their position could not, therefore, be affected
by the disgrace of M. de Choiseul, but they heard the
complaints of the nobility, of the clergy, of the parliament, and this noise, joined to their own murmurs, made
an uproar which intoxicated them.

The consequence of these feelings was regret, and a
sort of a quasi-popularity for the name of Choiseul.

All Paris—the word in this case can be justified by the
facts—accompanied the exile on his way to Chanteloup as
far as the town gates.

The people lined the road which the carriage was to
take, while the members of the parliament and the court,
who could not be received by the duke, stationed themselves in their carriages in front of the crowd of people,
that they might salute him as he passed, and bid him
adieu.

The procession was the densest at the Barrière d'Enfer,
which is on the road to Touraine, at which place there was
such a conflux of foot-passengers, horsemen, and carriages,
that the traffic was interrupted for several hours.

When the duke had crossed the barrière, he found him-

self escorted by more than a hundred carriages, which
formed a sort of triumphant procession around him.

Acclamations and sighs followed him on all sides, but
he had too much sense and penetration not to know that
all this noise was not so much occasioned by regret for him
personally as by the fear of those unknown people who
were to rise upon his ruin.

A short way from the barrière a post-chaise, galloping
along the crowded road, met the procession, and had it not
been for the skill of the postilion, the horses, white with
foam and dust, would have dashed against M. de Choiseul's
equipage.

A head bent forward out of the carriage window, and M.
de Choiseul leaned out also from his.

M. d'Aiguillon bowed profoundly to the fallen minister
whose heritage he had come to canvass.   M. de Choiseul
threw himself back in the carriage ; a single second had
sufficed to wither the laurels which had crowned his disgrace.

But at the same moment, as a compensation, no doubt,
a carriage drawn by eight horses and bearing the royal arms
of France, which was seen advancing along the cross-road
from Sèvres to St. Cloud, and which, whether by accident,
or on account of the crowd, did not turn into the high-
road, also crossed before M. de Choiseul's carriage.   The
dauphiness, with her lady of honor, Mme. de Noailles, was
on the back seat of the carriage, on the front was Mlle.
Andrée de Taverney.   M. de Choiseul, crimson with exul-
tation and joy, bent forward out of the door, and bowed
profoundly.

" Adieu, madame," said he, in a low voice.

" Au revoir, Monsieur de Choiseul," replied the dauphiness, with an imperial smile, and a majestic contempt
of all etiquette.

" Long live Monsieur de Choiseul ! " cried a voice, en-
thusiastically, after the dauphiness had spoken.

At the sound of the voice, Mlle. Andrée turned round
quickly.

" Make way ! make way ! " cried her highness's grooms,

forcing Gilbert, pale as death, and pressing forward in his eagerness to range himself with the other people on road.

It was indeed our hero, who, in his philosophical enthusiasm, had cried out, "Long live Monsieur de Choiseul."

CHAPTER XX.

THE DUKE D'AIGUILLON.

WHILE melancholy visages and red eyes were the order of the day on the road from Paris to Chanteloup, Luciennes was radiant with blooming faces and charming smiles.

It was because at Luciennes was enthroned not a mere mortal, although the most beautiful and most adorable of mortals, as the poets and courtiers declared, but the real divinity which governed France.

The evening after M. de Choiseul's disgrace, therefore, the road leading to Luciennes was thronged with the same carriages which, in the morning, had rolled after the exiled minister. There were, besides, the partisans of the chancellor, and the votaries of corruption and self-interest, and altogether they made an imposing procession.

But Mme. Dubarry had her police, and Jean knew, to a baron, the names of those who had strewn the last flowers over the expiring Choiseuls. He gave a list of these names to the countess, and they were pitilessly excluded, while the courage of the others in braving public opinion was rewarded by the protecting smile and the complete view of the goddess of the day. What joy and what congratulations echoed on all sides. Pressings of the hand, little smothered laughs, and enthusiastic applause, seemed to have become the habitual language of the inhabitants of Luciennes.

After the great throng of carriages, and the general crowd, followed the private receptions. Richelieu, the secret and modest hero, indeed, but yet the real hero of the day, saw the crowd of visitors and petitioners pass away, and remained the last in the countess's boudoir.

"It must be confessed," said the countess, "that the Count Balsamo, or De Fenix, whichever name you give him, marshal, is one of the first men of the age. It would be a thousand pities if such sorcerers were still burned."

"Certainly, countess, he is a great man," replied Richelieu.

"And a very handsome man, too; I have taken quite a fancy to him, duke."

"You will make me jealous," said Richelieu, laughing, and eager besides to direct the conversation to a more positive and serious subject. "The Count de Fenix would make a dreadful minister of police."

"I was thinking of that," replied the countess; "only it would be impossible."

"Why, countess?"

"Because he would render colleagues impossible."

"How so?"

"Knowing everything—seeing into their hand——"

Richelieu blushed beneath his rouge.

"Countess," replied he, "if he were my colleague I would wish him to see into mine always, and communicate the cards to you; for you would ever see the knave of hearts on his knees before the queen, and prostrate at the feet of the king."

"Your wit puts us all to the blush, my dear duke," replied the countess. "But let us talk a little of our ministry. I think you mentioned that you warned your nephew D'Aiguillon of what would take place."

"He has arrived, madame, and with what Roman augurs would have called the best conjunction of omens possible; his carriage met Choiseul's leaving Paris."

"That is indeed a favorable omen," said the countess. "Then he is coming here?"

"Madame, I thought that if Monsieur d'Aiguillon was seen at Luciennes at such a time, it would give rise to unpleasant comment; I begged him, therefore, to remain in the village, until I should send for him according to your orders."

"Send for him immediately then, marshal, for we are alone, or very nearly so."

" The more willing that we quite understand each other;
do we not, countess? "

" Certainly, duke, you prefer war to finance, do you not;
or do you wish for the marine? "

" I prefer war, madame; I can be of most service in
that department."

" True, I will speak of it to the king; you have no antipathies."

" For whom? "

" For any colleagues his majesty might present to you."

" I am the least difficult man in the world to live with,
countess, but allow me to send for my nephew, since you
are good enough to grant him the favor of an audience."

Richelieu approached the window and looked into the
courtyard, now illuminated by the last rays of the setting
sun.   He made a sign to one of his footmen, who was
keeping his eye fixed upon the window, and who darted
off as soon as he received the signal.

Lights were now brought in.

Ten minutes after the footman had disappeared a carriage rolled into the courtyard.   The countess turned
quickly toward the window.

Richelieu saw the movement, which seemed to him an
excellent prognostic for M. d'Aiguillon's affairs, and consequently for his own.

" She likes the uncle," said he to himself; " and she is
in a fair way to like the nephew; we shall be masters here."

While he was feasting on these chimerical visions, a
slight noise was heard at the door, and the confidential
valet-de-chambre throwing it open, announced the Duke
d'Aiguillon.

He was an extremely handsome and graceful nobleman,
richly, and at the same time elegantly and tastefully
dressed.   M. d'Aiguillon had passed his earliest prime,
but he was one of those men who, whether judged by their
looks or minds, seem young until old age renders them in-
firm.

The cares of government had traced no wrinkles on his
brow; they had only enlarged the natural fold which seems
to be the birthplace of great thoughts both in statesmen

and in poets. His air and carriage were lofty and commanding, and his handsome features wore an expression at once of intelligence and melancholy, as if he knew that the hatred of ten millions of men weighed upon his head, but at the same time wished to prove that the weight was not beyond his strength.

M. d'Aiguillon had the most beautiful hands in the world; they looked white and delicate even when buried in the softest folds of lace. A well-turned leg was prized very highly at that period, and the duke's was a model of manly elegance and aristocratic form. He combined the suavity of the poet with the nobility of the lord and the suppleness and ease of the dashing guardsman. He was thus a *beau-ideal* for the countess in the three several qualities which the instinct of this beautiful sensualist taught her to love.

By a remarkable coincidence, or, rather, by a chain of circumstances skilfully combined by M. d'Aiguillon, these two objects of public animadversion, the favorite and the courtier, had, with all their mutual advantages, never yet met each other face to face at court.

For the last three years M. d'Aiguillon had managed to be very busy, either in Brittany or in his closet, and had not once shown himself at court, knowing well that a favorable or unfavorable crisis must soon take place. In the first case, it would be better to be comparatively unknown; in the second, to disappear without leaving any trace behind, and thus be able easily to emerge from the gulf under new auspices, and in a new character.

Another motive influenced his calculations—a motive which is the mainspring of romance, but which, nevertheless, was the most powerful of all.

Before Mme. Dubarry was a countess, and every evening touched the crown of France with her lips, she had been a lovely, smiling, and adored creature—she had been loved, a happiness she could no longer hope for since she was feared.

Among all the young, rich, powerful, and handsome men who had paid court to Jeanne Vaubernier, among all the rhymers who had coupled her in their verses with the epithets of angel and divinity, the Duke d'Aiguillon had formerly figured in the first rank; but whether it was that the duke was not sufficiently ardent, or whether Mlle. Lange was not so easily pleased as her detractors pretended, or lastly, whether the sudden attachment of the king had separated the two hearts ready to unite, is not known; but the fact remains that M. d'Aiguillon got his verses, acrostics, bouquets, and perfumes returned, and Mlle. Lange closed her door in the Rue des Petits Champs against him. The duke hastened to Brittany, suppressing his sighs; Mlle. Lange wafted all hers toward Versailles, to the Baron de Gonesse, that is, the King of France.

D'Aiguillon's sudden disappearance had troubled Mme. Dubarry very little, for she feared the remembrances of the past; but when subsequently she saw the silent attitude of her former adorer, she felt at first perplexed, then astonished, and, being in a good position for judging of men, she ended by thinking him a man of profound tact and discretion.

For the countess this was a great distinction, but it was not all, and the moment was perhaps come when she might think D'Aiguillon a man of heart.

We have seen that the marshal, in all his conversations with Mme. Dubarry, had never touched upon the subject of his nephew's acquaintance with Mlle. Lange. This silence from a man accustomed, as the old duke was, to say the most difficult things in the world, had much surprised and even alarmed the countess. She therefore impatiently awaited M. d'Aiguillon's arrival to know how to conduct herself, and to ascertain whether the marshal had been discreet or merely ignorant.

The duke entered, respectful, but at the same time easy, and sufficiently master of himself to draw the distinction in his salutation between the reigning sultana and the court lady. By this discriminating tact he instantly gained a protectress quite disposed to find good perfect, and perfection wonderful.

M. d'Aiguillon then took his uncle's hand, and the latter advancing toward the countess, said, in his most insinuating voice:

"The Duke d'Aiguillon, madame. It is not so much my nephew as one of your most ardent servants, whom I have the honor to present to you."

The countess glanced at the duke as the marshal spoke, and looked at him like a woman, that is to say, with eyes which nothing can escape. But she saw only two heads, bowing respectfully before her, and two faces erect, serene, and calm after the salutation was over.

"I know, marshal, that you love the duke," said the countess. "You are my friend. I shall request Monsieur d'Aiguillon, therefore, in deference to his uncle, to imitate him in all that will be agreeable to me."

"That is the conduct I had traced out beforehand for myself, madame," said D'Aiguillon, with another bow.

"You have suffered much in Brittany?" asked the countess.

"Yes, madame, and it is not yet over," replied D'Aiguillon.

"I believe it is, sir! besides, there is Monsieur de Richelieu who will be a powerful assistance to you."

D'Aiguillon looked at Richelieu as if surprised.

"Ah," said the countess, "I see that the marshal has not yet had time to have any conversation with you. That is very natural, as you have just arrived from a journey. Well, you must have a thousand things to say to each other, and I shall therefore leave you, marshal, for the present. My lord duke, pray consider yourself at home here."

So saying, the countess retired; but she did not proceed far. Behind the boudoir there opened a large closet, filled with all sorts of fantastic baubles with which the king was very fond of amusing himself when he came to Luciennes. He preferred this closet to the boudoir, because in it one could hear all that was said in the next room. Mme. Dubarry therefore was certain to hear the whole conversation between the duke and his nephew, and she calculated upon forming from it a correct and irrevocable opinion of the latter.

But the duke was not duped; he knew most of the secrets of every royal and ministerial residence. To listen when other people were speaking of him was one of his means; to speak while others were overhearing him was one of his ruses.

He determined, therefore, still joyous at the reception which D'Aiguillon had met with, to proceed in the same vein, and to reveal to the favorite, under cover of her supposed absence, such a plan of secret happiness and of lofty power, complicated with intrigues, as would present a double bait too powerful for a pretty woman, and above all, for a court lady, to resist.

He desired the duke to be seated, and commenced:

"You see, duke, I am installed here."

"Yes, sir, I see it."

"I have had the good fortune to gain the favor of the charming woman, who is looked upon as a queen here, and who is one in reality."

D'Aiguillon bowed.

"I must tell you, duke," continued Richelieu, "what I could not say in the open street—that Madame Dubarry has promised me a portfolio."

"Ah!" said D'Aiguillon, "that is only your desert, sir."

"I do not know if I deserve it or not, but I am to have it—rather late in the day, it is true. Then, situated as I shall be, I shall endeavor to advance your interests, D'Aiguillon."

"Thank you, my lord duke; you are a kind relative, and have often proved it."

"You have nothing in view, D'Aiguillon?"

"Absolutely nothing, except to escape being degraded from my title of duke and peer, as the parliament insists upon my being."

"Have you supporters anywhere?"

"Not one."

"You would have fallen, then, had it not been for the present circumstances?"

"I would have bit the dust, my lord duke."

"Ah! you speak like a philosopher. Diable! that is the reason that I am so harsh, my poor D'Aiguillon, and address you more like a minister than an uncle."

"My uncle, your goodness penetrates me with gratitude."

"When I sent for you in such a hurry, you may be certain it was because I wished you to play an important part here. Let me see; have you reflected on the part Monsieur de Choiseul played for ten years?"

"Yes; certainly his was an enviable position."

"Enviable! Yes, enviable, when, along with Madame de Pompadour, he governed the king and exiled the Jesuits; but very sad when having quarreled with Madame Dubarry, who is worth a hundred Pompadours, he was dismissed from office in four-and-twenty hours. You do not reply."

"I am listening, sir, and endeavoring to discover your meaning."

"You like Monsieur de Choiseul's first part best, do you not?"

"Certainly."

"Well, my dear duke, I have decided upon playing this part."

D'Aiguillon turned abruptly toward his uncle.

"Do you speak seriously?" said he.

"Yes. Why not?"

"You intend to be a candidate for Madame Dubarry's favor?"

"Ah! diable! you proceed too fast. But I see you understand me. Yes, Choiseul was very lucky: he governed the king, and governed his favorite also. It is said he was attached to Madame de Pompadour—in fact, why not? Well, no, I cannot act the lover; your cold smile tells me plainly so. You, with your young eyes, look compassionately at my furrowed brow, my bending knees, and my withered hands, which were once so beautiful. In place of saying, when I was speaking of Choiseul's part, that I would play it, I should have said we will play it."

"Uncle!"

"No, she cannot love me, I know it; nevertheless—I may confess it to you without fear, for she will never learn it—I could have loved this woman beyond everything—but——"

D'Aiguillon frowned. "But," said he.

"I have a splendid project," continued the marshal. "This part which my age renders impossible for me, I will divide into two."

"Ha!" said D'Aiguillon.

"Some one of my family," continued Richelieu, "will love Madame Dubarry. Parbleu! a glorious chance—such an accomplished woman!"

And Richelieu in saying these words raised his voice.

"You know it cannot be Fronsac. A degenerate wretch, a fool, a coward, a rogue, a gambler—duke, will you be the man?"

"I?" cried D'Aiguillon; "are you mad, uncle?"

"Mad? What! you are not already on your knees before him who gives you this advice? What! you do not bound with joy? You do not burn with gratitude? You are not already out of your senses with delight at the manner in which she receives you? You are not yet mad with love? Go! go!" cried the old marshal, "since the days of Alcibiades there has been but one Richelieu in the world, and I see there will be no more after him."

"My uncle," replied the duke, with much agitation, either feigned, and in that case it was admirably counterfeited, or real, for the proposition was sudden, "my uncle, I perceive all the advantage you would gain by the position of which you speak; you would govern with the authority of Monsieur de Choiseul, and I should be the lover who would constitute that authority. The plan is worthy of the cleverest man in France, but you have forgotten one thing in projecting it."

"What!" cried Richelieu, uneasily, "is it possible you do not love Madame Dubarry? Is that it—fool!—triple fool!—wretch!—is that it?"

"Ah, no! that is not it, my dear uncle," cried D'Aiguillon, as if he knew that not one of his words was lost. "Madame Dubarry, whom I scarcely know, seems to me the most charming of women. I should, on the contrary, love Madame Dubarry madly, I should love her only too well—that is not the question."

"What is it, then?"

"This, my lord duke. Madame Dubarry will never love me, and the first condition of such an alliance is love. How do you imagine the beautiful countess could distinguish among all the gentlemen of this brilliant court—surrounded as she is by the homage of so much youth and beauty—how should she distinguish one who has no merit, who is already no longer young, who is overwhelmed with sorrows, and who hides himself from all eyes because he feels that he will soon disappear forever? My uncle, if I had known Madame Dubarry in the period of my youth and beauty, when women admired in me all that is lovable in a man, then she might have given me a place in her memory. That would have been much. But now there is no hope—neither past, nor present, nor future. No, uncle, we must renounce this chimera. You have pierced my heart by presenting it to me in such bright and glowing colors."

During this tirade, which was delivered with a fire which Mole might have envied, and Lekain would have thought worthy of imitation, Richelieu bit his lips, muttering to himself:

"Has the man guessed that the countess is listening? Peste! he is a clever dog. He is a master of his craft. In that case, I must take care!"

Richelieu was right; the countess was listening, and every word D'Aiguillon spoke sunk deep into her heart. She eagerly drank in the charm of this confession, and appreciated this exquisite delicacy in not betraying the secret of their former intimacy to his nearest confidant, for fear of throwing a shadow over a perhaps still dearly cherished portrait.

"Then you refuse?" said Richelieu.

"Oh! as for that, yes, my uncle, for unfortunately I see it is impossible."

"But try, at least, unfortunate that you are."

"And how?"

"You are here, one of us—you will see the countess very day; please her, morbleu!"

"With an interested aim? Never! If I should be so unfortunate as to please her with this unworthy view, I should flee to the end of the world, for I should be ashamed of myself."

Richelieu scratched his chin.

" The thing is settled," said he to himself, " or D'Aiguillon is a fool."

All at once a noise was heard in the courtyard, and several voices cried out, " The king!"

" Diable!" cried Richelieu; " the king must not see me here; I shall make my escape."

" And I?" said the duke.

" It is different with you; he must see you. Remain; and, for God's sake, do not throw the handle after the ax."

With these words Richelieu stole out by the back stairs, saying, as he left the room:

" Adieu till to-morrow."

CHAPTER XXI.

THE KING DIVIDES THE SPOILS.

WHEN the Duke d'Aiguillon was left alone he felt at first somewhat embarrassed. He had perfectly understood all his uncle had said to him—perfectly understood that Mme. Dubarry was listening—perfectly understood, in short, that, for a clever man, it was necessary to this conjecture to seem a man of heart, and to play alone that part in which the old marshal sought to obtain a share.

The king's arrival luckily interrupted the explanation which must have resulted from the puritanical declaration of M. d'Aiguillon.

The marshal was not a man to remain long a dupe, nor above all one who would make another's virtue shine with exaggerated brilliancy at the expense of his own.

But, being left alone, D'Aiguillon had time to reflect.

The king had in truth arrived. Already his pages had opened the door of the antechamber, and Zamore had darted toward the monarch, begging for bonbons, a touching familiarity which Louis, when he was in a bad temper, punished by sundry fillips on the nose or boxes on the ears, both exceedingly disagreeable to the young African.

The king installed himself in the Chinese cabinet; and what convinced D'Aiguillon that Mme. Dubarry had not lost a word of his conversation with his uncle, was the fact that he, D'Aiguillon, overheard the entire interview between Mme. Dubarry and the king.

His majesty seemed fatigued, like a man who has raised an immense weight. Atlas was less enfeebled when his day's work was done than when he had held the world suspended on his shoulders for twelve hours.

Louis XV. allowed his favorite to thank, applaud, and caress him, and tell him the whole particulars of M. de Choiseul's departure, which amused him exceedingly.

Then Mme. Dubarry ventured. It was fair weather for politics; and besides, she felt herself strong enough at that moment to have raised one of the four quarters of the world.

"Sire," said she, "you have destroyed, that is well; you have demolished, that is superb; but now you must think about rebuilding."

"Oh! it is done," said the king, carelessly.

"You have a ministry?"

"Yes."

"What! all at once, without breathing?"

"See what it is to want common sense. Oh! woman that you are! before sending away your cook, must you not, as you said the other day, have a new one in readiness?"

"Repeat to me that you have formed the cabinet."

The king raised himself upon the immense sofa upon which he was lying rather than sitting, using the shoulders of the beautiful countess for his principal cushion.

"One would think, Jeannette," said he, "to hear you making yourself so uneasy, that you know my ministry, and wish to find fault with them, or propose another."

"Well," said the countess, "that would not be so absurd as you seem to imagine."

"Indeed? Then you have a ministry?"

"You have one, have you not?" replied she.

"Oh! it is my place to have one, countess. Let me see your candidates."

"By no means; tell me yours."

"Most willingly, to set you the example."

"In the first place, then, who have you for the navy, where that dear Monsieur de Praslin was?"

"Ah! something new, countess; a charming man, who has never seen the sea."

"Who is it?"

"'Pon honor, it is a splendid idea. I shall make myself very popular, and I shall be crowned in the most distant seas—in effigy, of course."

"But who, sire? Who is it?"

"I would wager you do not guess in a thousand attempts. It is a member of parliament, my dear—the first president of the parliament of Besançon."

"Monsieur de Boynes?"

"The same. Peste! how learned you are! You know all these people!"

"I cannot help it; you talked parliament to me the whole day. Why, the man would not know an oar if he saw it."

"So much the better. Monsieur de Praslin knew his duties too well, and made me pay dearly for all his naval constructions."

"Well, the finance department, sire?"

"Oh! that is a different affair; I have chosen a special man."

"A financier?"

"No; a soldier. The financiers have crushed me too long already."

"Good heavens! And the war department?"

"Do not be uneasy, for that I have chosen a financier, Terray. He is a terrible scrutinizer of accounts! He will find errors in all Monsieur de Choiseul's additions. I may tell you that I had some idea of putting a wonderful man in the war department—every inch a man, as they say. It was to please the philosophers."

"Good. But who? Voltaire?"

"Almost. The Chevalier de Muy—a Cato."

" Oh, Heaven ! You alarm me."

" It was all arranged.   I had sent for the man, his commission was signed, he had thanked me, when my good or my evil genius—judge which—prompted me to ask him to come to Luciennes this evening to sup and chat with us."

" Fy ! Horrible ! "

" Well, countess, that was exactly what De Muy replied."

" He said that to you ? "

" Expressed in other words, countess.   He said that his most ardent wish was to serve the king, but as for serving Madame Dubarry, it was impossible."

" Well, that was polite of your philosopher."

" You must know, countess, I held out my hand to him —for his brevet, which I tore in pieces with a most patient smile, and the chevalier disappeared.   Louis XIV. would have let the rascal rot in one of those ugly dens in the Bastile; but I am Louis XV., and I have a parliament which gives me the whip, in place of my giving it to the parliament.   Ha ! "

" No matter, sire," said the countess, covering her royal lover with kisses, " you are not the less a clever man."

" That is not what the world in general says.   Terray is execrated."

" Who is not?   And for foreign affairs? "

" That honest fellow, Bertin, whom you know."

" No."

" Then whom you do not know."

" But, among them all, I cannot find one good minister."

" So be it; now tell me yours."

" I will only tell you one."

" You dare not tell me; you are afraid."

" The marshal."

" The marshal?   What marshal? " said the king, making a wry face.

" The Duke de Richelieu."

" That old man?   That chicken-hearted wretch ? "

" Good!   The conqueror of Mahon a chicken-hearted wretch ! "

" That old debauchee ? "

" Sire, your companion."

"A immoral man, who frightens all the women."

"That is only since he no longer runs after them."

"Do not speak to me of Richelieu; he is my raw-head-and-bloody-bones. The conqueror of Mahon took me into all the gaming-houses in Paris. We were lampooned. No! no!—Richelieu! The very name puts me beside myself."

"You hate them so much?"

"Whom?"

"The Richelieus."

"I abhor them."

"All?"

"All. What a worthy duke and peer Monsieur Fronsac makes. He has deservèd the rack twenty times."

"I give him up; but there are more Richelieus in the world than he."

"Ah! yes, D'Aiguillon."

"Well?"

The reader may judge, if, at these words, the ears of the nephew were not strained in the boudoir.

"I ought to hate him more than all the others, for he hounds all the bawlers in France upon me—and yet—it is a weakness which I cannot conquer—he is bold, and does not displease me."

"He is a man of spirit!" cried the countess.

"A brave man, and zealous in the defense of the royal prerogative. He is a model of a peer."

"Yes, yes—a hundred times yes! Make something of him."

The king looked at the countess and folded his arms.

"What, countess! Is it possible that you propose such a thing to me, when all France demands that I should exile and degrade this man?"

Mme. Dubarry folded her arms in her turn.

"Just now," said she, "you called Richelieu chicken-hearted—the name belongs more properly to yourself."

"Oh, countess!"

"You are very proud because you have dismissed Monsieur de Choiseul."

"Well, it was not an easy task."

"You have done it, and you have done well; but you are afraid of the consequences."

"I!"

"Of course. What do you accomplish by sending away Monsieur de Choiseul?"

"Give the parliament a kick in the seat of honor."

"And you will not give them two! Diable! Raise both your feet—one after the other, be it understood. The parliament wished to keep Choiseul; you send him away. They want to send away D'Aiguillon; keep him."

"I do not send him away."

"Keep him—improve and considerably enlarged."

"You want an office for this fire-brand?"

"I want a recompense for him who defended you at the risk of his position and fortune."

"Say of his life, for he will be stoned some fine morning along with your friend Maupeou."

"You would encourage your defenders very much, if they could only hear you."

"They pay me back with interest, countess."

"Do not say so; facts contradict you in this case."

"Ah, well! But why this eagerness for D'Aiguillon?"

"Eagerness! I do not know him; I have seen and spoken to him to day for the first time."

"Ah! that is a different affair. Then it is from conviction of his merit—and I respect conviction in others, because I never have it myself."

"Then give Richelieu something in D'Aiguillon's name, since you will not give D'Aiguillon anything in his own."

"Richelieu! nothing! Never, never, never!"

"Then something to Monsieur d'Aiguillon, since you refuse Richelieu!"

"What! give him a portfolio? That is impossible at present."

"I understand that; but after some time, perhaps. Remember that he is a man of resources and action, and that with Terray, D'Aiguillon, and Maupeou, you will have the three heads of Cerberus. Remember, too, that your ministry is only a jest which cannot last."

"You are mistaken, countess, it will last three months."

" In three months, then, I have your promise? "

" Oh! oh! countess."

" That is enough; in the meantime something for the present."

" But I have nothing."

" You have the light horse; Monsieur d'Aiguillon is an officer—what is called a sword; give him your light horse."

" Very well, he shall have them."

" Thanks! " exclaimed the countess, transported with joy, " a thousand thanks! "

And M. d'Aiguillon could hear a very plebeian kiss resound on the cheeks of his Majesty Louis XV.

" In the meantime," said the king, " order supper to be served, countess."

" No," said she, " there is nothing here; you have overpowered me with politics. My people have made speeches and fireworks, but no supper."

" Then come to Marly; I will take you with me."

" Impossible! My poor head is splitting in pieces."

" With headache? "

" Dreadful headache."

" You must go to bed, countess."

" I am just going to do so, sire."

" Adieu! then."

" Au revoir, rather."

" I am somewhat like Monsieur de Choiseul; I am dismissed."

" Yes, but accompanied, feasted, cajoled," said the giddy creature, pushing the king gently toward the door, and from thence to the foot of the stairs, laughing loudly and turning round at each step.

On the peristyle the countess stopped, candle in hand.

" Countess," said the king, turning round and asceding a step.

" Sire? "

" I trust the poor marshal will not die of it."

" Of what? "

" Of the portfolio which he has missed."

" Countess," said the king, turning round and ascending him with another loud laugh.

And his majesty drove off, very much delighted with his last quodlibet upon the duke, whom he really hated.

When Mme. Dubarry returned to her boudoir, she found D'Aiguillon on his knees before the door, his hands clasped, his eyes ardently fixed upon her.

She blushed.

" I have failed," said she.   " The poor marshal ! "

" Oh, I know all ! " said he ; " I could hear—thanks, madame—thanks ! "

" I thought I owed you that," she replied, with a sweet smile ; " but rise, duke ; else I shall think your memory is as retentive as your mind is highly cultivated."

" That may well be, madame ; my uncle has told you I am nothing but your admiring and zealous servant."

" And the king's : to-morrow you must go and pay your respects to his majesty.   Rise, I beg."

And she gave him her hand, which he kissed respectfully.

The countess seemed to be deeply moved, for she did not add a single word.

M. d'Aiguillon was also silent, as deeply moved as she. At last, Mme. Dubarry, raising her head, said :

" Poor marshal ! he must know this defeat."

M. d'Aiguillon looked upon these words as a dismissal, and bowed.

" Madame," said he, " I am going to him."

" Oh, duke ! unpleasant news is always soon enough told ; do something better—sup with me."

The day was gained.   D'Aiguillon, as we have seen, was the lucky man.

CHAPTER XXII.

THE ANTECHAMBERS OF THE DUKE DE RICHELIEU.

M. DE RICHELIEU, like all the courtiers, had an hotel at Versailles, one at Paris, a house at Marly, and another at Luciennes ; a residence, in short, near each of the palaces or residences of the king.

Louis XIV., when he multiplied his places of residence

so much, had imposed on all men of rank—on all those privileged to attend the grand and little receptions and levees, the obligation of being very rich, that they might keep pace at once with the splendor of his household and the flights of his whims.

At the period of the disgrace of MM. de Choiseul and De Praslin, M. de Richelieu was living in his house at Versailles; and it was there that he returned after having presented his nephew to Mme. Dubarry at Luciennes.

Richelieu had been seen in the forest of Marly with the countess; he had been seen at Versailles after the minister's disgrace; his long and secret audience at Luciennes was known; and this, with the indiscretions of Jean Dubarry, was sufficient for the whole court to think themselves obliged to go and pay their respects to M. de Richelieu.

The old marshal was now going in his turn to inhale that delightful incense of praises, flatteries, and caresses which every interested person offered without discrimination to the idol of the day.

M. de Richelieu, however, was far from expecting all that was to happen to him; but he rose that morning with the firm resolution of closing his nostrils against the incense, as Ulysses closed his ears with wax against the songs of the sirens. The result which he expected could not be known until the next day, when the nomination of the new ministry would be announced by the king himself

Great was the marshal's surprise, therefore, when he awoke, or, rather, was awakened by the loud noise of carriages, to hear from his valet that the courtyards of the hotel, as well as the anterooms and saloons, were filled with visitors.

" Oh! " said he, " it seems I make some noise already."

" It is still early, my lord marshal," said his valet de chambre, seeing the duke's haste in taking off his nightcap.

" Henceforward," replied the duke, " there will be no such word as early for me—remember that."

" Yes, sir."

" What did you reply to the visitors? "

" That you were not up yet."

" Nothing more ? "

" Nothing more."

" That was exceedingly stupid. You should have added that I was up late last night; or, better still, you should have—let me see, where is Rafte ? "

" Monsieur Rafte is asleep," said the valet.

" What! asleep! Let him be called, the wretch! "

" Well," said a fresh and smiling old man, who appeared at the door, " here is Rafte ; what is he wanted for ? "

All the duke's bombast ceased at these words.

" Ah! I was certain that you were not asleep."

" And if I had been asleep, where would have been the wonder? It is scarcely daylight."

" But, my dear Rafte, you see that I do not sleep."

" That is another thing, you are a minister—how should you sleep ? "

" Oh! now you are going to scold me," said the marshal, making a wry face before the glass; " you are not satisfied ? "

" I! What benefit is that to me? You will fatigue yourself to death and then you will be ill. The consequence will be that I shall have to govern the state, and that is not so amusing, sir."

" How old you are getting, Rafte."

" I am just four years younger than yourself, sir. Yes, I am getting old."

The marshal stamped with impatience.

" Did you come through the antechambers? " asked he.

" Yes."

" Who is there ? "

" All the world."

" What do they speak of ? "

" Every one is telling what favors he is going to ask from you."

" That is very natural. But what did you hear about my appointment ? "

" Oh! I would much rather not tell you that."

" What! Criticisms already ? "

" Yes, and from those who have need of your assistance! What will they say, sir, whose assistance you need ? "

"Ah, Rafte!" said the old man, affecting to laugh, "those who would say you flatter me——"

"Well, sir," said Rafte, "why the devil did you harness yourself to this wagon called a ministry? Are you tired of living and of being happy?"

"My dear fellow, I have tasted everything but that."

"Corbleu! you have never tasted arsenic! Why do you not take some in your chocolate, from curiosity?"

"Rafte, you are an idle dog; you think that, as my secretary, you will have more work, and you shrink—you confessed as much, indeed."

The marshal dressed himself with care.

"Give me a military air," said he to his valet, "and hand me my military orders."

"It seems we are in the war department," said Rafte.

"Good heavens! yes. It seems we are there."

"Oh! But I have not seen the king's appointment," continued Rafte; "it is not confirmed yet."

"The appointment will come in good time, no doubt."

"Then, *no doubt* is the official word to-day?"

"You become more disagreeable, Rafte, as you get older. You are a formalist, and superstitiously particular. If I had known that, I would not have allowed you to deliver my inauguration speech at the Academie; that made you pedantic."

"But listen, my lord; since we are in the government, let us be regular. This is a very odd affair."

"What is odd?"

Monsieur the Count de la Vaudraye, whom I met just now in the street, told me that nothing had yet been settled about the ministry."

Richelieu smiled.

Monsieur de la Vaudraye is right," said he. "But have you already been out, then?"

"Pardieu! I was obliged. This cursed noise of carriages awoke me; I dressed, put on my military orders also, and took a turn in the town."

"Ah! Monsieur Rafte makes merry at my expense."

"Oh, my lord, God forbid! But——"

" But what? "

" On my walk, I met some one."

" Whom? "

" The secretary of the Abbé Terray."

" Well? "

" Well, he told me that his master was appointed to the war department."

" Oh, ho! " said Richelieu, with his eternal smile.

" What does monseigneur conclude from this? "

" That if Monsieur Terray is appointed to the war department, I am not; that if he is not, I may perhaps be."

Rafte had satisfied his conscience; he was a bold, indefatigable, ambitious man, as clever as his master, and much better armed than he, for he knew himself to be of low origin and dependent, two defects in his coat of mail which for forty years had exercised all his cunning, strength, and acuteness to obviate. When Rafte saw his master so confident, he believed he had nothing more to fear.

" Come, my lord," said he, " make haste; do not oblige them to wait too long; that would be a bad commencement."

" I am ready; but tell me once more who is there? "

" Here is the list."

He presented a long list to his master, who saw with increasing satisfaction the names of the first among the nobility, the law, and the finance.

" Suppose I should be popular, hey, Rafte? "

" We are in the age of miracles," replied the latter.

" Ha! Taverney! " said the marshal, continuing to peruse the list. " What does he come here for? "

" I have not the least idea, my lord marshal; but come, make your entrée;" and the secretary, with an authoritative air, almost pushed his master into the grand saloon.

Richelieu ought to have been satisfied; his reception might have contented the ambition of a prince of the blood royal. But the refined cunning and craft which characterized the period and particularly the class of society we are speaking of, only too well assisted Richelieu's unlucky

star, which had such a disagreeable contretemps in store
for him.

From propriety and respect for etiquette all this crowded
levee abstained from pronouncing the word minister before
Richelieu; some were bold enough to venture as far as the
word congratulation, but they knew that they must pass
quickly over the word, and that Richelieu would scarcely
reply to it.

For one and all this morning visit was a simple demonstration of respect, a mere expression of good will; for at
this period such almost imperceptible shades of policy
were frequently understood and acted upon by the general
mass of the community.   There were certain of the courtiers who even ventured, in the course of conversation, to
express some wish, desire or hope.

The one would have wished, he said, to have his government rather nearer Versailles; and it gratified him to have
an opportunity of speaking on the subject to a man of such
great influence as M. de Richelieu.

Another said he had been three times forgotten by M. de
Choiseul in the promotions of the knights of the order, and
he reckoned upon M. de Richelieu's obliging memory to refresh the king's, now that there existed no obstacle in the
way of his majesty's good will.   In short, a hundred requests, more or less grasping, but all veiled by the highest
art, were preferred to the delighted ears of the marshal.

Gradually the crowd retired; they wished, as they said,
to leave the marshal to his important occupations.

One man alone remained in the saloon; he had not approached as the others had; he had asked for nothing, he
had not even presented himself.

When the courtiers had gone, this man advanced toward
the duke with a smile upon his lips.

" Ah! Monsieur de Taverney!" said the marshal; "I
am enchanted to see you, truly enchanted."

" I was waiting, duke, to pay you my compliments, and
to offer you my sincere congratulations."

" Ah! indeed, and for what?" replied Richelieu, for the
cautious reserve of his visitors had imposed upon him the
necessity of being discreet and even mysterious.

" On your new dignity, duke."

" Hush, hush! " said the marshal, " let us not speak of that; nothing is settled; it is a mere rumor."

" Nevertheless, my dear marshal, there are many people of my opinion, for your saloons were full."

" In truth, I do not know why."

" Oh! I know very well."

" Why then? Why? "

" One word from me."

" What word? "

" Yesterday I had the honor of paying my respects to the king at Trianon. His majesty spoke to me of my children, and ended by saying: ' You know Monsieur de Richelieu, I think; pay your compliments to him.' "

" Ah! his majesty said that? " replied Richelieu, with a glow of pride as if these words had been the official brevet the destination of which Rafte doubted, or at least deplored its delay.

" So that," continued Taverney, " I soon suspected the truth—in fact, it was not difficult to do so, when I saw the eagerness of all Versailles—and I hastened to obey the king by paying my compliments to you, and to gratify my own feelings by reminding you of our old friendship."

The duke had now reached a pitch of intoxication. It is a defect in our nature from which the highest minds cannot always preserve themselves. He saw in Taverney only one of those expectants of the lowest order—poor devils who have fallen behind on the road of favor, who are useless even as protégés, useless as acquaintances, and who are reproached with coming forth from their obscurity after a lapse of twenty years, to warm themselves at the sun of another's prosperity.

" I see what you are aiming at," said the marshal, harshly; " you have some favor to ask of me."

" You have said it, duke."

" Ah! " grumbled Richelieu, seating himself on, or, rather, plumping into a sofa.

" I told you I had two children," continued Taverney, pliant and cunning, for he perceived the coolness of his great friend, and therefore only advanced the more

eagerly; " I have a daughter whom I love very dearly,
and who is a model of virtue and beauty. She is placed
with her highness the dauphiness, who has been conde-
scending enough to grant her her particular esteem. Of
my beautiful Andrée, therefore, I need not speak to you.
Her path is smoothed, her fortune is made. Have you seen
my daughter? Did I not once present her to you somewhere? Have you not heard of her?"

" Pshaw! I don't know," said Richelieu, carelessly,
" perhaps so."

" No matter," pursued Taverney, " there is my daughter settled. For my own part, I want nothing; the king
grants me a pension upon which I can live. I confess I
would like to have some emolument to enable me to re-
build Maison Rouge, where I wish to end my days, and
with your interest and my daughter's——"

" Ha! " thought Richelieu, who until now had not listened, so lost was he in contemplation of his grandeur,
but whom the words, " my daughter's interest," had roused
from his reverie. " Oh! ho! your daughter! Why, she is
a young beauty who annoys our countess; she is a little
scorpion who is sheltering herself under the wings of the
dauphiness, in order to bite some one at Luciennes. Come,
I will not be a bad friend, and as for gratitude, this dear
countess, who has made me a minister, shall see if I am
wanting in time of need." Then aloud:

" Proceed," said he to the Baron de Taverney, in a
haughty tone.

" Faith, I am near the end," replied the latter, promising himself to laugh in his sleeve at the vain marshal if
he could only get what he wanted from him. " I am
anxious, therefore, about my son Philip, who bears a lofty
name, but who will never be able to support it worthily
unless some one assists him. Philip is a bold and thoughtful youth; rather too thoughtful, perhaps, but that is the
result of his embarrassed position. You know the horse
which is reined in too tightly droops its head."

" What is all this to me? " thought Richelieu, giving
most unequivocal signs of weariness and impatience.

" I want some one," continued Taverney, remorselessly,

"some one in authority like yourself, to procure a company for Philip. Her highness the dauphiness on entering Strasbourg raised him to the rank of captain, but he still wants a hundred thousand livres to enable him to purchase a company in some privileged regiment of cavalry. Procure that for me, my powerful friend."

"Your son," said Richelieu, "is the young man who rendered the dauphiness a service, is he not?"

"A most essential service," replied Taverney; "it was he who forced the last relay for her royal highness from that Dubarry who wanted to seize it by force."

"Oh, ho!" thought Richelieu, "that is just it; the most violent enemies of the countess. He comes at the right time, this Taverney! He advances claims that are sufficient to damn him forever."

"You do not answer, duke?" said Taverney, rather soured by the marshal's obstinate silence.

"It is perfectly impossible, my dear Monsieur de Taverney," replied the marshal, rising to show that the audience was over.

"Impossible? Such a trifle impossible? An old friend tell me that?"

"Why not? Is it any reason, because you are a friend, as you say, that you should seek to make me commit treason both against friendship and justice? You never came to see me for twenty years, for during that time I was nothing; now that I am a minister, you come."

"Monsieur de Richelieu, it is you who are unjust at this moment."

"No, my dear friend, no; I do not wish to see you dangling in antechambers; I am a true friend; and therefore——"

"You have some reasons for refusing me, then?"

"I!" exclaimed Richelieu, much alarmed at the suspicion Taverney might perhaps form—"I! a reason?"

"Yes, I have enemies."

The duke might have replied what he thought, but that would have been to discover to the baron that he tried to please Mme. Dubarry from gratitude; it would have been to confess that he was the minister of the favorite, and

that the marshal would not have confessed for an empire.
He therefore hastily replied:

"You have no enemy, my dear friend; but I have many.
To grant requests at once, without examining claims,
would expose me to the accusations of continuing the
Choiseul system. My dear sir, I wish to leave behind
some trace of my administration of affairs. For twenty
years I have projected reforms, improvements, and now
they shall blossom. Favoritism is the ruin of France; I
will protect merit. The writings of our philosophers are
bright torches whose light has not shone for me in vain;
they have dissipated all the mists of ignorance and superstition which brooded over the past, and it was full time it
should be so, for the well-being of the state. I shall therefore examine your son's claims, neither more nor less than
I should do those of any other citizen. I must make this
sacrifice to my conscience—a grievous sacrifice, no doubt,
but which, after all, is only that of one man for the benefit of three hundred thousand. If your son, Monsieur
Philip de Taverney, proves that he merits my favor, he
shall have it, not because his father is my friend, not because he bears the name he does, but because he is a man of
merit. That is my plan of conduct."

"You mean your system of philosophy," replied the old
baron, biting his nails with rage, and adding to his anger
by reflecting how much humiliation and how many petty
cowardices this interview had cost him.

"Philosophy, if you will, sir; it is a noble word."

"Which dispenses good things, marshal, does it not?"

"You are a bad courtier," said Richelieu, with a cold
smile.

"Men of my rank are courtiers only of the king."

"Oh! Monsieur Rafte, my secretary, has a thousand of
your rank in my antechambers every day," replied Richelieu; "they generally come from some obscure den or
other in the provinces, where they have learned to be rude
to their pretended friends while they preach concord."

"Oh! I am well aware that a Maison Rouge, a title
which dates from the Crusades, does not understand concord so well as a Vignerol fiddler."

The marshal had more tact than Taverney. He could have had him thrown out of the windows, but he only shrugged his shoulders, and replied:

"You are rather behind the time, most noble scion of the Crusades; you only remember the calumnious memoir presented by parliament in 1720, and have not read that of the peers and dukes in reply. Be kind enough to walk into my library, my dear sir; Rafte will give it to you to read."

As he was bowing his antagonist out with his apt repartee, the door opened, and a man entered noisily, crying:

"Where is my dear duke?"

This man, with ruddy visage, eyes dilated with satisfaction, and joyous air, was neither more nor less than Jean Dubarry.

On seeing this newcomer, Taverney started back with surprise and vexation.

Jean saw the movement, recognized the face, and turned his back.

"I understand," said the baron, quietly, "and I shall retire. I leave the minister in most distinguished company."

And he left the room with dignity.

CHAPTER XXIII.

RICHELIEU IS DISABUSED.

FURIOUS at this extremely provoking exit, Jean made two steps after the baron; then returning to the marshal, he said, shrugging his shoulders:

"You receive such people here?"

"Oh! my dear sir, you mistake; on the contrary, I send such people away."

"Do you know who this gentleman is?"

"Alas! Yes."

"No, but do you know really?"

"He is a Taverney."

" He is a man who wishes to make his daughter the king's favorite."

" Oh, come ! "

" A man who wishes to supplant us, and who takes all possible means to do so. But Jean is there, and Jean has his eyes about him."

" You think he wishes——"

" It is a very difficult matter to see what he wishes, is it not? One of the dauphin's party, my dear sir; and they have their little stabber, too."

" Bah ! "

" A young man who looks quite ready to fly at people's throats—a bully, who pinks Jean's shoulder—poor Jean ! "

" Yours? It is a personal enemy of yours, my dear count? " asked Richelieu, feigning surprise.

" Yes; he was my adversary in that affair of the relay, you know."

" Indeed ! What a strange sympathy. I did not know that, and yet I refused all his demands; only if I had known, I should not only have refused him, but kicked him out. But do not be uneasy, count, I have now this worthy bully under my thumb, and he shall find it out to his cost."

" Yes, you can cure him of his taste for attacking people on the highway. For in fact—ha! by the bye, I have not yet congratulated you."

" Why, yes, count; it seems the affair is definitely settled."

" Oh! it is all completed. Will you permit me to embrace you ? "

" With all my heart."

" Faith, there was some trouble; but the trouble is nothing when you succeed. You are satisfied, are you not ? "

" Shall I speak frankly? Yes; but I think I can be useful."

" No doubt of that. But it is a bold stroke; there will be some growling."

" Am I not liked by the public ? "

" You? Why, there is no question of you, either one way or the other; it is he who is execrated."

" He? " said Richelieu, with surprise; " who?—he? "

" Of course," interupted Jean. " Oh! the parliament will revolt, it will be a second edition of the flagellation of Louis XIV. They are whipped, duke, they are whipped."

" Explain."

" Why, it explains itself. The parliament, of course, hate the author of their persecutions."

" Ah! you think that? "

" I am certain of it, as all France is. No matter, duke, it was a capital stroke of you to send for him that way, just at the very heat of the affair."

" Whom? Whom, duke? I am on thorns—I do not understand one word of what you say."

" Why, I speak of Monsieur d'Aiguillon, your nephew."

" Well, what then? "

" Well, I say it was well advised of you to send for him."

" Ah! very good, very good. You mean to say he will assist me? "

" He will assist us all. Do you know he is on the best terms with little Jeanne? "

" Oh! indeed? "

" On the best terms. They have already had a chat together, and understand each other perfectly, as it seems to me."

" You know that? "

" Why, I saw D'Aiguillon's carriage leave Luciennes late yesterday evening, and as he only arrived yesterday morning in Paris, it seems to me that he must be a great favorite with Jeanne to obtain an audience so early."

" Yes, yes," said Richelieu, rubbing his hands; " he must have supped there. Bravo, D'Aiguillon! "

" And so there you are all three, like Orestes and Pylades, with the addition of another Pylades."

At this moment, and as the marshal was rubbing his hands with great glee, D'Aiguillon entered the saloon.

The nephew saluted his uncle with an air of condolence which was sufficient to enable Richelieu, without understanding the whole truth, at least to guess the greatest part of it.

He turned pale as though he had received a mortal wound. It flashed across his mind that at court there exists neither friends nor relatives, and that every one seeks only his own aggrandizement.

"I was a great fool!" thought he. "Well, D'Aiguillon?" continued he aloud, repressing a deep sigh.

"Well, marshal?"

"It is a heavy blow to the parliament," said Richelieu, repeating Jean's words.

D'Aiguillon blushed.

"You know it?" said he.

"The countess has told me all," replied Richelieu; "even your late stay at Luciennes last night. Your appointment is a triumph for my family."

"Be assured, marshal, of my extreme regret."

"What the devil does he mean by that?" said Jean, folding his arms.

"Oh, we understand each other," interrupted Richelieu; "we understand each other."

"That is a different affair; but for my part I do not understand you. Regret! Ah! yes, because he will not be recognized as minister immediately—yes, yes, I see."

"Oh! there will be an interim?" said the marshal, feeling a ray of hope—that constant guest in the heart of the ambitious man and the lover—once more dawn in his breast.

"Yes, marshal, an interim."

"But, in the meantime," cried Jean, "he is tolerably well paid; the finest command in Versailles."

"Ah! a command?" said Richelieu, pierced by a new wound.

"Monsieur Dubarry perhaps exaggerates a little," said the Duke d'Aiguillon.

"But, in one word, what is this command?"

"The king's light horse."

Richelieu again felt his furrowed cheeks grow pale.

"Oh! yes," said he, with a smile which it would be impossible to describe; "yes, it is indeed a trifling appointment for such a charming man. But what can you expect, duke—the loveliest woman in the world, were she even the king's favorite, can only give what she has."

It was now D'Aiguillon's turn to grow pale.

Jean was scrutinizing the beautiful Murillos which adorned Richelieu's walls.

Richelieu slapped his nephew on the shoulder.

"Luckily," said he, "you have the promise of approaching advancement. Accept my congratulations, duke— my sincere compliments. Your address, your cleverness in negotiations, is only equaled by your good fortune. Adieu; I have some business to transact. Do not forget me in the distribution of your favors, my dear minister."

D'Aiguillon only replied:

"Your interests and mine, my lord marshal, are henceforth one and the same."

And, saluting his uncle, he left the room with the dignity which was natural to him, thus escaping from one of the most embarrassing positions he had ever experienced in a life strewn with so many difficulties.

"An admirable trait in D'Aiguillon's character," said Richelieu, the moment the former had disappeared, to Jean, who was rather at a loss to know what to think of this exchange of politeness between the nephew and uncle —"and one that I admire particularly, is his artlessness. He is at once frank and high-spirited; he knows the court, and is withal as simple-minded as a girl."

"And then he loves you so well!" said Jean.

"Like a lamb."

"Oh," said Jean, "he is more like your son than Monsieur de Fronsac."

"By my faith, yes, count—by my faith, yes."

While replying thus, Richelieu kept walking round his chair in great agitation; he sought but could not find.

"Ah, countess," he muttered, "you shall pay me for this!"

"Marshal," said Jean, with a cunning look, "we four will realize that famous fagot of antiquity; you know, the one that could not be broken."

" We four, my dear Monsieur Jean; how do you understand that?"

" My sister as power, D'Aiguillon as authority, you as advice, and I as vigilance."

" Very good! very good!"

" And now let them attack my sister. I defy them all!"

" Pardieu!" said Richelieu, whose brain was boiling.

" Let them set up rivals now!" exclaimed Jean, in ecstasies with his plans and his visions of triumph.

" Oh!" said Richelieu, striking his forehead.

" Well, my dear marshal, what is the matter?"

" Nothing; I think your idea of a league admirable."

" Is it not?"

" And I enter body and soul into your plans."

" Bravo!"

" Does Taverney live at Trianon with his daughter?"

" No; he lives in Paris."

" The girl is very handsome, my dear count."

" If she were as beautiful as Cleopatra—or my sister, I do not fear her, now that we are leagued together."

" You said Taverney lives in Paris; in the Rue St. Honoré, I think."

" I did not say the Rue St. Honoré; it is the Rue Coq Heron in which he lives. Have you any plan of chastising these Taverneys, that you ask?"

" Yes, count; I think I have found a capital plan."

" You are an incomparable man. But I must leave you now; I wish to see what they say in town."

" Adieu, then, count. Apropos, you have not told me who the new ministers are."

" Oh, mere birds of passage; Terray, Bertin, and I know not who else. Mere counters in the hands of D'Aiguillon—the real minister, though his appointment is deferred for a short time."

" Perhaps indefinitely adjourned," thought the marshal, directing his most gracious smile to Jean, as an affectionate adieu.

Jean retired, Rafte entered. He had heard all, and knew how to conduct himself; all his suspicions were now realized. He did not utter a word to his master, he knew

him too well. He did not even call the valet de chambre;
he assisted him with his own hands to undress, and conducted him to his bed, in which the old marshal, shivering
with fever, immediately buried himself, after taking a
pill which his secretary made him swallow.

Rafte drew the curtains and retired. The antechamber
was thronged with eager, listening valets. Rafte took the
head valet aside.

"Attend to the marshal carefully," said he, "he is ill.
He has had a serious vexation this morning; he was obliged to disobey the king."

"Disobey the king!" exclaimed the alarmed valet.

"Yes; his majesty sent a portfolio to my lord, but as he
was aware that he owed it to the solicitations of the Dubarry, he refused. Oh! it was a noble resolve, and the
Parisians ought to build him a triumphal arch; but the
shock was great, and our master is ill. Look to him carefully."

After these words, whose circulating power he knew
beforehand, Rafte returned to his closet.

A quarter of an hour afterward, all Versailles was informed of the noble conduct and lofty patriotism of the
marshal, who in the meantime slept soundly upon the
popularity his secretary had gained for him.

CHAPTER XXIV.

THE DAUPHIN'S FAMILY REPAST.

THE same day, about three o'clock, Mlle. Taverney
left her apartment to attend upon the dauphiness, who was
in the habit of being read to for a short time before
dinner.

The abbé who had held the post of first reader to her
royal highness no longer exercised his functions, as for
some time previous, ever since certain diplomatic intrigues
in which he had displayed a very great talent for business,
he had employed himself entirely in important political
affairs.

Mlle. Taverney therefore set out, dressed as well as circumstances would permit, to fulfil her office. Like all the guests at Trianon, she still suffered considerable inconvenience from the rather sudden installation in her new abode, and had not yet been able to arrange her furniture, or make the necessary provisions for establishing her modest household. She had therefore on the present occasion been assisted in her toilet by one of the femmes de chambre of Mme. de Noailles, that starched lady of honor whom the dauphiness nicknamed Mme. Etiquette.

Andrée was dressed in a blue silk robe, with long waist, which fitted admirably to her slender figure. This robe opened in front, and displayed a muslin skirt relieved with three falls of embroidery. Short sleeves, also of muslin, embroidered in the same manner as her dress, and festooned and tapering to the shoulder, were admirably in keeping with a habit shirt, worked à la paysanne, which modestly concealed her neck and shoulders. Her beautiful hair, which fell in long and luxuriant ringlets upon her shoulders, was simply tied with a ribbon of the same color as her dress, a mode of arrangement which harmonized infinitely better with the noble yet modest and retiring air of the lovely young girl, and with her pure and transparent complexion never yet sullied by the touch of rouge, than the feathers, ornaments, and laces which were then in vogue.

As she walked, Andrée drew on a pair of white silk mittens upon the slenderest and roundest fingers in the world, while the tiny points of her high-heeled shoes of pale blue satin left their traces on the gravel of the garden-walk.

When she reached the pavilion of Trianon, she was informed that the dauphiness was taking a turn in the grounds with her architect and her head-gardener. In the apartments of the first story overhead, she could hear the noise of a turning-lathe with which the dauphin was making a safety lock for a coffer which he valued very highly.

In order to rejoin the dauphiness, Andrée had to cross the parterre, where, notwithstanding the advanced period of the season, flowers carefully covered through the night, raised their pale heads to bask in the setting rays of a sun even paler than themselves. And as the evening was already closing in, for in that season it was dark at six o'clock, the gardener's apprentices were employed in placing the bell-glasses over the most delicate plants in each bed.

While traversing a winding alley of evergreens clipped into the form of a hedge, bordered on each side by beds of Bengal roses, and opening on a beautiful lawn, Andrée all at once perceived one of these gardeners, who, when he saw her, raised himself upon his spade, and bowed with a more refined and studied politeness than was usual in one of his station.

She looked, and in this workman recognized Gilbert, whose hands, notwithstanding his labor, were yet white enough to excite the envy of M. de Taverney.

Andrée blushed in spite of herself; it seemed to her that Gilbert's presence in this place was too remarkable a coincidence to be the result of chance.

Gilbert repeated his bow, and Andrée returned it, but without slackening her pace.

She was too upright and too courageous, however, to resist the promptings of her heart, and leave the question of her restless soul unanswered. She turned back, and Gilbert, whose cheeks had already become as pale as death, and whose dark eyes followed her retreating steps with a somber look, felt as if suddenly restored to life, and bounded forward to meet her.

" You here, Monsieur Gilbert? " said Andrée, coldly.

" Yes, mademoiselle."

" By what chance? "

" Mademoiselle, one must live, and live honestly."

" But do you know that you are very fortunate? "

" Oh, yes, mademoiselle, very fortunate," said Gilbert.

" I beg your pardon—what did you say? "

" I said, mademoiselle, that I am, as you think, very fortunate."

" Who introduced you here? "

" Monsieur de Jussieu, a protector of mine."

"Ah!" said Andrée, surprised; "then you know Monsieur de Jussieu?"

"He is a friend of my first protector—of my master, Monsieur Rousseau."

"Courage, then, Monsieur Gilbert," said Andrée, making a movement to proceed.

"Do you find yourself better, mademoiselle?" asked Gilbert, in a trembling voice.

"Better? How so?" said Andrée, coldly.

"Why—the accident!"

"Oh, yes, thank you, Monsieur Gilbert, I am better; it was nothing."

"Oh! you were nearly perishing," said Gilbert, almost speechless with emotion; "the danger was terrible."

Andrée now began to think that it was high time to cut short this interview with a workman in the most public part of the royal park.

"Good day, Monsieur Gilbert," said she.

"Will mademoiselle not accept a rose?" said Gilbert, trembling, and the drops of perspiration standing on his forehead.

"But, sir," replied Andrée, "you offer me what is not yours to give."

Gilbert, surprised and overwhelmed by this reply, could not utter a word. His head drooped, but as he saw Andrée looking at him with something like a feeling of joy at having manifested her superiority, he drew himself up, tore a branch covered with flowers from the finest of the rose-trees, and began to pull the roses to pieces with a coolness and dignity which surprised and startled the young girl.

She was too just and too kind-hearted not to see that she had gratuitously wounded the feelings of an inferior who had unthinkingly committed a breach of propriety. But like all proud natures who feel themselves in the wrong, she preserved silence, when, perhaps, an apology or a reparation was hovering upon her lips.

Gilbert added not a word either; he threw away the branch and resumed his spade; but his character was a mixture of pride and cunning, and while stooping to his work, he kept his eye stealthily fixed on Andrée's retreating figure. At the end of the walk she could not help looking round. She was a woman.

This weakness was sufficient for Gilbert; he said to himself that in this last struggle he had been victorious.

"She is weaker than I am," thought he, "and I shall govern her. Proud of her beauty, of her name, of her advancing fortunes, indignant at my love which she perhaps suspects, she is only the more an object of adoration to the poor working-man who trembles while he looks at her. Oh! this trembling, this emotion, unworthy of a man! Oh! these acts of cowardice which she makes me commit, she shall one day repay me for them all! But to-day I have worked enough," added he; "I have conquered the enemy. I who ought to have been the weakest, since I love, have been a hundred times stronger than she."

He repeated these words once more with a wild burst of joy, as he convulsively dashed back the dark hair from his thoughtful brow. Then he stuck his spade deep into the flower-bed, bounded through the hedge of cypress and yew-trees with the speed of a roebuck, and, light as the wind, threaded a parterre of plants under bell-glasses, not one of which he touched, notwithstanding the furious rapidity of his career, and posted himself at the extremity of a turn which he had reached by describing a diagonal course before Andrée, who followed the winding of the path.

From his new position he saw her advancing, thoughtful and almost humbled, her lovely eyes cast down, her moist and motionless hand gently rustling her dress as she walked. Concealed behind the thick hedge, Gilbert heard her sigh twice as if she were speaking to herself. At last she passed so close to the trees which sheltered him, that had he stretched out his arm he might have touched hers, as a mad and feverish impulse prompted him to do.

But he knit his brow with an energetic movement almost akin to hatred, and placing his trembling hand upon his heart:

"Coward again!" said he to himself. Then he added softly: "But she is so beautiful!"

Gilbert might have remained for a considerable time sunk in contemplation, for the walk was long and Andrée's step was slow and measured, but this walk was crossed by others, from which some troublesome visitor might at any moment make his appearance, and fate treated Gilbert so scurvily that a man did in fact advance from the first alley upon the left—that is to say, almost opposite the clump of evergreens behind which he was concealed.

This intruder walked with a methodic and measured step; he carried his head erect, held his hat under his right arm, and his left hand resting upon his sword. He wore a velvet coat underneath a pelisse lined with sable fur, and pointed his foot as he walked, which he did with the easy grace of a man of high rank and breeding.

This gentleman, as he advanced, perceived Andrée, and the young girl's figure evidently pleased him, for he quickened his pace, and crossed over in an oblique direction, so as to reach as soon as possible the path on which Andrée was walking and intercept her course.

When Gilbert perceived this personage he involuntarily gave a slight cry, and took to flight like a startled lapwing. The intruder's maneuver was successful; he was evidently accustomed to it, and in less than three minutes he was in advance of Andrée, whom three minutes before he had been following at some distance.

When Andrée heard his footsteps behind her, she moved aside a little to let the man pass, and when he had passed she looked at him in her turn. The gentleman looked also, and most eagerly; he even stopped to see better, and returning after he had seen her features:

"Ah! mademoiselle," said he, in a very kind voice, "whither are you hastening so quickly, may I ask?"

At the sound of this voice Andrée raised her head, and saw about twenty paces behind her two officers of the guards following slowly; she spied a blue ribbon peeping from beneath the sable pelisse of the person who addressed her, and pale and startled at this unexpected rencontre, and at being accosted thus graciously, she said, bending very low:

" The king ! "

" Mademoiselle," replied Louis XV., approaching her; " excuse me ; I have such bad eyes that I am obliged to ask your name."

" Mademoiselle de Taverney," stammered the young girl, so confused and trembling that her voice was scarcely audible.

" Oh! yes—I remember. I esteem myself fortunate in meeting you in Trianon, mademoiselle," said the king.

" I was proceeding to join her royal highness the dauphiness, who expects me," said Andrée, trembling more and more.

" I will conduct you to her, mademoiselle," replied Louis XV., " for I am just going to pay a visit to my daughter in my quality of country 'neighbor. Be kind enough to take my arm as we are proceeding in the same direction."

Andrée felt a cloud pass before her eyes, and the blood flowed in tumultuous waves to her heart. In fact, such an honor for the poor girl as the king's arm, the sovereign lord of all France, such an unhoped-for, incredible piece of good fortune, a favor which the whole court might envy, seemed to her more like a dream than reality.

She made such a deep and reverential courtesy that the king felt himself obliged to bow a second time. When Louis XV. was inclined to remember Louis XIV., it was always in matters of ceremonial and politeness. Such traditions, however, dated further back and were handed down from Henri IV.

He offered his hand therefore to Andrée, who placed the burning points of her fingers upon the king's glove, and they both continued to advance toward the pavilion, where they had been informed that the dauphiness, with her architect and her head gardener, would be found.

We can assure the reader that Louis XV., although not particularly fond of walking, chose the longest road to conduct Andrée to the little Trianon. Although the king was apparently unaware of his error, the two officers who walked behind perceived it but too plainly, and bemoaned themselves bitterly, as they were lightly clad and the weather was cold.

They arrived too late to find the dauphiness where they had expected, as Marie Antoinette had just set out for Trianon, that she might not keep the dauphin waiting, who liked to sup between six and seven o'clock.

Her royal highness arrived therefore at the exact hour, and as the punctual dauphin was already upon the threshold of the saloon, that he might lose no time in reaching the dining-room the moment the maître d'hôtel appeared, the dauphiness threw her mantle to a femme de chambre, took the dauphin's arm with a winning smile, and drew him into the dining-room.

The table was laid for the two illustrious hosts. They occupied each the center of the table, so as to leave the place of honor vacant, which, since several unexpected visits of the king, was never occupied in his majesty's absence, even when the room was filled with guests.

At this end of the table the king's cover and cadenas occupied a considerable space; but the maître d'hôtel, not calculating upon it being occupied this evening, was conducting the service on this side.

Behind the dauphiness's chair, leaving the necessary space between for the valets to pass, was stationed Mme. de Noailles, stiff and upright, and yet wearing as amiable an expression on her features as she could conjure up for the festive occasion.

Near Mme. de Noailles were some other ladies, whose position at the court gave them the right or the merited privilege of being present at the supper of their royal highnesses.

Three times a week Mme. de Noailles supped at the same table with the dauphin and dauphiness: but on the days when she did not sit up with them, she would not for anything in the world have missed being present. Besides, it was a delicate mode of protesting against the exclusion of the four days out of seven.

Opposite the Duchess de Noailles, surnamed by the dauphiness Mme. Etiquette, was the Duke de Richelieu, on a raised seat very similar to her own.

He was also a strict observer of forms; but his etiquette was undistinguishable to a casual observer, being always veiled beneath the most perfect elegance and sometimes beneath the wittiest raillery.

The result of this antithesis between the first gentleman of the bed-chamber and the first lady of honor of the dauphiness was that the conversation, always dropped by the Duchess de Noailles, was incessantly renewed by M. de Richelieu.

The marshal had traveled through all the courts of Europe, and had adopted the tone of elegance in each which was best suited to his character; so that from his admirable tact and propriety he knew exactly what anecdote to relate at the table of the youthful couple, and what would be suitable to the private supper of Mme. Dubarry.

Perceiving this evening that the dauphiness had a good appetite, and that the dauphin was voracious, he concluded that they would give no heed to the conversation going on around them, and that he had consequently only to make Mme. de Noailles suffer an hour of purgatory in anticipation.

He began therefore to speak of philosophy and theatrical affairs, a twofold subject of conversation doubly obnoxious to the venerable duchess. He related the subject of one of the last philanthropic sallies of the philosopher of Ferney, the name already given to the author of the "Henriade," and when he saw the duchess on the squabbles hooks, he changed the text and detailed all the squabbles and disputes which, in his office of gentleman of the chamber, he had to undergo in order to make the actresses in ordinary to the king play more or less badly.

The dauphiness loved the arts, and above all the theater; she had sent a complete costume for "Clytemnestra" to Mlle. Raucourt, and she therefore listened to M. de Richelieu not only with indulgence but with pleasure.

Then the poor lady of honor, in violation of all etiquette, was forced to fidget on her bench, blow her nose noisily, and shake her venerable head, without thinking of the cloud of powder which at each movement fell upon her forehead, like the cloud of snow which surrounds the summit of Mont Blanc at every gust of the east wind.

But it was not enough to amuse the dauphiness; the dauphin must also be pleased. Richelieu abandoned the subject of the theater, for which the heir to the crown had never displayed any great partiality, to discourse of humanity and philosophy. When he spoke of the English, he did so with all the warmth and energy which Rousseau displays in drawing the character of Edward Bromston.

Now, Mme. de Noailles hated the English as much as she did the philosophers. To admit a new idea was a fatiguing operation for her, and fatigue deranged the economy of her whole person. Mme. de Noailles, who felt herself intended by nature for a conserver, growled at all new ideas like a dog at a frightful mask.

Richelieu, in playing this game, had a double end in view; he tormented Mme. Etiquette, which evidently pleased the dauphiness, and he threw in, here and there, some virtuous apophthegm, some axiom in mathematics, which was rapturously received by the dauphin, the royal amateur of exact sciences.

He was paying his court, therefore, with great skill and address, and from time to time directing an eager glance toward the door, as if he expected some one who had not yet arrived, when a cry from the foot of the staircase echoed along the arched corridors, was repeated by two valets stationed at regular intervals from the entrance door, and at last reached the dining saloon.

" The king ! "

At this magic word Mme. de Noailles started bolt up-right from her seat, as if moved by a spring; Richelieu rose more slowly, and with easy grace; the dauphin hastily wiped his mouth with his napkin, and stood up before his seat, his face turned toward the door.

As for the dauphiness, she hastened toward the stair-case to meet the king, and do the honors of her mansion to him.

CHAPTER XXV.

THE QUEEN'S HAIR.

THE king still held Mlle. de Taverney by the hand when they reached the landing-place, and it was only on arriving there that he bowed to her, so courteously and so low, that Richelieu had time to see the bow, to admire its grace, and to ask himself to what lucky mortal it was addressed.

His ignorance did not last long. Louis XV. took the arm of the dauphiness, who had seen all that had passed, and had already recognized Andrée.

"My daughter," said he, "I come without ceremony to ask you for my supper. I crossed the entire park in my way hither, and happening to meet Mademoiselle de Taverney, I requested her to accompany me."

"Mademoiselle de Taverney!" murmured Richelieu, almost dizzy at this unexpected stroke. "On my faith, I am almost too fortunate!"

"I shall not only not be angry with mademoiselle, who is late," replied the dauphiness, graciously, "but I have to thank her for bringing your majesty to us."

Andrée, whose cheeks were dyed with as deep a red as the ripe and tempting cherries which graced the epergne in the center of the table, bowed without replying.

"Diable! Diable! she is indeed beautiful," thought Richelieu; "and that old scoundrel Taverney said no more for her than she deserves."

The king had already taken his seat at the table, after having saluted the dauphin. Gifted, like his grandfather, with an obliging appetite, the monarch did justice to the improvised supper which the maître d'hôtel placed before him as if by magic. But while eating, the king, whose back was turned toward the door, seemed to seek something, or rather some one.

In fact Mlle. de Taverney, who enjoyed no privilege

as her position in the dauphiness's household was not yet
fixed, had not entered the dining-room, and after her profound reverence in reply to the king's salutation, had returned to the dauphiness's apartment lest her services
might be required, as they had been once or twice already, to read to her highness after she had returned to
bed.

The dauphiness saw that the king was looking for the
beautiful companion of his walk:

"Monsieur de Coigny," said she to a young officer of
the guards who was standing behind the king, "pray request Mademoiselle de Taverney to come up; with Madame de Noailles' permission we will discard etiquette for
this evening."

M. de Coigny left the room, and almost immediately
afterward returned, introducing Andrée, who, totally at a
loss to comprehend the reason for such a succession of unusual favors, entered trembling.

"Seat yourself there, mademoiselle," said the dauphiness, "beside Madame de Noailles."

Andrée mounted timidly on the raised seat; but she
was so confused that she had the audacity to seat herself
only about a foot distant from the lady of honor. She
received in consequence such a terrific look that the poor
child started back at least four feet, as if she had come
in contact with a Leyden jar highly charged.

The king looked at her and smiled.

"Ah! ça," said the duke to himself, "it is scarcely
worth my while to meddle with the affair; everything is
progressing of itself."

The king turned and perceived the marshal, who was
quite prepared to meet his look.

"Good day, duke," said Louis; "do you agree well
with the Duchess de Noailles?"

"Sire," replied the marshal, "the duchess always does
me the honor to treat me as a madcap."

"Oh! Were you also on the road to Chanteloup,
duke?"

"I, sire? Faith, no; I am too grateful for the favors
your majesty has showered on my family."

The king did not expect this blow; he was prepared to rally, but he found himself anticipated.

"What favors have I showed, duke?"

"Sire, your majesty has given command of your light horse to the Duke d'Aiguillon."

"Yes; it is true, duke."

"And that is a step which must have put all the energy, all the skill of your majesty to the task. It is almost a coup d'état."

The meal was now over; the king waited for a moment, and then rose from the table.

The conversation was taking an embarrassing turn, but Richelieu was determined not to let go his prey. Therefore, when the king began to chat with Mme. de Noailles, the dauphiness, and Mlle. de Taverney, Richelieu maneuvered so skilfully that he soon found himself in the full fire of a conversation, which he directed according to his pleasure.

"Sire," said he, "your majesty knows that success emboldens."

"Do you say so for the purpose of informing us that you are bold, duke?"

"Sire, it is for the purpose of requesting a new favor from your majesty, after the one the king has already deigned to grant. One of my best friends, an old servant of your majesty, has a son in the gendarmes; the young man is highly deserving, but poor. He has received from an august princess the brevet title of captain, but he has not yet got a company."

"The princess! my daughter?" asked the king, turning toward the dauphiness.

"Yes, sire," said Richelieu, "and the father of this young man is called the Baron de Taverney."

"My father!" involuntarily exclaimed Andrée, "Philip! Is it for Philip, my lord duke, that you are asking for a company?"

Then ashamed of this breach of etiquette, Andrée made a step backward, blushing and clasping her hands with emotion.

The king turned to admire the blush which mantled

on the cheek of the lovely girl, and then glanced at Richelieu with a pleased look, which informed the courtier how
agreeable his request had been.

"In truth," said the dauphiness, "he is a charming
young man, and I had promised to make his fortune.
How unfortunate princes are! When God gives them the
best intentions, He deprives them of the memory and
reasoning powers necessary to carry their intentions into
effect. Ought I not to have known that this young man
was poor, and that it was not sufficient to give him the
epaulet without at the same time giving him the company?"

"Oh! madame! how could your royal highness have
known that?"

"Oh, I knew it!" replied the dauphiness, quickly,
with a gesture which recalled to Andrée's memory the
modest but yet happy home of her childhood; "yes, I knew
it, but I thought I had done everything necessary in giving a step to Monsieur Philip de Taverney. He is called
Philip, is he not, mademoiselle?"

"Yes, madame."

The king looked round on these noble and ingenuous
faces, and then rested his gaze on Richelieu, whose face
was also brightened by a ray of generosity, borrowed,
doubtless, from his august neighbor.

"Duke," said he, in a low voice, "I shall embroil myself with Luciennes."

Then, addressing Andrée, he added, quickly:

"Say that it will give you pleasure, mademoiselle."

"Ah, sire!" said Andrée, clasping her hands, "I request it as a boon from your majesty."

"In that case, it is granted," said Louis. "You will
choose a good company for this young man, duke. I will
furnish the necessary funds, if the charges are not already
paid and the post vacant."

This good action gladdened all who were present. It
procured the king a heavenly smile from Andrée, and
Richelieu a warm expression of thanks from those beautiful lips, from which, in his youth, he would have asked
for even more.

Several visitors arrived in succession, among whom was the Cardinal de Rohan, who, since the installation of the dauphiness at Trianon, had paid his court assiduously to her.

But during the whole evening the king had kind looks and pleasant words only for Richelieu. He even commanded the marshal's attendance when, after bidding farewell to the dauphiness, he set out to return to his own Trianon. The old marshal followed the king with a heart bounding with joy.

While the king, accompanied by the duke and his two officers, gained the dark alleys which led from the palace, the dauphiness had dismissed Andrée.

"You will be anxious to write this good news to Paris, mademoiselle," said the princess. "You may retire."

And, preceded by a footman carrying a lantern, the young girl traversed the walk, of about a hundred paces in length, which separates Trianon from the offices.

Also in advance of her, concealed by the thick foliage of the shrubbery, bounded a shadowy figure which followed all her movements with sparkling eyes. It was Gilbert.

When Andrée had arrived at the entrance, and begun to ascend the stone staircase, the valet left her and returned to the antechambers of Trianon.

Then Gilbert, gliding into the vestibule, reached the courtyard, and climbed by a small staircase, as steep as a ladder, into his attic, which was opposite Andrée's windows, and was situated in a corner of the building.

From this position he could see Andrée call a femme de chambre of Mme. de Noailles to assist her, as that lady had her apartments in the same corridor. But when the girl had entered the room, the window-curtains fell like an impenetrable veil between the ardent eyes of the young man and the object of his wishes.

At the palace there now only remained M. de Rohan, redoubling his gallant attentions to the dauphiness, who received them but coldly.

The prelate, fearing at last to be indiscreet, inasmuch as the dauphin had already retired, took leave of her royal highness with an expression of the deepest and most tender respect. As he was entering his carriage, a waiting-woman of the dauphiness approached and almost leaned inside the door.

" Here," said she.

And she put into his hand a small paper parcel, carefully folded, the touch of which made the cardinal start.

" Here," he replied, hastily thrusting into the girl's hand a heavy purse, the contents of which would have been a handsome salary. Then, without losing time, the cardinal ordered the coachman to drive to Paris and to ask for fresh orders at the barriere. During the whole way, in the darkness of the carriage, he felt the paper, and kissed the contents like some intoxicated lover. At the barriere he cried: " Rue St. Claude." A short time afterward he crossed the mysterious courtyard, and once more found himself in the little saloon occupied by Fritz, the silent usher.

Balsamo kept him waiting about a quarter of an hour. At last he appeared, and gave as a reason for his delay the lateness of the hour which had prevented him from expecting the arrival of visitors.

In fact it was now nearly eleven o'clock at night.

" That is true, baron," said the cardinal; " and I must request you to excuse my unseasonable visit. But you may remember you told me one day, that to be assured of certain secrets——"

" I must have a portion of the person's hair of whom we were speaking on that day," interrupted Balsamo, who had already spied the little paper which the unsuspecting prelate held carelessly in his hand.

" Precisely, baron."

" And you have brought me this hair, sir; very well."

" Here it is. Do you think it would be possible to return it to me again after the trial? "

" Unless fire should be necessary; in which case——"

" Of course, of course," said the cardinal. " However, I can procure some more. Can I have a reply? "

" To-day? "

" You know I am impatient."

"I must first ascertain, my lord."

And Balsamo took the packet of hair and hastily mounted to Lorenza's apartment.

"I shall now know," said he, on the way, "the secret of this monarchy—the mysterious fate which destiny has in store for it!"

And from the other side of the wall, even before opening the secret door, he plunged Lorenza into the magnetic sleep. The young girl received him, therefore, with an affectionate embrace. Balsamo could scarcely extricate himself from her arms. It would be difficult to say which was the most grievous for the poor baron, the reproaches of the beautiful Italian when she was awake, or her caresses when she slept. When he had succeeded in loosening the chain which her snowy arms formed around his neck:

"My beloved Lorenza," said he, putting the paper in her hand, "can you tell me to whom this hair belongs?"

Lorenza took it and pressed it against her breast, and then to her forehead. Though her eyes were open, it was only by means of her head and breast that she could see in her sleep.

"Oh!" said she, "it is an illustrious head from which this hair has been taken."

"Is it not?—and a happy head, too? Speak."

"She may be happy."

"Look well, Lorenza."

"Yes, she may be happy; there is no shadow as yet upon her life."

"Yet she is married?"

"Oh!" said Lorenza, with a sigh. "Strange," said she, "strange indeed! She is married like myself, pure and spotless as I am; but, unlike me, dear Balsamo, she does not love her husband."

"Oh, fate!" said Balsamo. "Thanks, Lorenza. I know all I wished to know."

He embraced her, put the hair carefully into his pocket, and then cutting off a lock of the Italian's black tresses, he burned it at the wax-light and inclosed the ashes in the paper which had been wrapped round the hair of the dauphiness.

Then he left the room, and while descending the stairs, he awoke the young woman.

The prelate, agitated and impatient, was waiting and doubting.

"Well, count?" said he.

"Well, my lord, the oracle has said you may hope."

"It said so!" exclaimed the prince, transported with joy.

"Draw what conclusion you please, my lord; the oracle said that this woman did not love her husband."

"Oh!" said M. de Rohan, with a thrill of joy.

"I was obliged to burn the hair to obtain the revelation by its-essence. Here are the ashes, which I restore to you most scrupulously, after having gathered them up as if each atom were worth a million."

"Thanks, sir, a thousand thanks; I can never repay you."

"Do not speak of that, my lord. I must recommend you, however, not to swallow these ashes in wine, as lovers sometimes do; it causes such a dangerous sympathy that your love would become incurable, while the lady's heart would cool toward you."

"Oh! I shall take care," said the prelate, almost terrified. "Adieu, count, adieu."

Twenty minutes afterward his eminence's carriage crossed M. de Richelieu's at the corner of the Rue des Petits Champs, so suddenly, that it was nearly upset in a deep trench which had been dug for the foundation of a new building.

The two noblemen recognized each other.

"Ha! prince," said Richelieu, with a smile.

"Ha! duke," replied de Rohan, with his fingers upon his lips.

And they disappeared in different directions.

CHAPTER XXVI.

M. DE RICHELIEU APPRECIATES NICOLE.

M. DE RICHELIEU drove straight to M. de Taverney's modest hotel in the Rue Coq Heron.

Thanks to the privilege we possess in common with the devil on two sticks, of entering every house, be it ever so carefully locked, we are aware before M. de Richelieu that the baron was seated before the fireplace, his feet resting upon the immense andirons which supported a smoldering log, and was lecturing Nicole, sometimes pausing to chuck her under the chin in spite of the rebellious and scornful poutings of the young waiting-maid. But whether Nicole would have been satisfied with the caresses without the sermon, or whether she would have preferred the sermon without the caresses, we can give no satisfactory information.

The conversation between the master and the servant turned upon the very important point, that at a certain hour of the evening Nicole never came when the bell was rung; that she had always something to do in the garden or in the greenhouse; and that everywhere but in these two places she neglected her business.

Nicole, turning backward and forward with a charming and voluptuous grace, replied:

" So much the worse! I am dying with weariness here; you promised I should go to Trianon with mademoiselle."

It was thereupon that the baron thought it proper in charity to pat her cheeks and chuck her chin, no doubt to distract her thoughts from dwelling on so unpleasant a subject; but Nicole continued in the same vein, and, refusing all consolation, deplored her unhappy lot.

" Yes," sighed she, " I am shut up within four horrible walls, I have no company, I have no air; while I had the prospect of a pleasant and fortunate future before me."

" What prospect? " said the baron.

" Trianon," replied Nicole; " Trianon, where I should

have seen the world—where I should have looked about me—where I should have been looked at."

"Oh, ho! my little Nicole," said the baron.

"Well, sir, I am a woman, and as well worth looking at as another, I suppose."

"Cordieu! how she talks," said the baron to himself. "What fire! what ambition!"

And he could not help casting a look of admiration at so much youth and beauty. Nicole seemed at times thoughtful and impatient.

"Come, sir," said she, "will you retire to bed, that I may go to mine?"

"One word more, Nicole."

All at once the noise of the street-bell made Taverney start and Nicole jump.

"Who can be coming," said the baron, "at half-past eleven o'clock at night? Go, child, and see."

Nicole hastened to open the door, asked the name of the visitor, and left the street-door half open. Through this lucky opening a shadow, which had apparently emerged from the courtyard, glided out, not without making noise enough to attract the attention of the marshal, for it was he who turned and saw the flight. Nicole preceded him, candle in hand, with a beaming look.

"Oh, ho!" said the marshal, smiling and following her into the room, "this old rogue of a Taverney only spoke to me of his daughter."

The duke was one of those men who do not require a second glance to see, and see completely. The shadowy figure which he had observed escaping made him think of Nicole, and Nicole of the shadow. When he saw her pretty face he guessed what errand the shadow had come upon, and, judging from her saucy and laughing eyes, her white teeth, and her small waist, he drew a tolerably correct picture of her character and tastes.

At the door of the saloon, Nicole, not without a palpitation of the heart, announced:

"His lordship, the Duke de Richelieu."

This name was destined to cause a sensation that evening. It produced such an effect upon the baron that he arose from his armchair and walked straight to the door, not being able to believe the evidence of his ears.

" The duke ! " he stammered.

" Yes, my dear friend, the duke himself," replied Richelieu, in his most winning voice.   " Oh ! that surprises you after your visit the other day ?   Well, nevertheless, nothing can be more real.   In the meantime, your hand, if you please."

" My lord duke, you overwhelm me."

" Where have your wits fled to, my dear friend ? " said the old marshal, giving his hat and cane to Nicole and seating himself comfortably in an armchair, " you are getting rusty, you dote; you seem no longer to know the world."

" But yet, duke," replied Taverney, much agitated, " it seems to me that the reception you gave me the other day was so significant that I could not mistake its purport."

" Hark ye, my old friend," answered Richelieu, " the other day you behaved like a schoolboy and I like a pedant. Between us there was only a difference of the ferula.   You are going to speak—I will save you the trouble; you might very probably say some foolish things to me, and I might reply in the same vein.   Let us leave the other day aside, therefore, and come direct to the present time.   Do you know what I have come for this evening ? "

" No, certainly."

" I have come to bring you the company which you asked me for your son the other day, and which the king has granted.   Diable ! can you not understand the difference?   The day before yesterday I was but a quasi-minister, and to ask a favor was an injustice; but to-day, when I am simply Richelieu and have refused the portfolio, it would be absurd not to ask.   I have therefore asked and obtained, and now I bring it to you."

" Duke, can this be true?   And is this kindness on your part——"

" It is the natural consequence of my duty as your friend. The minister refused, Richelieu asks and gives."

" Ah, duke, you enchant me—you are a true friend ! "

" Pardieu ! "

" But the king—the king, who confers such a favor on me——"

" The king scarcely knows what he has done; or perhaps I am mistaken, and he knows very well."

" What do you mean ? "

" I mean that his majesty has, no doubt, some motive for provoking Madame Dubarry just now; and you owe this favor which he bestows upon you more to that motive than to my influence."

" You think so ? "

" I am certain of it, for I am aiding and abetting. You know it is on account of this creature that I refused the portfolio ? "

" I was told so, but——"

" But you did not believe it. Come, say it frankly."

" Well, I confess that——"

" You always thought me not likely to be troubled by many scruples of conscience—is that it ? "

" At least, that I thought you without prejudices."

" My friend, I am getting old, and I no longer care for pretty faces except when they can be useful to me. And besides, I have some other plans. But, to return to your son; he is a splendid fellow."

" But on bad terms with that Dubarry who was at your house when I had the folly to present myself."

" I am aware of it, and that is why I am not a minister."

" Oh! you refused the portfolio in order not to displease my son ? "

" If I told you so, you would not believe me. No, that is not the reason. I refused it because the requirements of the Dubarrys, which commenced with the exclusion of your son, would have ended in enormities of all kinds."

" Then you have quarreled with these creatures ? "

" Yes and no. They fear me—I despise them; it is tit for tat."

" It is heroic, but imprudent."

" Why ? "

" The countess has still some power."

" Pooh! " said Richelieu.

" How you say that! "

" I say it like a man who feels the weakness of his position, and who, if necessary, would place the miner in a good position to blow up the whole place."

" I see the true state of the case; you do my son a favor partly to vex the Dubarrys."

" Principally for that reason, and your perspicacity is not at fault. Your son serves me as a grenade; I shall cause an explosion by his means. But, apropos, baron, have not you also a daughter? "

" Yes."

" Young—lovely as Venus—and who lives at present at Trianon? "

" Ah! then, you know her? "

" I have spent the evening in her company, and have conversed about her for a full hour with the king."

" With the king? " cried Taverney, his cheeks in a flame. " The king has spoken of my daughter—of Mademoiselle de Taverney? "

" The king himself, my friend. Do I vex you in telling you this? "

" Vex me? No, certainly not. The king honors me by looking at my daughter—but—the king——"

" Is immoral; is that what you are going to say? "

" Heaven forbid that I should talk evil of his majesty. He has a right to adopt whatever morals he chooses."

" Well! what does this astonishment mean, then? Do you pretend to say that Mademoiselle Andrée is not an accomplished beauty, and that therefore the king may not have looked upon her with admiration? "

Taverney did not reply; he only shrugged his shoulders and fell into a reverie, during which the unrelenting inquisitorial eye of the Duke de Richelieu was still fixed upon him.

" Well, I guess what you would say, if instead of thinking to yourself, you would speak aloud," continued the old marshal, approaching his chair nearer the baron's. " You would say that the king is accustomed to bad society, that he mixes with low company, and that therefore he is not likely to admire this noble girl, so modest in her demeanor

and so pure and lofty in her ideas, and is not capable
of appreciating the treasures of her grace and beauty."

" Certainly you are a great man, duke; you have guessed
my thoughts exactly," said Taverney.

" But confess, baron," continued Richelieu, " that our
master should no longer force us gentlemen, peers and
companions of the King of France, to kiss the vile, open
hand of a creature like Dubarry. It is time that he should
restore us to our proper position. After having sunk
from La Chateauroux, who was a marquise and of a stuff
to make duchesses, to La Pompadour, who was the daughter and the wife of a farmer of the public revenue, and
from La Pompadour to the Dubarry, who calls herself
simply Jeanneton, may he not fall still further and plunge
us into the lowest pitch of degradation? It is humiliating for us, baron, who wear a coronet on our caps, to bow
the head before such trumpery creatures."

" Oh! you only speak the truth," said Taverney. " How
evident is it that the court is deserted on account of these
new fashions."

" No queen, no ladies, no courtiers. The king elevates
a grisette to the rank of a consort, and the people are upon
the throne, represented by Mademoiselle Jeanne Vaubernier, a seamstress of Paris."

" It is so, and yet——"

" You see then, baron," interrupted the marshal, " what
a noble career there is open for a woman of mind who
should reign over France at present."

" Without doubt," said Taverney, whose heart was beating fast, " but, unluckily, the place is occupied."

" For a woman," continued the marshal, " who would
have the boldness of these creatures without their vice, and
who would direct her views and calculations to a loftier
aim. For a woman who would advance her fortune so high
that she should be talked of when the monarchy itself
should no longer exist. Do you know if your daughter has
intellect, baron?"

" Lofty intellect, and above all, good sense."

" She is very lovely."

" Is she not?"

"Her beauty is of that soft and charming character which pleases men so much, while her whole being is stamped with that air of candor and virgin purity which imposes respect even upon women. You must take great care of that treasure, my old friend."

"You speak of her with such fire——"

"I! I am madly in love with her, and would marry her to-morrow were I twenty instead of seventy-four years of age. But is she comfortably placed? Has she the luxury which befits such a lovely flower? Only think, baron; this evening she returned alone to her apartments, without waiting-woman or lackey. A servant of the dauphin carried a lantern before her! That looks more like a servant than a lady of her rank."

"What can I do, duke; you know I am not rich?"

"Rich or not, your daughter must at least have a waiting-maid."

Taverney sighed.

"I know very well," said he, "that she wants one, or at least that she ought to have one."

"Well! have you none?"

The baron did not reply.

"Who is that pretty girl you had here just now?" continued Richelieu. "A fine, spirited-looking girl, i'faith."

"Yes, but—I—I cannot send her to Trianon."

"Why not, baron? On the contrary, she seems to me perfectly suited for the post; she would make a capital femme de chambre."

"You did not look at her face, then, duke?"

"I! I did nothing else."

"You looked at her and did not remark the strange resemblance?"

"To whom?"

"To—guess. Come hither, Nicole."

Nicole advanced; like a true waiting-woman, she had been listening at the door. The duke took her by both hands and looked her steadily in the face, but the impertinent gaze of this great lord and debauchee did not alarm or embarrass her for a moment.

"Yes," said he, "it is true; there is a resemblance."

" You know to whom, and you see therefore that it is impossible to expose the fortunes of our house to such an awkward trick of fate. Would it be thought agreeable that this little minx of a Nicole should resemble the most illustrious lady in France? "

" Oh, ho! " replied Nicole, sharply, and disengaging herself from the marshal's grasp the better to reply to M. de Taverney, " is it so certain that this little minx resembles this illustrious lady so exactly? Has this lady the low shoulder, the quick eye, the round ankle, and the plump arm of the little minx? "

Nicole was crimson with rage, and therefore ravishingly beautiful.

The duke once more took her pretty hands in his, and with a look full of caresses and promises.

" Baron," said he, " Nicole has certainly not her equal at court, at least, in my opinion. As for the illustrious lady to whom she has, I confess, a slight resemblance, we shall know how to spare her self-love. You have fair hair of a lovely shade, Mademoiselle Nicole; you have eyebrows and a nose of a most imperial form; well, in one quarter of an hour employed before the mirror, these imperfections, since the baron thinks them such, will disappear. Nicole, my child, would you like to be at Trianon? "

" Oh! " said Nicole, and her soul full of longing was expressed in this monosyllable.

" You shall go to Trianon then, my dear, and without prejudicing in any way the fortunes of others. Baron, one word more."

" Speak, my dear duke."

" Go, my pretty child," said Richelieu, " and leave us alone a moment."

Nicole retired. The duke approached the baron.

" I press you the more to send your daughter a waiting-maid, because it will please the king. His majesty does not like poverty, and pretty faces do not frighten him. Let me alone, I understand what I am about."

" Nicole shall go to Trianon, if you think it will please the king," replied the baron, with a meaning smile.

" Then, if you will allow me, I will bring her with me, she can take advantage of the carriage."

" But still, her resemblance to the dauphiness! We must think of that, duke."

" I have thought of it. This resemblance will disappear in a quarter of an hour under Rafte's hands, I will answer for it. Write a note to your daughter to tell her of what importance it is that she should have a femme de chambre, and that this femme de chambre should be Nicole ? "

" You think it important that it should be Nicole ? "

" I do."

" And that no other than Nicole would do ? "

" Upon my honor, I think so."

" Then I will write immediately."

And the baron sat down and wrote a letter which he handed to Richelieu.

" And the instructions, duke ? "

" I will give them to Nicole. Is she intelligent ? "

The baron smiled.

" Then you confide her to me, do you not ? " said Richelieu.

" That is your affair, duke; you asked me for her, I give her to you; make of her what you like."

" Mademoiselle, come with me," said the duke, rising and calling into the corridor, " and that quickly."

Nicole did not wait to be told twice. Without asking the baron for his consent, she made up a packet of clothes in five minutes, and, light as a bird, she flew down-stairs and took her place beside the coachman.

Richelieu took leave of his friend, who repeated his thanks for the service he had rendered Philip. Of Andrée not a word was said; it was necessary to do more than speak of her.

CHAPTER XXVII.

THE TRANSFORMATION.

NICOLE was overjoyed. To leave Taverney for Paris was not half so great a triumph as to leave Paris for Trianon. She was so gracious with M. de Richelieu's coachman, that the next morning the reputation of the new femme de chambre was established throughout all the coach-houses and antechambers, in any degree aristocratic, of Paris and Versailles.

When they arrived at the Hotel de Hanover, M. de Richelieu took the little waiting-maid by the hand and led her to the first story, where M. Rafte was waiting his arrival, and writing a multitude of letters, all on his master's account.

Amid the various acquirements of the marshal, war occupied the foremost rank, and Rafte had become, at least in theory, such a skilful man of war, that Polybius and the Chevalier de Fobard, if they had lived at that period, would have esteemed themselves fortunate could they have perused the pamphlets on fortifications and maneuvering, of which Rafte wrote one every week. M. Rafte was busy revising the plan of attack against the English in the Mediterranean, when the marshal entered, and said:

" Rafte, look at this child, will you? "

Rafte looked.

" Very pretty," said he, with a most significant movement of the lips.

" Yes, but the likeness, Rafte? It is of the likeness I speak."

" Oh! true. What the deuce! "

" You see it, do you not? "

" It is extraordinary; it will either make or mar her fortune."

" It will ruin her in the first place; but we shall arrange all that. You observe she has fair hair, Rafte; but that will not signify much, will it? "

" It will only be necessary to make it black, my lord,"

replied Rafte, who had acquired the habit of completing his master's thoughts, and sometimes even of thinking entirely for him.

"Come to my dressing-table, child," said the marshal; "this gentleman, who is a very clever man, will make you the handsomest and the least easily recognized waiting-maid in France."

In fact, ten minutes afterward, with the assistance of a composition which the marshal used every week to dye the white hairs beneath his wig black, a piece of coquetry which he often affected to confess by the bedside of some of his acquaintance, Rafte had dyed the beautiful auburn hair of Nicole a splendid jet black.

Then he passed the end of a pin, blackened in the flame of a candle, over her thick fair eyebrows, and by this means gave such a fantastic look to her joyous countenance, such an ardent and even somber fire to her bright clear eyes, that one would have said she was some fairy bursting by the power of an incantation from the magic prison in which her enchanter had held her confined.

"Now, my sweet child," said Richelieu, after having handed a mirror to the astonished Nicole, "look how charming you are, and how little like the Nicole you were just now. You have no longer a queen to fear, but a fortune to make."

"Oh, my lord!" exclaimed the young girl.

"Yes, and for that purpose it is only necessary that we understand each other."

Nicole blushed and looked down, the cunning one expected, no doubt, some of those flattering words which Richelieu knew so well how to say.

The duke perceived this, and to cut short all misunderstanding, said:

"Sit down in this armchair beside Monsieur Rafte, my dear child. Open your ears wide, and listen to me. Oh! do not let Monsieur Rafte's presence embarrass you; do not be afraid; he will, on the contrary, give us his advice. You are listening are you not?"

"Yes, my lord," stammered Nicole, ashamed at having thus been led away by her vanity.

The conversation between M. de Richelieu, M. Rafte, and Nicole lasted more than an hour, after which the marshal sent the little femme de chambre to sleep with the other waiting-maid in the hotel.

Rafte returned to his military pamphlet, and Richelieu retired to bed, after having looked over the different letters which conveyed to him intelligence of all the acts of the provincial parliaments against M. d'Aiguillon and the Dubarry clique.

Early the next day, one of his carriages, without his coat of arms, conducted Nicole to Trianon, set her down at the gate with her little packet, and immediately disappeared. Nicole, with head erect, mind at ease, and hope dancing in her eyes, after having made the necessary inquiries, knocked at the door of the offices.

It was ten o'clock in the morning. Andrée, already up and dressed, was writing to her father to inform him of the happy event of the preceding day, of which M. de Richelieu, as we have already seen, had made himself the messenger. Our readers will not have forgotten that a flight of stone steps led from the garden to the little chapel of Trianon; that on the landing-place of this chapel a staircase branched off toward the right to the first story, which contained the apartments of the ladies-in-waiting, which apartments opened off a long corridor, like an alley, looking upon the garden.

Andrée's apartment was the first upon the left hand in this corridor. It was tolerably large, well lighted by windows looking upon the stable court, and preceded by a little bedroom with a closet on either side. This apartment, however insufficient, if one considers the ordinary household of the officers of a brilliant court, was yet a charming retreat, very habitable, and very cheerful as an asylum from the noise and bustle of the palace. There an ambitious soul could fly to devour the affronts or the mistakes of the day, and there, too, an humble and melancholy spirit could repose in silence and in solitude, apart from the grandeur of the gay world around.

In fact, the stone steps once ascended, and the chapel passed, there no longer existed either superiority, duty, or display. There reigned the calm of a convent and the personal liberty of prison life. The slave of the palace was a monarch when she had crossed the threshold of her modest dwelling. A gentle yet lofty soul, such as Andrée's, found consolation in this reflection; not that she flew here to repose after the fatigues of a disappointed ambition, or of unsatisfied longings, but she felt that she could think more at her ease in the narrow bounds of her chamber than in the rich saloons of Trianon, or those marble halls which her feet trod with a timidity amounting almost to terror.

From this sequestered nook, where the young girl felt herself so well and so appropriately placed, she could look without emotion on all the splendor which, during the day, had met her dazzled eye. Surrounded by her flowers, her harpsichord, and her German books—such sweet companions to those who read with the heart—Andrée defied fate to inflict on her a single grief or to deprive her of a single joy.

"Here," said she, when in the evening, after her duties were over, she returned to throw around her shoulders her dressing-gown with its wide folds, and to breathe with all her soul, as with all her lungs—"here I possess nearly everything I can hope to possess till my death. I may one day perhaps be richer, but I can never be poorer than I now am. There will always be flowers, music, and a consoling page to cheer the poor recluse."

Andrée had obtained permission to breakfast in her own apartment when she felt inclined. This was a precious boon to her; for she could thus remain in her own domicile until twelve o'clock, unless the dauphiness should command her attendance for some morning reading or some early walk. Thus free, in fine weather, she set out every morning with a book in her hand, and transversed alone the extensive woods which lie between Versailles and Trianon; then, after a walk of two hours, during which she gave full play to meditation and reverie, she returned to breakfast, often without having seen either nobleman or servant, man or livery.

When the heat began to pierce through the thick foliage,

Andrée had her little chamber so fresh and cool with the double current of air from the door and the window. A small sofa, covered with Indian silk, four chairs to match, a simple yet elegant bed, with a circular top, from which the curtains of the same material as the covering of the furniture fell in deep folds, two china vases placed upon the chimney-piece, and a square table with brass feet, composed her little world, whose narrow confines bounded all her hopes and limited all her wishes.

Andrée was seated in her apartment, therefore, as we have said, and busily engaged in writing to her father when a little modest knock at the door of the corridor attracted her attention.

She raised her head on seeing the door open, and uttered a slight cry of astonishment when the radiant face of Nicole appeared entering from the little antechamber.

CHAPTER XXVIII.

HOW PLEASURE TO SOME IS DESPAIR TO OTHERS.

" Good-day, mademoiselle, it is I," said Nicole, with a joyous courtesy, which, nevertheless, from the young girl's knowledge of her mistress's character, was not unmixed with anxiety.

" You! And how do you happen to be here?" replied Andrée, putting down her pen, the better to follow the conversation which was thus commenced.

" Mademoiselle had forgotten me, so I came——"

" But if I forgot you, mademoiselle, it was because I had my reasons for so doing. Who gave you permission to come?"

" Monsieur, the baron, of course, mademoiselle," said Nicole, smoothing the handsome black eyebrows which she owed to the generosity of M. Rafte, with a very dissatisfied air.

" My father requires your services in Paris, and I do not require you here at all. You may return, child."

" Oh, then, mademoiselle does not care—I thought mademoiselle had been more pleased with me—it is well worth while loving," added Nicole, philosophically, " to meet with such a return at last."

And she did her utmost to bring a tear to her beautiful eyes.

There was enough of heart and feeling in this reproach to excite Andrée's compassion.

" My child," said she, " I have attended here already, and I cannot permit myself unnecessarily to increase the household of the dauphiness by another mouth."

" Oh! as if this mouth was so large! " said Nicole, with a charming smile.

" No matter, Nicole, your presence here is impossible."

" On account of this resemblance? " said the young girl. " Then you have not looked at my face, mademoiselle? "

" In fact, you seem changed."

" I think so! A fine gentleman, he who got the promotion for Monsieur Philip, came to us yesterday, and as he saw the baron quite melancholy at your being here without a waiting-maid, he told him that nothing was easier than to change me from fair to dark. He brought me with him, dressed me as you see, and here I am."

Andrée smiled.

" You must love me very much," said she, " since you are determined at all risks to shut yourself up in Trianon, where I am almost a prisoner."

Nicole cast a rapid but intelligent glance round the room.

" The chamber is not very gay," said she; " but you are not always in it? "

" I? Of course not," replied Andrée! " but you? "

" Well, I! "

" You, who will never enter the saloons of madame the dauphiness; you, who will have neither the resources of the theater, nor the walk, nor the evening circle, but will always remain here, you will die of weariness."

" Oh! " said Nicole, " there is always some little window or other, one can surely see some little glimpse of the gay world without, were it only through the chinks of the door.

If a person can see they can also be seen—that is all I require; so do not be uneasy on my account."

" I repeat, Nicole, that I cannot receive you without express orders from my father."

" Is that your settled determination ? "

" It is."

Nicole drew the Baron Taverney's letter from her bosom.

" There," said she, " since my entreaties and my devotion to you have had no effect, let us see if the order contained in this will have more power."

Andrée read the letter, which was in the following terms :

" I am aware, and indeed it is already remarked, my dear Andrée, that you do not occupy the position at Trianon which your rank imperatively requires. You ought to have two femmes de chambre and a valet, as I ought to have clearly twenty thousand pounds per annum; but as I am satisfied with one thousand pounds, imitate my example, and content yourself with Nicole, who in her own person is worth all the servants you ought to have.

" Nicole is quick, intelligent, and devoted to you, and will readily adopt the tone and manners of her new locality. Your chief care, indeed, will be not to stimulate her, but to repress her anxiety. Keep her, then; and do not imagine that I am making any sacrifice in depriving myself of her services. In case you should think so, remember that his majesty, who had the goodness to think of us, remarked on seeing you (this was confided to me by a good friend), that you required a little more attention to your toilet and general appearance. Think of this; it is of great importance.

" YOUR AFFECTIONATE FATHER."

This letter threw Andrée into a state of grief and perplexity. She was then to be haunted, even in her new prosperity, by the remembrance of that poverty which she alone did not feel to be a fault, while all around seemed to consider it as a crime.

Her first impulse was to break her pen indignantly, to tear the letter she had commenced, and to reply to her father's epistle by some lofty tirade expressive of philosophical self-denial, which Philip would have approved of with all his heart. But she imagined she saw the baron's satirical smile on reading this chef-d'œuvre, and her resolution vanished. She merely replied to the baron's order, therefore, by a paragraph annexed to the news of Trianon which she had already written to him according to his request.

"My father," she added, "Nicole has this moment arrived, and I receive her since you wish it; but what you have written on this subject has vexed me. Shall I be less ridiculous with this village girl as waiting-maid, than when I was alone amid this wealthy court? Nicole will be unhappy at seeing me humbled; she will be discontented; for servants feel proud or humbled in proportion to the wealth or poverty of their masters. As to his majesty's remark, my father, permit me to tell you that the king has too much good sense to be displeased at my incapacity to play the grand lady, and, besides, his majesty has too much heart to have remarked or criticized my poverty without transforming it into a wealth to which your name and services would have had a legitimate claim in the eyes of all."

This was Andrée's reply, and it must be confessed that her ingenuous innocence, her noble pride, had an easy triumph over the cunning and corruption of her tempters.

Andrée said no more respecting Nicole. She agreed to her remaining, so that the latter, joyous and animated, she well knew why, prepared on the spot a little bed in the cabinet on the right of the antechamber, and made herself as small, as aerial, and as exquisite as possible, in order not to inconvenience her mistress by her presence in this modest retreat. One would have thought she wished to imitate the rose leaf which the Persian sages let fall upon a vase filled with water to show that something could be added without spilling the contents.

Andrée set out for Trianon about one o'clock. She had never been more quickly or more gracefully attired. Nicole had surpassed herself; politeness, attention, and zeal—nothing had been wanting in her services.

When Mlle. de Taverney was gone, Nicole felt herself mistress of the domicile, and instituted a thorough examination of it. Everything was scrutinized, from the letters to the smallest knick-knack on the toilet-table, from the mantelpiece to the most secret corners of the closets. Then she looked out of the windows to take a survey of the neighborhood.

Below her was a large courtyard, in which several hostlers were dressing and currying the splendid horses of the dauphiness. Hostlers? pshaw! Nicole turned away her head.

On the right was a row of windows on the same story as those of Andrée's apartment. Several heads appeared at these windows, apparently those of chambermaids and floor-scrubbers. Nicole disdainfully proceeded in her examination.

On the opposite side, in a large apartment, some music-teachers were drilling a class of choristers and instru-mentalists for the mass of St. Louis. Without ceasing her dusting operations. Nicole commenced to sing after her own fashion, thus distracting the attention of the masters, and causing the choristers to sing false.

But this pastime could not long satisfy Mlle. Nicole's ambition. When the masters and the singers had quar-reled, and been mystified sufficiently, the little waiting-maid proceeded to the inspection of the higher story. All the windows were closed, and moreover they were only attics, so Nicole continued her dusting. But a moment afterward, one of these attic windows was opened without her being able to discover by what mechanism, for no one appeared. Some person, however, must have opened this window; this some person must have seen Nicole and yet not have remained to look at her, thereby proving himself a most impertinent some person. At least such was Nicole's opinion. But she, who examined everything so conscientiously, could not avoid examining the features of this impertinent; and she therefore returned every moment from her different avocations to the window to give a glance at this attic—that is, at this open eye from which the eyeball was so obstinately absent.   Once she imagined that the person fled as she approached; but this was incredible, and she did not believe it.

On another occasion she was almost certain of the fact, having seen the back of the fugitive, surprised, no doubt, by a prompter return than he had anticipated.   Then Nicole had recourse to stratagem.   She concealed herself behind the curtain, leaving the window wide open to drown all suspicion.

She waited a long time, but at last a head of black hair made its appearance; then came two timid hands, which supported, buttress-like, a body bending over cautiously; and finally, a face showed itself distinctly at the window. Nicole almost fell, and grasped the curtain so tightly, in her surprise, that it shook from top to bottom.

It was M. Gilbert's face, which was looking at her from this lofty attic.   But the moment Gilbert saw the curtain move, he comprehended the trick, and appeared no more. To mend the matter, the attic window was closed.

No doubt Gilbert had seen Nicole; he had been astonished, and had wished to convince himself of the presence of his enemy; and when he found himself discovered instead, he had fled in agitation and in anger.   At least Nicole interpreted the scene thus, and she was right, for this was the exact state of the case.

In fact, Gilbert would rather have seen his satanic majesty in person than Nicole.   The arrival of this spy caused him a thousand terrors.   He felt an old leaven of jealousy against her, for she knew his secret of the garden in the Rue Coq Heron.

'Gilbert had fled in agitation, but not in agitation alone, but also in anger, and biting his nails with rage.

"Of what use now is my foolish discovery of which I was so proud?" said he to himself.   "Even if Nicole had a lover in Paris, the evil is done, and she will not be sent away from this on that account; but if she tells what I did in the Rue Coq Heron, I shall be dismissed from

Trianon. It is not I who govern Nicole—it is she who governs me. Oh, fury!"

And Gilbert's inordinate self-love, serving as a stimulant to his hatred, made his blood boil with frightful violence. It seemed to him that Nicole in entering that apartment had chased from it, with a diabolical smile, all the happy dreams which Gilbert from his garret had wafted thither every night along with his vows, his ardent love, and his flowers. Had Gilbert been too much occupied to think of Nicole before, or had he banished the subject from his thoughts on account of the terror with which it inspired him? We cannot determine; but this we do know, at least, that Nicole's appearance was a most disagreeable surprise for him.

He saw plainly that, sooner or later, war would be declared between them; but as Gilbert was prudent and politic, he did not wish the war to commence until he felt himself strong enough to make it energetic and effective. With this intention he determined to counterfeit death until chance should present him with a favorable opportunity of reviving, or until Nicole, from weakness or necessity, should venture on some step which would deprive her of her present vantage ground. Therefore, all eye, all ear, where Andrée was concerned, but at the same time ceaselessly vigilant, he continued to make himself acquainted with the state of affairs in the first apartment of the corridor, without Nicole's ever having once met him in the gardens.

Unluckily for Nicole, she was not irreproachable, and even had she been so for the present, there was always one stumbling-block in the past over which she could be made to fall.

At the end of a week's ceaseless watching, morning, noon, and night, Gilbert at last saw through the bars of his window a plume which he fancied he recognized. The plume was a source of constant agitation to Nicole, for it belonged to M. Beausire, who, following the rest of the court, had emigrated from Paris to Trianon.

For a long time Nicole was cruel; for a long time she left M. Beausire to shiver in the cold, and melt in the sun, and her prudence drove Gilbert to despair; but one fine morning, when M. Beausire had, doubtless, overleaped the barrier of mimic eloquence, and found an opportunity of bringing persuasive words to his aid, Nicole profited by Andrée's absence to descend to the courtyard and join M. Beausire, who was assisting his friend, the superintendent of the stables, to train a little Shetland pony.

From the court they passed into the garden, and from thence into the shady avenue which leads to Versailles. Gilbert followed the amorous couple with the ferocious joy of a tiger who scents his prey. He counted their steps, their sighs, learned by heart all he heard of their conversation, and it may be presumed that the result pleased him, for the next day, freed from all embarrassment, he displayed himself openly at his attic window, humming a song and looking quite at ease, and so far from fearing to be seen by Nicole, that, on the contrary, he seemed to brave her look.

Nicole was mending an embroidered silken mitten belonging to her mistress; she heard the song, raised her head, and saw Gilbert. The first evidence she gave of his presence was a contemptuous pouting, which bordered on the bitter, and breathed of hostility at a league's distance. But Gilbert sustained this look with such a singular smile, and there was such provoking intelligence in his air and in his manner of singing, that Nicole looked down and blushed.

"She understands me," thought Gilbert; "that is all I wished." On subsequent occasions Gilbert continued the same behavior, and it was now Nicole's turn to tremble. She went so far as to long for an interview with him, in order to free her heart from the load with which the satirical looks of the young gardener had burdened it.

Gilbert saw that she sought him. He could not misunderstand the short dry coughs which sounded near the window whenever Nicole knew him to be in his attic, nor the goings and comings of the young girl in the corridor when she supposed he might be ascending or descending the stairs. For a short time he was very proud of this triumph, which he attributed entirely to his strength of

character and wise precautions. Nicole watched him so
well that once she spied him as he mounted to his attic.
She called him, but he did not reply.

Prompted either by curiosity or fear, Nicole went still
further. One evening she took off her pretty little high-
heeled slippers, a present from Andrée, and with a trembling and hurried step she ventured into the corridor at the
end of which she saw Gilbert's door. There was still sufficient daylight to enable Gilbert, aware of Nicole's approach, to see her distinctly through the joining or, rather,
through the crevices of the panels. She knocked at the
door, knowing well that he was in his room, but Gilbert
did not reply.

It was, nevertheless, a dangerous temptation for him.
He could at his ease humble her who thus came to entreat
his pardon, and prompted by this thought he had already
raised his hand to draw the bolt which, with his habitual
precaution and vigilance, he had fastened to avoid surprise.

" But no," thought he, " no. She is all calculation; it
is from fear or interest alone that she comes to seek me.
She therefore hopes to gain something by her visit; but if
so, what may I not lose? "

And with this reasoning he let his hand fall again by
his side. Nicole, after having knocked at the door two or
three times, retired, frowning. Gilbert therefore kept all
his advantages, and Nicole had only to redouble her cunning in order not to lose hers entirely. At last all these
projects and counter-projects reduced themselves to this
dialogue, which took place between the belligerent parties
one evening at the chapel door, where chance had brought
them together.

" Ha! Good evening, Monsieur Gilbert; you are here,
then, are you? "

" Oh! Good evening, Mademoiselle Nicole; you are at
Trianon? "

" As you see—waiting-maid to mademoiselle."

" And I am assistant gardener."

Then Nicole made a deep courtesy to Gilbert, who returned her a most courtly bow, and they separated. Gilbert ascended to his attic as if he had been on his way

thither, and Nicole left the offices and proceeded on her errand; but Gilbert glided down again stealthily, and followed the young femme de chambre, calculating that she was going to meet M. Beausire.

A man was indeed waiting for her beneath the shadows of the alley; Nicole approached him. It was too dark for Gilbert to recognize M. Beausire; and the absence of the plume puzzled him so much that he let Nicole return to her domicile, and followed the man as far as the gate of Trianon.

It was not M. Beausire, but a man of a certain age, or rather certainly aged, with a distinguished air and a brisk gait notwithstanding his advanced years. When he approached, Gilbert, who carried his assurance so far as almost to brush past him, recognized M. de Richelieu.

"Peste!" said he, "first an officer, now a marshal of France! Mademoiselle Nicole ascends in the scale."

CHAPTER XXIX.

THE PARLIAMENTS.

WHILE all these minor intrigues, hatched and brought to light beneath the linden-trees, and amid the alleys of Trianon, formed a sufficiently animated existence for the insects of this little world, the great intrigues of the town, like threatening tempests, spread their vast wings over the palace of Themis, as M. Jean Dubarry wrote in mythological parlance to his sister.

The parliaments, those degenerate remains of the ancient French opposition, had taken breath beneath the capricious government of Louis XV.; but since their protector, M. de Choiseul, had fallen, they felt the approach of danger, and they prepared to meet it by measures as energetic as their circumstances would permit.

Every general commotion is kindled at first by some personal quarrel, as the pitched battles of armies commence by skirmishes of outposts. Since M. de la Chalotais

had attacked M. d'Aiguillon, and in doing so had person-
ified the struggle of the tiers-état with the feudal lords,
the public mind had taken possession of the question, and
would not permit it to be deferred or displaced.

Now the king—whom the parliament of Brittany and
of all France had deluged with floods of petitions, more
or less submissive and foolish—the king, thanks to Mme.
Dubarry, had just given his countenance to the feudal
against the tiers party by nominating M. d'Aiguillon to
the command of his light horse.

M. Jean Dubarry had described it very correctly; it
was a smart fillip to "the dear and trusty counselors,
sitting in high court of parliament."

"How would the blow be taken?" Town and court
would ask itself this question every morning at sunrise;
but members of parliament are clever people, and where
others are much embarrassed they see clearly. They began
with agreeing among themselves as to the application and
result of this blow, after which they adopted the following
resolution, when it had been clearly ascertained that the
blow had been given and received:

"The court of parliament will deliberate upon the conduct of the ex-Governor of Brittany, and give its opinion
thereon."

But the king parried the blow by sending a message to
the peers and princes, forbidding them to repair to the
palace, or to be present at any deliberation which might
take place concerning M. d'Aiguillon. They obeyed to the
letter.

Then the parliament, determined to do its business
itself, passes a decree, in which, after declaring that the
Duke d'Aiguillon was seriously inculpated and tainted
with suspicion, even on matters which touched his honor,
it proclaimed that that peer was suspended from the functions of the peerage, until, by a judgment given in the
court of peers, which the forms and solemnities prescribed
by the laws and customs of the kingdom, the place of
which nothing can supply, he had fully cleared himself

from the accusations and suspicions now resting on his honor.

But such a decree, passed merely in the court of parliament before those interested, and inscribed in these reports, was nothing; public notoriety was wanting, and above all that uproar which song alone ventures to raise in France, and which makes song the sovereign controller of events and rulers. This decree of parliament must be heightened and strengthened by the power of song.

Paris desired nothing better than to take part in this commotion. Little disposed to view either court or parliament with favor, Paris in its ceaseless movement was waiting for some good subject for a laugh, as a transition from all the causes for tears which had been furnished it for centuries.

The decree was therefore properly and duly passed, and the parliament appointed commissioners who were to have it printed under their own eyes. Ten thousand copies of the decree were to be struck off, and the distribution organized without delay.

Then, as it was one of their rules that the person interested should be informed of what the court had done respecting him, the same commissioner proceeded to the hotel of the Duke d'Aiguillon, who had just arrived in Paris for an important interview, no less indeed than to have a clear and open explanation, which had become necessary between the duke and his uncle, the marshal.

Thanks to Rafte, all Versailles had been informed within an hour of the noble resistance of the old duke to the king's orders touching the portfolio of M. de Choiseul. Thanks to Versailles, all Paris and all France had learned the same news; so that Richelieu had found himself for some time past on the summit of popularity, from which he made political grimaces at Mme. Dubarry and his dear nephew.

The position was unfavorable for M. d'Aiguillon, who was already so unpopular. The marshal, hated, but at the same time feared by the people, because he was the living type of that nobility which was so respected and so respectable under Louis XV.—the marshal so Protean in his character, that after having chosen a part, he was able to withdraw from it without difficulty when circumstances required it, or when a bonmot might be the result —Richelieu, we repeat, was a dangerous enemy, the more so as the worst part of his enmity was always that which he concealed, in order, as he said, to create a surprise.

The Duke d'Aiguillon, since his interview with Mme. Dubarry, had two flaws in his coat of mail. Suspecting how much anger and thirst for revenge Richelieu concealed under the apparent equality of his temper, he acted as mariners do in certain cases of difficulty—he burst the waterspout with his cannon, assured that the danger would be less if it were faced boldly. He set about looking everywhere for his uncle therefore, in order to have a serious conversation with him; but nothing was more difficult to accomplish than this step, since the marshal had discovered his wish.

Marches and countermarches commenced. When the marshal saw his nephew at a distance, he sent him a smile, and immediately surrounded himself by people who rendered all communication impossible, thus putting the enemy at defiance as from an impregnable fort.

The Duke d'Aiguillon burst the waterspout. He simply presented himself at his uncle's hotel at Versailles; but Rafte, from his post at the little window of the hotel looking upon the court, recognized the liveries of the duke, and warned his master. The duke entered the marshal's bedroom, where he found Rafte alone, who, with a most confidential smile, was so indiscreet as to inform the nephew that his uncle had not slept at home that night.

M. d'Aiguillon bit his lips and retired. When he returned to his hotel, he wrote to the marshal to request an audience. The marshal could not refuse to reply. If he replied, he could not refuse an audience; and if he granted the audience, how could he refuse a full explanation? M. d'Aiguillon resembled too much those polite and engaging duelists who hide their evil designs under a fascinating and graceful exterior, lead their man upon the ground with bows and reverences, and there put him to death without pity.

The marshal's self-love was not so powerful as to mislead him; he knew his nephew's power. Once in his presence, his opponent would force from him either a pardon or a concession. Now, Richelieu never pardoned any one, and concessions to an enemy are always a dangerous fault in politics. Therefore, on receipt of M. d'Aiguillon's letter, he pretended to have left Paris for several days.

Rafte, whom he consulted upon this point, gave him the following advice:

"We are on a fair way to ruin Monsieur d'Aiguillon. Our friends of the parliament will do the work. If Monsieur d'Aiguillon, who suspects this, can lay his hand upon you before the explosion, he will force from you a promise to assist him in case of misfortune; for your resentment is of that kind that you cannot openly gratify it at the expense of your family interest. If, on the contrary, you refuse, Monsieur d'Aiguillon will leave you knowing you to be his enemy and attributing all his misfortunes to you; and he will go away comforted, as people always are when they have found out the cause of their complaint, even although the complaint itself be not removed."

"That is quite true," replied Richelieu; "but I cannot conceal myself forever. How many days will it be before the explosion takes place?"

"Six days, my lord."

"Are you sure?"

Rafte drew from his pocket a letter from a counselor of the parliament. This letter contained only the two following lines:

"It has been decided that the decree shall be passed. It will take place on Thursday, the final day fixed on by the company."

"Then the affair is very simple," replied the marshal; "send the duke back his letter with a note from your own hand.

"'MY LORD DUKE.—You have doubtless heard of the departure of my lord marshal for   *   *   This change of air has been judged indispensable by the marshal's physician, who thinks him rather overworked. If, as I believe is the case, after what you did me the honor to tell me the other day, you wish to have an interview with my lord, I can assure you that on Thursday evening next, the duke, on his return from   *   *   will sleep in his hotel in Paris, where you will certainly find him.'

" And now," added the marshal, " hide me somewhere until Thursday."

Rafte punctually fulfilled these instructions; the letter was written and sent, the hiding-place was found. Only one evening Richelieu, who began to feel very much wearied, slipped out and proceeded to Trianon to speak to Nicole. He risked nothing, or thought he risked nothing, by this step, knowing the Duke d'Aiguillon to be at the pavilion of Luciennes. The result of this maneuver was, that even if M. d'Aiguillon suspected something, he could not foresee the blow which menaced him until he had actually met his enemy's sword.

The delay until Thursday satisfied him; on that day he left Versailles with the hope of at last meeting and combating this impalpable antagonist. This Thursday was, as we have said, the day on which parliament was to proclaim its decree.

An agitation, low and muttering as yet, but perfectly intelligible to the Parisians, who know so well the level of these popular waves, reigned in the wide streets through which M. d'Aiguillon's carriage passed. No notice was taken of him, for he had observed the precaution of coming in a carriage without a coat of arms or other heraldic distinctions.

Here and there he saw busy-looking crowds, who were showing one another some paper which they read with many gesticulations, and collecting in noisy groups, like ants round a piece of sugar fallen to the ground. But this was the period of inoffensive agitation; the people were then in the habit of congregating together in this manner for a corn tax, for an article in the " Gazette de

Holland," for a verse of Voltaire's, or for a song against Dubarry or Maupeou.

M. d'Aiguillon drove straight to M. de Richelieu's hotel. He found there only Rafte. " The marshal," the secretary said, " was expected every moment; some delay at the post must have detained him at the barriere."

M. d'Aiguillon proposed waiting, not without expressing some impatience to Rafte, for he took this excuse as a new defeat. His ill-humor increased, however, when Rafte told him that the marshal would be in despair on his return to find that M. d'Aiguillon had been kept waiting; that besides, he was not to sleep in Paris as he had at first intended; and that, most probably, he would not return from the country alone, and would just call in passing at his hotel to see if there was any news; that therefore M. d'Aiguillon would be wiser to return to his house, where the marshal would call as he passed.

" Listen, Rafte," said D'Aiguillon, who had become more gloomy during this mysterious reply; " you are my uncle's conscience, and I trust you will answer me as an honest man. I am played upon, am I not, and the marshal does not wish to see me ? Do not interrupt me, Rafte, you have been a valuable counselor to me, and I might have been, and can yet be, a good friend to you; must I return to Versailles ? "

" My lord duke, I assure you, upon my honor, you will receive a visit at your own house from the marshal in less than an hour."

" Then I can as well wait here, since he will come this way."

" I have had the honor of informing you that he will probably not be alone."

" I understand. I have your word, Rafte ? "

At these words the duke retired deep in thought, but with an air as noble and graceful as the marshal's was the reverse, when after his nephew's departure, he emerged from a closet through the glass door of which he had been peeping.

The marshal smiled like one of those hideous demons which Callot has introduced in his " Temptations."

"He suspects nothing, Rafte?" said he.

"Nothing, my lord."

"What hour is it?"

"The hour has nothing to do with the matter, my lord. You must wait until our little procureur of the Châtelet makes his appearance. The commissioners are still at the printer's."

Rafte had scarcely finished, when a footman opened a secret door, and introduced a personage, very ugly, very greasy, very black—one of these living pens for which M. Dubarry professed such a profound antipathy.

Rafte pushed the marshal into a closet, and hastened, smiling, to meet this man.

"Ah! it is you, Monsieur Flageot?" said he; "I am delighted to see you."

"Your servant, Monsieur Rafte. Well, the business is done."

"Is it printed?"

"Five thousand are struck off. The first proofs are already scattered over the town, the others are drying."

"What a misfortune, my dear Monsieur Flageot! What a blow to the marshal's family!"

M. Flageot, to avoid the necessity of answering—that is, of telling a lie—drew a large silver box from his pocket and slowly inhaled a pinch of Scotch snuff.

"Well, what is to be done now?" asked Rafte.

"The forms, my dear sir, the forms! The commissioners, now that they are sure of the printing and the distribution, will immediately enter their carriages, which are waiting at the door of the printing-office, and proceed to make known the decree to Monsieur the Duke d'Aiguillon, who happens, luckily—I mean unfortunately, Monsieur Rafte—to be in his hotel in Paris, where they can have an interview with him in person."

Rafte hastily seized an enormous bag of legal documents from a shelf, which he gave to M. Flageot, saying:

"These are the suits which I mentioned to you, sir; the marshal has the greatest confidence in your ability, and leaves this affair, which ought to prove most remunerative, entirely in your hands. I have to thank you for your

good offices in this deplorable conflict of Monsieur d'Aiguillon with the all-powerful parliament of Paris, and
also you for your very valuable advice."

And he gently, but with some haste, pushed M. Flageot,
delighted with the weight of his burden, toward the door
of the antechamber. Then releasing the marshal from his
prison:

"Quick, my lord, to your carriage! You have no time
to lose if you wish to be present at the scene. Take care
that your horses go more quickly than those of the commissioners."

CHAPTER XXX.

IN WHICH IT IS SHOWN THAT THE PATH OF A MINISTER IS NOT ALWAYS STREWN WITH ROSES.

THE Marshal de Richelieu's horses did go more quickly
than those of the commissioners, for the marshal entered
first into the courtyard of the Hôtel d'Aiguillon.

The duke did not expect his uncle, and was preparing
to return to Luciennes to inform Mme. Dubarry that the
enemy had been unmasked, when the announcement of the
marshal's arrival roused his discouraged mind from its
torpor.

The duke hastened to meet his uncle, and took both his
hands in his with a warmth of affection proportionate to
the fear he had experienced. The marshal was as affectionate as the duke; the tableau was touching. The Duke
d'Aiguillon, however, was manifestly endeavoring to
hasten the period of explanation, while the marshal, on
the contrary, delayed it as much as possible, by looking at
the pictures, the bronzes, or the tapestry, and complain-
ing of dreadful fatigue.

The duke cut off the marshal's retreat, imprisoned him
in an armchair, as M. de Villars imprisoned the Prince
Eugene in Marchiennes, and commenced the attack.

"Uncle," said he, "is it true that you, the most discriminating man in France, have judged so ill of me as to
think that my self-seeking did not extend to us both?"

There was no longer room for retreat; Richelieu decided
on his plan of action.

"What do you mean by that?" replied he, "and in
what do you perceive that I judged unfavorably of you or
the reverse, my dear nephew?"

"Uncle, you are offended with me."

"But for what, and how?"

"Oh! these loop-holes, my lord marshal, will not serve
you; in one word, you avoid me when I need your assistance."

"Upon my honor, I do not understand you."

"I will explain, then. The king refused to nominate
you for his minister, and because I, on my part, accepted
the command of the light horse, you imagine that I have
deserted and betrayed you. That dear countess, too, who
loves you so well."

Here Richelieu listened eagerly, but not to his nephew's
words alone.

"You say she loves me well, this dear countess?" he
added.

"And I can prove it."

"But, my dear fellow, I never doubted it. I send for
you to assist me to push the wheel; you are younger, and
therefore stronger than I am; you succeed, I fail. That
is in the natural course of things, and, on my faith, I cannot imagine why you have all these scruples. If you have
acted for my interest you will be a hundred-fold repaid,
if against me—well! I shall only return the fisticuff.
Does that require explanation?"

"In truth, uncle——"

"You are a child, duke. Your position is magnificent;
a peer of France, a duke, commander of the light horse,
minister in six weeks—you ought to be beyond the influence of all futile intrigues. Success absolves, my dear
child. Suppose—I like apologues—suppose that we are
the two mules in the fable. But what noise is that?"

"Nothing, my dear uncle; proceed."

"There is something; I hear a carriage in the courtyard."

"Do not let it interrupt you, uncle, pray; your conversation interests me extremely. I like apologues too."

"Well, my friend, I was going to say that when you are prosperous, you will never meet with reproaches, nor need you fear the spite of the envious; but if you limp, if you fall—diable! you must take care—then it is that the wolf will attack you. But you see I was right, there is a noise in the antechamber; it is the portfolio which they are bringing you, no doubt. The little countess must have exerted herself for you."

The usher entered.

"Messieurs the Commissioners of the parliament!" said he, uneasily.

"Ha!" exclaimed Richelieu.

"The Commissioners of parliament here? What do they want with me?" replied the duke, not at all reassured by his uncle's smile.

"In the king's name!" cried a sonorous voice at the end of the antechamber.

"Oh, ho!" cried Richelieu.

M. d'Aiguillon turned very pale; he rose, however, and advanced to the threshold of the apartment to introduce the two commissioners, behind whom were stationed two motionless ushers, and in the distance a host of alarmed footmen.

"What is your errand here?" asked the duke, in a trembling voice.

"Have we the honor of speaking to the Duke d'Aiguillon?" said one of the commissioners.

"I am the Duke d'Aiguillon, gentlemen."

The commissioner, bowing profoundly, drew from his belt the act in proper form, and read it in a loud and distinct voice.

It was the decree, detailed, complete, and circumstantial, which declared D'Aiguillon gravely arraigned and prejudiced by suspicions even regarding matters which affected his honor, and suspended him from his functions as peer of the realm.

The duke listened to the reading like a man thunderstruck. He stood motionless as a statue on its pedestal, and did not even hold out his hand to take the copy of the decree which the commissioners of the parliament offered him.

It was the marshal who, also standing, but alert and nimble, took the paper, read it, and returned the bow of Messieurs the Commissioners. They were already at some distance from the mansion, before the Duke d'Aiguillon recovered from his stupor.

"This is a severe blow," said Richelieu; "you are no longer a peer of France; it is humiliating."

The duke turned to his uncle as if he had only at that moment recovered the power of life and thought.

"You did not expect it?" asked Richelieu, in the same tone.

"And you, uncle?" rejoined D'Aiguillon.

"How do you imagine any one could suspect that the parliament would strike so bold a blow at the favored courtier of the king and his favorite; these people will ruin themselves."

The duke sat down, and leaned his burning cheek on his hand.

"But if," continued the old marshal, forcing the dagger deeper into the wound, "if the parliament degrades you from the peerage because you are nominated to the command of the light horse, they will decree you a prisoner and condemn you to the stake, when you are appointed minister. These people hate you, D'Aiguillon; do not trust them."

The duke bore this cruel irony with the fortitude of a hero; his misfortune raised and strengthened his mind. Richelieu thought this fortitude was only insensibility, or want of comprehension, perhaps, and that the wound had not been deep enough.

"Being no longer a peer," said he, "you will be less exposed to the hatred of these lawyers. Take refuge in a few years of obscurity. Besides, look you, this obscurity, which will be your safeguard, will come without your seeking it. Deprived of your functions of peer, you will have more difficulty in reaching the ministry, and may perhaps escape the business altogether. But if you will struggle, my dear fellow, why, you have Madame Dubarry on your side; she loves you, and she is a powerful support."

M. d'Aiguillon rose. He· did not even cast an angry look upon the marshal in return for all the suffering the old man had inflicted upon him.

" You are right, uncle," he replied, calmly, " and your wisdom is shown in this last advice. The Countess Dubarry, whom you had the goodness to present to me, and to whom you spoke so favorably of me, and with so much zeal, that every one at Luciennes can bear witness to it, Madame Dubarry will defend me. Thanks to Heaven, she likes me; she is brave, and exerts an all-powerful influence over the mind of the king. Thanks, uncle, for your advice; I fly thither as to a haven of safety. My horses! Bourgignon—to Luciennes!"

The marshal remained in the middle of an unfinished smile. M. d'Aiguillon bowed respectfully to his uncle and quitted the apartment, leaving the marshal very much perplexed, and, above all, very much confused at the eagerness with which he had attacked this noble and feeling victim.

There was some consolation for the old marshal in the mad joy of the Parisians when they read in the evening the ten thousand copies of the decree which was scrambled for in the streets. But he could not help sighing when Rafte asked for an account of the evening. Nevertheless, he told it without concealing anything.

" Then the blow is parried?" said the secretary.

" Yes and no, Rafte; but the wound is not mortal, and we have at Trianon something better which I reproach myself for not having made my sole care. We have started two hares, Rafte; it was very foolish."

" Why—if you seized the best?" replied Rafte.

" Oh, my friend, remember that the best is always the one we have not taken, and we would invariably give the one we hold for the one which has escaped."

Rafte shrugged his shoulders, and yet M. de Richelieu was in the right.

" You think," said he, " that Monsieur d'Aiguillon will escape? Do you think the king will, simpleton?"

" Oh! the king finds an opening everywhere; but this matter does not concern the king, that I know of."

" Where the king can pass, Madame Dubarry will pass, as she holds fast by his skirts; where Madame Dubarry has passed, D'Aiguillon will pass also—but you understand nothing of politics, Rafte."

" My lord, Monsieur Flageot is not of your opinion."

" Well, what does this Monsieur Flageot say?   But the first of all, tell me what he is."

" He is a procureur, sir."

" Well? "

" Well! Monsieur Flageot thinks that the king cannot get out of this matter."

" Oh, ho! and who will stop the lion? "

" Faith, sir, the rat! "

" And you believe him? "

" I always believe a procureur who promises to do evil."

" We shall see what means Monsieur Flageot means to employ, Rafte."

" That is what I say, my lord."

" Come to supper, then, that I may get to bed.   It has quite upset me to see that my poor nephew is no longer a peer of France, and will not be minister.   I am an uncle, Rafte, after all."

M. de Richelieu sighed, and then commenced to laugh.

" You have every quality, however, requisite for a minister," replied Rafte.

CHAPTER XXXI.

M. D'AIGUILLON TAKES HIS REVENGE.

THE morning succeeding the day on which the terrible decree had thrown Paris and Versailles into an uproar, when every one was anxiously awaiting the result of this decree, the Duke de Richelieu, who had returned to Versailles, and had resumed his regularly irregular life, saw Rafte enter his apartment with a letter in his hand.   The secretary scrutinized and weighed this letter with such an appearance of anxiety, that his emotion quickly communicated itself to his master.

" What is the matter now ? " asked the marshal.

" Something not very agreeable, I presume, my lord, and which is inclosed in this letter."

" Why do you imagine so ? "

" Because the letter is from the Duke d'Aiguillon."

" Ha! " said the duke, " from my nephew ? "

" Yes, my lord marshal; after the king's council broke up, an usher of the chamber called on me and handed me this paper for you. I have been turning it over and over for the last ten minutes, and I cannot help suspecting that it contains some evil tidings."

The duke held out his hand.

" Give it me," said he, " I am brave."

" I warn you," interrupted Rafte, " that when the usher gave me the paper he chuckled outrageously."

" Diable! that bodes ill," replied the marshal; " but give it me, nevertheless."

" And he added: ' Monsieur d'Aiguillon wishes the marshal to have this immediately.' "

" Pain? thou shalt not make me say that thou art an evil," said the marshal, breaking the seal with a firm hand.

And he read it.

" Ha! you change countenance," said Rafte, standing with his hands crossed behind him, in an attitude of observation.

" Is it possible! " exclaimed Richelieu, continuing to read.

" It seems, then, that it is serious? "

" You look quite delighted."

" Of course—I see that I was not mistaken."

The marshal read on.

" The king is good," said he, after a moment's pause.

" He appoints Monsieur d'Aiguillon minister? "

" Better than that."

" Oh! What, then? "

" Read and ponder."

Rafte, in his turn, read the note. It was in the hand-

writing of D'Aiguillon, and was couched in the following
terms :

" MY DEAR UNCLE,—Your good advice has borne its
fruit ; I confided my wrongs to that excellent friend of our
house, the Countess Dubarry, who has deigned to lay them
at his majesty's feet. The king is indignant at the violence with which the gentlemen of the parliament pursue
me, and in consideration of the services I have so faithfully rendered him, his majesty, in this morning's council,
has annulled the decree of parliament, and has commanded me to continue my functions as peer of France.

" Knowing the pleasure this news will cause you, my
dear uncle, I send you the tenor of the decision, which his
majesty in council came to to-day. I have had it copied
by a secretary, and you have the announcement before any
one else.

" Deign to believe in my affectionate respect, my dear
uncle, and continue to bestow on me your good will and
advice.

(Signed)   " DUKE D'AIGUILLON."

" He mocks at me into the bargain ! " cried Richelieu.

" Faith, I think so, my lord."

" The king throws himself into the hornets' nest ! "

" You would not believe me yesterday when I told you
so."

" I did not say he would not throw himself into it, Rafte ;
I said he would contrive to get out of it ! Now you see
he does get out of it."

" The fact is, the parliament is beaten."

" And I also."

" For the present—yes."

" Forever. Yesterday I foresaw it, and you consoled me
so well, that some misfortune could not fail to ensue."

" My lord, you despair a little too soon, I think."

" Master Rafte, you are a fool. I am beaten, and I must
pay the stake. You do fully comprehend, perhaps, how
disagreeable it is to me to be the laughing-stock of Luciennes ; at this moment, the duke is mocking me in company
with Madame Dubarry ; Mademoiselle Chon and Monsieur

Jean are roaring themselves hoarse at my expense, while
the little negro ceases to stuff himself with sweetmeats
to make game of me. Parbleu! I have a tolerably good
temper, but all this makes me furious!"

" Furious, my lord? "

" I have said it—furious! "

" Then you have done what you should not have done,"
said Rafte, philosophically.

" You urged me on, Master Secretary."

" I? "

" Yes, you."

" Why, what is it to me whether Monsieur d'Aiguillon
is a peer of France or not—I ask you, my lord? Your
nephew does me no injury, I think."

" Master Rafte, you are impertinent."

" You have been telling me so for the last forty-nine
years, my lord."

" Well, I shall repeat it again."

" Not for forty-nine years more, that is one comfort."

" Rafte, is this the way you care for my interests——"

" The interests of your little passions? No, my lord
duke, never! Man of genius as you are, you sometimes
commit follies which I could not forgive even in an
understrapper like myself."

" Explain yourself, Rafte, and if I am wrong, I will
confess it."

" Yesterday you thirsted for vengeance, did you not?
You wished to behold the humiliation of your nephew;
you wished, as it were, to be the bearer of the decree of parliament; and gloat over the tremblings and palpitations of
your victim, as Monsieur Crebillon the younger says. Well,
my lord marshal, such sights as these must be well paid
for; such pleasures cost dear. You are rich—pay, pay,
my lord marshal! "

" What would you have done in my place, then, oh,
most skilful of tacticians? Come, let me see."

" Nothing. I would have waited without giving any
sign of life. But you itched to oppose the parliament to
the Dubarry, from the moment she found that Monsieur
d'Aiguillon was a younger man than yourself."

A grean was the marshal's only reply.

"Well!" continued Rafte, "the parliament was tolerably well prompted by you before it did what it has done. The decree once passed, you should have offered your services to your nephew, who would have suspected nothing."

"That is all well and good, and I admit that I did wrong; but you should have warned me."

"I hinder any evil! You take me for some one else, my lord marshal; you repeat to every one that comes that I am your creature, that you have trained me, and yet you would have me not delighted when I see a folly committed or a misfortune approaching! Fy, fy!"

"Then a misfortune will happen, Master Sorcerer?"

"Certainly."

"What misfortune?"

"You will quarrel, and Monsieur d'Aiguillon will become the link between the parliament and Madame Dubarry; then he will be minister, and you exiled, or at the Bastile."

The marshal in his anger upset the contents of his snuff-box upon the carpet.

"In the Bastile!" said he, shrugging his shoulders; "is Louis XV., think you, Louis XIV.?"

"No, but Madame Dubarry, supported by Monsieur d'Aiguillon, is quite equal to Madame Maintenon. Take care; I do not know any princess in the present day who would bring you bonbons and eggs."

"These are melancholy prognostics," replied the marshal, after a long silence. "You read the future; but what of the present, if you please?"

"My lord marshal is too wise for me to give him advice."

"Come, Master Witty-pate, are you, too, not mocking me?"

"I beg you to remark, my lord marshal, that you confound dates; a man is never called a witty-pate after forty; now I am sixty-seven."

"No matter, assist me out of this scrape—and quickly, too—quickly."

"By an advice?"

" By anything you please."

" The time has not come yet."

" Now you are certainly jesting."

" Would to Heaven I were! When I jest the subject shall be a jesting matter—and unfortunately this is not."

" What do you mean by saying that it is not time? "

" No, my lord, it is not time. If the announcement of the king's decree were known in Paris beforehand, I would not say, Shall we send a courier to the president, D'Aligre? "

" That they may laugh at us all the sooner? "

" What ridiculous self-love, my lord marshal! You would make a saint lose patience. Stay, let me finish my plan of a descent on England, and you can finish drowning yourself in your portfolio intrigue, since the business is already half done."

The marshal was accustomed to these sullen humors of his secretary. He knew that when his melancholy had once declared itself, he was dangerous to touch ungloved fingers.

" Come," said he, " do not pout at me, and if I did not understand, explain yourself."

" Then my lord wishes me to trace out a line of conduct for him? "

" Certainly, since you think I cannot conduct myself."

" Well, then, listen."

" I am all attention."

" You must send by a trusty messenger to Monsieur d'Aligre," said Rafte, abruptly, " the Duke d'Aiguillon's letter, and also the decree of the king in council. You must then wait till the parliament has met and deliberated upon it, which will take place immediately; whereupon you must order your carriage, and pay a little visit to your procureur, Monsieur Flageot."

" Eh? " said Richelieu, whom this name made start as it had done on the previous day; " Monsieur Flageot again! What the deuce has Monsieur Flageot to do with all this, and what am I to do at his house? "

" I have had the honor of telling you, my lord, that Monsieur Flageot is your procureur."

"Well! what, then?"

"Well, if he is your procureur, he has certain bags of yours—certain lawsuits on hand; you must go and ask him about them."

"To-morrow?"

"Yes, my lord marshal, to-morrow."

"But all this is your affair, Monsieur Rafte."

"By no means! by no means! When Monsieur Flageot was a simple scribbling drudge, then I could treat with him as an equal; but as, dating from to-morrow, Monsieur Flageot is an Attila, a scourge of kings—neither more nor less—it is not asking too much of a duke, a peer, a marshal of France, to converse with this all-powerful man."

"Is this serious, or are we acting a farce?"

"You will see to-morrow if it is serious, my lord."

"But tell me what will be the result of my visit to your Monsieur Flageot?"

"I should be very sorry to do so; you would endeavor to prove to me to-morrow that you had guessed it before-hand. Good night, my lord marshal. Remember; a courier to Monsieur d'Aligre immediately—a visit to Monsieur Flageot to-morrow. Oh! the address? The coachman knows it; he has driven me there frequently during the last week."

CHAPTER XXXII.

IN WHICH THE READER WILL ONCE MORE MEET AN OLD
ACQUAINTANCE WHOM HE THOUGHT LOST, AND WHOM
PERHAPS HE DID NOT REGRET.

THE reader will no doubt ask why M. Flageot is about to play so majestic a part in our story, was called procureur instead of avocat; and as the reader is quite right, we shall satisfy his curiosity.

The vacations had, for some time, been so frequent in the parliament, and the lawyers spoke so seldom, that their speeches were not worth speaking of. Master Flageot, foreseeing the time when there would be no pleading at all, made certain arrangements with Master Guildou, the procureur, in virtue of which the latter yielded him up office and clients in consideration of the sum of twenty-five thousand livres paid down. That is how Master Flageot became a procureur. But if we are asked how he managed to pay the twenty-five thousand livres, we reply, by marrying Mme. Marguerite, to whom this sum was left as an inheritance about the end of the year 1770—three months before M. de Choiseul's exile.

Master Flageot had been long distinguished for his persevering adherence to the opposition party. Once a procureur, he redoubled his violence; and by this violence succeeded in gaining some celebrity. It was this celebrity, together with the publication of an incendiary pamphlet on the subject of the conflict between M. d'Aiguillon and M. de la Chalotais, which attracted the attention of M. Rafte, who had occasion to keep himself well informed concerning the affairs of parliament.

But, notwithstanding his new dignity and his increasing importance, Master Flageot did not leave the Rue du Petit Lion St. Sauveur. It would have been too cruel a blow for Mme. Marguerite not to have heard the neighbors call her Mme. Flageot, and not to have inspired respect in the breast of M. Guildou's clerks, who had entered the service of the new procureur.

The reader may readily imagine what M. de Richelieu suffered in traversing Paris—the filthy Paris of that region—to reach the disgusting hole which the Parisian magistrature dignified with the name of street.

In front of M. Flageot's door M. de Richelieu's carriage was stopped by another carriage which pulled up at the same moment. The marshal perceived a woman's head-dress protruding from the window of this carriage, and as his sixty-five years of age had not quenched the ardor of his gallantry, he hastily jumped out on the muddy pavement, and proceeded to offer his hand to the lady, who was unaccompanied.

But this day the marshal's evil star was in the ascendant. A long, withered leg, which was stretched out to reach the step, betrayed the old woman. A wrinkled face, adorned with a dark streak of rouge, proved further that the old woman was not only old but decrepit.

Nevertheless, there was no room for retreat; the marshal had made the movement, and the movement had been seen. Besides, M. de Richelieu himself was no longer young. In the meantime, the litigant—for what woman with a carriage would have entered that street had she not been a litigant?—the litigant, we say, did not imitate the duke's hesitation; with a ghastly smile she placed her hand in Richelieu's.

"I have seen that face somewhere before," thought Richelieu; then he added:

"Does madame also intend to visit Monsieur Flageot?"

"Yes, duke," replied the old lady.

"Oh, I have the honor to be known to you, madame!" exclaimed the duke, disagreeably surprised, and stopping on the threshold of the dark passage.

"Who does not know the Duke de Richelieu?" was the reply. "I should not be a woman if I did not."

"This she-ape thinks that she is a woman!" murmured the conqueror of Mahon, and he made a most graceful bow.

"If I may venture to ask the question," added he, "to whom have I the honor of speaking?"

"I am the Countess de Béarn, at your service," replied the old lady, courtesying with courtly reverence upon the dirty floor of the passage, and about three inches from the open trap-door of a cellar, into which the marshal wickedly awaited her disappearance at the third bend.

"I am delighted, madame—enchanted," said he, "and I return a thousand thanks to fate. You also have lawsuits on hand, countess?"

"Oh, duke! I have only one; but what a lawsuit! Is it possible that you have never heard of it?"

"Oh, frequently, frequently—that great lawsuit. True; I entreat your pardon. How the deuce could I have forgotten that?"

"Against the Saluces?"

"Against the Saluces, yes, countess; the lawsuit about which the song was written."

"A song?" said the old lady, piqued; "what song?"

"Take care, madame; there is a trap-door here," said the duke, who saw that the old woman was decided not to throw herself into the cellar; "take hold of the balustrade—I mean, the cord."

The old lady mounted the first steps. The duke followed her.

"Yes, a very humorous song," said he.

"A humorous song on my lawsuit!"

"Dame! I shall leave you to judge—but perhaps you know it?"

"Not at all."

"It is to the tune of Bourbonnaise; it runs so:

> " ' Embarrassed, countess, as I stand,
> Give me, I pray, a helping hand,
> And I am quite at your command.'

It is Madame Dubarry who speaks, you must understand."

"That is very impertinent toward her."

"Oh! what can you expect? The ballad-mongers respect no one. Heavens! how greasy this cord is! Then you reply as follows:

> " ' I'm very old and stubborn, too;
> I'm forced at law my rights to sue;
> Ah, who can help me? tell me who?" '

"Oh, sir, it is frightful!" cried the countess; "a woman of quality is not to be insulted in this manner."

"Madame, excuse me, if I have sung out of tune; these stairs heat me so. Ah! here we are at last. Allow me to pull the bell."

The old lady, grumbling all the time, made way for the duke to pass.

The marshal rang, and Mme. Flageot, who, in becoming a procureur's wife, had not ceased to fill the functions of portress and cook, opened the door. The two litigants were ushered into M. Flageot's study, where they found that worthy in a state of furious excitement, and with a pen in his mouth, hard at work dictating a terrible plea to his head clerk.

" Good heavens, Master Flageot! what is the matter? "
cried the countess, at whose voice the attorney turned
round.

" Ah! madame, your most humble servant—a chair here
for the Countess de Béarn. This gentleman is a friend of
yours, madame, I presume. But surely—oh! I cannot be
mistaken—the Duke de Richelieu in my house! Another
chair, Bernardet—another chair."

" Master Flageot," said the countess, " how does my
lawsuit get on, pray? "

" Ah, madame! I was just now working for you."

" Very good, Master Flageot, very good."

" And after a fashion, my lady, which will make some
noise, I hope."

" Hum! Take care."

" Oh! madame, there is no longer any occasion for cau-
tion."

" Then if you are busy about my affair you can give an
audience to the duke."

" Excuse me, my lord duke," said Master Flageot, " you
are too gallant not to understand——"

" I understand, Master Flageot, I understand."

" But now I can attend to you exclusively."

" Don't be uneasy. I shall not abuse your good-nature;
you are aware what brings me here? "

" The bags which Monsieur Rafte gave me the other
day."

" Some papers relative to my lawsuit of—my suit about
—deuce take it! You must know which suit I mean,
Master Flageot? "

" Your lawsuit about the lands of Chapenat."

" Very probably; and will you gain it for me? That
would be very kind on your part."

" My lord, it is postponed indefinitely."

" Postponed! And why? "

" It will not be brought forward in less than a year, at
the earliest."

" For what reason, may I ask? "

" Circumstances, my lord, circumstances—you have
heard of his majesty's decree? "

"I think so—but which one?   His majesty publishes so many."

"The one which annuls ours."

"Very well; and what, then?"

"Well, my lord duke, we shall reply by burning our ships."

"Burning your ships, my dear friend?   You will burn the ships of the parliament?   I do not quite comprehend you—I was not aware that the parliament had ships."

"The first chamber refuses to register, perhaps?" inquired the Countess de Béarn, whom Richelieu's lawsuit in no way prevented from thinking of her own.

"Better than that."

"The second one also?"

"That would be a mere nothing.   Both chambers have resolved not to give any judgments until the king shall have dismissed Monsieur d'Aiguillon."

"Bah!" exclaimed the marshal, rubbing his hands.

"Not adjudicate! on what?" asked the countess, alarmed.

"On the lawsuits, madame."

"They will not adjudicate on my lawsuit," exclaimed the Countess de Béarn, with a dismay which she did not even attempt to conceal.

"Neither on yours, madame, nor the duke's."

"It is iniquitous!   It is rebellion against his majesty's orders, that!"

"Madame," replied the procureur, majestically, "the king has forgotten himself—we shall forget also."

"Monsieur Flageot, you will be sent to the Bastile, remember, I warn you."

"I shall go singing, madame, and if I am sent thither, all my fellow-members of parliament will follow me, carrying palms in their hands."

"He is mad!" said the countess to Richelieu.

"We are all the same," replied the procureur.

"Oh, ho!" said the marshal, "that is becoming rather curious."

"But, sir, you said just now that you were working for me," replied Madame de Béarn.

"I said so, and it is quite true.   You, madame, are the
first example I cite in my narration; here is the paragraph
which relates to you."

He snatched the draft from his clerk's hand, fixed his
spectacles upon his nose, and read with emphasis:

"Their position ruined, their fortune compromised, their
duties trampled under foot!   His majesty will understand
how much they must have suffered.   Thus the petitioner
had intrusted to his care a very important suit upon which
the fortune of one of the first families in the kingdom depends; by his zeal, his industry, and, he ventures to say,
his talents, this suit was progressing favorably, and the
rights of the most noble and most powerful lady, Ange-
lique Charlotte Veronique, Countess de Béarn, were on the
point of being recognized, proclaimed, when the breath
of discord—ingulfing——"

"I had just go so far, madame," said the procureur,
drawing himself up, "but I think the simile is not amiss."

"Monsieur Flageot," said the countess, "it is forty
years ago since I first employed your father, who proved
most worthy of my patronage; I continued that patronage
to you, you have gained ten or twelve thousand livres by
my suit, and you would probably have gained as many
more."

"Write down all that," said M. Flageot eagerly to his
clerk; "it is a testimony, a proof.   It shall be inserted in
the confirmation."

"But now," interrupted the countess, "I take back
all my papers from your charge; from this moment you
have lost my confidence."

Master Flageot, thunderstruck with this disgrace, remained for a moment almost stupefied; but all at once,
rising under the blow like a martyr who dies for his religion:

"Be it so," said he.   "Bernardet, give the papers back
to madame; and you will insert this fact," added he, "that
the petitioner preferred his conscience to his fortune."

"I beg your pardon, countess," whispered the marshal in the countess's ear, "but it seems to me that you have acted without reflection.'"

"In what respect, my lord duke?"

"You take back your papers from this honest procureur, but for what purpose?"

"To take them to another procureur, to another avocat!" exclaimed the countess.

Master Flageot raised his eyes to heaven, with a mournful smile of self-denial and stoic resignation.

"But," continued the marshal, still whispering in the countess's ear, "if it has been decided that the Chambers will not adjudicate, my dear madame, another procureur can do no more than Master Flageot."

"It is a league, then?"

"Pardieu! do you think Master Flageot fool enough to protest alone, to lose his practise alone, if his fellow-lawyers were not agred to do the same, and consequently support him?"

"But you, my lord duke, what will you do?"

"For my part, I declare that I think Master Flageot a very honest procureur, and that my papers are as safe in his possession as in my own. Consequently, I shall leave them with him, of course paying him as if my suit were going on."

"It is well said, my lord marshal, that you are a generous, liberal-minded man!" exclaimed Master Flageot; "I shall spread your fame far and wide, my lord."

"You absolutely overwhelm me, my dear procureur," replied Richelieu, bowing.

"Bernardet," cried the enthusiastic procureur to his clerk, "you will insert in the peroration a eulogy on Marshal de Richelieu."

"No, no! by no means, Master Flageot! I beg you will do nothing of the kind," replied the marshal, hastily. "Diable! that would be a pretty action! I love secrecy in what it is customary to call good actions. Do not disoblige me, Master Flageot—I shall deny it, look you—I shall positively contradict it—my modesty is susceptible. Well, countess, what say you?"

"I say my suit *shall* be judged. I must have a judgment, and I will.'"

"And I say, madame, that if your suit is judged, the king must first send the Swiss guards, the light horse, and twenty pieces of cannon into the great hall," replied Master Flagcot, with a belligerent air, which completed the consternation of the litigant.

"Then you do not think his majesty can get out of this scrape," said Richelieu, in a low voice to Flegeot.

"Impossible, my lord marshal. It is an unheard-of case. No more justice in France! It is as if you were to say, no more bread."

"Do you think so?"

"You will see."

"But the king will be angry."

"We are resolved to brave everything."

"Even exile?"

"Even death, my lord marshal! We have a heart, although we wear the gown."

And M. Flageot struck his breast vigorously.

"In fact, madame," said Richelieu to his companion, "I believe that this is an unfortunate step for the ministry."

"Oh, yes!" replied the old countess, after a pause, "it is very unfortunate for me, who never meddle in anything that passes, to be dragged into this conflict."

"I think, madame," said the marshal, "there is some one who could help you in this affair—a very powerful person. But would that person do it?"

"Is it displaying too much curiosity, duke, to ask the name of this powerful person?"

"Your goddaughter," said the duke.

"Oh! Madame Dubarry?"

"The same."

"In fact, that is true—I am obliged to you for the hint."

The duke bit his lips.

"Then you will go to Luciennes?" asked he.

"Without hesitation."

"But the Countess Dubarry cannot overcome the opposition of parliament."

"I will tell her I must have my suit judged, and as she can refuse me nothing, after the service I have rendered her, she will tell the king she wishes it. His majesty will speak to the chancellor, and the chancellor has a long arm, duke, Master Flageot, be kind enough to continue to study my case well; it may come on sooner than you think. Mark my words."

Master Flageot turned away his head with an air of incredulity which did not shake the countess in the least. In the meantime the duke had been reflecting.

"Well, madame, since you are going to Luciennes, will you have the goodness to present my most humble respects?"

"Most willingly, duke."

"We are companions in misfortune; your suit is in abeyance, and mine also. In supplicating for yourself you will do so for me, too. Moreover, you may express *yonder* the sort of pleasure these stubborn headed parliament men cause me; and you will add that it was I who advised you to have recourse to the divinity of Luciennes."

"I will not fail to do so, duke. Adieu, gentlemen."

"Allow me the honor of conducting you to your carriage."

"Once more adieu, Monsieur Flageot; I leave you to your occupations."

The marshal handed the countess to her carriage.

"Rafte was right," said he, "the Flageots will cause a revolution. Thank Heaven! I am supported on both sides —I am of the court, and of the parliament. Madame Dubarry will meddle with politics and fall, alone if she resists. I have my little pretty face at Trianon. Decidedly Rafte is of my school, and when I am minister he shall be my chief secretary."

CHAPTER XXXIII.

THE CONFUSION INCREASES.

MME. DE BEARN followed Richelieu's advice literally. Two hours and a half after the duke had left her, she was waiting in the antechamber at Luciennes, in the company of M. Zamore.

It was some time since she had been seen at Mme. Dubarry's, and her presence therefore excited a feeling of curiosity in the countess's boudoir when her name was announced.

M. d'Aiguillon had not lost any time either, and he was plotting with the favorite when Chon entered to request an audience for Mme. de Béarn. The duke made a movement to retire, but the countess detained him.

"I would rather you would remain," said she. "In case my old alms-giver comes to ask a loan, you would be most useful to me, for she will ask less."

The duke remained. Mme. de Béarn, with a face composed for the occasion, took the chair opposite the countess, which the latter offered her, and after the first civilities were exchanged:

"May I ask to what fortunate chance I am indebted for your presence, madame?" said Mme. Dubarry.

"Ah, madame!" said the old litigant, "a great misfortune."

"What! madame—a misfortune?"

"A piece of news which will deeply afflict his majesty."

"I am all impatience, madame——"

"The parliament——"

"Oh, ho!" grumbled the Duke d'Aiguillon.

"The Duke d'Aiguillon," said the countess, hastily introducing her guest to her lady visitor for fear of some unpleasant contretemps. But the old countess was as cunning as all the other courtiers put together, and never caused a misunderstanding, except willingly, and when the misunderstanding seemed likely to benefit her.

"I know," said she, "all the baseness of these lawyers, and their want of respect for merit and high birth."

This compliment, aimed directly at the duke, drew a most graceful bow from him, which the litigant returned with an equally graceful courtesy.

"But," continued she, "it is not the duke alone who is now concerned, but the entire population—the parliament refuse to act."

"Indeed!" exclaimed Mme. Dubarry, throwing herself back upon the sofa; "there will be no more justice in France. Well! What change will that produce?"

The duke smiled. As for Mme. de Béarn, instead of taking the affair pleasantly, her morose features darkened still more. "It is a great calamity, madame," said she.

"Ah! indeed?" replied the favorite.

"It is evident, madame, that you are happy enough to have no lawsuit."

"Hem!" said D'Aiguillon, to recall the attention of Mme. Dubarry, who at last comprehended the insinuation of the litigant.

"Alas! madame," said she, "it is true; you remind me that if I have no lawsuit, you have a very important one."

"Ah! yes, madame, and delay will be ruinous to me."

"Poor lady!"

"Unless, countess, the king takes some decided step."

"Oh! madame, the king is right well inclined to do so. He will exile Messieurs the Councilors, and all will be right."

"But, madame, that would be an indefinite adjournment."

"Do you see any remedy, then? Will you be kind enough to point it out to us?"

The litigant concealed her face beneath her hood, like Cæsar expiring under his toga.

"There is one remedy, certainly," said D'Aiguillon, "but perhaps his majesty might shrink from employing it."

"What is it?" asked the plaintiff, with anxiety.

"The ordinary resource of royalty, in France, when it is rather embarrassed. It is to hold a bed of justice, and to say, ' I will! ' when all the opponents say, ' I will not.' "

"An excellent idea!" exclaimed Mme. de Béarn, with enthusiasm.

"But which must not be divulged," replied D'Aiguillon, diplomatically, and with a gesture which Mme. de Béarn fully comprehended.

"Oh, madame!" said she instantly, "you who have so much influence with the king, persuade him to say, "I will have the suit of Madame de Béarn judged.' Besides, you know it was promised long ago."

M. d'Aiguillon bit his lips, glanced an adieu to Mme. Dubarry, and left the boudoir. He had heard the sound of the king's carriage in the courtyard.

"Here is the king," said Mme. Dubarry, rising to dismiss her visitor.

"Oh, madame! why will you not permit me to throw myself at his majesty's feet?"

"To ask him for a bed of justice?" replied the countess, quickly. "Most willingly! Remain here, madame, since such is your desire."

Scarcely had Mme. de Béarn adjusted her headdress when the king entered.

"Ah!" said he, "you have visitors, countess!"

"Madame de Béarn, sire."

"Sire, justice!" exclaimed the old lady, making a most profound reverence.

"Oh!" said Louis XV., in a bantering tone, imperceptible to those who did not know him, "has any one offended you, madame?"

"Sire, I ask for justice."

"Against whom?"

"Against the parliament."

"Ah! good," said the king, rubbing his hands; "you complain of my parliament. Well! do me the pleasure to bring them to reason. I too have to complain of them, and I beg you to grant me justice also," added he, imitating the courtesy of the old countess.

"But, sire, you are the king—the master."

"The king—yes; the master—not always."

"Sire, proclaim your will."

"I do that every evening, madame, and they proclaim

theirs every morning. Now, as these two wills are diametrically opposed to each other, it is with us as with the
earth and the moon which are ever running after each
other without meeting."

" Sire, your voice is powerful enough to drown all the
bawlings of these fellows."

" There you are mistaken. I am not a lawyer, as they
are. If I say yes, they say no—it is impossible for us to
come to any arrangement. If, when I have said yes, you
can find any means to prevent their saying no, I will make
an alliance with you."

" Sire, I have the means."

" Let me hear it quickly."

" I will, sire. Hold a bed of justice."

" That is another embarrassment," said the king; " a
bed of justice—remember, madame—is almost a revolution."

" It is simply telling these rebellious subjects that you
are the master. You know, sire, that when the king pro-
claims his will in this manner, he alone has a right .to
speak; no one answers. You say to them, *I will,* and they
bow their assent."

" The fact is," said the Countess Dubarry, " the idea is
a magnificent one."

" Magnificent it may be, but not good," replied Louis.

" But what a noble spectacle ! " resumed Mme. Dubarry,
with warmth; " the procession, the nobles, the peers, the
entire military staff to the king ! Then the immense crowd
of people; then the bed of justice, composed of five cushions embroidered with golden fleur-de-lis—it would be
a splendid ceremony."

" You think so ? " said the king, rather shaken in his
resolution.

" Then the king's magnificent dress—the cloak lined
with ermine, the diamonds in the crown, the golden scepter
—all the splendor which so well suits an august and noble
countenance. Oh ! how handsome you would look, sire ! "

" It is a long time since we had a bed of justice," said
Louis, with affected carelessness.

" Not since your childhood, sire," said Mme. de Béarn.

" The remembrance of your brilliant beauty on that occasion has remained engraven on the hearts of all."

" And then," added Mme. Dubarry, " there would be an excellent opportunity for the chancellor to display his keen and concise eloquence—to crush these people with his truth, dignity, and power."

" I must wait for the parliament's next misdeed," said Louis; " then I shall see."

" What can you wait for, sire, more outrageous than what they have just committed? "

" Why, what have they done? "

" Do you not know? "

" They have teased Monsieur d'Aiguillon a little, but that is not a hanging offense—although," said the king, looking at Mme. Dubarry, " although this dear duke is a friend of mine. Besides, if the parliament has teased the duke a little, I have punished them for their ill-nature by my decree of yesterday or the day before—I do not remember which. We are now even."

" Well, sire," said Mme. Dubarry, with warmth, " Madame de Bearn has just informed us that this morning these black-gowned gentlemen have taken the start of you."

" How so? " said the king, frowning.

" Speak, madame, the king permits it," said the favorite.

" Sire, the counselors have determined not to hold a court of parliament until your majesty yields to their wishes."

" What say you? " said the king. " You mistake, madame; that would be an act of rebellion, and my parliament dares not revolt, I hope."

" Sire, I assure you——"

" Oh, madame! it is a mere rumor."

" Will your majesty deign to hear me? "

" Speak, countess."

" Well, my procureur has this morning returned me all the papers relating to my lawsuit. He can no longer plead, since they will no longer judge."

" Mere reports, I tell you—attempts at intimidation."

But while he spoke, the king paced up and down the boudoir in agitation.

"Sire, will your majesty believe Monsieur de Richelieu, if you will not believe me? In my presence his papers were returned to him also, and the duke left the house in a rage."

"Some one is tapping at the door," said the king, to change the conversation.

"It is Zamore, sire."

Zamore entered.

"A letter, mistress," said he.

"With your permission, sire," said the countess. "Ah! good heavens!" exclaimed she, suddenly.

"What is the matter?"

"From the chancellor, sire. Monsieur de Maupeou, knowing that your majesty has deigned to pay me a visit, solicits my intervention to obtain an audience for him."

"What is in the wind now?"

"Show the chancellor in," said Mme. Dubarry. The Countess de Béarn rose to take her leave.

"You need not go, madame," said the king. "Good day, Monsieur de Maupeou. What news?"

"Sire," said the chancellor, bowing, "the parliament embarrassed you; you have no longer a parliament."

"How so? Are they all dead? Have they taken arsenic?"

"Would to heavens they had. No, sire, they live; but they will not sit any longer, and have sent in their resignations. I have just received them in a mass."

"The counselors?"

"No, sire, the resignations."

"I told you, sire, that it was a serious matter," said the countess, in a low voice.

"Most serious," replied Louis, impatiently. "Well, chancellor, what have you done?"

"Sire, I have come to receive your majesty's orders."

"We shall exile these people, Maupeou."

"Sire, they will not judge any better in exile."

"We shall command them to judge. Bah! injunctions are out of date—letters of order likewise——"

"Ah! sire, this time you must be determined."

"Yes, you are right."

"Courage!" said Mme. de Béarn, aside to the countess.

"And act the master, after too often having acted only the father," said the countess.

"Chancellor," said the king, slowly, "I know only one remedy; it is serious, but efficacious. I will hold a bed of justice; these people must be made to tremble once for all."

"Ah, sire!" exclaimed the chancellor, "that is well spoken; they must bend or break."

"Madame," added the king, addressing Mme. de Béarn, "if your suit be not judged, you see it will not be my fault."

"Sire, you are the greatest monarch in the world!"

"Oh! yes," echoed the countess, Chon and the chancellor.

"The world does not say so, however," murmured the king.

CHAPTER XXXIV.

THE BED OF JUSTICE.

THIS famous bed of justice took place with all the ceremonies which royal pride, on the one hand, and the intrigues which drove the master to this step, on the other, demanded.

The household of the king was placed under arms; an abundance of short-robed archers, soldiers of the watch, and police officers were commissioned to protect the lord chancellor, who, like a general upon the decisive day, would have to expose his sacred person to secure the success of the enterprise.

The chancellor was execrated. Of this he was well aware, and if his vanity made him fear assassination, those better versed in the sentiments of the public toward him could, without exaggerating, have predicted some downright insults, or at least hootings, as likely to fall to his share. The same perquisites were promised to M. d'Aiguillon, who was equally obnoxious to the popular instincts, improved perhaps by parliamentary debates. The king affected serenity, yet he was not easy. But he donned with great satisfaction his magnificent robes, and straightway came to the conclusion that nothing protects so surely as majesty. He might have added, " and the love of the people." But this phrase had been so frequently repeated to him at Metz during his illness, that he imagined he could not repeat it now without being guilty of plagiarism.

The dauphiness, for whom the sight was a new one, and who at heart perhaps wished to see it, assumed her plaintive look, and wore it during the whole way to the ceremony—which disposed public opinion very favorably toward her.

Mme. Dubarry was brave. She possessed that confidence which is given by youth and beauty. Besides, had not everything been said that could be said of her. What could be added now? She appeared radiant with beauty, as if the splendor of her august lover had been reflected upon her.

The Duke d'Aiguillon marched boldly among the peers who preceded the king. His noble and impressive countenance betrayed no symptoms of grief or discontent, nor did he bear himself triumphantly. To see him walking thus, none would have guessed that the struggle of the king with his parliament was on his account.

The crowd pointed him out in the crowd, terrible glances were darted at him from the parliament, and that was all. The great hall of the Palais was crammed to overflowing; actors and spectators together made a total of more than three thousand persons.

Outside the Palais the crowd, kept in order by the staves of the officers, and the batons and maces of the archers, gave token of its presence only by that indescribable hum which is not a voice, which articulates nothing, but which nevertheless makes itself heard, and which may justly be called the sound of the popular flood.

The same silence reigned in the great hall, when, the sound of footsteps having ceased, and every one having

taken his place, the king, majestic and gloomy, had commanded his chancellor to begin the proceedings.

The parliament knew beforehand what the bed of justice
held in reserve for them. They fully understood why they
had been convoked. They were to hear the unmitigated
expression of the royal will; but they knew the patience,
not to say the timidity, of the king, and if they feared, it
was rather for the consequences of the bed of justice, than
for the sitting itself.

The chancellor commenced his address. He was an excellent orator; his exordium was clever, and the amateurs
of a demonstrative style found ample scope for study in
it. As it proceeded, however, the speech degenerated into
a tirade so severe, that all the nobility had a smile on
their lips, while the parliament felt very ill at ease.

The king, by the mouth of his chancellor, ordered them
to cut short the affairs of Brittany, of which he had had
enough. He commanded them to be reconciled to the Duke
d'Aiguillon, whose services pleased him; and not to interrupt the service of justice; by which means everything
should go on as in that happy period of the golden age,
when the flowing streams murmured judicial or argumen-
tative discourses, when the trees were loaded with bags of
law papers, placed within reach of the lawyers and attor-
neys, who had the right to pluck them as fruit belonging
to them.

These flippancies did not reconcile the parliament to the
lord chancellor, nor to the Duke d'Aiguillon. But the
speech had been made, and all reply was impossible.

The members of the parliament, although scarcely able
to contain their vexation, assumed, with that admirable
unity which gives so much strength to constituted bodies,
a calm and indifferent demeanor, which highly displeased
his majesty and the aristocratic world upon the platform.

The dauphiness turned pale with anger. For the first
time she found herself in the presence of popular resistance, and she coldly calculated its power. She had come
to this bed of justice with the intention of opposing, at
least by her look, the resolution which was about to be
adopted there, but gradually she felt herself drawn to

make common cause with those of her own caste and race, so that in proportion as the chancellor attacked the parliament more severely, this proud young creature was indignant to find his words so weak. She fancied she could have found words which would have made this assembly start like a troop of oxen under the goad. In short, she found the chancellor too feeble and the parliament too strong.

Louis XV. was a physiognomist, as all selfish people would be if they were not sometimes idle as well as selfish. He cast a glance around to observe the effect of his will, expressed in words which he thought tolerably eloquent. The paleness and the compressed lip of the dauphiness showed him what was passing in her mind. As a counterpoise he turned to look at Mme. Dubarry; but instead of the victorious smile he hoped to find there, he only saw an anxious desire to attract the king's looks, as if to judge what he thought. Nothing intimidates weak minds so much as being forestalled by the minds and wills of others. If they find themselves observed by those who have already taken a resolution, they conclude that they have not done enough—that they are about to be, or have been ridiculous—that people had a right to expect more than they have done.

Then they pass to extremes; the timid man becomes furious, and a sudden manifestation betrays the effect of this reaction produced by fear upon a fear less powerful than itself.

The king had no need to add a single word to those his chancellor had already spoken; it was not according to etiquette—it was not even necessary. But on this occasion he was possessed by the babbling demon, and, making a sign with his hand, he signified that he intended to speak. Immediately attention was changed to stupor.

The heads of the members of parliament were all seen to wheel round toward the bed of justice, with the precision of a file of soldiers upon drill. The princes, peers, and military felt uneasy. It was not impossible that after so many excellent things had been said, his most Christian majesty might add something which, to say the least, would be quite useless. Their respect prevented them from giving any other title to the words which might fall from the royal lips.

M. de Richelieu, who had affected to keep aloof from his nephew, was now seen to approach the most stubborn of the parliamentarians, and exchange a glance of mysterious intelligence. But his glances, which were becoming rebellious, met the penetrating eye of Mme. Dubarry. Richelieu possessed, as no one else did, the precious power of transition; he passed easily from the satirical to the admiring tone, and chose the beautiful countess as the point of intersection between these two extremes. He sent a smile of gallantry and congratulation, therefore, to Mme. Dubarry in passsing, but the latter was not duped by it; the more so that the old marshal, who had commenced a correspondence with the parliament, and the opposing princes, was obliged to continue it, that he might not appear what he really was.

What sights there are in a drop of water—that ocean for an observer. What centuries in a second—that indescribable eternity. All we have related took place while Louis was preparing to speak, and was opening his lips.

" You have heard," said he in a firm voice, " what my chancellor has told you of my wishes. Prepare therefore to execute them, for such are my intentions, and I shall never change them ! "

Louis XV. uttered these last words with the noise and force of a thunderbolt. The whole assembly was literally thunder-struck.

A shudder passed over the parliament, and was quickly communicated, like an electric spark, to the crowd. A like thrill was felt by the partisans of the king. Surprise and admiration were on every face and in every heart.

The dauphiness involuntarily thanked the king by a lightning glance from her beautiful eyes. Mme. Dubarry, electrified, could not refrain from rising, and would have clapped her hands, but for the very natural fear of being stoned as she left the house, or of receiving hundreds of couplets the next morning, each more odious than the other.

Louis could from this moment enjoy his triumph. The parliament bent low, still with the same unanimity. The king rose from his embroidered cushions. Instantly the captain of the guards, the commandant of the household, and all the gentlemen of the king's suite rose. Drums beat and trumpets sounded outside. The almost silent stir of the people on the arrival was now changed into a deep murmur, which died away in the distance, repressed by the soldiers and archers.

The king proudly crossed the hall, without seeing anything on the way but humble foreheads. The Duke d'Aiguillon still preceded his majesty without abusing his triumph.

The chancellor, having reached the door of the hall, saw the immense crowd of people extending on all sides, and heard their execrations, which reached his ears, notwithstanding the distance. He trembled, and said to the archers:

" Close around me."

M. de Richelieu bowed low to the Duke d'Aiguillon, as he passed, and whispered:

" These heads are very low, duke—some day or other they will rise devilish high. Take care! "

Mme. Dubarry was passing at the moment, accompanied by her brother, the Marchioness de Mirepoix, and several other ladies. She heard the marshal's words, and as she was more inclined to repartee than malice, she said:

" Oh, there is nothing to fear, marshal; did you not hear his majesty's words? The king, I think, said he would never change."

" Terrible words, indeed, madame," replied the duke, with a smile; " but happily for us, these poor parliament men did not remark that while saying he would never change, the king looked at you."

And he finished this compliment with one of those inimitable bows which are no longer seen, even upon the stage.

Mme. Dubarry was a woman, and by no means a politician. She only saw the compliment where D'Aiguillon detected plainly the epigram and the threat. Therefore, she replied with a smile, while her ally turned pale and bit his lips with vexation, to see the marshal's anger endure so long.

The effect of the bed of justice was, for the moment, favorable to the royal cause. But it frequently happens that a great blow only stuns, and it is remarked that after the stunning effect has passed away, the blood circulates with more vigor and purity than before. Such at least were the reflections made by a little group of plainly dressed persons, who were stationed as spectators at the corner of the Quai aux Fleurs and the Rue de la Barillerie, on seeing the king, attended by his brilliant cortége, leave the hall.

They were three in number. Chance had brought them together at this corner, and from thence they seemed to study with interest the impressions of the crowd; and, without knowing each other, after once exchanging a few words, they had discussed the sitting even before it was over.

"These passions are well ripened," said one of them, an old man with bright eyes, and a mild and honest expression. "A bed of justice is a great work."

"Yes," replied a young man, smiling bitterly; "yes, if the work realize the title."

"Sir," replied the old man, turning around, "I think I should know you—I fancy I have seen you before."

"On the night of the thirty-first of May. You are not mistaken, Monsieur Rousseau."

"Oh! you are that young surgeon—my countryman, Monsieur Marat."

"Yes, sir, at your service."

The two men exchanged salutations. The third had not yet spoken. He was also young, eminently handsome, and aristocratic in appearance, and during the whole ceremony had unceasingly observed the crowd. The young surgeon moved away the first and plunged into the densest mass of the people, who, less grateful than Rousseau, had already forgotten him, but whose memory he calculated upon refreshing one day or other.

The other young man waited until he was gone, and then, addressing Rousseau:

" Sir," said he, " you do not go? "

" Oh! I am too old to venture among such a mob."

" In that case," said the unknown, lowering his voice; " I will see you again this evening in the Rue Plastriere, Monsieur Rousseau—do not fail."

The philosopher started as if a phantom had risen before him. His complexion, always pale, became livid. He made an effort to reply to this strange appeal, but the man had already disappeared.

CHAPTER XXXV.

THE INFLUENCE OF THE WORDS OF THE UNKNOWN UPON J. J. ROUSSEAU.

On hearing those singular words, spoken by a man whom he did not know, Rousseau, trembling and unhappy, plunged into the crowd; and without remembering that he was old and naturally timid, elbowed his way through it. He soon reached the bridge of Notre Dame; then, still plunged in his reverie, and muttering to himself, he crossed the quarter of La Grève, which was the shortest way to his own dwelling.

" So," said he to himself, " this secret, which the initiated guard at the peril of their lives, is in possession of the first comer. This is what mysterious associations gain by passing through the popular sieve. A man recognizes me, who knows that I shall be his associate, perhaps his accomplice, yonder. Such a state of things is absurd and intolerable."

And while he spoke, Rousseau walked forward quickly —he, usually so cautious, especially since his accident in the Rue Menil Montant.

" Thus," continued the philosopher, " I must wish, forsooth, to sound the bottom of these plans of human regeneration which some spirits who boast of the title of *illuminati* propose to carry out. I was foolish enough to imagine that any good ideas could come from Germany— that land of beer and fog—and may have compromised my name by joining it to those of fools or plotters, whom it will serve as a cloak to shelter their folly. Oh, no! it shall not be thus; no, a flash of lightning has shown me the abyss, and I will not cheerfully throw myself into it."

And Rousseau paused to take a breath, resting upon his cane, and standing motionless for a moment.

" Yet it was a beautiful chimera," pursued the philosopher. " Liberty in the midst of slavery—the future conquered without noise and struggle—the snare mysteriously woven while earth's tyrants slept. It was too beautiful; I was a fool to believe it. I will not be the sport of fears, of suspicions, of shadows, which are unworthy of a free spirit and an independent body."

He had got thus far, and was continuing his progress, when the sight of some of M. de Sartines' agents gazing around with their ubiquitous eyes, frightened the free spirit, and gave such an impulse to the independent body, that it plunged into the deepest shadows of the pillars under which it was walking.

From these pillars it was not far to the Rue Plastriere. Rousseau accomplished the distance with the speed of lightning, ascended the stairs to his domicile—breathing like a stag pursued by the hunters—and sunk upon a chair, unable to utter a word in answer to all Therese's questions.

At last he recovered sufficiently to account for his emotion; it was the walk, the heat, the news of the king's angry remarks at the bed of justice, the commotion caused by the popular terror—a sort of panic, in short, which had spread among all who witnessed what had happened.

Therese grumblingly replied that all that was no reason for allowing the dinner to cool; and that, moreover, a man ought not to be such a soft chicken-hearted wretch as to be frightened at the least noise.

Rousseau could make no reply to this last argument, which he himself had so frequently stated in other terms.

Therese added, that these philosophers, these imagina-

tive people, were all the same, that they always talked
very grandly in their writings; they said that they feared
nothing; that God and man were very little to them; but,
at the slightest barking of the smallest poodle, they cried
" Help! " at the least feverishness they exclaimed, " Oh,
heavens, I am dead."

This was one of Therese's favorite themes, that which
most excited her eloquence, and to which Rousseau, who
was naturally timid, found it most difficult to reply.
Rousseau, therefore, pursued his own thoughts to the
sound of this discordant music—thoughts which were certainly well worth Therese's, notwithstanding the abuse the
latter showered so plentifully on him.

" Happiness," said he, " is composed of perfume and
music; now, noise and odor are conventional things. Who
can prove that the onion smells less sweet than the rose,
or the peacock sings less melodiously than the nightin-
gale? "

After which axiom, which might pass for an excellent
paradox, they sat down to table.

After dinner, Rousseau did not as usual sit down to
his harpischord. He paced up and down the apartment
and stopped a hundred times to look out of the window,
apparently studying the physiogonomy of the Rue Plastriere. Therese was forthwith seized with one of those
fits of jealousy which peevish—that is to say, the least
really jealous—people in the world often indulge in for
the sake of opposition. For if there is a disagreeable affectation in the world, it is the affectation of a fault; the
affectation of virtue may be tolerated.

Therese, who held Rousseau's age, complexion, mind,
and manners in the utmost contempt—who thought him
old, sickly, and ugly—did not fear that any one should run
off with her husband; she never dreamed that other women
might look upon him with different eyes from herself.
But as the torture of jealousy is woman's most dainty
punishment, Therese sometimes indulged herself in this
treat. Seeing Rousseau, therefore, approaching the window so frequently, and observing his dreaming and restless air, she said:

"Very good; I understand your agitation—you have just left some one."

Rousseau turned to her with a startled look which served as an additional proof of the truth of her suspicions.

"Some one you wish to see again," she continued.

"What do you say?" asked Rousseau.

"Yes, we make assignations, it seems."

"Oh!" said Rousseau, comprehending that Therese was jealous—"an assignation! You are mad, Therese."

"I know perfectly well that it would be madness in you," said she; "but you are capable of any folly. Go—go, with your papier-maché complexion, your palpitations and your coughs—go, and make conquests. It is one way of getting on in the world."

"But, Therese, you know there is not a word of truth in what you are saying," said Rousseau, angrily; "let me think in peace."

"You are a libertine," said Therese, with the utmost seriousness.

Rousseau reddened as if she had hit the truth, or as if he had received a compliment.

Therese forthwith thought herself justified in putting on a terrible countenance, turning the whole household upside down, slamming the doors violently, and playing with Rousseau's tranquillity, as children with those metal rings which they shut up in a box and shake to make a noise. Rousseau took refuge in his closet; this uproar had rather confused his ideas.

He reflected that there would doubtless be some danger in not being present at the mysterious ceremony of which the stranger had spoken at the corner of the quai.

"If there are punishments for traitors, there will also be punishments for the lukewarm or careless," thought he. "Now I have always remarked that great dangers mean in reality nothing, just like loud threats. The cases in which either are productive of any result are extremely rare; but petty revenges, underhand attacks, mystifications, and other such small coin—these we must be on our guard against. Some day the masonic brothers may repay my contempt by stretching a string across my staircase; I shall stumble over it and break a leg or the six or eight teeth I have left. Or else they will have a stone ready to fall upon my head when I am passing under a scaffolding; or, better still, there may be some pamphleteer belonging to the fraternity, living quite near me, upon the same floor, perhaps, looking from his windows into my room. That is not impossible, since the reunions take place even in the Rue Plastriere. Well! this wretch will write stupid lampoons on me, which will make me ridiculous all over Paris. Have I not enemies everywhere?"

A moment afterward Rousseau's thoughts took a different turn.

"Well," said he to himself, "but where is courage? where is honor? Shall I be afraid of myself? Shall I see in my glass only the face of a coward—a slave? No, it shall not be so. If the whole world should combine to ruin me—if the very street should fall upon me—I will go. What pitiable reasoning does fear produce? Since I met this man, I have been continually turning in a circle of absurdities. I doubt every one, and even myself. That is not logical—I know myself. I am not an enthusiast; if I thought I saw wonders in this projected association, it is because there are wonders in it. Who will say I may not be the regenerator of the human race, I who am sought after, I whom on the faith of my writings the mysterious agents of an unlimited power have eagerly consulted? Shall I retreat when the time has come to follow up my word, to substitute practise for theory?"

Rousseau became animated.

"What can be more beautiful. Ages roll on; the people rise out of their brutishness; step follows step into the darkness, hand follows hand into the shadows; the immense pyramid is raised, upon the summit of which, as its crowning glory, future ages shall place the bust of Rousseau, citizen of Geneva, who risked his liberty, his life, that he might act as he had spoken—that he might be faithful to his motto: *Vitam impendere vero."*

Thereupon Rousseau, in a fit of enthusiasm, seated himself at his harpsichord, and exalted his imagination by the loudest, the most sonorous, and most warlike melodies he could call forth from its sounding cavity.

Night closed in. Therese, wearied with her vain endeavors to torment her captive, had fallen asleep upon her chair. Rousseau, with a beating heart, took his new coat as if to go out on a pleasure excursion, glanced for a moment in the glass at the play of his black eyes, and he was charmed to find that they were sparkling and expressive.

He grasped his knotted stick in his hand, and slipped out of the room without awakening Therese. But when he arrived at the foot of the stairs, and had drawn back the bolt of the street door, Rousseau paused and looked out, to assure himself as to the state of the locality.

No carriage was passing; the street, as usual, was full of idlers gazing at one another, as they do at this day, while many stopped at the shop windows to ogle the pretty girls. A newcomer would therefore be quite unnoticed in such a crowd. Rousseau plunged into it; he had not far to go. A ballad-singer with a cracked violin was stationed before the door which had been pointed out to him. This music, to which every true Parisian ear is extremely sensitive, filled the street with echoes which repeated the last bars of the air sung by the violin or by the singer himself. Nothing could be more unfavorable, therefore, to the free passage along the street than the crowd gathered at this spot, and the passers-by were obliged to turn either to the right or left of the group. Those who turned to the left took the center of the street, those to the right brushed along the side of the house indicated, and *vice versa*.

Rousseau remarked that several of these passers-by disappeared on the way as if they had fallen into some trap. He concluded that these people had come with the same purpose as himself, and determined to imitate their maneuver. It was not difficult to accomplish. Having stationed himself in the rear of the assembly of listeners, as if to join their number, he watched the first person whom he saw entering the open alley. More timid than they, probably because he had more to risk, he waited until a particularly favorable opportunity should present itself.

He did not wait long. A cabriolet which drove along the street divided the circle, and caused the two hemispheres to fall back upon the houses on either side. Rousseau thus found himself driven to the very entrance of the passage; he had only to walk on. Our philosopher observed that all the idlers were looking at the cabriolet and had turned their backs on the house; he took advantage of this circumstance, and disappeared in the dark passage.

After advancing a few steps he perceived a lamp, beneath which a man was seated quietly, like a stall-keeper after the day's business was over, and read, or seemed to read, a newspaper. At the sound of Rousseau's footsteps this man raised his head and visibly placed his finger upon his breast, upon which the lamp threw a strong light. Rousseau replied to this symbolic gesture by raising his finger to his lips.

The man then immediately rose, and, pushing open a door at his right hand, which door was so artificially concealed in the wooden panel of which it formed a part as to be wholly invisible, he showed Rousseau a very steep staircase, which descended underground. Rousseau entered, and the door closed quickly but noiselessly after him.

The philosopher descended the steps slowly, assisted by his cane. He thought it rather disrespectful that the brothers should cause him, at this his first interview, to run the risk of breaking his neck or his legs.

But the stairs, if steep, was not long. Rousseau counted seventeen steps, and then felt as if suddenly plunged into a highly heated atmosphere.

The moist heat proceeded from the breath of a considerable number of men who were assembled in the low hall. Rousseau remarked that the walls were tapestried with red and white drapery, on which figures of various implements of labor, rather symbolic doubtless than real, were depicted. A single lamp hung from the vaulted ceiling, and threw a gloomy light upon the faces of those present, who were conversing with one another on the wooden

benches, and who wore the appearance of honest and respectable citizens.

The floor was neither polished nor carpeted, but was
covered with a thick mat of plaited rushes, which dead-
ened the sound of the footsteps. Rousseau's entrance,
therefore, produced no sensation.

No one seemed to have remarked it.

Five minutes previously Rousseau had longed for nothing so much as such an entrance; and yet, when he had
entered, he felt annoyed that he had succeeded so well.
He saw an unoccupied place on one of the back benches,
and installed himself as modestly as possible on this seat,
behind all the others.

He counted thirty-three heads in the assembly. A desk,
placed upon a platform, seemed to wait for a president.

CHAPTER XXXVI.

THE HOUSE IN THE RUE PLASTRIERE.

ROUSSEAU remarked that the conversation of those
present was very cautious and reserved. Many did not
open their lips; and scarcely three or four couples exchanged a few words.

Those who did not speak endeavored even to conceal
their faces, which was not difficult—thanks to the great
body of shadow cast by the platform of the expected
president. The refuge of these last, who seemed to be the
timid individuals of the assembly, was behind this platform. But in return, two or three members of this corpo-
ration gave themselves a great deal of trouble to recognize
their colleagues. They came and went, talked among
themselves, and frequently disappeared through a door before which was drawn a black curtain ornamented with
red flames.

In a short time a bell was rung. A man immediately
rose from the end of the bench upon which he was seated,
and where he was previously confounded with the other
freemasons, and took his place upon the platform.

After making some signs with the hands and fingers, which were repeated by all those present, and adding a last sign more explicit than the others, he declared the sitting commenced.

This man was entirely unknown to Rousseau. Beneath the exterior of a working-man in easy circumstances, he concealed great presence of mind, aided by an elocution as flowing as could have been wished for in an orator.

His speech was brief and to the point. He declared that the lodge had been assembled to proceed to the election of a new brother.

" You will not be surprised," said he, " that we have assembled you in a place where the usual trials cannot be attempted. These trials have seemed useless to the chiefs; the brother whom we are to receive to-day is one of the lights of contemporary philosophy—a thoughtful spirit who will be devoted to us from conviction, not from fear. One who has discovered all the mysteries of nature and of the human heart cannot be treated in the same manner as the simple mortal from whom we demand the help of his arm, his will, and his gold. In order to have the co-operation of his distinguished mind, of his honest and energetic character, his promise and his assent are sufficient."

The speaker, when he had concluded, looked round to mark the effect of his words.

Upon Rousseau the effect had been magical; the Genevese philosopher was acquainted with the preparatory mysteries of freemasonry, and looked upon them with the repugnance natural to enlightened minds. The concessions, absurd because they were useless, which the chiefs required from the candidates, this simulating fear when every one knew there was nothing to fear, seemed to him to be the acme of puerility and senseless superstition.

Besides this, the timid philosopher, an enemy to all personal exhibitions and manifestations, would have felt most unhappy had he been obliged to serve as a spectacle for people whom he did not know, and who would have certainly mystified him more or less.

To dispense with these trials in his case was therefore

more than a satisfaction to him. He knew the strictness with which equality was enforced by the masonic principles, therefore an exception in his favor constituted a triumph.

He was preparing to say some words in reply to the gracious address of the president, when a voice was heard among the audience.

"At least," said this voice, which was sharp and discordant, "since you think yourself obliged to treat in this princely fashion a man like ourselves, since you dispense in his case with physical pains, as if the pursuit of liberty through bodily suffering were not one of our symbols, we hope you will not confer a precious title upon an unknown person without having questioned him according to the usual ritual, and without having received his profession of faith."

Rousseau turned round to discover the features of the aggressive person who so rudely jostled his triumphant car, and with the greatest surprise recognized the young surgeon whom he had that morning met upon the Quai aux Fleurs. A conviction of his own honesty of purpose, perhaps also a feeling of disdain for the precious title, prevented him from replying.

"You have heard?" said the president, addressing Rousseau.

"Perfectly," replied the philosopher, who trembled slightly at the sound of his voice as it echoed through the vaulted roof of the dark hall, "and I am more surprised at the interpellation when I see from whom it proceeds. What! A man whose profession it is to combat what is called physical suffering, and to assist his brethren, who are common men as well as freemasons—preaches the utility of physical suffering! He chooses a singular path through which to lead the creature to happiness, the sick to health."

"We do not here speak of this or that person," replied the young man warmly; "I am supposed to be unknown to the candidate, and he to me. I am merely the utterer of an abstract truth, and I assert that the chief has done wrong in making an exception in favor of any one. I do not recognize in him," pointing to Rousseau, " the philosopher, and he must not recognize the surgeon in me. We shall walk side by side through life, without a look or gesture betraying our intimacy, which, nevertheless, thanks to the laws of the association, is more binding than all vulgar friendships. I repeat, therefore, that if it has been thought well to spare this candidate the usual trials, he ought at least to have the usual questions put to him."

Rousseau made no reply. The president saw depicted on his features disgust at this discussion, and regret at having engaged in the enterprise.

" Brother," said he authoritatively to the young man, " you will please be silent when the chief speaks, and do not venture on light grounds to blame his actions, which are sovereign here."

" I have a right to speak," replied the young man, more gently.

" To speak, yes; but not to blame. The brother who is about to enter our association is so well known that we have no wish to add to our masonic relations a ridiculous and useless mystery. All the brothers here present know his name, and his name itself is a perfect guarantee. But as he himself, I am certain, loves equality, I request him to answer the questions which I shall put to him merely for form."

" What do you seek in this association ? "

Rousseau made two steps forward in advance of the crowd, and his dreamy and melancholy eyes wandered over the assembly.

" I seek," said he, " that which I do not find—truths, not sophisms. Why should you surround me with poniards which do not wound, with poisons which are only clear water, and with traps under which mattresses are spread? I know the extent of human endurance. I know the vigor of my physical frame. If you were to destroy it, it would not be worth your while to elect me a brother, for when dead I could be of no use to you. Therefore you do not wish to kill me, still less to wound me; and all the doctors in the world would not make me approve of an initiation in the course of which my limbs had been broken. I have served a longer apprenticeship to pain than any of you; I have sounded the body, and probed even to the soul. If I consented to come among you when I was solicited "— and he laid particular emphasis on the word—" it was because I thought I might be useful. I give, therefore; I do not receive. Alas! before you could do anything to defend me, before you could restore me to liberty were I imprisoned—before you could give me bread if 1 were starving, or consolation were I afflicted—before, I repeat, you could do anything—the brother whom you admit to-day, if this gentleman," turning to Marat, " permits it— this brother will have paid the last tribute of nature; for progress is halting, light is slow, and from the grave into which he will be thrown, none of you can raise him."

" You are mistaken, illustrious brother," said a mild and penetrating voice, which charmed Rousseau's ear; " there is more than you think in the association into which you are about to enter; there is the whole future destiny of the world. The future, you are aware, is hope —is science; the future is God, who will give His light to the world, since he has promised to give it, and God cannot lie."

Astonished at this elevated language, Rousseau looked around and recognized the young man who had made the appointment with him in the morning at the bed of justice. This man, who was dressed in black, with great neatness, and, above all, with a marked air of distinction in his appearance, was leaning against the side of the plat-form, and his face, illumined by the lamp, shone in all its beauty, grace, and expressiveness.

" Ah!" said Rousseau, " science—the bottomless abyss! You speak to me of science, consolation, futurity, hope; another speaks of matter, of rigor, and of violence; whom shall I believe? Shall it be then in this assembly of brothers, as it is among the devouring wolves of the world which stirs above us? Wolves and sheep! Listen to my profession of faith since you have not read it in my books."

" Your books!" exclaimed Marat. " They are sublime. I confess it; but they are Utopias. You are useful in the same point of view as Pythagoras, Solon, and Cicero the sophist. You point out the good; but it is an artificial, unsubstantial, unattainable good. You are like one who would feed a hungry crowd with air-bubbles, more or less illumined by the sun."

"Have you ever seen," said Rousseau, frowning, "great commotions of nature take place without preparation? Have you seen the birth of a man—that common and yet sublime event? Have you not seen him collect substance and life in the womb of his mother for nine months? Ah! you wish me to regenerate the world with actions? That is not to regenerate, sir—it is to revolutionize."

"Then," retorted the young surgeon, violently, "you do not wish for independence—you do not wish for liberty?"

"On the contrary," replied Rousseau, "independence is my idol—liberty is my goddess. But I wish for a mild and radiant liberty—a liberty which warms and vivifies. I wish for an equality which will connect men by ties of friendship, not by fear. I wish for education, for the instruction òf each element of the social body, as the mechanic wishes for harmonious movement—as the cabinet-maker wishes for the perfect exactness, for the closest fitting, in each piece of his work. I repeat it, I wish for that which I have written—progress, concord, devotion."

A smile of disdain flitted over Marat's lips.

"Yes," he said, "rivulets of milk and honey. Elysian fields like Virgil's poetic dreams, which philosophy would make a reality."

Rousseau made no reply. It seemed to him too hard that he should have to defend his moderation—he whom all Europe called a violent innovation.

He took his seat in silence, after having satisfied his ingenuous and timid mind by appealing for and obtaining the tacit approbation of the person who had just before defended him.

The president rose.

"You have all heard?" said he.

"Yes," replied the entire assembly.

"Does the candidate appear to you worthy of entering the association, and does he comprehend its duties?"

" Yes," replied the assembly again; but this time with a reserve which did not evince much unanimity.

" Take the oath," said the president to Rousseau.

" It would be disagreeable to me," said the philosopher, with some pride, " to displease any members of this association; and I must repeat the words I made use of just now, as they are the expression of my earnest conviction. If I were an orator, I would put them in a more eloquent manner; but my organ of speech is rebellious, and always betrays my thoughts when I ask it for an immediate translation. I wish to say that I can do more for the world and for you out of this assembly than I could were I strictly to follow your usages. Leave me, therefore, to my work, to my weakness, to my loneliness. I have told you I am descending to the grave; grief, infirmity, and want hurry me on. You cannot delay this great work of nature. Abandon me; I am not made for the society of men; I hate and fly them. Nevertheless, I serve them, because I am a man myself; and in serving them I fancy them better than they are. Now you have my whole thoughts; I shall not say another word."

" Then you refuse to take the oath?" said Marat, with some emotion.

" I refuse positively; I do not wish to join the association. I see too many convincing proofs to assure me that I should be useless to it."

" Brother," said the unknown personage with the conciliatory voice, " allow me to call you so, for we are brothers, independently of all combinations of the human mind—brother! do not give way to a very natural feeling of irritation; sacrifice your legitimate pride; do for us what is repulsive to yourself. Your advice, your ideas, your presence, are light to our paths. Do not plunge us in the two-fold darkness of your absence and your refusal."

" You are in error," said Rousseau; " I take nothing from you, since I should never have given you more than I have given to the whole world—to the first chance reader, to the first consulter of the journals. If you wish for the name and essence of Rousseau——"

" We do wish for them!" said several voices, politely.

" Then make a collection of my books ; place them upon the table of your president ; and when you are taking the opinions of the meeting, and my turn to give one comes, open my books—you will find my counsel and my vote there."

Rousseau made a step toward the door.

" Stop one moment," said the surgeon; " mind is free, and that of the illustrious philosopher more than any other ; but it would not be regular to have allowed a stranger even to enter our sanctuary, who, not being bound by any tacit agreement, might, without dishonesty, reveal our mysteries."

Rousseau smiled compassionately.

" You want an oath of secrecy ? " said he.

" You have said it."

" I am ready."

" Be good enough to read the formula, venerable brother," said Marat.

The venerable brother read the following form of oath:

" I swear, in the presence of the eternal God, the architect of the universe, and before my superiors, and the respectable assembly which surrounds me, never to reveal or to make known or write anything which has happened in my presence, under penalty, in case of indiscretion, of being punished according to the laws of the Great Founder, of my superiors, and the anger of my fathers."

Rousseau had already raised his hand to swear, when the unknown, who had followed the progress of the debate with a sort of authority which no one seemed to dispute, although he was not distinguished from the crowd, approached the president, and whispered some words in his ear.

" True," said the venerable chief; and he added:

" You are a man, not a brother ; you are a man of honor, placed toward us only in the position of a fellowman. We here abjure, therefore, our distinguishing peculiarity, and ask from you merely your word of honor to forget what has passed between us."

" Like a dream of the morning—I swear it upon my honor." said Rousseau, with emotion.

With these words he retired, and many of the members followed him.

CHAPTER XXXVII.

THE REPORT.

WHEN the members of the second and third orders had gone, seven associates remained in the lodge. They were the seven chiefs. They recognized one another by means of signs, which proved their initiation to a superior degree.

Their first care was to close the doors. Then their president made himself known by displaying a ring, on which were engraved the mysterious letters, L. P. D.*

This president was charged with the most important correspondence of the order. He was in communication with the six other chiefs, who dwelt in Switzerland, Russia, America, Sweden, Spain, and Italy.

He brought with him some of the most important documents he had received from his colleagues, in order to communicate their contents to the superior circles of initiated brothers, who were above the others but beneath him.

We have already recognized this chief—it was Balsamo.

The most important of the letters contained a threatening advice. It was from Sweden, and written by Swedenborg.

" Watch the South, brothers," he said; " under its burning rays has been hatched a traitor who will ruin you.

" Watch in Paris, brothers—the traitor dwells there; he possesses the secrets of the order; a feeling of hatred urges him on.

" A murmuring voice, a rustling flight, whispers the denunciation in my ear. I see a terrible vengeance coming, but perhaps it will be too late. In the meantime, brothers, watch! watch! A traitorous tongue, even though it be uninstructed, is sometimes sufficient to overthrow our most skilfully constructed plans."

* Lilia pedibus destrue.

The brothers looked at one another in mute surprise. The language of the fierce old sage, his prescience which had acquired an imposing authority from many striking examples, contributed in no small degree to cast a gloom over the meeting at which Balsamo presided. Balsamo himself, who placed implicit faith in Swedenborg's second sight, could not resist the saddening influence which this letter had on the assembly.

"Brothers," said he, "the inspired prophet is rarely deceived. Watch, then, as he bids you. You know now, as I do, that the struggle commences. Let us not be conquered by these ridiculous enemies, whose power we sap in the utmost security. You must not forget that they have mercenary swords at their command. It is a powerful weapon in this world, among those who do not see beyond the limits of our terrestrial life. Brothers, let us distrust these hired traitors."

"These fears seem to me puerile," said a voice; "we gather strength daily, and we are directed by brilliant genius and powerful hands."

Balsamo bowed his thanks for the flattering eulogy.

"Yes, but as our illustrious president has said, treason creeps everywhere," replied a brother, who was no other than the surgeon Marat, promoted, notwithstanding his youth, to a superior grade, in virtue of which he now sat for the first time on a consulting committee. "Remember, brothers, that by doubling the bait, you make a more important capture. If Monsieur de Sartines, with a bag of crown-pieces, can purchase the revelations of one of our obscurer brothers, the minister, with a million, or with holding out the hope of advancement, may buy over one of our superiors. Now, with us, the obscurer brother knows nothing. At the most, he is cognizant of the names of some of his colleagues, and these names signify nothing. Ours is an excellent constitution, but it is an eminently aristocratic one; the inferiors know nothing, can do nothing. They are called together to say or to hear trifles, and yet they contribute their time and their money to increase the solidity of our edifice. Reflect that the workman brings only the stone and the mortar, but without stone and mortar could you build the house? Now, the workman receives a very small salary, but I consider him equal to the architect who plans, creates, and superintends the whole work; and I consider him equal because he is a man, and in the eyes of a philosopher one man is worth as much as another, seeing that he bears his misfortunes and his fate equally, and, because, even more than another man, he is exposed to the fall of a stone or the breaking of a scaffold."

"I must interrupt you, brother," said Balsamo. "You diverge from the question which alone ought to occupy our thoughts. Your failing, brother, is that you are over-zealous, and apt to generalize discussions. Our business on the present occasion is not to decide whether our constitution be good or bad, but to uphold the integrity of that constitution in all its strength. If I wished, however, to discuss the point with you, I would answer, no; the instrument which receives the impulse is not equal to the architect; the brain is not the equal of the arm."

"Suppose Monsieur de Sartines should seize one of our least important brethren," cried Marat, warmly, "would he not send him to rot in the Bastile equally with you or me?"

"Granted; but the misfortune in that case is for the individual only, not for the order, which is with us the all-important point. If, on the contrary, the chief were imprisoned, the whole conspiracy is at an end. When the general is absent, the army loses the battle. Therefore, brother, watch over the safety of the chiefs."

"Yes, but let them in return watch over ours."

"That is their duty."

"And let their faults be doubly punished."

"Again, brother, you wander from the constitution of the order. Have you forgotten that the oath which binds all the members of the association is the same, and threatens all with the same punishment?"

"The great ones always escape."

"That is not the opinion of the great themselves, brother. Listen to the conclusion of the letter which one of the greatest among us, our prophet Swedenborg, has written. This is what he adds:

" ' The blow will come from one of the mighty ones, one of the mightiest of the order; or if it comes not directly from him, the fault will be traceable to him. Remember that fire and water may be accomplices; one gives light, the other revelation.

" ' Watch, brothers, over all and over each, watch ! ' "

" Then," said Marat, seizing upon those points in Balsamo's speech and Swedenborg's letter which suited his purpose, " let us repeat the oath which binds us together, and let us pledge ourselves to maintain it in its utmost vigor, whosoever he may be who shall betray us, or be the cause of our betrayal."

Balsamo paused for a moment, and then rising from his seat, he pronounced the consecrated words, with which our readers are already acquainted, in a slow, solemn, terrible voice.

" In the name of the crucified Son, I swear to break all the bonds of nature which unite me to father, mother, brother, sister, wife, relation, friend, mistress, king, benefactor, and to any being whatsoever to whom I have promised faith, obedience, gratitude, or service !

" I swear to reveal to the chief, whom I acknowledge according to the statutes of the order, all that I have seen or done, read or guessed, and even to search out and penetrate that which may not of itself be openly present to my eyes.

" I will honor poison, steel, and fire as a means of ridding the world, by death or idiocy, of the enemies of truth and liberty.

" I subscribe to the law of silence. I consent to die, as if struck by lightning, on the day when I shall have merited this punishment, and I await without murmuring the knife which will reach me in whatsoever part of the world I may be."

Then, the seven men who composed this solemn assembly repeated the oath, word for word, standing, and with uncovered heads.

When the words of the oath had been repeated by all:

"We are now guaranteed against treachery," said Balsamo; "let us no longer mingle extraneous matter with our discussion. I have to make my report to the committee of the principal events of the year.

"My summary of the affairs of France may have interest for enlightened and zealous minds like yours; I will commence with it.

"France is situated in the center of Europe, as the heart in the center of the body; it lives and radiates life. It is in its palpitations that we must look for the cause of all the disorder in the general organization.

"I came to France, therefore, and approached Paris as a physician approaches the heart. I listened, I felt, I experimented. When I entered it a year ago, the monarchy harassed it; to-day, vices kill it. I required to hasten the effect of these fatal debauches, and therefore I assisted them.

"An obstacle was in my way; this obstacle was a man, not only the first, but the most powerful man in the state, next to the king.

"He was gifted with some of those qualities which please other men. He was too proud, it is true, but his pride was applied to his works. He knew how to lighten the hardships of the people by making them believe and even feel sometimes that they were a portion of the state; and by sometimes consulting them on their grievances, he raised a standard around which the mass will always rally—the spirit of nationality.

"He hated the English, the natural enemies of the French; he hated the favorite, the natural enemy of the working classes. Now, if this man had been a usurper—if he had been one of us—if he would have trodden in our path, acted for our ends, I would have assisted him, I would have kept him in power, I would have upheld him by the resources I am able to create for my protégés; for, instead of patching up decayed royalty, he would have assisted us in overthrowing it on the appointed day. But he belonged to the aristocracy; he was born with a feeling of respect for that first rank, to which he could not aspire, for the monarchy, which he dared not attack; he served royalty while despising the king; he did worse—he acted as a shield to this royalty against which our blows were directed. The parliament and the people, full of respect for this living dyke which opposed itself to any encroachment on the royal prerogative, limited themselves to a moderate resistance, certain as they were of having in him a powerful assistant when the moment should arrive.

"I understood the position—I undertook Monsieur de Choiseul's fall.

"This laborious task, at which for ten years so much hatred and interest had labored in vain, I commenced and terminated in a few months, by means which it would be useless to reveal to you. By a secret which constitutes one of my powers—a power the greater because it will remain eternally hidden from the eyes of all, and will manifest itself only by its effects—I overthrew and banished Monsieur de Choiseul, and attached to his overthrow a long train of regret, disappointment, lamentation, and anger.

"You see now that my labor bears its fruit; all France asks for Choiseul, and rises to demand him back, as orphans turn to heaven when God has taken away their earthly parents.

"The parliament employs the only right it possesses—inertia; it has ceased to act. In a well-organized body, as a state of the first rank ought to be, the paralysis of any essential organ is fatal. Now, the parliament in the social is what the stomach is in the human body. When the parliament ceases to act, the people—the intestines of the state—can work no longer; and, consequently, must cease to pay, and the gold—that is, the blood—will be wanting.

"There will be a struggle, no doubt; but who can combat against the people? Not the army—that daughter of the people—which eats the bread of the laborer and drinks the wine of the vine-grower. There remain then the king's household, the privileged classes, the guards, the Swiss, the musketeers—in all, scarce five or six thousand men. What can this handful of pygmies do when the nation will rise like a giant?"

" Let them rise, then—let them rise ! " cried several
voices.

" Yes, yes ! to the work ! " exclaimed Marat.

" Young man, I have not yet consulted you," said Balsamo, coldly. " This sedition of the masses," continued
he, " this revolt of the weak, become strong by their number, against the powerful, single-handed—less thoughtful,
less ripened, less experienced minds would stimulate immediately, and would succeed with a facility which terrifies me ; but I have reflected and studied—I have mixed
with the people, and, under their dress, with their perseverance, even their coarseness, I have viewed them so
closely, that I have made myself, as it were, one of themselves. I know them now ; I cannot be deceived in them.
They are strong, but ignorant ; irritable, but not revengeful. In a word, they are not yet ripe for sedition
such as I mean and wish for. They want the instruction
which will make them see events in the double light of
example and utility ; they want the memory of their past
experience.

" They resemble those daring young men whom I have
seen in Germany, at the public festivals, eagerly climb a
vessel's mast, at the top of which were hung a ham and a
silver cup. They started at first burning with eagerness,
and mounted with surprising rapidity ; but when they had
almost reached the goal—when they had only to extend the
arm to seize their prize--their strength abandoned them,
and they slipped to the bottom amid the hootings of the
crowd.

" The first time it happened as I told you ; the second
time they husbanded their strength and their breath ; but
taking more time, they failed by their slowness, as they
had before failed from too great haste. At last—the third
time—they took a middle course between precipitation and
delay, and this time they succeeded. This is the plan I
propose : efforts—never-ceasing efforts—which gradually
approach the goal, until the day arrives when infallible
success will crown our attempts."

Balsamo ceased, and looked around upon his audience,

among whom the passions of youth and inexperience were boiling over.

"Speak, brother," said he to Marat, who was more agitated than the others.

"I will be brief," said he. "Efforts soothe the people when they do not discourage them. Efforts! that is the theory of Monsieur Rousseau, citizen of Geneva, a great poet, but a slow and timid genius—a useless citizen, whom Plato would have driven from his republic. Wait! Ever wait! Since the emancipation of the commons, since the revolt of the *mailotins*—for seven centuries we have waited! Count the generations which have died in the meantime, and then dare to pronounce the fatal word, *wait!* as your motto of the future. Monsieur Rousseau speaks to us of opposition, as it was practised in the reign of the Grand Monarque—as Molière practised it in his comedies, Bolieu in his satires, and Lafontaine in his fables—whispering in the ear of marchionesses, and prostrating it at the feet of kings. Poor and feeble opposition, which has not advanced the cause of humanity one jot. Lisping children recite these sudden theories without understanding them, and go to sleep while they recite. Rabelais was also a politician, in your sense of the word; but at such politics people laugh, and correct nothing. Have you seen one single abuse redressed for the last three hundred years? Enough of poets and theoreticians. Let us have deeds, not words. We have given France up to the care of physicians for three hundred years, and it is time now that surgery should enter in its turn, scalpel and saw in hand. Society is gangrened; let us stop the gangrene with the steel. He may wait, who rises from his table to recline upon a couch of roses, from which the ruffled leaves are blown by the breath of his slaves; for the satisfied stomach exhales grateful vapors which mount into the brain, and recreate and vivify it. But hunger, misery, despair, are not satiated nor consoled with verses, with sentences and fables. They cry out loudly in their sufferings; deaf indeed must he be who does not hear their lamentations—accursed he who does not reply to them! A revolt, even should it be crushed, will enlighten the minds more

than a thousand years of precepts, more than three centuries of examples. It will enlighten the kings, if it does
not overthrow them. That is much—that is enough!"

A murmur of admiration rose from several lips.

"Where are our enemies?" pursued Marat. "Above
us. They guard the doors of the palaces, they surround
the steps of the throne. Upon this throne is their palladium, which they guard with more care and with more fear
than the Trojans did theirs. This palladium, which
makes them all-powerful, rich, and insolent, is royalty.
This royalty cannot be reached save by passing over the
bodies of those who guard it, as one can only reach the
general by overthrowing the battalion by which he is surrounded. Well! History tells us of many battalions
which have been captured—many generals who have been
overthrown—from Darius down to King John, from Reg-
ulus down to Duguesclin.

"If we overthrow the guard, we reach the idol. Let us
begin by striking down the sentinels—we can afterward
strike down the chief. Let the first attack be on the courtiers, the nobility, the aristocracy; the last will be upon the
kings. Count the privileged heads; there are scarcely two
hundred thousand. Walk through this beautiful garden,
called France, with a sharp switch in your hand, and cut
down these two hundred thousand heads as Tarquin did
the poppies of Latium, and all will be done. There will
then be only two powers opposed to each other, the people
and the kingship. Then let this kingship, the emblem,
try to struggle with the people, this giant—and you will
see! When dwarfs wish to overthrow a colossus, they commence with the pedestal. When the woodmen wish to cut
down the oak, they attack it at the foot. Woodmen! woodmen! seize the hatchet—attack the oak at its roots, and
the ancient tree with its proud branches will soon bite
the dust!"

"And will crush you like pygmies in its fall, unfortunate wretches that you are!" exclaimed Balsamo, in a voice
of thunder. "Ah! you rail against the poets, and you
speak in metaphors even more poetical and more imagina-
tive than theirs! Brother, brother!" continued he, ad-

dressing Marat, " I tell you, you have quoted these sentences from some romance which you are composing in your garret ! "

Marat reddened.

" Do you know what a revolution is? " continued Balsamo; " I have seen two hundred, and can tell you. I have seen that of ancient Egypt, that of Assyria, those of Rome and Greece, and that of the Netherlands. I have seen those of the Middle Ages, when the nations rushed one against the other—East against the West, West against the East—and murdered without knowing why. From the Shepherd Kings to our own time there have been, perhaps, a hundred revolutions, and yet now you complain of being slaves. Revolutions, then, have done no good. And why? Because those who caused the revolution were all struck with the same vertigo—they were too hasty. Does God, who presides over the revolutions of the world, as genius presides over the revolutions of men—does He hasten?

" ' Cut down the oak ! ' you cry. And you do not calculate that the oak, which needs but a second to fall, covers as much ground when it falls as a horse at a gallop would cross in thirty seconds? Now, those who throw down the oak, not having time to avoid the unforeseen fall, would be lost, crushed, killed beneath its immense trunk. That is what you want, is it not? You will never get that from me. I shall be patient. I carry my fate—yours—the world's—in the hollow of this hand. No one can make me open this hand, full of overwhelming truth, unless I wish to open it. There is thunder in it, I know. Well, the thunder-bolt shall remain in it, as if hidden in the murky cloud. Brethren, brethren ! descend from these sublime heights, and let us once more walk upon the earth.

" Sirs, I tell you plainly, and from my inmost soul, that the time has not yet come. The king who is on the throne is the last reflection of the great monarch whom the people still venerate; and in this fading monarchy there is yet something dazzling enough to outweigh the lightning shafts of your petty anger. This man was born a king, and will die a king. His race is insolent but pure. You can read his origin on his brow, in his gestures, in his words—he will always be king. Overthrow him, and the same will happen to him as happened to Charles the First —his executioners will kneel before him, and the courtiers who accompanied him in his misfortune, like Lord Capel, will kiss the ax which struck off the head of their master.

"Now, sirs, you all know that England was too hasty. King Charles the First died upon the scaffold, indeed; but King Charles the Second, his son, died upon the throne.

"Wait! wait, brethren, for the time will soon be propitious. You wish to destroy the lilies. That is our motto—*Lilia pedibus destrue.* But not a single root must leave the flower of St. Louis the hope of blooming again. You wish to destroy royalty, to destroy royalty forever! You must first weaken her prestige, as well as her essence. You wish to destroy royalty! Wait till royalty is no longer a sacred office, but merely a trade—till it is practised in a shop, not in a temple. Now, what is most sacred in royalty—viz., the legitimate transmission of the throne, authorized for centuries by God and the people—is about to be lost forever. Listen, listen! This invincible, this impervious barrier between us nothings and these *quasi-* divine creatures—this limit which the people have never dared to cross, and which is called legitimacy—this word, brilliant as a lighted watch-tower, and which until now has saved the royal family from shipwreck—this word will be extinguished by the breath of a mysterious fatality!

"The dauphiness—called to France to perpetuate the race of kings by the admixture of imperial blood—the dauphiness, married now for a year to the heir of the French crown—approach, brethren, for I fear to let the sound of my words pass beyond your circle——"

"Well?" asked the six chiefs, with anxiety.

"Well, brethren, the dauphiness will never have an heir, or if one be born to her, he will die early."

A sinister murmur, which would have frozen the monarchs of the world with terror had they heard it—such deep hatred, such revengeful joy did it breathe—escaped like a deadly vapor from the little circle of six heads, which almost touched one another, Balsamo's being bent over them from his rostrum.

" Now, gentlemen, you know this year's work; you see the progress of our mines. Be assured that we shall only succeed by the genius and the courage of some, who will serve as the eyes and the brain—by the perseverance and labor of others, who will represent the arms—by the faith and the devotion of others again, who will be the heart.

" Above all, remember the necessity of a blind submission, which ordains that even your chief must sacrifice himself to the will of the statutes of the order, whenever those statutes require it.

" After this, gentlemen, and beloved brothers, I would dissolve the meeting, if there were not still a good act to perform, an evil to point out.

" The great writer who came among us this evening, and who would have been one of us but for the stormy zeal of one of our brothers who alarmed his timid soul—this great author proved himself in the right before our assembly, and I deplore it as a misfortune that a stranger should be victorious before a majority of brothers who are imperfectly acquainted with our rules, and utterly ignorant of our aim.

" Rousseau, triumphing over the truths of our association with the sophisms of his books, represents a fundamental vice which I would extirpate by steel and fire, if I had not the hope of curing it by persuasion. The self-love of one of our brothers has developed itself most unfortunately. He has given us the worst in the discussion. No similar fact, I trust, will again present itself, or else I shall have recourse to the laws of discipline.

" In the meantime, gentlemen, propagate the faith by gentleness and persuasion. Insinuate it; do not impose it —do not force it into rebellious minds with wedges and blows, as the inquisitors tortured their victims. Remember that we cannot be great until after we have been acknowledged good; and that we cannot be acknowledged good but by appearing better than those who surround us. Remember, too, that among us the great, the good, the best, are nothing without science, art, and faith—nothing, in short, compared with those whom God has marked with a peculiar stamp, as if giving them an authority to govern over men and rule empires.

"Gentlemen, the meeting is dissolved."

After pronouncing these words, Balsamo put on his hat and folded himself in his cloak.

Each of the initiated left in his turn, alone and silently, in order not to awaken suspicion.

CHAPTER XXXVIII.

THE BODY AND THE SOUL.

THE last who remained beside the master was Marat, the surgeon. He was very pale, and humbly approached the terrible orator, whose power was unlimited.

"Master," said he, "have I indeed committed a fault?"

"A great one, sir," said Balsamo; "and, what is worse, you do not believe that you have committed one."

"Well, yes; I confess that not only do I not believe that I committed a fault, but I think that I spoke as I ought to have done."

"Pride, pride!" muttered Balsamo; "pride—destructive demon! Men combat the fever in the blood of the patient; they dispel the plague from the water and the air —but they let pride strike such deep roots in their hearts that they cannot exterminate it."

"Oh, master!" said Marat, "you have a very despicable opinion of me. Am I indeed so worthless that I cannot count for anything among my fellows? Have I gathered the fruits of my labor so ill that I cannot utter a word without being taxed with ignorance? Am I such a lukewarm adept that my earnestness is suspected? If I had no other good quality, at least I exist through my devotion to the holy cause of the people."

"Sir," replied Balsamo, "it is because the principle of good yet struggles in you against the principle of evil, which appears to me likely to carry you away one day, that

I will try to correct these defects in you. If I can succeed—if pride has not yet subdued every other sentiment
in your breast—I shall succeed in one hour."

" In one hour? " said Marat.

" Yes; will you grant me that time? "

" Certainly."

" Where shall I see you? "

" Master, it is my place to seek you in any place you may
choose to point out to your servant."

" Well," said Balsamo, " I will come to your house."

" Mark the promise you are making, master. I live in
an attic in the Rue des Cordeliers. An attic, remember! "
said Marat, with an affectation of proud simplicity, with a
boasting display of poverty, which did not escape Balsamo
—" while you——"

" Well, while I? "

" While you, it is said, inhabit a palace."

Balsamo shrugged his shoulders, as a giant who looks
down with contempt on the anger of a dwarf.

" Well, even so, sir," he replied; " I will come to see you
in your garret."

" And when, sir? "

" To-morrow."

" At what time? "

" In the morning."

" At daybreak I go to my lecture-room, and from thence
to the hospital."

" That is precisely what I want. I would have asked
you to take me with you, had you not proposed it."

" But early, remember," said Marat; " I sleep little."

" And I do not sleep at all," replied Balsamo. " At daybreak, then."

" I shall expect you."

Thereupon they separated, for they had reached the
door opening on the street, now as dark and solitary as it
had been noisy and populous when they entered. Balsamo turned to the left, and rapidly disappeared. Marat
followed his example, striding toward the right with his
long, meager limbs.

Balsamo was punctual; the next morning, at six o'clock,

he knocked at Marat's door, which was the center one of six opening on a long corridor which formed the topmost story of an old house in the Rue des Cordeliers.

It was evident that Marat had made great preparations to receive his illustrious guest. The small bed of walnut-tree, and the wooden chest of drawers beside it, shone bright beneath the sturdy arm of the charwoman who was busily engaged scrubbing the decayed furniture.

Marat himself lent a helping hand to the old woman, and was refreshing the withered flowers which were arranged in a blue delf pot, and which formed the principal ornament of the attic. He still held a duster underneath his arm, which showed that he had not touched the flowers until after having given a rub to the furniture.

As the key was in the door, and as Balsamo had entered without knocking, he interrupted Marat in his occupation. Marat, at the sight of the master, blushed much more deeply than was becoming in a true stoic.

"You see, master," said he, stealthily throwing the telltale cloth behind a curtain, "I am a domestic man, and assist this good woman. It is from preference that I choose this task, which is, perhaps, not quite plebeian, but it is still less aristocratic."

"It is that of a poor young man who loves cleanliness," said Balsamo, coldly, "nothing more. Are you ready sir? You know my moments are precious."

"I have only to slip on my coat, sir. Dame Grivette, my coat! She is my portress, sir—my footman, my cook, my housekeeper, and she costs me one crown a month."

"Economy is praisworthy," said Balsamo; "it is the wealth of the poor, and the wisdom of the rich."

"My hat and cane!" said Marat.

"Stretch out your hand," said Balsamo; "there is your hat, and no doubt this cane which hangs beside your hat is yours."

"Oh, I beg your pardon, sir; I am quite confused."

"Are you ready?"

"Yes, sir. My watch, Dame Grivette."

Dame Grivette bustled about the room as if in search of something, but did not reply.

"You have no occasion for a watch, sir, to go to the amphitheater and the hospital; it will perhaps not be easily found, and that would cause some delay."

"But, sir, I attach great value to my watch, which is an excellent one, and which I bought with my savings." '

"In your absence, Dame Grivette will look for it," replied Balsamo, with a smile; "and if she searches carefully, it will be found when you return."

"Oh, certainly," said Dame Grivette, "it will be found, unless monsieur has left it somewhere else. Nothing is lost here."

"You see," said Balsamo. "Come, sir, come!"

Marat did not venture to persist, and followed Balsamo, grumbling.

When they reached the door, Balsamo said:

"Where shall we go first?"

"To the lecture-room, if you please, master; I had marked a subject which must have died last night of acute meningitis. I want to make some observations on the brain, and I do not wish my colleagues to take it from me."

"Then let us go to the amphitheater, Monsieur Marat."

"Moreover, it is only a few yards from here; the amphitheater is close to the hospital, and I shall only have to go in for a moment; you may even wait for me at the door."

"On the contrary, I wish to accompany you inside, and hear your opinion of this subject."

"When it was alive, sir?"

"No; since it has become a corpse."

"Take care," said Marat, smiling; "I may gain a point over you, for I am well acquainted with this part of my profession, and am said to be a skilful anatomist."

"Pride! pride! ever pride!" murmured Balsamo.

"What do you say?" asked Marat.

"I say that we shall see, sir," replied Balsamo. "Let us enter."

Marat preceded Balsamo in the narrow alley leading to

the amphitheater, which was situated at the extremity of the Rue Hautefeuille. Balsamo followed him unhesitatingly until they reached a long, narrow room, where two corpses, a male and a female, lay stretched upon a marble table.

The woman had died young; the man was old and bald. A soiled sheet was thrown over their bodies, leaving their faces half uncovered.

They were lying side by side upon this cold bed; they who had perhaps never met before in the world, and whose souls, then voyaging in eternity, must, could they have looked down on earth, have been struck with wonderment at the proximity of their mortal remains.

Marat, with a single movement, raised and threw aside the coarse linen which covered the two bodies, whom death had thus made equal before the anatomist's scalpel.

"Is not the sight of the dead repugnant to your feelings?" asked Marat, in his usual boasting manner.

"It makes me sad," replied Balsamo.

"Want of custom," said Marat. "I who see this sight daily, feel neither sadness nor disgust. We practitioners live with the dead, and do not interrupt any of the functions of our existence on their account."

"It is a sad privilege of your profession, sir."

"Besides," added Marat, "why should I be sad, or feel disgust? In the first case, reflection forbids it; in the second, custom."

"Explain your ideas," said Balsamo; "I do not understand you clearly. Reflection first."

"Well, why should I be afraid? Why should I fear an inert mass—a statue of flesh instead of stone, marble, or granite?"

"In short, you think there is nothing in a corpse."

"Nothing—absolutely nothing.'"

"Do you believe that?"

"I am sure of it."

"But in the living body?"

"There is motion," said Marat, proudly.

"And the soul?—you do not speak of it, sir."

" I have never found it in the bodies which I have dissected."

" Because you have only dissected corpses."

" Oh, no, sir; I have frequently operated upon living bodies."

" And you have found nothing more in them than in the corpses ? "

" Yes, I have found pain. Do you call pain the soul ? "

" Then you do not believe in it ? "

" In what ? "

" In the soul."

" I believe in it, because I am at liberty to call it motion if I wish."

" That is well. You believe in the soul; that is all I asked. I am glad you believe in it."

" One moment, master; let us understand each other, and, above all, let us not exaggerate," said Marat, with his serpent smile. " We practitioners are rather disposed to materialism."

" These bodies are very cold," said Balsamo, dreamily, " and this woman was very beautiful."

" Why, yes."

" A lovely soul would have been suitable in this lovely body."

" Ah ! there is the mistake in Him who created her. A beautiful scabbard, but a vile sword. This corpse, master, is that of a wretched woman who had just left St. Lazarus, when she died of cerebral inflammation in the Hotel Dieu. Her history is long, and tolerably scandalous. If you call the motive power which impelled this creature, soul, you wrong our souls, which must be of the same essence, since they are derived from the same source."

" Her soul should have been cured," said Balsamo; " it was lost for want of the only Physician who is indispensable—the Physician of the Soul."

" Alas ! master, that is another of your theories. Medicine is only for the body," replied Marat, with a bitter smile. " Now you have a word on your lips which Molière has often employed in his comedies, and it is this word which makes you smile."

"No," said Balsamo; "you mistake; you cannot guess why I smile. What we concluded just now was, that these corpses are void, was it not?"

"And insensible," added Marat, raising the young woman's head, and letting it fall noisily upon the marble, while the body neither moved nor shuddered.

"Very well," said Balsamo, "let us now go to the hospital."

"Wait one moment, master, I entreat you, until I have separated from the trunk this head, which I am most anxious to have, as it was the seat of a very curious disease. Will you allow me?"

"Do you ask?" said Balsamo.

Marat opened his case, and took from it a bistoury, and picked up in the corner a large wooden mallet stained with blood. Then, with a practised hand, he made a circular incision, which separated all the flesh and the muscles of the neck, and having thus reached the bone, he slipped his bistoury between the juncture of the vertebral column, and struck a sharp blow upon it with the mallet.

The head rolled upon the table, and from the table upon the floor; Marat was obliged to seize it with his damp hands. Balsamo turned away, not to give too much joy to the triumphant operator.

"One day," said Marat, who thought he had hit the master in a weak point, "one day some philanthropist will occupy himself with the details of death as others do of life, and will invent a machine which shall sever a head at a single blow, and cause instantaneous annihilation, which no other instrument of death does. The wheel, quartering, and hanging are punishments suitable for savages, but not for civilized people. An enlightened nation, as France is, should punish, but not revenge. Those who condemn to the wheel, who hang or quarter, revenge themselves upon the criminal by inflicting pain before punishing him by death, which, in my opinion, is too much by half."

"And in mine also, sir. But what kind of an instrument do you mean?"

"I can fancy a machine cold and impassible as the law itself. The man who is charged with fulfilling the last office is moved at the sight of his fellow-man, and sometimes strikes badly, as it happened to the Duke o fMonmouth and to Chalais. This could not be the case with a machine—with two arms of oak wielding a cutlass, for instance."

"And do you believe, sir, that because the knife would pass with the rapidity of lightning between the base of the occiput and the trapezoid muscles, that death would be instantaneous, and the pain momentary?"

"Certainly; death would be instantaneous, for the iron would sever at a blow the nerves which cause motion. The pain would be momentary, for the blade would separate the brain, which is the seat of the feelings, from the heart, which is the center of life."

"Sir," said Balsamo, "the punishment of decapitation exists in Germany."

"Yes, but by the sword; and, as I said before, a man's hand may tremble."

"Such a machine exists in Italy; an arm of oak wields it. It is called the *mannaja.*"

"Well?"

"Well, sir, I have seen criminals, decapitated by the executioner, raise their headless bodies from the bench on which they were seated, and stagger five or six paces off, where they fell. I have picked up heads which had rolled to the foot of the mannaja, as that head you are holding by the hair has just rolled from the marble table, and on pronouncing in their ears the name by which those persons had been called, I have seen the eyes open again and turn in their orbit, in their endeavors to see who had called them back again to earth."

"A nervous movement—nothing else."

"Are the nerves not the organs of sensibility?"

"What do you conclude from that, sir?"

"I conclude that it would be better, instead of inventing a machine which kills to punish, that man should seek a means of punishing without killing. The society which will invent this means, will assuredly be the best and the most enlightened of societies."

"Utopias again! always Utopias!" said Marat.

"Perhaps you are right," said Balsamo; "time will

show. But did you not speak of the hospital? Let us go!"

"Come, then," said Marat; and he tied the woman's head in his pocket-handkerchief, carefully knotting the four corners. "Now I am sure, at least," said he, as he left the hall, "that my comrades will only have my leavings."

They took the way to the Hotel Dieu—the dreamer and the practician, side by side.

"You have cut off this head very coolly and skilfully, sir," said Balsamo; "do you feel less emotion when you operate upon the living than the dead? Does the sight of suffering affect you more than that of immobility? Have you more pity for living bodies than for corpses?"

"No; that would be as great a fault as for the executioner to be moved. You may kill a man by cutting his thigh unskilfully, just as well as by severing the head from the body. A good surgeon operates with his hand, not with his heart; though he knows well, at the same time, in his heart, that for one moment of suffering he gives years of life and health. That is the fair side of our profession, master."

"Yes, sir; but in the living bodies you meet with the soul, I hope."

"Yes, if you will agree with me that the soul is motion, or sensibility. Yes, certainly, I meet with it; and it is very troublesome, too; for it kills far more patients than any scalpel."

They had by this time arrived at the threshold of the Hotel Dieu, and now entered the hospital. Guided by Marat, who still carried his ominous burden, Balsamo penetrated to the hall where the operations were performed, in which the head-surgeon and the students in surgery were assembled. The attendant had just brought in a young man who had been run over the preceding week by a heavy carriage, the wheel of which had crushed his foot. A hasty operation, performed upon the limb when benumbed by pain, had not been sufficient; the inflammation had rapidly extended, and the amputation of the leg had now become urgent.

The unfortunate man, stretched upon his bed of anguish, looked with a horror which would have melted tigers, at the band of eager students who were watching for the moment of his martyrdom, perhaps of his death, that they might study the science of life—that marvelous phenomenon behind which lies the gloomy phenomenon of death.

He seemed to implore a pitying look, a smile, or a word of encouragement from each of the students and attendants, but the beatings of his heart were responded to only by indifference, his beseeching looks with glances of iron. A surviving emotion of pride kept him silent. He reserved all his strength for the cries which pain would soon wring from him. But when he felt the heavy hand of the attendant upon his shoulder, when the arms of the assistants twined around him like the serpents of Laocoon, when he heard the operator's voice cry, " Courage! " the unfortunate man ventured to break the silence, and asked, in a plaintive voice:

" Shall I suffer much? "

" Oh, no; make your mind easy," replied Marat, with a hypocritical smile, which was affectionate to the patient but ironical to Balsamo.

Marat saw that Balsamo had understood him; he approached and whispered:

" It is a dreadful operation. The bone is full of cracks and fearfully sensitive. He will die, not of the wound, but of the pain. That is what the soul does for this poor man."

" Then why do you operate? why do you not let him die in peace? "

" Because it is the surgeon's duty to attempt a cure, even when the cure seems impossible."

" And you say he will suffer? "

" Fearfully."

" And that his soul is the cause? "

" His soul, which has too much sympathy with the body."

" Then, why not operate upon the soul? Perhaps the tranquillity of the one would cause the cure of the other."

"I have done so," said Marat, while the attendants continued to bind the patient.

"You have prepared his soul?"

"Yes."

"How so?"

"As one always does, by words. I spoke to his soul, his intelligence, his sensibility—to that organ which caused the Greek philosopher to exclaim, 'Pain, thou art no evil'—the language suitable for it. I said to him, 'You will not suffer.' That is the only remedy hitherto known, as regards the soul—falsehood! Why is this she-devil of a soul connected with the body? When I cut off this head just now, the body said nothing, yet the operation was a serious one. But motion had ceased, sensibility was extinguished, the soul had fled, as you spiritualists say. This is the reason why the head I severed said nothing, why the body which I mutilated allowed me to do so; while this body which is yet inhabited by a soul—for a short time, indeed, but still inhabited—will cry out fearfully. Stop your ears well, master, you who are moved by this union of body and soul, which will always destroy your theory until you succeed in isolating the body from the soul."

"And you believe we shall never arrive at this isolation?"

"Try," said Marat; "this is an excellent opportunity."

"Well, yes, you are right," said Balsamo; "the opportunity is a good one, and I will make the attempt."

"Yes, try."

"I will."

"How so?"

"This young man interests me; he shall not suffer."

"You are an illustrious chief," said Marat, "but you are not the Almighty, and you cannot prevent this wretch from suffering."

"If he were not to feel the pain, do you think he would recover?"

"His recovery would be more probable, but not certain."

Balsamo cast an inexpressible look of triumph upon Marat, and placing himself before the young patient, whose frightened eyes, already dilated with the anguish· of terror, met his.

" Sleep," said he, not alone with his lips, but with his look, with his will—with all the heat of his blood, all the vital energy of his body.

The head-surgeon was just commencing to feel the injured leg, and to point out the aggravated nature of the case to his students; but, at Balsamo's command, the young man, who had raised himself upon his seat, oscillated for a moment in the arms of his attendants, his head drooped, and his eyes closed.

" He is ill," said Marat.

" No, sir."

" But do you not see that he loses consciousness? "

" He is sleeping."

" What, he sleeps? "

" Yes."

Every one turned to look at the strange physician, whom they took for a madman. An incredulous smile hovered on Marat's lips.

" Is it usual for people to talk while in a swoon? " asked Balsamo.

" No."

" Well, question him; he will reply."

" Halloo, young man! " cried Marat.

" You need not speak so loud," said Balsamo; " speak in your usual voice."

" Tell us what is the matter with you."

" I was ordered to sleep, and I do sleep," replied the patient.

His voice was perfectly calm, and formed a strange contrast to that they had heard a few moments before.

All the attendants looked at one another.

" Now," said Balsamo, " release him."

" That is impossible," said the head-surgeon; " the slightest movement will spoil the operation."

" He will not stir."

" Who can assure me of that? "

" I, and he also. Ask him."

" Can you be left untied, my friend? "

" Yes."

" And will you promise not to move ? "

" I will promise it if you command me."

" I command it."

" Faith! sir, you speak so positively that I am tempted to make the trial."

" Do so, sir, and fear nothing."

" Untie him."

The assistants obeyed.

Balsamo advanced to the bedside.

" From this moment," said he, " do not stir until I order you."

A carved statue upon a tombstone could not have been more motionless than the patient upon this injunction.

" Now operate, sir," said Balsamo; " the patient is quite ready."

The surgeon took his bistoury; but, when upon the point of using it, he hesitated.

" Cut, sir, cut! " said Balsamo, with the air of an inspired prophet.

And the surgeon yielding—like Marat, like the patient, like every one present—to the irresistible influence of Balsamo's words, raised the knife. The sound of the knife passing through the flesh was heard, but the patient never stirred, nor even uttered a sigh.

" From what country do you come, my friend? " asked Balsamo.

" I am a Breton, sir," replied the patient, smiling.

" And you love your country? "

" Oh, sir, it is so beautiful! "

In the meantime the surgeon was making the circular incisions in the flesh, by means of which, in amputations, the bone is laid bare.

" You quitted it when young? " asked Balsamo.

" At ten years of age, sir."

The incisions were made—the surgeon placed the saw on the bone.

" My friend," said Balsamo, " sing me that song which the salt-makers of Batz chant as they return to their

homes after the day's work is over.   I can only remember
the first line:

> " ' My salt covered o'er with its mantle of foam.' "

The saw was now severing the bone; but at Balsamo's
command the patient smiled, and commenced in a low,
melodious, ecstatic voice, like a lover or like a poet, the
following verses:

> " My salt covered o'er with its mantle of foam,
>   The lake of pure azure that mirrors my home,
>   My stove where the peats ever cheerfully burn,
>   And the honeyed wheat-cake which awaits my return ;
>
> ' 'The wife of my bosom—my silver-haired sire—
>   My urchins who sports round my evening fire—
>   And there where the wild flowers, in brightest of bloom,
>   Their fragrance diffuse round my loved mother's tomb.
>
> ' ' Blest, blest be ye all !   Now the day's task is o'er,
>   And I stand once again at my own cottage door ;
>   And richly will love my brief absence repay,
>   And the calm joys of eve the rude toils of the day.' "

The leg fell upon the bed while the patient was still
singing.

CHAPTER XXXIX.

BODY AND SOUL.

EVERY one looked with astonishment at the patient—
with admiration at the surgeon.   Some said that both were
mad.   Marat communicated this opinion to Balsamo, in a
whisper.

"Terror has made the poor devil lose his senses," said
he ; "that is why he feels no pain."

" I think not," replied Balsamo; " and far from having
lost his senses, I am sure that if I asked him he could tell
us the day of his death, if he is to die, or the period of his
convalescence, if he is to recover."

Marat was almost inclined to adopt the general opinion

—that Balsamo was as mad as his patient. In the meantime, however, the surgeon was tying up the arteries, from which spouted streams of blood.

Balsamo drew a small vial from his pocket, poured a few drops of the liquid it contained upon a little ball of lint, and begged the chief surgeon to apply the lint to the arteries. The latter obeyed with a certain feeling of curiosity. He was one of the most celebrated practitioners of that period—a man truly enamored of his profession; who repudiated none of its mysteries, and for whom chance was but the makeshift of doubt.

He applied the lint to the artery, which quivered, bubbled,. and then only allowed the blood to escape drop by drop. He could now tie up the artery with the greatest facility.

This time Balsamo obtained an undoubted triumph, and all present asked him where he had studied, and of what school he was.

"I am a German physician of the school of Gottingen," replied he, "and I have made this discovery you have just witnessed. However, gentlemen and fellow practitioners, I wish this discovery to remain a secret for the present, as I have a wholesome terror of the stake, and the parliament of Paris might perhaps resume their functions once more for the pleasure of condemning a sorcerer."

The chief surgeon was still plunged in a reverie. Marat also seemed thoughtful, but he was the first to break the silence.

"You said just now," said he, "that if you were to question this man about the result of this operation, he would reply truly, though the result is still veiled in futurity."

"I assert it again," replied Balsamo.

"Well, let us have the proof."

"What is this poor fellow's name?"

"Havard," replied Marat.

Balsamo turned to the patient, whose lips were yet murmuring the last words of the plaintive air.

"Well, my friend," asked he, "what do you augur from the state of this poor Havard?"

"What do I augur from his state?" replied the patient; "stay, I must return from Brittany, where I was, to the Hotel Dieu, where he is."

"Just so; enter, look at him, and tell me the truth respecting him."

"Oh! he is very ill; his leg has been cut off."

"Indeed!" said Balsamo. "And has the operation been successful?"

"Exceedingly so; but——"

The patient's face darkened.

"But what?" asked Balsamo.

"But," resumed the patient, "he has a terrible trial to pass through. The fever——"

"When will it commence?"

"At seven o'clock this evening."

All the spectators looked at one another.

"And this fever?" asked Balsamo.

"Oh! it will make him very ill; but he will recover from the first attack."

"Are you sure?"

"Oh, yes!"

"Then, after this first attack, will he be saved?"

"Alas! no," said the wounded man, sighing.

"Will the fever return, then?"

"Oh, yes, and more severely than before. Poor Havard! poor Havard!" he continued, "he has a wife and several children." And his eyes filled with tears.

"Must his wife be a widow, then, and his children orphans?" asked Balsamo.

"Wait, wait!"

He clasped his hands.

"No, no!" he exclaimed, his features lighting up with an expression of sublime faith. "No; his wife and children have prayed, and their prayers have found favor in the sight of God."

"Then he will recover?"

"Yes."

"You hear, gentlemen," said Balsamo, "he will recover."

"Ask him in how many days," said Marat.

" In how many days, do you say ? "

" Yes, you said he could indicate the phases, and the duration of his convalescence."

" I ask nothing better than to question him on the subject."

" Well, then, question him now."

" And when do you think Havard will recover ? " said Balsamo.

" Oh ! his cure will take a long time, a month, six weeks, two months. He entered this hospital five days ago, and he will leave it two months and fourteen days after having entered."

" And he will leave it cured ? "

" Yes."

" But," said Marat, " unable to work, and consequently to maintain his wife and children."

Havard again clasped his hands.

" Oh ! God is good, God will provide for him."

" And how will God provide for him ? " asked Marat. " As I am in the way of hearing something new to-day, I might as well hear that."

" God has sent to his bedside a charitable man who has taken pity upon him, and who has said to himself, ' Poor Havard shall not want.' "

The spectators were amazed; Balsamo smiled.

" Ha ! this is in truth a strange scene," said the chief surgeon, at the same time taking the patient's hand, feeling his chest and forehead; " this man in dreaming."

" Do you think so ? " said Balsamo.

Then darting upon the sick man a look of authority and energy :

" Awake, Havard ! " said he.

The young man opened his eyes with some difficulty, and gazed with profound surprise upon all these spectators, who had so soon laid aside their threatening character, and assumed an inoffensive one toward him.

" Well," said he, sadly, " have you not operated yet ? Are you going to make me suffer still more ? "

Balsamo replied hastily. He feared the invalid's emotion. But there was no need for such haste ; the surprise of all the spectators was so great that none would have anticipated him.

"My friend," said he, "be calm. The head-surgeon has operated upon your leg in such a manner as to satisfy all the requirements of your position. It seems, my poor fellow, that you are not very strong-minded, for you fainted at the first incision."

"Oh, so much the better," said the Breton, smilingly; "I felt nothing, and my sleep was even sweet and refreshing. What happiness! my leg will not be cut off."

But just at that moment the poor man looked down, and saw the bed full of blood, and his amputated leg lying near him. He uttered a scream, and this time fainted in reality.

"Now question him," said Balsamo, coldly, to Marat, "you will see if he replies."

Then, taking the head-surgeon aside, while the nurses carried the poor young man back to his bed:

"Sir," said Balsamo, "you heard what your poor patient said?"

"Yes, sir, that he would recover."

"He said something else; he said that God would take pity upon him, and would send him wherewithal to support his wife and children."

"Well?"

"Well, sir, he told the truth on this point as on the others. Only you must undertake to be the charitable medium of affording him this assistance. Here is a diamond worth about twenty thousand livres; when the poor man is cured, sell it and give him the proceeds. In the meantime, since the soul, as your pupil, Monsieur Marat, said very truly, has a great influence upon the body, tell Havard as soon as he is restored to consciousness that his future comfort and that of his children is secured."

"But, sir," said the surgeon, hesitating to take the ring which Balsamo offered him, "if he should not recover?"

"He will recover."

"Then allow me at least to give you a receipt."

"Sir!"

" That is the only condition upon which I can receive a jewel of such value."

" Do as you think right, sir."

" Your name, if you please ? "

" The Count de Fenix."

The surgeon passed into the adjoining apartment while Marat, overwhelmed, confounded, but still struggling against the evidence of his senses, approached Balsamo.

In five minutes the surgeon returned, holding in his hand the following receipt, which he gave Balsamo:

" I have received from the Count de Fenix a diamond, which he affirms to be worth twenty thousand livres, the price of which is to be given to the man Havard when he leaves the Hotel Dieu.

" This 15th of September, 1771.

"   GUILLOTIN, M. D."

Balsamo bowed to the doctor, took the receipt, and left the room, followed by Marat.

" You are forgetting your head," said Balsamo, for whom the wandering of the young student's thoughts was a great triumph.

" Ah ! true," said he.

And he again picked up his dismal burden. When they emerged into the street, both walked forward very quickly without uttering a word; then, having reached the Rue des Cordeliers, they ascended the steep stairs which led to the attic.

Marat, who had not forgotten the disappearance of his watch, stopped before the lodge of the portress, if the den which she inhabited deserved that name, and asked for Dame Grivette.

A thin, stunted, miserable-looking child, of about seven years old, replied, in a whining voice:

" Mamma is gone out; she said that when you came home I was to give you this letter."

" No, no, my little friend," said Marat; " tell her to bring it me herself."

" Yes. sir."

And Marat and Balsamo proceeded on their way.

"Ah!" said Marat, pointing out a chair to Balsamo, and falling upon a stool himself, "I see the master has some noble secrets."

"Perhaps I have penetrated further than most men into the confidence of nature, and into the works of God," replied Balsamo.

"Oh!" said Marat, "how science proves man's omnipotence, and makes us proud to be a man!"

"True; and a physician, you should have added."

"Therefore, I am proud of you, master," said Marat.

"And yet," replied Balsamo, smiling, "I am but a poor physician of souls."

"Oh, do not speak of that, sir; you who stopped the patient's bleeding by material means."

"I thought my best cure was that of having prevented him from suffering. True, you assured me he was mad."

"He was so for a moment, certainly."

"What do you call madness? Is it not an abstraction of the soul?"

"Or of the mind," said Marat.

"We will not discuss the point. The soul serves me as a term for what I mean. When the object is found, it matters little how you call it."

"There is where we differ, sir; you pretend you have found the thing, and seek only the name, I maintain that you seek both the object and the name."

"We shall return to that immediately. You said then that madness was a temporary abstraction of the mind?"

"Certainly."

"Involuntarily, is it not?"

"Yes. I have seen a madman at Bicetre who bit the iron bars of his cell, crying out all the time, 'Cook, your pheasants are very tender, but they are badly dressed.'"

"But you admit, at least, that this madness passes over the mind like a cloud, and that when it has passed, the mind resumes its former brightness?"

"That scarcely ever happens."

"Yet you saw our patient recover his senses perfectly after his insane dream."

"I saw it, but I did not understand what I saw. It is an exceptional case—one of those strange events which the Israelites called miracles."

"No, sir," said Balsamo; "it is simply the abstraction of the soul—the twofold isolation of spirit and matter. Matter—that inert thing—dust—which will return to dust; and soul, the divine spark which was inclosed for a short period in that dark-lantern called the body, and which, being the child of Heaven, will return to Heaven after the body has sunk to earth."

"Then you abstracted the soul momentarily from the body?"

"Yes, sir; I commanded it to quit the miserable abode which it occupied. I raised it from the abyss of suffering in which pain had bound it, and transported it into pure and heavenly regions. What, then, remained for the surgeon? The same that remained for your dissecting-knife, when you severed that head you are carrying from the dead body—nothing but inert flesh, matter, clay."

"And in whose name did you command the soul?"

"In His name who created all the souls by His breath —the souls of the world, of men—in the name of God."

"Then," said Marat, "you deny free will?"

"I?" said Balsamo. "On the contrary; what am I doing at this moment? I show you, on the one hand, free will; on the other, abstraction. I show you a dying man a prey to excruciating pain; this man has a stoical soul, he anticipates the operation, he asks for it, he bears it, but he suffers. That is free will. But when I approach the dying man—I, the ambassador of God, the prophet, the apostle—and taking pity upon this man who is my fellow-creature, I abstract, by the powers which the Lord has given me, the soul from the suffering body, this blind, inert, insensible body becomes a spectacle which the soul contemplates with a pitying eye from the height of its celestial sphere. Did you not hear Havard, when speaking of himself, say, 'Poor Havard'? He did not say '*myself.*' It was because this soul had in truth no longer any connection with the body—it was already winging its way to Heaven."

"But, by this way of reckoning, man is nothing," said Marat, "and I can no longer say to the tyrant, ' You have power over my body, but none over my soul.' "

"Ah! now you pass from truth to sophism; I have already told you, sir, it is your failing. God lends the soul to the body, it is true; but it is no less true that during the time the soul animates this body, there is a union between the two—an influence of one over the other—a supremacy of matter over mind, or mind over matter, according as, for some purpose hidden from us, God permits either the body or the soul to be the ruling power. But it is no less true that the soul which animates the beggar is as pure as that which reigns in the bosom of the king. That is the dogma which you, an apostle of equality, ought to preach. Prove the equality of the spiritual essences in these two cases, since you can establish it by the aid of all that is most sacred in the eyes of men, by holy books and traditions, by science and faith. Of what importance is the equality of matter? With physical equality you are only men; but spiritual equality makes you gods. Just now, this poor wounded man, this ignorant child of the people, told you things concerning his illness which none among the doctors would have ventured to pronounce. How was that? It was because his soul, temporarily freed from earthly ties, floated above this world, and saw from on high a mystery which our opaqueness of vision hides from us."

Marat turned his dead head back and forward upon the table, seeking a reply which he could not find.

"Yes," muttered he, at last; "yes, there is something supernatural in all this."

"Perfectly natural, on the contrary, sir. Cease to call supernatural what has its origin in the functions and destiny of the soul. These functions are natural, although perhaps not known."

"But, though unknown to us, master, these functions cannot surely be a mystery to you. The horse, unknown to the Peruvians, was yet perfectly familiar to the Spaniards who had tamed him."

"It would be presumptuous in me to say 'I know.' I am more humble, sir; I say 'I believe.'"

"Well, what do you believe?"

"I believe that the first, the most powerful, of all laws is the law of progress. I believe that God has created nothing without having a beneficent design in view; only, as the duration of this world is uncalculated and incalculable, the progress is slow. Our planet, according to the Scriptures, was sixty centuries old, when printing came like some vast lighthouse to illuminate the past and the future. With the advent of printing, obscurity and forgetfulness vanished. Printing is the memory of the world. Well, Guttenberg invented printing, and my confidence returned."

"Ah!" said Marat, ironically; "you will, perhaps, be able at last to read men's hearts."

"Why not?"

"Then you will open that little window in men's breasts which the ancients so much desired to see?"

"There is no need for that, sir. I shall separate the soul from the body; and the soul—the pure, immaculate daughter of God—will reveal to me all the turpitudes of the mortal covering it is condemned to animate."

"Can you reveal material secrets?"

"Why not?"

"Can you tell me, for instance, who has stolen my watch?"

"You lower science to a base level, sir. But, no matter. God's greatness is proved as much by a grain of sand as by the mountain—by the flesh-worm as by the elephant. Yes, I will tell you who has stolen your watch."

Just then, a timid knock was heard at the door. It was Marat's servant, who had returned, and who came, according to the young surgeon's order, to bring the letter.

CHAPTER ⌐.

THE door opened, and Dame Grivette entered. This woman, whom we have not before taken the trouble to sketch, because she was one of those characters whom the painter keeps in the background so long as he has no occasion for them—this woman now advances in the moving picture of this history, and demands her place in the immense picture we have undertaken to unroll before the eyes of our readers, in which, if our genius equaled our goodwill, we would introduce all classes of men, from the beggar to the king, from Caliban to Ariel.

We shall now, therefore, attempt to delineate Dame Grivette, who steps forth out of the shade, and advances toward us.

She was a tall, withered creature, of from thirty to five-and-thirty years of age, with dark, sallow complexion, and blue eyes encircled with black rings—the fearful type of that decline, that wasting away, which is produced in densely populated towns by poverty, bad air, and every sort of degradation, mental as well as bodily, among those creatures whom God created so beautiful, and who would otherwise have become magnificent in their perfect development, as all living denizens of earth, air, and sky are when man has not made their life one long punishment —when he has not tortured their limbs with chains, and their stomachs with hunger, or with food almost as fatal.

Thus Marat's portress would have been a beautiful woman if from her fifteenth year she had not dwelt in a den without air or light—if the fire of her natural instinct, fed by this oven-like heart, or by the icy cold, had not ceaselessly burned. She had long, thin hands, which the needle of the seamstress had furrowed with little cuts, which the suds of the wash-house had cracked and softened—which the burning coals of the kitchen had roasted and tanned—but in spite of all, hands which, by their form, that indelible trace of the divine mold, would have been called royal, if, instead of being blistered by the broom, they had wielded the scepter. So true is it that this poor human body is only the outward sign of our profession.

But in this woman, the mind, which rose superior to the body, and which, consequently, had resisted external circumstances better, kept watch like a lamp; it illumined, as it were, the body by a reflected light, and at times a ray of beauty, youth, intelligence, and love was seen to glance from her dulled and stupid eyes—a ray of all the finest feelings of the human heart.

Balsamo gazed attentively at the woman, or, rather,. at this singular nature, which had from the first struck his observing eye.

The portress entered holding the letter in her hand, and in a soft, insinuating voice, like that of an old woman —for women condemned to poverty are old at thirty— said:

" Monsieur Marat, here is the letter you asked for."

" It was not the letter I wanted," said Marat; " I wished to see you."

" Well, here I am at your service, Monsieur Marat " (Dame Grivette made a courtesy) ; " what do you want with me ? "

" You know very well what I want. I wish to know something about my watch."

" Ah, dame ! I can't tell what has become of it. I saw it all day yesterday hanging from the nail over the mantelpiece."

" You mistake. All day yesterday it was in my fob; but when I went out at six o'clock in the evening, I put it under the candlestick, because I was going among a crowd, and I feared it might be stolen."

" If you put it under the candlestick, it must be there yet."

And with feigned simplicity, which she was far from suspecting to be so transparent, she raised the very candlestick of the pair which ornamented the mantelpiece, under which Marat had concealed his watch.

"Yes, that is the candlestick, sure enough," said the young man; "but where is the watch?"

"No; I see it is no longer there. Perhaps you did not put it there, Monsieur Marat."

"But when I tell you I did."

"Look for it carefully."

"Oh, I have looked carefully enough," said Marat, with an angry glance.

"Then you have lost it."

"But I tell you that yesterday I put it under that candlestick myself."

"Then some one must have entered," said Dame Grivette; "you see so many people, so many strangers."

"All an excuse," cried Marat, more and more enraged. "You know very well that no one has been here since yesterday. No, no; my watch is gone where the silver top of my last cane went, where the little silver spoon you know of is gone to, and my knife with the six blades. I am robbed. Dame Grivette, I have borne much, but I shall not tolerate this; so take notice!"

"But, sir," said Dame Grivette, "do you mean to accuse me?"

"You ought to take care of my effects."

"I have not even the key."

"You are the portress."

"You give me a crown a month, and you expect to be as well served as if you had ten domestics."

"I do not care about being badly served; but I do care whether I am robbed or not."

"Sir, I am an honest woman."

"Yes; an honest woman whom I shall give in charge to the police, if my watch is not found in an hour."

"To the police?"

"Yes."

"To the police—an honest woman like me?"

"An honest woman, do you say? Honest! that's good."

"Yes; and of whom nothing bad can be said; do you hear that?"

"Come, come! enough of this, Dame Grivette."

" Ah! I thought that you suspected me when you went out."

" I have suspected you ever since the top of my cane disappeared."

" Well, Monsieur Marat, I will tell you something, in my turn."

" What will you tell me? "

" While you were away I have consulted my neighbors."

" Your neighbors! For what purpose? "

" Respecting your suspicions."

" I had said nothing of them to you at the time."

" But I saw them plainly."

" And the neighbors? I am curious to know what they said."

" They said that if you suspect me, and have even gone so far as to impart your suspicions to another person, you must pursue the affair to the end."

" Well? "

" That is to say, you must prove that the watch has been taken."

" It has been taken, since it was there, and is now gone."

" Yes; but taken by me—taken by me; do you understand? Oh, justice requires proofs; your word will not be sufficient, Monsieur Marat; you are no more than ourselves, Monsieur Marat."

Balsamo, calm as ever, looked on during this scene. He saw that though Marat's conviction was not altered, he had, nevertheless, lowered his tone.

" Therefore," continued the portress, " if you do not render justice to my probity—if you do not make some reparation to my character—it is I who will send for the police, as our landlord just now advised me to do."

Marat bit his lips. He knew there was a real danger in this. The landlord was an old, rich, retired merchant. He lived on the third story; and the scandal-mongers of the quarter did not hesitate to assert that, some ten years before, he had not been indifferent to the charms of the portress, who was then kitchen-maid to his wife.

Now, Marat attended mysterious meetings. Marat was a young man of not very settled habits, besides being addicted to concealment and suspected by the police; and, for all these reasons, he was not anxious to have an affair with the commissary, seeing that it might tend to place him in the hands of M. de Sartines, who liked much to read the papers of young men such as Marat, and to send the authors of such noble writings to houses of meditation, such as Vincennes, the Bastile, Charenton, and Bicetre.

Marat, therefore, lowered his tone; but in proportion as he did so, the portress raised hers. The result was, that this nervous and hysterical woman raged like a flame which suddenly meets with a current of fresh air.

Oaths, cries, tears—she employed all in turn; it was a regular tempest.

Then Balsamo judged that the time had come for him to interfere. He advanced toward the woman, and looking at her with an ominous and fiery glance, he stretched two fingers toward her, uttering, not so much with his lips as with his eyes, his thought, his whole will, a word which Marat could not hear.

Immediately Dame Grivette became silent, tottered, and, losing her equilibrium, staggered backward, her eyes fearfully dilated, and fell upon the bed without uttering a word.

After a short interval, her eyes closed and opened again, but this time the pupil could not be seen; her tongue moved convulsively, but her body was perfectly motionless, and yet her hands trembled as if shaken by fever.

" Ha ! " said Marat, " like the wounded man in the hospital."

" Yes."

" Then she is asleep? "

" Silence ! " said Balsamo.

Then addressing Marat:

" Sir," said he, " the moment has now come when all your incredulity must cease. Pick up that letter which this woman was bringing you, and which she dropped when she fell."

Marat obeyed.

" Well ? " he asked.

" Wait."

And taking the letter from Marat's hands:

" You know from whom this letter comes ? " asked Balsamo of the somnambulist.

" No, sir," she replied.

Balsamo held the sealed letter close to the woman.

" Read it to Monsieur Marat, who wishes to know the contents."

" She cannot read," said Marat.

" Yes, but you can read ? "

" Of course."

" Well, read it, and she will read it after you in proportion as the words are engraven upon your mind."

Marat broke the seal of the letter and read it, while Dame Grivette, standing, and trembling beneath the allpowerful will of Balsamo, repeated word for word, as Marat read them to himself, the following words:

" MY DEAR HIPPOCRATES,—Appelles has just finished his portrait; he has sold it for fifty francs, and those fifty francs are to be eaten to-day at the tavern in the Rue St. Jacques. Will you come ?

" P.S.—It is understood that part is to be drunk.

" Your friend,   L. DAVID."

It was word for word what was written.

Marat let the paper fall from his hand.

" Well," said Balsamo, " you see that Dame Grivette also has a soul, and that this soul wakes while she sleeps."

" And a strange soul," said Marat; " a soul which can read when the body cannot."

" Because the soul knows everything—because the soul can reproduce by reflection. Try to make her read this when she is awake—that is to say, when the body has wrapped the soul in its shadow—and you will see."

Marat was dumb; his whole material philosophy rebelled within him, but he could not find a reply.

" Now," continued Balsamo, " we shall pass on to what interests you most: that is to say, as to what has become of your watch. Dame Grivette," said he, turning to her "who has taken Monsieur Marat's watch?"

The somnambulist made a violent gesture of denial.

"I do not know," said she.

"You know perfectly well," persisted Balsamo, "and you shall tell me."

Then, with more decided exertion of his will:

"Who has taken Monsieur Marat's watch—speak?"

"Dame Grivette has not stolen Monsieur Marat's watch. Why does Monsieur Marat believe she has?"

"If it is not she who has taken it, tell me who has?"

"I do not know."

"You see," said Marat, "conscience is an impenetrable refuge."

"Well, since you have only this last doubt," said Balsamo, "you shall be convinced."

Then turning again to the portress:

"Tell me who took the watch; I insist upon it."

"Come, come," said Marat, "do not ask an impossibility."

"You heard?" said Balsamo. "I have said you must tell it."

Then, beneath the pressure of this imperious command, the unhappy woman began to wring her hands and arms as if she were mad; a shudder like that of an epileptic fit ran through her whole body; her mouth was distorted with a hideous expression of terror and weakness; she threw herself back rigid, as if she were in a painful convulsion, and fell upon the bed.

"No, no," said she; "I would rather die!"

"Well," said Balsamo, with a burst of anger which made the fire flash from his eyes, "you shall die if necessary, but you shall speak. Your silence and your obstinacy are sufficient indications for us; but for an incredulous person we must have irrefragable proofs. Speak! I will it; who has taken the watch?"

The nervous excitement was at its height; all the strength and power of the somnambulist struggled against Balsamo's will; inarticulate cries escaped from her lips, which were stained with a reddish foam.

" She will fall into an epileptic fit," said Marat.

" Fear nothing; it is the demon of falsehood who is in her, and who refuses to come out."

Then, turning toward the woman, and throwing in her face as much fluid as his hands could contain:

" Speak," said he; " who has taken the watch?"

" Dame Grivette," replied the somnambulist, in an almost inaudible voice.

" When did she take it?"

" Yesterday evening."

" Where was it?"

" Underneath the candlestick."

" What has she done with it?"

" She has taken it to the Rue St. Jacques."

" Where in the Rue St. Jacques?"

" To No. 29."

" Which story?"

" The fifth."

" To whom did she give it?"

" To a shoemaker's apprentice."

" What is his name?"

" Simon."

" What is this man to her?"

The woman was silent.

" What is this man to her?"

The somnambulist was again silent.

" What is this man to her?" repeated Balsamo.

The same silence.

Balsamo extended toward her his hand, impregnated with the fluid, and the unfortunate woman, overwhelmed by this terrible attack, had only strength to murmur:

" Her lover."

Marat uttered an exclamation of astonishment.

" Silence!" said Balsamo; " allow consicence to speak."

Then, continuing to address the woman, who was trembling all over, and bathed in perspiration:

" And who advised Dame Grivette to steal the watch?" asked he.

" No one. She raised the candlestick by accident, she saw the watch, and the demon tempted her."

" Did she do it from want? "

" No; for she did not sell the watch."

" She gave it away, then? "

" Yes."

" To Simon? "

The somnambulist made a violent effort.

" To Simon," said she.

Then she covered her face with her hands, and burst into a flood of tears.

Balsamo glanced at Marat, who, with gaping mouth, disordered hair, and dilated eyes, was gazing at the fearful spectacle.

" Well, sir," said he, " you see, at last, the struggle between the body and the soul. You see conscience forced to yield, even in a redoubt which it had believed impregnable. Do you confess now that God has forgotten nothing in this world, and that all is in everything? Then deny no longer that there is a conscience—deny no longer that there is a soul—deny no longer the unknown, young man! Above all, do not deny faith, which is power supreme; and since you are ambitious, Monsieur Marat, study; speak little, think much, and do not judge your superiors lightly. Adieu; my words have opened a vast field before you; cultivate this field, which contains hidden treasures. Adieu! Happy will you be if you can conquer the demon of incredulity which is in you, as I have conquered the demon of falsehood which was in this woman."

And with these words, which caused the blush of shame to tinge the young man's cheeks, he left the room.

Marat did not even think of taking leave of him. But after his first stupor was over, he perceived that Dame Grivette was still sleeping. This sleep struck terror to his soul. Marat would rather have seen a corpse upon his bed, even if M. de Sartines should interpret the fact after his own fashion.

He gazed on this lifeless form, these turned-up eyes, these palpitations, and he felt afraid. His fear increased when the living corpse rose, advanced toward him, took his hand, and said:

" Come with me, Monsieur Marat."

" Where to ? "

" To the Rue St. Jacques."

" Why ? "

" Come, come; he commands me to take you."

Marat, who had fallen upon a chair, rose.

Then Dame Grivette, still asleep, opened the door and descended the stairs with the stealthy pace of a cat, scarcely touching the steps.

Marat followed, fearing every moment that she would fall, and, in falling, break her neck.

Having reached the foot of the stairs, she crossed the threshold, and entered the street, still followed by the young man, whom she led in this manner to the house and the garret she had pointed out.

She knocked at the door; Marat felt his heart beat so violently that he thought it must be audible.

A man was in the garret; he opened the door. In this man Marat recognized a workman of from five-and-twenty to thirty years of age, whom he had several times seen in the porter's lodge.

Seeing Dame Grivette followed by Marat, he started back.

But the somnambulist walked straight to the bed, and putting her hand under the thin bolster, she drew out the watch, which she gave to Marat; while the shoemaker Simon, pale with terror, dared not utter a word, and watched with alarmed gaze the least movement of the woman, whom he believed to be mad.

Scarcely had her hand touched Marat's, in returning him the watch, than she gave a deep sigh and murmured:

" He awakes me!   He awakes me ! "

Her nerves relaxed like a cable freed from the capstan, the vital spark again animated her eyes, and finding herself face to face with Marat, her hand in his, and still holding the watch—that is to say, the irrefragable proof of her crime—she fell upon the floor of the garret in a deep swoon.

" Does conscience really exist, then ? " asked Marat of himself, as he left the room, doubt in his heart and reverie in his eyes.

CHAPTER XLI.

THE MAN AND HIS WORKS.

WHILE Marat was employing his time so profitably in philosophizing on conscience and a dual existence, another philosopher in the Rue Plastriere was also busy in reconstructing, piece by piece, every part of the preceding evening's adventures, and asking himself if he were or were not a very wicked man. Rousseau, with his elbows leaning upon the table, and his head drooping heavily on his left shoulder, was deep in thought.

His philosophical and political works, "Emilius" and the "Social Contract," were lying open before him.

From time to time, when his reflections required it, he stooped down to turn over the leaves of these books, which he knew by heart.

"Ah! good heavens!" said he, reading a paragraph from "Emilius" upon liberty of conscience, "what incendiary expressions! What philosophy! Just Heaven! was there ever in the world a firebrand like me?"

"What!" added he, clasping his hands above his head, "have I written such violent outbursts against the throne —the altar of society? I can no longer be surprised if some dark and brooding minds have outstripped my sophisms, and have gone astray in the paths which I have strewn for them with all the flowers of rhetoric. I have acted as the disturber of society."

He rose from his chair, and paced the floor in great agitation.

"I have," continued he, "abused those men in power who exercise tyranny over authors. Fool! barbarian that I was! Those people are right—a thousand times right! What am I, if not a man dangerous to the state? My words, written to enlighten the masses—at least, such was the pretext I gave myself—have become a torch which will set the world on fire. I have sown discourses on the inequality of ranks, projects of universal fraternity, plans of education—and now I reap a harvest of passions so ferocious that they would overturn the whole framework of society, of intestine wars capable of depopulating the world, and of manners so barbarous that they would roll back the civilization of ten centuries! Oh, I am a great criminal."

He read once more a page of his " Savoyard Vicar."

" Yes, that is it. ' Let us unite to form plans for our happiness.' I have written it. ' Let us give our virtues the force which others give to their vices.' I have written that also."

And Rousseau became still more agitated and unhappy than before.

" Thus, by my fault," said he, " brothers are united to brothers, and one day or other some of these concealed places of meeting will be invaded by the police; the whole nest of these men, who have sworn to eat one another in case of treachery, will be arrested, and one bolder than the others will take my book from his pocket, and will say: ' What do you complain of? We are disciples of Monsieur Rousseau; we are going through a course of philosophy.' Oh, how Voltaire will laugh at that! There is no fear of that courtier's ever getting into such a wasp's nest ! "

The idea that Voltaire would ridicule him put the Genevese philosopher into a violent rage.

" I a conspirator ! " muttered he; " I must be in my dotage, certainly. Am I not, in truth, a famous conspirator ? "

He was at this point when Therese entered with the breakfast, but he did not see her. She perceived that he was attentively reading a passage in the " Reveries of a Recluse."

" Very good," said she, placing the hot milk noisily upon the very book; " my peacock is looking at himself in the glass. Monsieur reads his books. Monsieur Rousseau admires himself."

" Come, Therese," said the philosopher, " patience—leave me; I am in no humor for laughing."

" Oh, yes, it is magnificent, is it not? " said she, mock-
ingly. " You are delighted with yourself. What vanity
authors have and how angry they are to see it in us poor
women. If I only happen to look in my mirror, monsieur
grumbles and calls me a coquette."

She proceeded in this strain, making him the most unhappy man in the world, as if Rousseau had not been
richly enough endowed by nature in this respect. He
drank his milk without steeping his bread. He reflected.

" Very good," said she; " there you are, thinking again.
You are going to write another book full of horrible
things."

Rousseau shuddered.

" You dream," continued Therese, " of your ideal woman, and you write books which young girls ought not
to read, or else profane works which will be burned by the
hands of the common executioner."

The martyr shuddered again. Therese had touched him
to the quick.

" No," replied he; " I will write nothing more which can
cause an evil thought. On the contrary, I wish to write
a book which all honest people will read with transports
of joy."

" Oh, oh! " said Therese, taking away the cup; " that is
impossible; your mind is full of obscene thoughts. Only
the other day I heard you read some passage or other, and
in it you spoke of women whom you adored. You are a
satyr, a magus! "

This word *magus* was one of the most abusive in
Therese's vocabulary; it always made Rousseau shudder.

" There, there, now! " said he; " my dear woman, you
will find that you shall be satisfied. I intend to write that
I have found the means of regenerating the world without
causing pain to a single individual by the changes which
will be effected. Yes, yes; I will mature the project.
No revolutions! Great heavens! my good Therese, no
revolutions! "

" Well, we shall see," said the housekeeper.

" Stay! some one rings."

Therese went out and returned almost immediately with

a handsome young man, whom she requested to wait in the outer apartment. Then, rejoining Rousseau, who was already taking notes with his pencil:

"Be quick," said she, "and lock all these infamous things past. There is some one who wishes to see you."

"Who is it?"

"A nobleman of the court."

"Did he not tell you his name?"

"A good idea! as if I would receive a stranger."

"Tell it me, then."

"Monsieur de Coigny."

"Monsieur de Coigny!" exclaimed Rousseau. "Monsieur de Coigny, gentleman-in-waiting to the dauphin?"

"It must be the same; a charming youth, a most amiable young man."

"I will go, Therese."

Rousseau gave a glance at himself in the mirror, dusted his coat, wiped his slippers, which were only old shoes trodden down in the heels by long wear, and entered the dining-room where the gentleman was waiting.

The latter had not sat down. He was looking with a sort of curiosity at the dried plants pasted by Rousseau upon paper and inclosed in frames of black wood. At the noise Rousseau made in entering, he turned, and bowing most courteously:

"Have I the honor," said he, "of speaking to Monsieur Rousseau?"

"Yes, sir," replied the philosopher, in a morose voice, not unmingled, however, with a kind of admiration for the remarkable beauty and unaffected elegance of the person before him.

M. de Coigny was, in fact, one of the handsomest and most accomplished gentlemen in France. It must have been for him, and such as him, that the costume of that period was invented. It displayed to the greatest advantage the symmetry and beauty of his well-turned leg, his broad shoulders and deep chest; it gave a majestic air to his exquisitely formed head, and added to the ivory whiteness of his aristocratic hands.

His examination satisfied Rousseau, who, like a true artist, admired the beautiful wherever he met with it.

"Sir," said he, "what can I do for you?"

"You have been, perhaps, informed, sir," replied the young nobleman, "that I am the Count de Coigny. I may add that I come from her royal highness the dauphiness."

Rousseau reddened and bowed. Therese, who was standing in a corner of the dining-room, with her hands in her pockets, gazed with complacent eyes at the handsome messenger of the greatest princess in France.

"Her royal highness wants me—for what purpose?" asked Rousseau. "But take a chair, if you please, sir."

Rousseau sat down, and M. de Coigny drew forward a straw-bottomed chair, and followed his example.

"Monsieur, here is the fact. The other day, when his majesty dined at Trianon, he expressed a good deal of admiration for your music, which is indeed charming. His majesty sung your prettiest airs, and the dauphiness, who is always anxious to please his majesty in every respect, thought that it might give him pleasure to see one of your comic operas performed in the theater at Trianon."

Rousseau bowed low.

"I come, therefore, to ask you, from the dauphiness——"

"Oh, sir," interrupted Rousseau, "my permission has nothing to do in the matter. My pieces and the airs belonging to them are the property of the theater where they are represented. The permission must, therefore, be sought from the comedians, and her royal highness will, I am assured, find no obstacle in that quarter. The actors will be too happy to play and sing before his majesty and the court."

"That is not precisely what I am commissioned to request, sir," said M. de Coigny. "Her royal highness the dauphiness wishes to give a more complete and more recherché entertainment to his majesty. He knows all your operas, sir."

Another bow from Rousseau.

"And sings them charmingly."

Rousseau bit his lips.

"It is too much honor," stammered he.

" Now," pursued M. de Coigny, " as several ladies of the court are excellent musicians, and sing delightfully, and as several gentlemen also have studied music with some success, whichever of your operas the dauphiness may choose shall be performed by this company of ladies and gentlemen, the principal actors being their royal highnesses."

Rousseau bounded in his chair.

" I assure you, sir," said he, " that this is a signal honor conferred upon me, and I beg you will offer my most humble thanks to the dauphiness."

" Oh! that is not all," said M. de Coigny, with a smile.

" Ah! "

" The troupe thus composed is more illustrious certainly than that usually employed, but also more inexperienced. The superintendence and the advice of a master are, therefore, indispensable. The performance ought to be worthy of the august spectator who will occupy the royal box, and also of the illustrious author."

Rousseau rose to bow again. This time the compliment had touched him, and he saluted M. de Coigny most graciously.

" For this purpose, sir," continued the gentleman-in-waiting, " her royal highness requests your company at Trianon, to superintend the general rehearsal of the work."

" Oh! " said Rousseau, " her royal highness cannot surely think of such a thing. I at Trianon! "

" Well," said M. de Coigny, with the most natural air possible.

" Oh, sir, you are a man of taste and judgment, you have more tact than the majority of men—answer me, on your conscience, is not the idea of Rousseau, the philosopher, the outlaw, the misanthrope, attending at court, enough to make the whole cabal split their sides with laughter? "

" I do not see," replied M. de Coigny, coldly, " how the laughter and the remarks of the foolish set which persecutes you should disturb the repose of a gallant man, and an author who may lay claim to be the first in the kingdom. If you have this weakness, Monsieur Rousseau, conceal it carefully; it alone would be sufficient to raise a laugh at your expense. As to what remarks may be made, you will confess that those making them had better be careful on that point, when the pleasure and the wishes of her royal highness the dauphiness, presumptive heiress of the French kingdom, are in question."

"Certainly," said Rousseau, "certainly."

"Can it be, possibly, a lingering feeling of false shame?" said M. de Coigny, smiling. "Because you have been severe upon kings, do you fear to humanize yourself? Ah, Monsieur Rousseau, you have given valuable lessons to the human race, but I hope you do not hate them. And, besides, you certainly except the ladies of the blood royal."

"Sir, you are very kind to press me so much; but think of my position—I live retired, alone, unhappy."

Therese made a grimace.

"Unhappy!" said she. "He is hard to please."

"Whatever effort I may make, there will always be something in my features and manner unpleasing to the eyes of the king and the princesses, who seek only joy and happiness. What should I do there—what should I say?"

"One would think you distrusted yourself. But, sir, do you not think that he who has written the 'Nouvelle Héloïse' and the 'Confessions' must have more talent for speaking and acting than all of us put together, no matter what position we occupy."

"I assure you, sir, it is impossible."

"That word, sir, is not known to princes."

"And for that very reason, sir, I shall remain at home."

"Sir, you would not inflict the dreadful disappointment of returning vanquished and disgraced to Versailles on me, the venturous messenger who undertook to satisfy her royal highness? It would be such a blow to me that I should immediately retire into voluntary exile. Come, my dear Monsieur Rousseau, grant to me, a man full of the deepest sympathy for your works, this favor—a favor which you would refuse to supplicating kings."

"Sir, your kindness gains my heart, your eloquence is irresistible, and your voice touches more than I can express."

"Will you allow yourself to be persuaded?"

"No, I cannot—no, decidedly; my health forbids such a journey."

"A journey! oh, Monsieur Rousseau, what are you thinking of? An hour and a quarter in a carriage."

"Yes; for you and your prancing horses."

"But all the equipages of the court are at your disposal, Monsieur Rousseau. The dauphiness charged me to tell you that there is an apartment prepared for you at Trianon; for she is unwilling that you should have to return so late to Paris. The dauphin, who knows all your works by heart, said, before the whole court, that he would be proud to show the room in his palace where Monsieur Rousseau had slept."

Therese uttered a cry of admiration, not for Rousseau, but for the good prince.

Rousseau could not withstand this last mark of goodwill.

"I must surrender," said he, "for never have I been so well attacked."

"Your heart only is vanquished, sir," replied De Coigny; "your mind is impregnable."

"I shall go, then, sir, in obedience to the wishes of her royal highness."

"Oh, sir, receive my personal thanks. As regards the dauphiness's, permit me to abstain. She would feel annoyed at being forestalled, as she means to pay them to you in person this evening. Besides, you know, it is the man's part to thank a young and adorable lady who is good enough to make advances to him."

"True, sir," replied Rousseau, smiling; "but old men have the privilege of pretty women—they are sought after."

"If you will name your hour, Monsieur Rousseau, I shall send my carriage for you; or, rather, I will come myself to take you up."

"No, thank you, sir. I must positively refuse your kind offer. I will go to Trianon, but let me go in whatever manner I may choose. From this moment leave me to myself. I shall come, that is all. Tell me the hour."

"What, sir! you will not allow me to introduce you? I

know I am not worthy of the honor, and that a name like yours needs no announcement——"

"Sir, I am aware that you are more at court than I am anywhere in the world. I do not refuse your offer, therefore, from any motives personal to yourself, but I love my liberty. I wish to go as if I were merely taking a walk, and—in short, that is my ultimatum."

"Sir, I bow to your decision, and should be most unwilling to displease you in any particular. The rehearsal commences at six o'clock."

"Very well. At a quarter before six I shall be at Trianon."

"But by what conveyance?"

"That is my affair—these are my horses."

He pointed to his legs, which were well formed, and displayed with some pretension.

"Five leagues!' said M. de Coigny, alarmed; "you will be knocked up—take care, it will be a fatiguing evening!"

"In that case, have my carriage—and my horses also —a fraternal carriage—the popular vehicle, which belongs to my neighbor as well as to myself, and which costs only fifteen sous."

"Oh, good heavens! The stage-coach! You make me shudder."

"Its benches, which seem to you so hard, are to me like the Sybarite's couch. To me they seem stuffed with down or strewn with rose leaves. Adieu, sir, till this evening."

M. de Coigny, seeing himself thus dismissed, took his leave after a multitude of thanks, indications more or less precise, and expressions of gratitude for his services. He descended the dark staircase, accompanied by Rousseau to the landing, and by Therese half-way down the stairs.

M. de Coigny entered his carriage, which was waiting in the street, and drove back to Versailles, smiling to himself.

Therese returned to the apartment, slamming the door with angry violence which foretold a storm for Rousseau.

CHAPTER XLII.

ROUSSEAU'S TOILET.

WHEN M. de Coigny was gone, Rousseau, whose ideas this visit had entirely changed, threw himself into a little armchair, with a deep sigh, and said, in a sleepy tone:

"Oh! how tiresome this is. How these people weary me with their persecutions!"

Therese caught the last words as she entered, and placing herself before Rousseau:

"How proud we are!" said she.

"I?" asked Rousseau, surprised.

"Yes; you are a vain fellow—a hypocrite!"

"I?"

"Yes, you; you are enchanted to go to court, and you conceal your joy under this false indifference."

"Oh, good heavens!" replied Rousseau, shrugging his shoulders, and humiliated at being so truly described.

"Do you not wish to make me believe that it is not a great honor for you to perform for the king the airs you thump here upon your spinet, like a good-for-nothing, as you are?"

Rousseau looked angrily at his wife.

"You are a simpleton!" said he; "it is no honor for a man such as I am to appear before a king. To what does this man owe that he is on the throne? To a caprice of nature, which gave him a queen as his mother; but I am worthy of being called before the king to minister to his recreation. It is to my works I owe it and to the fame acquired by my works."

Therese was not a woman to be so easily conquered.

"I wish Monsieur de Sartines heard you talking in this style; he would give you a lodging in Bicetre or a cell at Charenton."

"Because this Monsieur de Sartines is a tyrant in the pay of another tyrant, and because man is defenseless

against tyrants with the aid of his genius alone.   But if
Monsieur de Sartines were to persecute me——"

"Well, what, then?" asked Therese.

"Ah, yes!" sighed Rousseau, "yes, I know that would
delight my enemies."

"Why have you enemies?" continued Therese.   "Because you are ill-natured, and because you have attacked
every one.   Ah, Monsieur de Voltaire knows how to
make friends, he does!"

"True," said Rousseau, with an angelic smile.

"But, dame!   Monsieur de Voltaire is a gentleman—
he is the intimate friend of the King of Prussia; he has
horses, he is rich, and lives at his château at Ferney.   And
all that he owes to his merit.   Therefore, when he goes to
court, he does not act the disdainful man—he is quite at
home there."

"And do you think," said Rousseau, "that I shall not be
at home there?   Think you that I do not know where all
the money that is spent there comes from, or that I am
duped by the respect which is paid to the master.   Oh,
my good woman, who judgest everything falsely, remember
if I act the disdainful, it is because I really feel contempt
—remember that if I despise the pomp of these courtiers,
it is because they have stolen their riches."

"Stolen!" said Therese, with inexpressible indignation.

"Yes, stolen from you—from me—from every one.   All
the gold they have upon their fine clothes should be restored to the poor wretches who want bread.   That is the
reason why I, who know all these things, go so reluctantly
to court."

"I do not say that the people are happy—but the king
is always the king."

"Well, I obey him; what more does he want?"

"Ah! you obey because you are afraid.   You must not
say, in my hearing, that you go against your will, or that
you are a brave man, for if so, I shall reply that you are a
hypocrite, and that you are very glad to go."

"I do not fear anything," said Rousseau, superbly.

"Good!   Just go and say to the king one quarter of
what you have been telling me the last half-hour."

"I shall assuredly do so, if my feelings prompt me."

"You?"

"Yes. Have I ever recoiled?"

"Bah! You dare not take a bone from a cat when she is gnawing it, for fear she should scratch you. What would you be if surrounded by guards and swordsmen? Look you. I know you as well as if I were your mother. You will just now go and shave yourself afresh, oil your hair, and make yourself beautiful; you will display your leg to the utmost advantage; you will put on your interesting little winking expression, because your eyes are small and round, and if you opened them naturally, that would be seen, while, when you wink, you make people believe that they are as large as carriage entrances. You will ask me for your silk stockings; you will put on your chocolate-colored coat with steel buttons and your beautiful new wig; you will order a coach, and my philosopher will go and be adored by the ladies! And to-morrow—ah!—to-morrow, there will be such ecstatic reveries, such interesting languor! You will come back amorous, you will sigh and write verses, and you will dilute your coffee with your tears. Oh! how well I know you."

"You are wrong, my dear," said Rousseau. "I tell you, I am reluctantly obliged to go to court. I go because, after all, I fear to cause scandal, as every honest citizen should do. Moreover, I am not one of those who refuse to acknowledge the supremacy of one citizen in a republic; but as to making advances, as to brushing my new coat against the gold spangles of these gentlemen of the Œil-de-Bœuf—no, no; I shall do nothing of the sort, and if you catch me doing so, laugh at me as much as you please."

"Then you will not dress?" said Therese, sarcastically.

"No."

"You will not put on your new wig?"

"No."

"You will not wink with your little eyes?"

"I tell you I shall go like a free man, without affectation and without fear. I shall go to court as if I were going to the theater, and let the actors like me or not, I care not for them."

"Oh! you will at least trim your beard," said Therese; "it is half a foot long."

"I tell you I shall make no change."

Therese burst into so loud and prolonged a laugh that Rousseau was obliged to take refuge in the next room. But the housekeeper had not finished her persecutions; she had them of all colors and kinds.

She opened the cupboard and took out his best coat, his clean linen, and beautifully polished shoes. She spread all these articles out upon the bed and over the chairs in the apartment; but Rousseau did not seem to pay the least attention.

At last Therese said:

"Come, it is time you should dress. A court toilet is tedious. You will have barely time to reach Versailles at the appointed hour."

"I have told you, Therese, that I shall do very well as I am. It is the same dress in which I present myself every day among my fellow-citizens. A king is but a citizen like myself."

"Come, come," said Therese, trying to tempt him and bring him to her purpose by artful insinuation; "do not pout, Jacques, and don't be foolish. Here are your clothes. Your razor is ready; I have sent for the barber, in case you have your nervousness to-day."

"Thank you, my dear," replied Rousseau; "I shall only just give myself a brush, and take my shoes because I cannot go out in slippers."

"Is he going to be firm, I wonder?" thought Therese.

She tried to coax him, sometimes by coquetry, sometimes by persuasion, and sometimes by the violence of her raillery. But Rousseau knew her and saw the snare. He felt that the moment he should give way, he would be unmercifully disgraced and ridiculed by his better half. He determined, therefore, not to give way, and abstained from looking at the fine clothes, which set off what he termed his natural advantages.

Therese watched him. She had only one resource left; this was the glance which Rousseau never failed to give in the glass before he went out; for the philosopher was neat to an extreme, if there can be an extreme in neatness.

But Rousseau continued to be on his guard, and as he caught Therese's anxious look, he turned his back to the looking-glass. The hour arrived, the philosopher had filled his head with all the disagreeable remarks he could think of to say to the king.

He repeated some scraps of them to himself while he buckled his shoes, then tucked his hat under his arm, seized his cane, and taking advantage of a moment when Therese could not see him, he pulled down his coat and his waistcoat with both hands to smooth the creases.

Therese now returned, handed him a handkerchief, which he plunged into his huge pocket, and then accompanied him to the landing-place, saying:

" Come, Jacques, be reasonable; you look quite frightful—you have the air of some false moneyer."

" Adieu!" said Rousseau.

" You look like a thief, sir," said Therese; " take care!"

" Take care of fire," said Rousseau, " and do not touch my papers."

" You have just the air of a spy, I assure you!" said Therese, in despair.

Rousseau made no reply; he descended the steps, singing, and favored by the obscurity, he gave his hat a brush with his sleeve, smoothed his shirt frill with his left hand, and touched up his toilet with a rapid but skilful movement.

Arrived at the foot of the stairs, he bodily confronted the mud of the Rue Plastriere, walking upon tiptoe, and reached the Champs-Elysees, where those honest vehicles which, so rather affectedly called *pataches,* were stationed, and which, so late as ten years ago, still carried, or rather bundled, from Paris to Versailles those travelers who were obliged to use economy.

CHAPTER XLIII.

THE SIDE SCENES OF TRIANON.

THE adventures of the journey are of no importance. A Swiss, an assistant clerk, a citizen, and an abbé were of course among his traveling companions.

He arrived at half-past five. The court was already assembled at Trianon, and the performers were going over their parts while waiting for the king; for as to the author, no one thought of him. Some were aware that M. Rousseau, of Geneva, was to come to direct the rehearsal; but they took no greater interest in seeing M. Rousseau than M. Rameau, or M. Marmontel, or any other of those singular animals, to a sight of which the courtiers sometimes treated themselves in their drawing-rooms or country houses.

Rousseau was received by the usher in waiting, who had been ordered by M. de Coigny to inform him as soon as the philosopher should arrive.

This young nobleman hastened with his usual courtesy, and received Rousseau with the most amiable *empressement*...But scarcely had he cast his eyes over his person, than he stared with astonishment, and could not prevent himself from recommencing the examination.

Rousseau was dusty, pale, and disheveled, and his paleness rendered conspicuous such a beard as no master of the ceremonies had ever seen reflected in the mirrors of Versailles.

Rousseau felt deeply embarrassed under M. de Coigny's scrutiny, but more embarrassed still when, approaching the hall of the theater, he saw the profusion of splendid dresses, valuable lace, diamonds, and blue ribbons, which, with the gilding of the hall, produced the effect of a bouquet of flowers in an immense basket.

Rousseau felt ill at ease also when he breathed this perfumed atmosphere, so intoxicating for plebeian nerves.

Yet he was obliged to proceed and put a bold face on the matter. Multitudes of eyes were fixed upon him who thus formed a stain, as it were, on the polish of the assembly. M. de Coigny, still preceding him, led him to the orchestra, where the musicians were waiting for him.

When there, he felt rather relieved, and while his music was being performed, he seriously reflected that the worst danger was past, that the step was taken, and that all the reasoning in the world could now be of no avail.

Already the dauphiness was on the stage, in her costume as Colette; she waited for Colin.

M. de Coigny was changing his dress in his box.

All at once the king entered, surrounded by a crowd of bending heads. Louis smiled, and seemed to be in the best humor possible. The dauphin seated himself at his right hand, and the Count de Provence, arriving soon after, took his place on the left. On a sign from the king, the fifty persons who composed the assembly, private as it was, took their seats.

" Well, why do you not begin? " asked Louis.

" Sire," said the dauphiness, " the shepherds and shepherdesses are not yet dressed; we are waiting for them."

" They can perform in their evening-dresses," said the king.

" No, sire," replied the dauphiness, " for we wish to try the dresses and costumes by candle-light, to be certain of the effect."

" You are right, madame," said the king; " then let us take a stroll."

And Louis rose to make the circuit of the corridor and the stage. Besides, he was rather uneasy at not seeing Mme. Dubarry.

When the king had left the box, Rousseau gazed in a melancholy mood and with an aching heart at the empty hall and his own solitary position; it was a singular contrast to the reception he had anticipated.

He had pictured to himself that on his entrance all the groups would separate before him; that the curiosity of the courtiers would be even more importunate and more significative than that of the Parisians; he had feared questions and presentations; and, lo! no one paid any attention to him.

He thought that his long beard was not yet long enough; that rags would not have been more remarked than his old clothes, and he applauded himself for not having been so ridiculous as to aim at elegance. But at the bottom of his heart he felt humiliated at being thus reduced to the simple post of leader of the orchestra. Suddenly an officer approached and asked him if he was not M. Rousseau.

" Yes, sir," replied he.

" Her royal highness the dauphiness wishes to speak to you, sir," said the officer.

Rousseau rose, much agitated.

The dauphiness was waiting for him. She held in her hand the air of Colette.

' My happiness is gone."

The moment she saw Rousseau, she advanced toward him. The philosopher bowed very humbly, saying to himself, " Then his bow was for the woman, not for the princess."

The dauphiness, on the contrary, was as gracious toward the savage philosopher as she would have been to the most finished gentleman in Europe.

She requested his advice about the inflection she ought to get to the third strophe—

" Colin leaves me."

Rousseau forthwith commenced to develop a theory of declamation and melody, which, learned as it was, was interrupted by the noisy arrival of the king and several courtiers.

Louis entered the room in which the dauphiness was taking her lesson from the philosopher. The first impulse of the king's when he saw this carelessly dressed person was the same that M. de Coigny had manifested, only M. de Coigny knew Rousseau, and the king did not.

He stared, therefore, long and steadily, at our freeman, while still receiving the thanks and compliments of the dauphiness.

This look, stamped with royal authority—this look, not accustomed to be lowered before any one—produced a powerful effect upon Rousseau, whose quick eye was timid and unsteady.

The dauphiness waited until the king had finished his scrutiny, then, advancing toward Rousseau, she said:

"Will your majesty allow me to present our author to you?"

"Your author?" said the king, seeming to consult his memory.

During this short dialogue Rousseau was upon burning coals. The king's eye had successively rested upon and burned up—like the sun's rays under a powerful lens—the long beard, the dubious shirt-frill, the dusty garb, and the old wig of the greatest writer in his kingdom.

The dauphiness took pity on the latter.

"Monsieur Jean Jacques Rousseau, sire," said she, "the author of the charming opera we are going to execute before your majesty."

The king raised his head.

"Ah!" said he, coldly, "Monsieur Rousseau, I greet you."

And he continued to look at him in such a manner as to point out all the imperfections of his dress.

Rousseau asked himself how he ought to salute the king of France, without being a courtier, but also without impoliteness, for he confessed that he was in the prince's house.

But while he was making these reflections, the king addressed him with that graceful ease of princes who have said everything when they have uttered an agreeable or a disagreeable remark to the person before them. Rousseau, petrified, had at first stood speechless. All the phrases he had prepared for the tyrant were forgotten.

"Monsieur Rousseau," said the king, still looking at his coat and wig, "you have composed some charming music, which has caused me to pass some very pleasant moments."

Then the king, in a voice which was diametrically opposed to all diapason and melody, commenced singing:

> " Had I turned a willing ear,
>   The gallants of the town to hear,
>   Ah ! I had found with ease
>   Other lovers then to please."

" It is charming ! " said the king, when he had finished.
Rousseau bowed.

" I do not know if I shall sing it well," said the dauphiness.

Rousseau turned toward the dauphiness to make some
remark in reply; but the king had commenced again, and
was singing the romance of Colin:

> " From my hut, obscure and cold,
>   Care is absent never ;
>   Whether sun, or storm, or cold,
>   Suffering, toil, forever."

His majesty sung frightfully for a musician. Rousseau, half flattered by the monarch's good memory, half
wounded by his detestable execution, looked like a monkey
nibbling an onion—crying on one side of his face and
laughing on the other.

The dauphiness preserved her composure with that im-
perturbable self-possession which is only found at court.

The king, without the least embarrassment, continued:

> " If thou'lt come to cast thy lot
>   In thy Colin's humble cot,
>   My sweet shepherdess Colette,
>   I'll bid adieu to all regret."

Rousseau felt the color rising to his face.

" Tell me, Monsieur Rousseau," said the king, " is it true
that you sometimes dress in the costume of an Armenian ? "

Rousseau blushed more deeply than before, and his
tongue was so glued to his throat that not for a kingdom could he have pronounced a word at this moment.

The king continued to sing, without waiting for a reply:

> " Ah ! but little, as times go,
>   Doth love know
>   What he'd let or what he'd hinder."

"You live in the Rue Plastriere, I believe, Monsieur Rousseau?" said the king.

Rousseau made a gesture in the affirmative with his head; but that was the *ultimâ thule* of his strength. Never had he called up so much to his support.

The king hummed:

> "She is a child,
> She is a child."

"It is said that you are on bad terms with Voltaire, Monsieur Rousseau?"

At this blow Rousseau lost the little presence of mind he had remaining, and was totally put out of countenance. The king did not seem to have much pity for him, and, continuing his ferocious melomania, he moved off, singing:

> "Come, dance with me beneath the elms;
> Young maidens, come be merry."

with orchestral accompaniments which would have killed Apollo, as the latter killed Marsyas.

Rousseau remained alone in the center of the room. The dauphiness had quitted it to finish her toilet.

Rousseau, trembling and confused, regained the corridor; but on his way he stumbled against a couple dazzling with diamonds, flowers, and lace, who filled up the entire width of the corridor, although the young man squeezed his lovely companion tenderly to his side.

The young woman, with her fluttering laces, her towering headdress, her fan, and her perfumes, was radiant as a star. It was she against whom Rousseau brushed in passing.

The young man, slender, elegant, and charming, with his blue ribbon rustling against his English shirt-frill, every now and then burst into a laugh of most engaging frankness, and then suddenly interrupted it with little confidential whispers which made the lady laugh in her turn, and showed that they were on excellent terms.

Rousseau recognized the Countess Dubarry in this beautiful lady, this seducing creature; and the moment he perceived her, true to his habit of absorbing his whole thoughts on a single object, he no longer saw her companion.

The young man with the blue ribbon was no other than the Count d'Artois, who was merrily toying with his grandfather's favorite.

When Mme. Dubarry perceived Rousseau's dark figure, she exclaimed:

"Ah, good heavens!"

"What!" said the Count d'Artois, also looking at the philosopher; and already he had stretched out his hand to make way for his companion.

"Monsieur Rousseau!" exclaimed Mme. Dubarry.

"Rousseau of Geneva?" said the Count d'Artois, in the tone of a schoolboy in the holidays.

"Yes, my lord," replied the countess.

"Ah, good day, Monsieur Rousseau," said the young fop, seeing Rousseau make a despairing effort to force a passage; "good day; we are going to hear your music."

"My lord——" stammered Rousseau, seeing the blue ribbon.

"Ah! most charming music!" exclaimed the countess; "and completely in harmony with the heart and mind of the author."

Rousseau raised his head, and his eyes met the burning gaze of the countess.

"Madame!" said he, ill-humoredly.

"I will play Colin, madame," cried the Count d'Artois, "and I entreat that you, Madame la Comtesse, will play Colette."

"With all my heart, my lord; but I would never dare —I, who am not an artist—to profane the music of a master."

Rousseau would have given his life to look again at her; but the voice, the tone, the flattery, the beauty, had each planted a baited hook in his heart. He tried to escape.

"Monsieur Rousseau," said the prince, blocking up the passage, "I wish you would teach me the part of Colin."

"I dare not ask Monsieur Rousseau to give me his advice respecting Colette," said the countess, feigning timidity, and thus completing the overthrow of the philosopher."

But yet his eyes inquired why.

" Monsieur Rousseau hates me," said she to the prince, with her enchanting voice.

" You are jesting," exclaimed the Count d'Artois. " Who could hate you, madame? "

" You see it plainly," replied she.

" Monsieur Rousseau is too great a man and has written too many noble works to fly from such a charming woman," said the Count d'Artois.

Rousseau heaved a sigh as if he were ready to give up the ghost, and made his escape through a narrow loop-hole which the Count d'Artois had imprudently left between himself and the wall. But Rousseau was not in luck this evening. He had scarcely proceeded four steps when he met another group composed of two men, one old, the other young. The young one wore the blue ribbon; the other, who might be about fifty years of age, was dressed in red and looked austere and pale. These two men overheard the merry laugh of the Count d'Artois, who exclaimed loudly:

" Ah! Monsieur Rousseau, Monsieur Rousseau! I shall say that the countess put you to flight; and, in truth, no one would believe it."

" Rousseau! " murmured the two men.

" Stop him, brother! " said the prince, still laughing; " stop him, Monsieur de Vauguyon! "

Rousseau now comprehended on what rock his evil star had shipwrecked him. The Count de Provence and the governor of the royal youths were before him.

The Count de Provence also barred the way.

" Good day, sir," said he, with his dry, pedantic voice.

Rousseau, almost at his wits' end, bowed, muttering to himself:

" I shall never get away! "

" Ah! I am delighted to have met you," said the prince, with the air of a schoolmaster who finds a pupil in fault.

" More absurd compliments! " thought Rousseau. " How insipid these great people are! "

"I have read your translation of ' Tacitus,' sir."

"Ah! true," thought Rousseau; "this one is a pedant, a scholar."

"Do you know that it is very difficult to translate ' Tacitus'?"

"My lord, I said so in a short preface."

"Yes, I know, I know; you said in it that you had only a slight knowledge of Latin."

"It is true, my lord."

"Then, Monsieur Rousseau, why translate ' Tacitus'?"

"My lord, it improves one's style."

"Ah! Monsieur Rousseau, it was wrong to translate *imperatoriâ brevitate* by ' a grave and concise discourse.' "

Rousseau, uneasy, consulted his memory.

"Yes," said the young prince, with the confidence of an old *savant* who discovers a fault in Saumise; "yes, you translated it so. It is in the paragraph where Tacitus relates that Pison harangued his soldiers."

"Well, my lord?"

"Well, Monsieur Rousseau, *imperatoriâ brevitate* means, ' with the conciseness of a general,' or of a man accustomed to command. With the brevity of command; that is the expression, is it not, Monsieur de la Vauguyon?"

"Yes, my lord," replied the governor.

Rousseau made no reply. The prince added:

"That is an evident mistake, Monsieur Rousseau. Oh! I will find you another."

Rousseau turned pale.

"Stay, Monsieur Rousseau, there is one in the paragraph relating to Cecina. It commences thus: *At in superiore Germaniâ.* You know he is describing Cecina, and Tacitus says, *Cito sermone.*"

"I remember it perfectly, my lord."

"You translated that by ' speaking well.' "

"Yes, my lord, and I thought——"

"*Cito sermone* means ' speaking quickly,' that is to say, easily."

"I said, ' speaking well.' "

"Then it should have been *decoro,* or *ornato,* or *ele-*

ganti sermone; cito is a picturesque epithet, Monsieur
Rousseau. Just as in portraying the change in Otho's
conduct, Tacitus says: *Delatâ voluptate, dissimulatâ luxuriâ, cuncta que ad imperii decorem composita."*

"I have translated that: 'Dismissing luxury and ef-
feminacy to other times, he surprised the world by in-
dustriously applying himself to re-establish the glory of
the empire.'"

"Wrong, Monsieur Rousseau, wrong! In the first place,
you have run the three little phrases into one, which
obliges you to translate *dissimulatâ luxuriâ* badly. Then
you made a blunder in the last portion of the phrase.
Tacitus did not mean that the Emperor Otho applied
himself to re-establishing the glory of the empire; he
meant to say that, no longer gratifying his passions, and
dissimulating his luxurious habits, Otho accommodated
all, made all turn—all, you understand, Monsieur Rousseau—that is to say, even his passions and his vices—to the
glory of the empire. That is the sense—it is rather com-
plex; yours, however, is too restricted, is it not, Monsieur
de la Vauguyon?"

"Yes, my lord."

Rousseau perspired and panted under this pitiless in-
fliction.

The prince allowed him a moment's breathing time,
and then continued:

"You are much more in your element in philosophy,
sir."

Rousseau bowed.

"But your 'Emilius' is a dangerous book."

"Dangerous, my lord?"

"Yes, from the quantity of false ideas it will put into
the citizens' heads!"

"My lord, as soon as a man is a father, he can enter
into the spirit of my book, whether he be the first or the
last in the kingdom. To be a father—is—is——"

"Tell me, Monsieur Rousseau," asked the satirical
prince, all at once, "your 'Confessions' form a very amusing book. How many children have you had?"

Rousseau turned pale, staggered, and raised an angry

and stupefied glance to his young tormentor's face, the expression of which only increased the malicious humor of the Count de Provence.

It was only malice, for, without waiting for a reply, the prince moved away arm in arm with his preceptor, continuing his commentaries on the works of the man whom he had so cruelly crushed.

Rousseau, left alone, was gradually recovering from his stupefaction, when he heard the first bars of his overture executed by the orchestra.

He proceeded in that direction with a faltering step, and when he reached his seat, he said to himself. " Fool! coward! stupid ass that I am! Now only do I find the answer I should have made the cruel little pedant. ' My lord,' I should have said, ' it is not charitable in a young person to torment a poor old man! ' "

He had just reached this point, quite content with his phrase, when the dauphiness and M. de Coigny commenced their duet. The preoccupation of the philosopher was disturbed by the suffering of the musician—the ear was to be tortured after the heart.

CHAPTER XLIV.

THE REHEARSAL.

THE rehearsal once fairly commenced, and the general attention drawn to the stage, Rousseau was no longer remarked, and it was he on the contrary who became the observer. He heard court lords who sung completely out of tune to their shepherds' dresses, and saw ladies arrayed in their court dresses coqueting like shepherdesses.

The dauphiness sung correctly, but she was a bad actress; and her voice, moreover, was so weak that she could scarcely be heard. The king, not to intimidate any one, had retired to an obscure box, where he chatted with the ladies. The dauphin prompted the words of the opera, which went off royally badly.

Rousseau determined not to listen, but he felt it very difficult to avoid overhearing what passed. He had one consolation, however, for he had just perceived a charming face among the illustrious figurantes, and the village maiden, who was the possessor of this charming face, had incomparably the most delightful voice of the entire company.

Rousseau's attention became at once completely riveted, and from his position behind the desk, he gazed with his whole soul at the charming figurante, and listened with all his ears to drink in the enchanting melody of her voice.

When the dauphiness saw the author so deeply attentive, she felt persuaded, from his smile and his sentimental air, that he was pleased with the execution of his work, and, eager for a compliment—for she was a woman—she leaned forward to the desk, saying:

"Is our performance very bad, Monsieur Rousseau?"

But Rousseau, with lips apart and absent air, did not reply.

"Oh! we have made some blunders," said the dauphiness, "and Monsieur Rousseau dares not tell us! Pray do, Monsieur Rousseau."

Rousseau's gaze never left the beautiful personage, who on her side did not perceive in the least the attention which she excited.

"Ah!" said the dauphiness, following the direction of our philosopher's eyes, "it is Mademoiselle Taverney who has been in fault!"

Andrée blushed; she saw all eyes directed toward her.

"No! no!" exclaimed Rousseau; "it was not mademoiselle, for mademoiselle sings like an angel.

Mme. Dubarry darted at the philosopher a look keener than a javelin.

The Baron de Taverney, on the contrary, felt his heart bound with joy, and greeted Rousseau with a most enchanting smile.

"Do you think that young girl sings well?" said Mme. Dubarry to the king, who was evidently struck by Rousseau's words.

"In a chorus I cannot hear her distinctly," said

Louis XV.; "it requires a musician to be able to distinguish."

Meanwhile, Rousseau was busy in the orchestra directing the chorus:

> " Colin revient a sa bergère,
> Celebrons un retour si beau."

As he turned to resume his seat, he saw M. de Jussieu bowing graciously to him.

It was no slight pleasure for the Genevese to be seen thus giving laws to the court by a courtier who had wounded him a little by his superiority. He returned his bow most ceremoniously, and continued to gaze at Andrée, who looked even more lovely for the praises she had received.

As the rehearsal proceeded, Mme. Dubarry became furious; twice had she surprised Louis XV.'s attention, wandering distracted by the spectacle before him from the sweet speeches she whispered.

The spectacle in the eyes of the jealous favorite meant Andrée alone, but this did not prevent the dauphiness from receiving many compliments and being in charmingly gay spirits. M. de Richelieu fluttered around her with the agility of a young man, and succeeded in forming, at the extremity of the stage, a circle of laughers, of which the dauphiness was the center, and which rendered the Dubarry party extremely uneasy.

"It appears," said he aloud, "that Mademoiselle de Taverney has a sweet voice."

"Charming!" said the dauphiness; "and had I not been too selfish, I should have allowed her to play Colette; but as it is my amusement that undertook the character, I will not give it up to no one."

"Oh! Mademoiselle de Taverney would not sing it better than your royal highness," said Richelieu, "and——"

"Mademoiselle is an excellent musician," said Rousseau, with enthusiasm.

"Excellent!" responded the dauphiness; "and to confess the truth, it is she who teaches me my part; besides, she dances enchantingly, and I dance very badly."

The effect of this conversation upon the king, upon

Mme. Dubarry, and the whole crowd of curious news-mongers and envious intriguers, may be imagined. All either tasted the pleasure of inflicting a wound, or received a blow with shame and grief. There were no indifferent spectators, except perhaps Andrée herself.

The dauphiness, incited by Richelieu, ended by making Andrée sing the air:

> " I have lost my love—
> Colin leaves me."

The king's head was seen to mark the time with such evident tokens of pleasure, that Mme. Dubarry's rouge fell off, from her agitation, in little flakes, as paintings fall to pieces from damp.

Richelieu, more malicious than a woman, enjoyed his revenge. He had drawn near the elder Taverney, and the two old men formed a tableau which might have been taken for Hypocrisy and Corruption sealing a project of union.

Their joy increased the more as Mme. Dubarry's features grew by degrees darker and darker. She added the finishing stroke to it by rising angrily, which was contrary to all etiquette, as the king was still seated.

The courtiers, like ants, felt the storm approach, and hastened to seek shelter with the strongest. The dauphiness was more closely surrounded by her own friends, Mme. Dubarry was more courted by hers.

By degrees the interest of the rehearsal was diverted from its natural course, and was turned in quite a different direction. Colin and Colette were no more thought of, and many spectators thought it would soon be Mme. Dubarry's turn to sing:

> " I have lost my love—
> Colin leaves me."

" Do you mark," whispered Richelieu to Taverney, " your daughter's immense success?"

And he drew him into the corridor, pushing open a glass door, and causing a looker-on, who had been clinging to the framework, in order to see into the hall, to fall backward.

"Plague take the wretch!" grumbled Richelieu, dusting his sleeve, which the rebound of the door had brushed against, and seeming still more angry when he saw that the looker-on was dressed like a workman of the château.

It was in fact a workman with a basket of flowers under his arm, who had succeeded in climbing up behind the glass, from which position he commanded a view of the entire saloon.

He was pushed back into the corridor, and almost overturned; but, although he himself escaped falling, his basket was upset.

"Ah! I know the rascal!" said Taverney, angrily.

"Who is it?" asked the duke.

"What are you doing here, scoundrel?" asked Taverney.

Gilbert—for the reader has doubtless already recognized him—replied haughtily:

"You see—I am looking."

"Instead of being at your work?" said Richelieu.

"My work is done," said Gilbert, humbly addressing the duke, without deigning to look at Taverney.

"Am I fated to meet this lazy rascal everywhere?" said Taverney.

"Gently, sir," interrupted a voice; "gently. My little Gilbert is a good workman and an industrious botanist."

Taverney turned, and saw M. de Jussieu, who was patting Gilbert on the head. The baron reddened with anger and moved off.

"Valets here!" muttered he.

"Hush!" said Richelieu, "there is Nicole! look—up there, at the corner of the door. The little buxom witch! she is not making bad use of her eyes, either."

The marshal was correct. Partially concealed behind a score of the domestics of Trianon, Nicole raised her charming head above all the others, and her eyes, dilated with surprise and admiration, seemed to devour everything she saw.

Gilbert perceived her, and turned another way.

"Come, come!" said the duke to Taverney; "I fancy the king wishes to speak with you. He is looking this way."

And the two friends disappeared in the direction of the royal box.

Mme. Dubarry was standing behind the king, and interchanging signs with M. d'Aiguillon, who was also standing, and who did not lose one of his uncle's movements.

Rousseau, now left alone, admired Andrée; he was endeavoring, if we may use the expression, to fall in love with her.

The illustrious actors proceeded to disrobe in their boxes, which Gilbert had decorated with fresh flowers.

Taverney, left alone in the passage by M. de Richelieu, who had gone to rejoin the king, felt his heart alternately chilled and elated. At last the duke returned and placed his finger upon his lips. Taverney turned pale with joy, and advanced to meet his friend, who drew him beneath the royal box. There they overheard the following conversation, which was quite inaudible to the rest of the company. Mme. Dubarry was saying to the king:

"May I expect your majesty to supper this evening?"

And the king replied:

"I feel fatigued, countess, excuse me."

At the same moment the dauphin entered, treading almost on Mme. Dubarry's toes without seeming to see her.

"Sire," said he, "will your majesty do us the honor of supping with us at Trianon?"

"No, my son; I was just at this moment saying to the countess that I felt fatigued. Our young people have made me giddy; I shall sup alone."

The dauphin bowed and retired. Mme. Dubarry courtesied almost to the ground, and, trembling with rage, left the box. When she was gone the king made a sign to the Duke de Richelieu.

"Duke," said he, "I wish to speak to you about an affair which concerns you."

"Sire——"

"I am not satisfied. I wish you to explain——stay, I shall sup alone; you will keep me company."

And the king looked at Taverney.

"You know this gentleman, I think, duke?"

"Monsieur de Taverney? Yes, sire."

"Ah! the father of the charming singer?"

"Yes, sire."

"Listen, duke."

And the king stooped to whisper in Richelieu's ear. Taverney clinched his hand till the nails entered the flesh, to avoid showing any emotion. Immediately afterward Richelieu brushed past Taverney, and said:

"Follow me without making any remark."

"Whither?" asked Taverney, in the same tone.

"No matter; follow me."

The duke moved away. Taverney followed him at a little distance to the king's apartment. The duke entered; Taverney waited in the anteroom.

CHAPTER XLV.

THE CASKET.

M. DE TAVERNEY had not to wait long. Richelieu, having asked the king's valet for something his majesty had left upon his dressing-table, soon returned, carrying something the nature of which the baron could not distinguish on account of the covering of silk which enveloped it.

But the marshal soon relieved his friend from all anxiety. Drawing him into a corner of the gallery:

"Baron," said he, as soon as he saw that they were alone, "you have at times seemed to doubt my friendship for you."

"Never since our reconciliation," replied Taverney.

"At least you doubted your own good fortune and that of your children?"

"Oh! as for that—yes."

"Well, you are wrong. Your children's fortune and your own is made with a rapidity which might make you giddy."

" Bah ! " said Taverney, who suspected part of the truth, but who, as he was not quite certain, took care to guard against mistakes, " what do you mean ? "

" Monsieur Philip is already a captain, with a company paid for by the king."

" It is true—I owe that to you."

" By no means. Then we shall have Mademoiselle de Taverney a marchioness, perhaps."

" Come, come ! " exclaimed Taverney. " How ? my daughter ! "

" Listen, Taverney. The king has great taste; and beauty, grace, and virtue, when accompanied by talent, delight his majesty. Now Mademoiselle de Taverney unites all these qualities in a very high degree. The king is therefore delighted with Mademoiselle de Taverney."

" Duke," replied Taverney, assuming an air of dignity at which the marshal could scarcely repress a smile, " duke, what do you mean by ' delighted ' ? "

" Baron, I am not a great linguist. I am not even well versed in orthography. I have always thought that ' delighted ' signified ' content beyond measure.' If you are grieved beyond measure to see the king pleased with the beauty, the talent, the merit of your children, you have only to say so. I am about to return to his majesty."

And Richelieu turned on his heel and made a pirouette with truly juvenile grace.

" You misunderstand me, duke," exclaimed the baron, stopping him. " Ventre bleu ! how hasty you are ! "

" What did you say that you were not satisfied ? "

" I did not say so."

" You ask for explanations of the king's pleasure— plague take the fool ! "

" But, duke, I did not breathe a syllable of that. I am most certainly content."

" Ah ! you—well, who will be displeased ? Your daughter ? "

" Oh ! oh ! "

" My dear friend, you have brought up your daughter like a savage, as you are."

" My dear friend, the young lady educated herself; you

may easily imagine that I could not possibly trouble myself with any such matter. I had enough to do to support
life in my den at Taverney. Virtue in her sprung up spon-
taneously."

"And yet people say that country folk know how to
pull up weeds? In short, your daughter is a prude."

"You mistake; she is a dove."

Richelieu made a grimace. "Well," said he, "the poor
child must only look out for a good husband, for opportunities of making a fortune happen rarely with this defect."

Taverney looked uneasily at the duke.

"Fortunately for her," continued he, "the king is so
desperately in love with Dubarry, that he will never think
seriously of another."

Taverney's alarm was changed to anguish.

"Therefore," continued Richelieu, "you and your
daughter may make your minds easy. I will state the
necessary objections to his majesty, and the king will never
bestow another thought on the matter."

"But objections to what?—good heavens!" exclaimed
Taverney, turning pale, and holding his friend's arm.

"To his making a little present to Mademoiselle Andrée, my dear baron."

"A little present! What is it?" asked the baron, brim-
ful of hope and avarice.

"Oh! a mere trifle," said Richelieu, carelessly, and he
took a casket from its silken covering.

"A casket!"

"A mere trifle—a necklace worth a few millions of
livres, which his majesty, flattered at hearing her sing his
favorite air, wished to present to the fair singer. It is the
usual custom. But if your daughter is proud, we will say
no more about it."

"Duke, you must not think of it—that would be to offend the king!"

"Of course it would; but is it not the attribute of virtue
always to offend some person, or something?"

"But, duke, consider—the child is not so unreason-
able."

"That is to say, it is you, and not your child, who speaks?"

"Oh! I know so well what she will do and say."

"The Chinese are a very fortunate nation," said Richelieu.

"Why?" asked Taverney, astonished.

"Because they have so many rivers and canals in the country."

"Duke, you turn the conversation—do not drive me to despair; speak to me."

"I am speaking to you, baron, and am not changing the conversation at all."

"Then why do you speak of China? What have its rivers to do with my daughter?"

"A great deal. The Chinese, I repeat, have the happiness of being able to drown their daughters when they are too virtuous, and no one can forbid it."

"Come, duke, you must be just. Suppose you had a daughter yourself."

"Pardieu! I have one; and if any one were to tell me that she is too virtuous, it would be very ill-natured of him—that's all."

"In short, you would like her better otherwise, would you not?"

"Oh! for my part, I don't meddle with my children after they are eight years old."

"Listen to me, at least. If the king were to commission me to offer a necklace to your daughter, and if your daughter were to complain to you?"

"Oh, my dear sir! there is no comparison. I have always lived at court, you have lived like a North American Indian; there is no similarity. What you call virtue, I think folly. Remember for the future that nothing is more ill-bred than to say to people: 'What would you do in this or that case?' And besides, your comparisons are erroneous, my friend. It is not true that I am about to present a necklace to your daughter."

"You said so."

"I said nothing of the sort. I said that the king had directed me to bring him a casket for Mademoiselle de

Taverney, whose voice had pleased him; but I did not say his majesty had charged me to give it to her."

"Then in truth," said the baron, in despair, "I know not what to think. I do not understand a single word—you speak in enigmas. Why give this necklace if it is not to be given? Why do you take charge of it if not to deliver it?"

Richelieu uttered an exclamation as if he had seen a spider.

"Ah!" said he; "*pouah! pouah!* the huron—the ugly animal!"

"Who?"

"You, my good friend—you, my trusty comrade—you seem as if you had fallen from the clouds, baron."

"I am at my wits' end."

"No, you never had any. When a king makes a lady a present, and when he charges Monsieur de Richelieu with the commission, the present is noble and the commission well executed—remember that. I do not deliver caskets, my dear sir—that was Monsieur Lebel's office. Did you know Monsieur Lebel?"

"What is your office, then?"

"My friend," said Richelieu, tapping Taverney on the shoulder, and accompanying this amiable gesture by a sardonic smile, "when I have to do with such paragons of virtue as Mademoiselle Andrée, I am the most moral man in the world. When I approach a dove, as you call your daughter, I do not display the talons of the hawk. When I am deputed to wait on a young lady, I speak to her father. I speak to you, therefore, Taverney, and give you the casket to present to your daughter. Well, are you willing?" And he offered the casket. "Or do you decline?" And he drew it back.

"Oh, say at once!" exclaimed the baron; "say at once that I am commissioned by his majesty to deliver the present. If so, it assumes quite a correct and paternal character—it is, so to speak, purified from——"

"Purified! Why, you must have suspected his majesty of evil intentions!" said Richelieu, seriously. "Now, you cannot have dared to do that."

"Heaven forbid! But the world—that is to say, my daughter——"

Richelieu shrugged his shoulders.

"Will you take it—yes or no?" asked he.

Taverney rapidly held out his hand.

"You are certain it is moral?" said he to the duke, with a smile, the counterpart of that which the duke had just addressed to him.

"Do you not think it pure morality, baron," said the marshal, "to make the father, who, as you have just said, purifies everything, an intermediate party between the king's delights and your daughter's charms? Let Monsieur Rousseau of Geneva, who was hovering about here just now, be the judge. He would say that Cato of happy memory was impure compared to me."

Richelieu pronounced these few words with a calmness, an abrupt haughtiness, a precision, which silenced Taverney's objections, and assisted to make him believe that he ought to be convinced. He seized his illustrious friend's hand, therefore, and pressing it:

"Thanks to your delicacy," said he, "my daughter can accept this present."

"The source and origin of the good fortune to which I alluded at the commencement of our tiresome discussion on virtue."

"Thanks, dear duke—most hearty thanks!"

"One word more. Conceal this favor carefully from the Dubarrys. It might make Madame Dubarry leave the king and take flight."

"And the king would be displeased?"

"I don't know, but the countess would not thank us. As for me, I should be lost; be discreet, therefore——"

"Do not fear. But at least present my most humble thanks to the king."

"And your daughter's—I shall not fail. But you have not yet reached the limits of the favors bestowed upon you. It is you who are to thank the king, my dear sir; his majesty invites you to sup with him this evening."

"Me?"

"You, Taverney. We shall be a select party—his ma-

jesty, you, and myself. We will talk of your daughter's
virtue. Adieu, Taverney, I see Dubarry with Monsieur
d'Aiguillon. We must not be perceived together."

And, agile as a page, he disappeared at the further end
of the gallery, leaving Taverney gazing at his casket,
like a Saxon child who awakens and finds the Christmas
gifts which had been placed in his hands while he slept.

CHAPTER XLVI.

KING LOUIS XV.'S PETIT SOUPER.

THE marshal found the king in the little saloon
whither several of the courtiers had followed him, pre-
ferring rather to lose their supper than to allow the wandering glance of their sovereign to fall on any others than
themselves. But Louis XV. seemed to have something
else to do this evening than to look at these gentlemen.
He dismissed every one, saying that he did not intend to
sup, or that, if he did, it would be alone. All the guests
having thus received their dismissal, and fearing to displease the dauphin if they were not present at the fête
which he was to give at the close of the rehearsal, instantly
flew off like a cloud of parasite pigeons, and winged their
way to him whom they were permitted to see, ready to
assert that they had deserted his majesty's drawing-room
for him.

Louis XV., whom they left so rapidly, was far from be-
stowing a thought on them. At another time the little-
ness of all this swarm of courtiers would have excited a
smile, but on this occasion it awoke no sentiment in the
monarch's breast—a monarch so sarcastic, that he spared
neither bodily or mental defect in his best friend, always
supposing that Louis XV. ever had a friend.

No, at that moment Louis XV. concentrated his entire
attention on a carriage which was drawn up opposite the
door of the offices of Trianon, the coachman seeming to
wait only for the step which should announce the owner's
presence in the gilded vehicle, to urge on his horses. The

carriage was Mme. Dubarry's, and was lighted by torches. Zamore, seated beside the coachman, was swinging his legs backward and forward like a child at play.

At last Mme. Dubarry, who had, no doubt, delayed in the corridors in the hope of receiving some message from the king, appeared, supported on M. d'Aiguillon's arm. Her anger, or at least her disappointment, was apparent in the rapidity of her gait. She affected too much resolution not to have lost her presence of mind.

After Mme. Dubarry followed Jean, looking gloomy in the extreme, and absently crushing his hat beneath his arm. He had not been present at the representation, the dauphin having forgotten to invite him; but he had stolen into the anteroom somewhat after the fashion of a lackey, and stood pensive as Hippolytus, with his shirt-frill falling over his vest, embroidered with silver and red flowers, and not even looking at his tattered ruffles, which seemed in harmony with his sad thoughts. Jean had seen his sister look pale and alarmed, and had concluded from this that the danger was great. Jean was brave in diplomacy only when opposed in flesh and blood, never when opposed to phantoms.

Concealed behind the window-curtain, the king watched this funereal procession defile before him, and ingulf themselves in the countess's carriage like a troop of phantoms. Then, when the door was closed, and the footman had mounted behind the carriage, the coachman shook the reins, and the horses started forward with a gallop.

"Oh!" said the king, "without making an attempt to see me—to speak to me? The countess is furious!"

And he repeated aloud:

"Yes, the countess is furious!"

Richelieu, who had just glided into the room like an expected visitor, caught these last words.

"Furious, sire; and for what? Because your majesty is amused for a moment. Oh! that is not amiable of the countess."

"Duke," replied Louis XV., "I am not amused; on the contrary, I am wearied and wish for repose. Music enervates me. If I had listened to the countess, I ought to have supped at Luciennes; I ought to have eaten, and, above all, to have drunk. The countess's wines are too strong; I do not know from what vineyards they come, but they overpower me. S'death! I prefer to take my ease here."

"And your majesty is perfectly in the right," said the duke.

"Besides, the countess will find amusement elsewhere. Am I such an amiable companion? She may say so as much as she likes, but I do not believe her."

"Ah! this time your majesty is in the wrong," exclaimed the marshal.

"No, duke; no, in truth. I count my years and I reflect."

"Sire, the countess is well aware that she could not possibly have better company, and it is that which makes her furious."

"In truth, duke, I do not know how to manage. You still lead the women, as if you were twenty. At that age it is for man to choose; but at mine, duke——"

"Well, sire?"

"It is for the woman to make her calculations."

The marshal burst into a laugh.

"Well, sire," said he, "that is only an additional reason; if your majesty thinks the countess is amused, let us console ourselves as well as we can."

"I do not say she is amused, duke; I only say that she will in the end be driven to seek amusement."

"Ah! sire, I dare not assert that such things have never happened."

The king rose, much agitated.

"Who waits outside?" inquired he.

"All your suite, sire."

The king reflected for a moment.

"But have you any one there?"

"I have Rafte."

"Very good."

"What shall he do, sire?"

"He must find out if the countess really returned to Luciennes."

" The countess is already gone, I fancy, sire."

" Yes, ostensibly."

" But whither does your majesty think she is gone? "

" Who can tell? Jealousy makes her frantic, duke."

" Sire, is not rather your majesty——"

" How—what? "

" Whom jealousy——"

" Duke! "

" In truth, it would be very humiliating for us all, sire."

" I jealous? " said Louis, with a forced laugh; " are you speaking seriously, duke? "

Richelieu did not in truth believe it. It must even be confessed that he was very near the truth in thinking that, on the contrary, the king only wished to know if Mme. Dubarry was really at Luciennes, in order to be sure that she would not return to Trianon.

" Then, sire," said he, aloud, " it is understood that I am to send Rafte on a voyage of discovery? "

" Send him, duke."

" In the meantime, what will your majesty do before supper? "

" Nothing; we shall sup instantly. Have you spoken to the person in question? "

" Yes; he is in your majesty's antechamber."

" What did he say? "

" He expressed his deep thanks."

" And the daughter? "

" She has not been spoken to yet."

" Duke, Madame Dubarry is jealous, and might readily return."

" Ah! sire, that would be in very bad taste. I think the countess would be incapable of committing such an enormity."

" Duke, she is capable of anything in such moods, especially when hatred is combined with jealousy. She execrates you; I don't know if you were aware of that? "

Richelieu bowed.

" I know she does me that honor, sire."

" She execrates Monsieur de Taverney also."

"If your majesty would be good enough to reckon, I am sure there is a third person whom she hates even more than me—even more than the baron."

"Whom?"

"Mademoiselle Andrée."

"Ah!" said the king, "I think that is natural enough."

"Then——"

"Yes, but that does not prevent its being necessary to watch that Madame Dubarry does not cause some scandal this evening."

"On the contrary, it proves the necessity of such a measure."

"Here is the maître d'hôtel; hush! give your orders to Rafte and join me in the dining-room with—you know whom?"

Louis rose and passed into the dining-room, while Richelieu made his exit by the opposite door. Five minutes afterward, he rejoined the king accompanied by the baron.

The king in the most gracious manner bid Taverney good evening. The baron was a man of talent, and replied in that peculiar manner which betokens a person accustomed to good society, and which puts kings and princes instantly at their ease. They sat down to table. Louis XV. was a bad king but a delightful companion; when he pleased, his conversation was full of attraction for boon companions, talkers, and voluptuaries. The king, in short, had studied life carefully, and from its most agreeable side.

He ate heartily, made his guests drink, and turned the conversation on music.

Richelieu caught the ball at the rebound.

"Sire," said he, "if music makes men agree, as our ballet-master says, and as your majesty seems to think, will you say as much of women?"

"Oh, duke!" replied the king, "let us not speak of women. From the Trojan war to the present time, women have always exercised an influence the contrary of music. You especially have too many quarrels to compound with them to bring such a subject on the tapis. Among others there is one, and that not the least dangerous, with whom you are at daggers drawn."

"The countess, sire! Is that my fault?"

"Of course it is."

"Ah, indeed! Your majesty, I trust, will explain."

"In two words, and with the greatest pleasure," said the king, slyly.

"I am all ears, sire."

"What! she offers you the portfolio of I don't know which department, and you refuse, because, you say, she is not very popular?"

"I?" exclaimed Richelieu, a good deal embarrassed by the turn the conversation was taking.

"Dame! the report is quite public," said the king, with that feigned, off-hand good-nature which was peculiar to him. "I forget now who told it to me—most probably the gazette."

"Well, sire!" said Richelieu, taking advantage of the freedom which the unusual gaiety of the august host afforded his guest, "I must confess that on this occasion rumors and even the gazettes have reported something not quite so absurd as usual."

"What!" exclaimed Louis XV., "then you have really refused a portfolio, my dear duke?"

Richelieu, it may easily be imagined, was in an awkward position. The king well knew that he had refused nothing; but it was necessary that Taverney should continue to believe what Richelieu had told him. The duke had therefore to frame his reply so as to avoid furnishing matter for amusement to the king, without at the same time incurring the reproach of falsehood, which was already hovering upon the baron's lips and twinkling in his smile.

"Sire," said Richelieu, "pray let us not speak of effects, but of the cause. Whether I have, or have not refused a portfolio, is a state secret which your majesty is not bound to divulge over the bottle; but the cause for which I should have refused the portfolio, had it been offered to me, is the important point."

"Oh! oh! duke," said the monarch, laughing; "and this cause is not a state secret?"

"No, sire; and certainly not for your majesty, who is at this moment, I beg pardon of the divinity, the most amïable earthly Amphytrion in the universe for my friend the Baron de Taverney and myself. I have no secrets, therefore, from my king. I give my whole soul up to him, for I do not wish it to be said that the King of France has not one servant who would tell him the entire truth."

"Let us hear the truth, then, duke," said the king, while Taverney, fearing that Richelieu might go too far, pinched up his lips and composed his countenance scrupulously after the king's.

"Sire, in your dominions there are two powers which a minister must obey; the first is, your will; the second, that of your majesty's most intimate friends. The first power is irresistible, none dare to rebel against it; the second is yet more sacred, for it imposes duties of the heart on whomsoever serves you. It is termed your confidence. To obey it, a minister must have the most devoted regard for the favorite of the king."

Louis XV. laughed.

"Duke," said he, "that is a very good maxim, and one I am delighted to hear from your lips; but I dare you to proclaim it aloud by the sound of trumpet upon the Pont Neuf."

"Oh, I know, sire," said Richelieu, "that the philosophers would be up in arms; but I do not think that their objurgations would matter much to your majesty or to me. The chief point is that the two preponderating influences in the kingdom be satisfied. Well! the will of a certain person—I will confess it openly to your majesty, even should my disgrace, that is my death, be the consequence—Madame Dubarry's will I could not conform to."

Louis was silent.

"It occurred to me the other day," continued Richelieu, "to look around among your majesty's court, and, in truth, I saw so many noble girls, so many women of dazzling beauty, that had I been King of France I should have found it almost impossible to choose."

Louis turned to Taverney, who, seeing things take such a favorable turn for him, sat trembling with hope and fear, aiding the marshal's eloquence with eyes and breath, as if he would waft forward the vessel loaded with his fortunes to a safe harbor.

"Come, baron, what is your opinion?" said the king.

"Sire," replied Taverney, with swelling heart, "the duke, as it seems to me, has been discoursing most eloquently, and at the same time with profound discernment to your majesty, for the last few minutes."

"Then you are of his opinion, in what he says of lovely girls?"

"In fact, sire, I think there are indeed very lovely young girls at the French court."

"Then you are of his opinion?"

"Yes, sire."

"And, like him, you advise me to choose among the beauties of the court?"

"I would venture to confess that I am of the marshal's opinion, if I dared to believe that it was also your majesty's."

There was a short silence, during which the king looked complaisantly at Taverney.

"Gentlemen," said he, "no doubt I would follow your advice, if I were only thirty years of age. I should have a very natural predilection for it, but I find myself at present rather too old to be credulous."

"Credulous! Pray, sire, explain the meaning of the word."

"To be credulous, my dear duke, means to believe. Now, nothing will make me believe certain things."

"What are they?"

"That at my age it would be possible to inspire love."

"Ah, sire!" exclaimed Richelieu, "until this moment I thought your majesty was the most polite gentleman in your dominions, but with deep regret, I see that I have been mistaken."

"How so?" asked the king, laughing.

"Because, in that case, I must be old as Methusaleh, as I was born in '94. Remember, sire, I am sixteen years older than your majesty."

This was an adroit piece of flattery on the duke's part.

Louis XV. had always admired this man's age, who had out-lived so many younger men in his service; for, having this example before him, he might hope to reach the same advanced period.

"Granted," said Louis; "but I hope you no longer have the pretension to be loved for yourself, duke?"

"If I thought so, sire, I would instantly quarrel with two ladies who told me the contrary only this very morning."

"Well, duke," said Louis, "we shall see; Monsieur de Taverney, we shall see; youth is certainly catching, that is very true."

"Yes, yes, sire; and we must not forget that a powerful constitution like your majesty's always gains and never loses."

"Yet I remember," said Louis, "that my predecessor, when he became old, thought not of such toys as woman's love, but became exceedingly devout."

"Come, come, sire!" said Richelieu, "your majesty knows my great respect for the deceased king, who twice sent me to the Bastile, but that ought not to prevent me from saying that there is a vast difference between the ripe age of Louis XV. and that of Louis XIV. Diable! your most Christian majesty, although honoring fully your title of eldest son of the Church, need not carry ascetism so far as to forget your humanity."

"Faith, no!" said Louis. "I may confess it, since neither my doctor nor confessor is present."

"Well, sire! the king, your grandfather, frequently astonished Madame de Maintenon, who was even older than he, by his excess of religious zeal and his innumerable penances. I repeat it, sire, can there be any comparison made between your two majesties?"

The king, this evening, was in a good humor. Richelieu's words acted upon him like so many drops of water from the Fountain of Youth.

Richelieu thought the time had come; he touched Taverney's knee with his.

"Sire," said the latter, "will your majesty deign to

accept my thanks for the magnificent present you have
made my daughter?"

" You need not thank me for that, baron," said the king.
" Mademoiselle de Taverney pleased me by her modest and
ingenuous grace. I wish my daughters had still their
households to form; certainly Mademoiselle Andrée—that
is her name, is it not?"

" Yes, sire," said Taverney, delighted that the king
knew his daughter's Christian name.

" A very pretty name—certainly Mademoiselle Andrée
should have been the first upon the list; but every post in
my house is filled up. In the meantime, baron, you may
reckon upon my protection for your daughter. I think
I have heard she has not a rich dowry?"

" Alas! no, sire."

" Well, I will make her marriage my especial care."

Taverney bowed to the ground.

" Then your majesty must be good enough," said he,
" to select a husband; for I confess that, in our confined
circumstances—our almost poverty——"

" Yes, yes; rest easy on that point," said Louis; " but
she seems very young—there is no haste."

" The less, sire, that I am aware your majesty dislikes
marriages."

" Ha!" said Louis, rubbing his hands and looking at
Richelieu. " Well! at all events, Monsieur de Taverney,
command me whenever you are at all embarrassed."

Then, rising, the king beckoned the duke, who approached.

" Was the little one satisfied?" asked he.

" With what?"

" With the casket."

" You majesty must excuse my speaking low, but the
father is listening, and he must not overhear what I have
to tell you."

" Bah!"

" No, I assure you, sire."

" Well! speak."

" Sire, the little one has indeed a horror of marriage;

but of one thing I am certain—viz., that she has not a horror of your majesty."

Uttering these words in a tone of familiarity which pleased the king from its very frankness, the marshal, with his little pattering steps, hastened to rejoin Taverney, who, from respect, had moved away to the doorway of the gallery.

Both retired by the gardens. It was a lovely evening. Two servants walked before them, holding torches in one hand, and with the other pulling aside the branches of the flowering shrubs. The windows of Trianon were blazing with light, and, flitting across them, could be discerned a crowd of joyous figures, the honored guests of the dauphiness.

His majesty's band gave life and animation to the minuet, for dancing had commenced after supper, and was still kept up with undiminished spirit.

Concealed in a dense thicket of lilac and snowball shrubs, Gilbert, kneeling upon the ground, was gazing at the movements of the shadows through the transparent curtains. A thunder-bolt, cleaving the earth at his feet, would scarcely have distracted the attention of the gazer, so much was he entranced by the lovely forms he was following with his eyes through all the mazes of the dance. Nevertheless, when Richelieu and Taverney passed, and brushed against the thicket, in which this night-bird was concealed, the sound of their voices, and, above all, a certain word, made Gilbert raise his head; for this word was an all-important one for him.

The marshal, leaning upon his friend's arm, and bending down to his ear, was saying:

"Everything well weighed and considered, baron—it is a hard thing to tell you—but you must at once send your daughter to a convent."

"Why so?" asked the baron.

"Because, I would wager," replied the marshal, "that the king is madly in love with Mademoiselle de Taverney."

At these words Gilbert started and turned paler than the flaky snowberries which, at his abrupt movement, showered down upon his head.

CHAPTER XLVII.

PRESENTIMENTS.

THE next day, as the clock of Trianon was striking twelve, Nicole's voice was heard calling Andrée, who had not yet left her apartment :

"Mademoiselle, mademoiselle, here is Monsieur Philip ! "

The exclamation came from the bottom of the stairs.

Andrée, at once surprised and delighted, drew her muslin robe closely over her neck and shoulders, and hastened to meet the young man, who was in fact dismounting in the courtyard of Trianon and inquiring from the servants at what time he could see his sister.

Andrée therefore opened the door in person, and found herself face to face with Philip, whom the officious Nicole had run to summon from the courtyard, and was accompanying up the stairs.

The young girl threw her arms around her brother's neck, and they entered Andrée's apartment together, followed by Nicole.

It was then that Andrée for the first time remarked that Philip was more serious than usual—that his smile was not free from sadness—that he wore his elegant uniform with the most scrupulous neatness, and that he held a traveling-cloak over his arm.

" What is the matter, Philip ? " asked she, with the instinct of tender affection, of which a look is a sufficient revelation.

" My sister," said Philip, " this morning I received an order to join my regiment."

" And you are going ? "

" I must."

" Oh ! " said Andrée ; and with this plaintive exclamation all her courage, and almost all her strength, seemed to desert her.

And although his departure was a very natural occurrence, and one which she might have foreseen, yet she felt so overpowered by the announcement that she was obliged to lean for support on her brother's arm.

"Good heavens !" asked Philip, astonished, "does this departure afflict you so much, Andrée ? You know, in a soldier's life, it is a most commonplace event."

"Yes, yes, it is in truth common," murmured the young girl. "And whither do you go, brother ?"

"My garrison is at Rheims. You see, I have not a very long journey to undertake. But it is probable that from thence the regiment will return to Strasbourg."

"Alas !" said Andrée ; "and when do you set out ?"

"The order commands me to start immediately."

"You have come to bid me good-by, then ?"

"Yes, sister."

"A farewell !"

"Have you anything particular to say to me, Andrée ?" asked Philip, fearing that this extreme dejection might have some other cause than his departure.

Andrée understood that these words were meant to call her attention to Nicole, who, astonished at Andrée's extreme grief, was gazing at the scene with much surprise ; for, in fact, the departure of an officer to his garrison was not a catastrophe to cause such a flood of tears.

Andrée therefore saw at the same instant Philip's feelings and Nicole's surprise. She took up a mantle, threw it over her shoulders, and, leading her brother to the staircase :

"Come," said she, "as far as the park gates, Philip. I will accompany you through the covered alley. I have, in truth, many things to tell you, brother."

These words were equivalent to a dismissal for Nicole, who returned to her mistress's chamber, while the latter descended the staircase with Philip.

Andreé led the way to the passage, which still, even at the present day, opens from the chapel into the garden ; but although Philip's look anxiously questioned her, she remained for a long time silent, leaning upon his arm, and supporting her head upon his shoulder.

But at last her heart was too full; her features were overspread with a death-like paleness, a deep sigh escaped her lips, and tears rushed from her eyes.

"My dear sister—my sweet Andrée!" exclaimed Philip, "in the name of Heaven, what is the matter?"

"My friend—my only friend," said Andrée, "you depart—you leave me alone in this great world which I entered but yesterday, and yet you ask me why I weep? Ah, remember, Philip, I lost my mother at my birth; it is dreadful to acknowledge it, but I have never had a father. All my little griefs—all my little secrets—I could confide to you alone. Who smiled upon me? Who caressed me? Who rocked me in my cradle? It was you. Who has protected me since I grew up? You. Who taught me that God's creatures were not cast into the world only to suffer? You, Philip—you alone. For, since the hour of my birth, I have loved no one in the world but you, and no one but you has loved me in return. Oh! Philip, Philip," continued Andrée, sadly, "you turn away your head, and I can read your thoughts. You think I am young—that I am beautiful—and that I am wrong not to trust to the future and to love. And yet you see, alas! Philip, it is not enough to be young and handsome, for no one thinks of me.

"You will say the dauphiness is kind, and she is so. She is all perfection, at least, she seems so in my eyes, and I look upon her as a divinity. But it is exactly because she holds this exalted situation, that I can feel only respect for her, and not affection. And yet, Philip, affection is necessary for my heart, which, if always thrust back on itself, must at last break. My father—I tell you nothing new, Philip—my father is not only no protector or friend, but I cannot even look at him without feeling terror. Yes, yes, I fear him, Philip, and still more now since you are leaving me.

"You will ask, why should I fear him? I know not. Do not the birds of the air, and the flocks of the field, feel and dread the approaching storm ? You will say they are endowed with instinct ; but why will you deny the instinct of misfortune to our immortal souls ? For some time past everything has prospered with our family ; I know it well. You are a captain ; I am in the household, and almost in the intimacy, of the dauphiness. My father, it is said, supped last night almost *tête-à-tête* with the king. Well ! Philip, I repeat it, even should you think me mad, all this alarms me more than our peaceful poverty and obscurity at Taverney."

" And yet, dear sister," said Philip, sadly, " you were alone there also ; I was not with you there to console you."

" Yes, but at least I was alone—alone with the memories of childhood. It seemed to me as if the house where my mother lived and breathed her last, owed me, if I may so speak, a protecting care. All there was peaceful, gentle, affectionate. I could see you depart with calmness and welcome you back with joy. But whether you departed or returned, my heart was not all with you ; it was attached also to that dear house, to my gardens, to my flowers, to the whole scene of which formerly you were but a part. Now you are all to me, Philip, and when you leave me I am indeed alone."

" And yet, Andrée, you have now a protector more powerful than I am."

" True."

" A happy future before you."

" Who can tell ? "

" Why do you doubt it ? "

" I do not know."

" This is ingratitude toward God, my sister."

" Oh ! no, thank Heaven, I am not ungrateful to God. Morning and evening I offer up my thanks to Him ; but it seems to me as if instead of receiving my prayers with grace, every time I bend the knee, a voice from on high whispers to my heart : " Take care, young girl, take care ! "

" But against what are you to guard ? Answer me. I

will admit that a danger threatens you. Have you any presentiment of the nature of this misfortune ? Do you know how to act so as best to confront it, or how to avoid it ? ''

" I know nothing, Philip, except that my life seems to hang by a thread, that nothing will look bright to me from the moment of your departure. In a word, it seems as if during my sleep I had been placed on the declivity of a precipice too steep to allow me to arrest my progress when roused to a sense of my danger ; that I see the abyss, and yet am dragged down ; and that you, being far away, and your helping hand no longer ready to support me, I shall be dashed down and crushed in the fall."

" Dear sister ! my sweet Andrée !" said Philip, agitated in spite of himself by the expression of deep and unaffected terror in her voice and manner, " you exaggerate the extent of an affection for which I feel deeply grateful. Yes, you will lose your friend, but only for a time ; I shall not be so far distant but that you can send for me if necessity should arise. Besides, remember that except chimerical fears, nothing threatens you."

Andrée placed herself in her brother's way.

" Then, Philip," said she, " how does it happen that you, who are a man, and gifted with so much more strength, are at this moment as sad as I am ? Tell me, my brother, how do you explain that ? "

" Easily, dear sister," said Philip, arresting Andrée's steps, for she had again moved forward on ceasing to speak. " We are not only brother and sister by blood, but in heart and affection ; therefore we have lived in an intimate communion of thoughts and feelings, which, especially since our arrival in Paris, has become to me a delightful necessity. I break this chain, my sweet love, or rather it is broken by others, and I feel the blow in my inmost heart. I am sad, but only for the moment, Andrée. I can look beyond our separation ; I do not believe in any misfortune, except in that of not seeing you for some months, perhaps for a year ; I am resigned and do not say ' farewell,' but rather, ' we shall soon meet again.' ''

In spite of these consolatory words, Andrée could only reply by sobs and tears.

"Dearest sister," exclaimed Philip, grieved at this dejection, which seemed so incomprehensible to him, "dearest sister, you have not told me all—you hide something from me. In Heaven's name, speak!"

And he took her in his arms, pressing her to his heart, and gazing earnestly in her eyes.

"I!" said she. "No, no, Philip, I assure you solemnly. You know all the most secret recesses of my heart are open before you."

"Well, then, Andrée, for pity's sake, take courage; do not grieve me so."

"You are right," said she, "and I am mad. Listen: I never had a strong mind, as you, Philip, know better than any one; I have always been a timid, dreaming, melancholy creature. But I have no right to make so tenderly beloved a brother a sharer in my fears, above all, when he labors to give me courage, and proves to me that I am wrong to be alarmed. You are right, Philip; it is true, everything here is conducive to my happiness. Forgive me, Philip! You see I dry my tears—I weep no longer—I smile, Philip—I do not say adieu, but rather 'we shall soon meet again.'"

And the young maiden tenderly embraced her brother, hiding her head on his shoulder to conceal from his view a tear which still dimmed her eye, and which dropped like a pearl upon the golden epaulet of the young officer.

Philip gazed upon her with that infinite tenderness which partakes at the same time of a father's and a brother's affection.

"Andrée," said he, "I love to see you bear yourself thus bravely. Be of good courage; I must go, but the courier shall bring you a letter every week. And every week let me receive one from you in return."

"Yes, Philip," said Andrée; "yes, it will be my only happiness. But you have informed my father, have you not?"

"Of what?"

" Of your departure."

" Dear sister, it was the baron himself who brought me
the minister's order this morning.   Monsieur de Taverney
is not like you, Andrée, and, it seems, will easily part with
me.   He appeared pleased at the thought of my departure,
and in fact he was right.   Here I can never get forward,
while there many occasions may present themselves."

" My father is glad to see you go ? " murmured Andrée.
" Are you not mistaken, Philip ? "

" He has you," replied Philip, eluding the question ;
"that is a consolation for him, sister."

" Do you think so, Philip ?   He never sees me."

" My sister, he bid me tell you that this very day, after
my departure, he would come to Trianon.   Believe me,
he loves you ; only it is after his own fashion."

" What is the matter now, Philip ? you seem embarrassed."

" Dearest Andrée, I heard the clock strike—what hour
is it ? "

" A quarter to one."

" Well, dear sister, I seem embarrassed, because I ought
to have been on the road an hour ago, and here we are at
the gate where my horse is waiting.   Therefore——"

Andrée assumed a calm demeanor, and taking her
brother's hand :

" Therefore," said she, in a voice too firm to be entirely
natural, " therefore, brother, adieu ! "

Philip gave her one last embrace.

" To meet soon again," said he ; " remember your
promise."

" What promise ? "

" One letter a week, at least."

" Oh ! do you think it necessary to ask it ? "

She required a violent effort to pronounce these last
words.   The poor girl's voice was scarcely audible.

Philip waved his hand in token of adieu, and walked
quickly toward the gate.   Andrée followed his retreating
form with her eyes, holding in her breath in the endeavor
to repress her sighs.   Philip bounded lightly on horseback,

shouted a last farewell from the other side of the gate, and was gone. Andrée remained standing motionless till he was out of sight, then she turned, darted like a wounded fawn among the shady trees, perceived a bench, and had only strength sufficient to reach it, and to sink on it power-less and almost lifeless. Then heaving a deep and heart-rending sigh, she exclaimed :

" Oh, my God ! do not leave me quite alone upon earth ! "

She buried her face in her hands, while the big tears she did not seek to restrain made their way through her slender fingers. At this instant a slight rustling was heard amid the shrubs behind her. Andrée thought she heard a sigh. She turned, alarmed ; a melancholy form stood before her.

It was Gilbert.

CHAPTER XLVIII.

GILBERT'S ROMANCE.

As pale, as despairing as Andrée, Gilbert stood down-cast before her. At the sight of a man, and of a stranger, for such he seemed at first sight through the thick veil of tears which obscured her gaze, Andrée hastily dried her eyes, as if the proud young girl would have blushed to be seen weeping. She made an effort to compose herself, and restored calmness to her marble features only an in-stant before agitated with the shudder of despair. Gilbert was much longer in regaining his calmness, and his feat-ures still wore an expression of grief when Mlle. de Taver-ney, looking up, at last recognized him.

" Oh ! Monsieur Gilbert again ! " said Andrée, with that trifling tone which she affected to assume whenever chance brought her in contact with the young man.

Gilbert made no reply ; his feelings were still too deeply moved. The grief which had shaken Andrée's frame to the center had violently agitated his own. It was Andrée, therefore, who again broke the silence, wishing to have the last word with this apparition.

" But what is the matter, Monsieur Gilbert ? " inquired

she. " Why do you gaze at me in that wobegone manner ? Something must grieve you. May I ask what it is ? "

" Do you wish to know ? " asked Gilbert, mournfully, for he felt the irony concealed beneath this appearance of interest.

" Yes."

" Well, what grieves me, mademoiselle, is to see you suffer," replied Gilbert.

" And who told you that I am suffering ? "

" I see it."

" You mistake, sir ; I am not suffering," said Andrée, passing her handkerchief over her face.

Gilbert felt the storm rising, but he resolved to turn it aside by humility.

" I entreat your pardon, mademoiselle," said he, " but the reason I spoke was that I heard your sobs."

" Ah ! you were listening ? Better and better ! "

" Mademoiselle, it was by accident," stammered Gilbert, for he felt that he was telling a falsehood.

" Accident ! I regret exceedingly, Monsieur Gilbert, that chance should have brought you here. But even so, may I ask in what manner these sobs which you heard me utter grieved you ? Pray inform me."

" I cannot bear to see a woman weep," said Gilbert, in a tone which highly displeased Andrée.

" Am I then a woman in Monsieur Gilbert's eyes ? " replied the haughty young girl. " I sue for no one's sympathy, but Monsieur Gilbert's still less than any other's."

" Mademoiselle," said Gilbert, sadly, " you do wrong to taunt me thus. I saw you sad, and I felt grieved. I heard you say, that now Monsieur Philip was gone, you would be alone in the world. Never, mademoiselle ! for I am beside you, and never did a heart beat more devoted to you. I repeat it, Mademoiselle de Taverney cannot be alone in the world while my head can think, my heart beat, or my arm retain its strength."

While he spoke these words, Gilbert was indeed a model a manly elegance and beauty, although he pronounced them with all the humility which the most sincere respect commanded.

But it was fated that everything which the young man did should displease Andrée, should offend her, and urge her to offensive retorts—as if his very respect were an insult, and his prayers a provocation. At first she attempted to rise, that she might second her harsh words with as harsh gestures ; but a nervous shudder retained her on her seat. Besides, she reflected that if she were standing, she could be seen from a distance, and seen talking to Gilbert. She therefore remained seated ; for she was determined, once for all, to crush the importunate insect before her under her foot, and replied :

"I thought I had already informed you, Monsieur Gilbert, that you are highly displeasing to me, that your voice annoys me, that your philosophical speeches disgust me. Then why, when you know this, do you still persist in addressing me ? "

"Mademoiselle," replied Gilbert, pale, but self-possessed, " an honest-hearted woman is never disgusted by sympathy. An honest man is the equal of every human being ; and I, whom you maltreat so cruelly, deserve, more than any other, perhaps, the sympathy which I regret to perceive you do not feel for me."

At this word sympathy, thus twice repeated, Andrée opened her large eyes to their utmost extent, and fixed them impertinently upon Gilbert.

"Sympathy ! " said she—"sympathy between you and me, Monsieur Gilbert ? In truth, I was deceived in my opinion of you. I took you for insolent, and I find you are even less than that—you are only a madman."

" I am neither insolent nor mad," said Gilbert, with an apparent calm which must have cost his proud disposition much to assume. " No, mademoiselle ; nature has made me your equal, and chance has made you my debtor."

"Chance again ! " said Andrée, sarcastically.

"Perhaps I should have said Providence. I never intended to have spoken to you of this, but your insults refresh my memory."

" I your debtor, sir ?   Your debtor, I think you said ?
Explain yourself."

" I should be ashamed to find you ungrateful, mademoiselle.   God, who has made you so beautiful, has given
you, to compensate for your beauty, sufficient defects
without that."

This time Andrée rose.

" Stay ! pardon me ! " said Gilbert ; " at times you irritate me too much also, and then I forget for a moment
the interest with which you inspire me."

Andrée burst into a fit of laughter so prolonged that it
was calculated to rouse Gilbert's anger to the utmost ; but
to her great surprise Gilbert did not take fire.   He folded
his arms on his breast, retained the same hostile and determined expression in his fiery glance, and patiently
awaited the end of this insulting laugh.

When she had finished—

" Mademoiselle," said Gilbert, coldly, " will you con-
descend to answer me one question ?   Do you respect
your father ? "

" You take the liberty, of catechizing me, it seems,
Monsieur Gilbert ? " replied the young girl, with sovereign hauteur.

" Yes, you respect your father," continued Gilbert ;
" and it is not on account of his good qualities or his
virtues, but simply because he gave you life.   A father,
unfortunately—and you must know it, mademoiselle—a
father is respected only in one relation, but still it gives
him a claim.   Even more ; for this sole benefit "—and
Gilbert, in his turn, felt himself animated by an emotion
of scornful pity—" you are bound to love your benefactor.
Well, mademoiselle, this being established as a principle,
why do you insult me ? why do you scorn me ? why do
you hate him who did not indeed give you life, but who
saved it ? "

" You ! " exclaimed Andrée ; " you saved my life ? "

" Ah ! you did not even dream of that," said Gilbert,
" or, rather, you have forgotten it.   That is very natural ;
it occurred nearly a year ago.   Well, mademoiselle, I must

only therefore inform you of it, or recall it to your memory. Yes, I saved your life at the risk of my own."

"At least, Monsieur Gilbert," said Andrée, deathly pale, "you will do me the favor of telling me when and where."

"The day, mademoiselle, when a hundred thousand persons, crushed one against the other, fleeing from the fiery horses, and the sabers which thinned the crowd, left the long train of dead and dying upon the Place de Louis XV."

"Ah ! the thirty-first of May ? "

"Yes, mademoiselle."

Andrée seated herself, and her features again assumed a pitiless smile.

"And on that day, you say, you sacrificed your life to save mine, Monsieur Gilbert ? "

"I have already told you so."

"Then you are the Baron Balsamo ? I beg your pardon, I was not aware of the fact."

"No, I am not the Baron Balsamo," replied Gilbert, with flashing eye and quivering lip, "I am the poor child of the people, Gilbert, who has the folly, the madness, the misfortune to love you ; who, because he loved you like a madman, like a fool, like a sot, followed you into the crowd ; who, separating from you for a moment, recognized you by the piercing shriek you uttered when you lost your footing ; who, forcing his way to you, shielded you with his arms until twenty thousand arms, pressing against his, broke their strength ; who threw himself upon the stone wall against which you were about to be crushed, to afford you the softer repose of his corpse ; and, perceiving among the crowd that strange man who seemed to govern his fellow-men, and whose name you have just pronounced, collected all his strength, all his energy, and raised you in his exhausted arms, that this man might see you, seize hold of you, and save you ! Gilbert, who in yielding you up to a more fortunate protector than himself, retained nothing but a shred of your dress, which he pressed to his lips. And it was time, for already the blood was rushing to his heart, to his temples, to his brain. The rolling tide of executioners and victims swept over him, and buried him beneath its waves, while you ascended aloft from its abyss to a haven of safety ! ''

Gilbert, in these hurried words, had shown himself as he was—uncultivated, simple, almost sublime, in his resolution as in his love. Notwithstanding her contempt, Andrée could not refrain from gazing at him with astonishment. For a moment he believed that his narrative had been as irresistible as truth—as love. But poor Gilbert, did not take into his calculations incredulity, that demon prompted by hatred. Andrée, who hated Gilbert, did not allow herself to be moved by any of the forcible arguments of her despised lover.

She did not reply immediately, but looked at Gilbert, while something like a struggle took place in her mind. The young man, therefore, ill at ease during this freezing silence, felt himself obliged to add, as a sort of peroration:

'' And now, mademoiselle, do not detest me as you did formerly, for now it would not only be injustice, but ingratitude, to do so. I said so before, and I now repeat it.''

At these words Andrée raised her haughty brow, and in the most indifferent and cutting tone, she asked :

'' How long, Monsieur Gilbert, did you remain under Monsieur Rousseau's tutelage ? ''

'' Mademoiselle,'' said Gilbert, ingenuously, '' I think about three months, without reckoning a few days of my illness, which was caused by the accident on the thirty-first of May.''

'' You misunderstand me,'' said she ; '' I did not ask you whether you had been ill or not, or what accidents you may have received. They add an artistic finish to your story, but otherwise they are of no importance to me. I merely wished to tell you, that having resided only three months with the illustrious author, you have profited well by his lessons, and that the pupil at his first essay composes romances almost worthy of his master.''

Gilbert had listened with all calmness, believing that

Andrée was about to reply seriously to his impassioned narration ; but at this stroke of cutting irony, he fell from the summit of his buoyant hopes to the dust.

" A romance ! " murmured he, indignantly ; "you treat what I have told you as a romance ! "

"Yes, sir," said Andrée, "a romance—I repeat the word ; only you did not force me to read it—for that I have to thank you. I deeply regret that, unfortunately, I am not able to repay its full value ; but I would make the attempt in vain—the romance is invaluable."

" And this is your reply ? " stammered Gilbert, a pang darting through his heart, and his eyes becoming dim from emotion.

" I do not reply at all, sir," said Andrée, pushing him aside to allow her room to pass on.

The fact was, that Nicole had at this moment made her appearance at the end of the alley, calling her mistress while still a considerable distance off, in order not to interrupt this interview too suddenly, ignorant as she was as to whom Andrée's companion might be, for she had not recognized Gilbert through the foliage. But as she approached she saw the young man, recognized him, and stood astounded. She then repented not having made a détour in order to overhear what Gilbert had to say to Mlle. Taverney. The latter, addressing her in a softened voice, as if to mark more strongly to Gilbert the haughtiness with which she had spoken to him :

" Well, child," said she, " what is the matter ? "

" The Baron de Taverney and the Duke de Richelieu have come to present their respects to mademoiselle," replied Nicole.

" Where are they ? "

" In mademoiselle's apartments."

" Come, then."

And Andrée moved away ; Nicole followed, not without throwing, as she passed, a sarcastic glance back at Gilbert, who, livid with agitation, and almost frantic with rage, shook his clenched hand in the direction of his departing enemy, and, grinding his teeth, muttered :

"Oh! creature without heart, without soul! I saved your life, I concentrated all my affection on you, I extinguished every feeling which might offend your purity, for in my madness I looked upon you as some superior being —the inhabitant of a higher sphere! Now that I have seen you more nearly, I find you are no more than a woman —and I am a man! But one day or other, Andrée de Taverney, I shall be revenged!"

He rushed from the spot, bounding through the thickest of the shrubs like a young wolf wounded by the hunters, who turns and shows his sharp teeth and his bloodshot eyeballs.

CHAPTER XLIX.

FATHER AND DAUGHTER.

WHEN she reached the opposite extremity of the alley, Andrée saw her father and the marshal walking up and down before the vestibule, waiting for her. The two friends seemed in high spirits, and as they stood with their arm interlaced, presented the most perfect representation of Orestes and Pylades the court had ever witnessed. As Andrée approached, the two old men seemed still more joyous, and remarked to each other on her radiant beauty, heightened by her walk and by the emotion she had previously undergone.

The marshal saluted Andrée as he would have done a declared Mme. Pompadour. This distinction did not escape Taverney, who was delighted at it, but it surprised Andrée from its mixture of respect and gallantry; for the cunning courtier could express as many shades of meaning in a bow as Covielle could French phrases by a single Turkish word.

Andrée returned the marshal's salutation, made one equally ceremonious to her father, and then with fascinating grace she invited both to follow her to her apartment.

The marshal admired the exquisite neatness which was the only ornament of the furniture and architecture of this retreat. With a few flowers and a little white muslin, Andrée had made her rather gloomy chamber, not a palace indeed, but a temple.

The duke seated himself upon an armchair covered with green chintz, beneath a Chinese cornucopia from which dropped bunches of perfumed acacia and maple, mingled with iris and Bengal roses.

Taverney occupied a similar chair ; and Andrée sunk upon a folding stool, her arm resting on a harpsichord, also ornamented with flowers, and arranged in a large Dresden vase.

"Mademoiselle," said the marshal, "I come as the bearer, on the part of his majesty, of the compliments which your charming voice and your musical talents drew from every auditor of yesterday's rehearsal. His majesty feared to arouse jealousy by praising you too openly at the time, and he therefore charged me to express to you the pleasure you have caused him."

Andrée blushed, and her blush made her so lovely that the marshal proceeded as if speaking on his own account.

"The king has assured me," said he, "that he never saw any one at his court who united to such a high degree the gifts of mind and the charms of personal beauty."

"You forget those of the heart," said Taverney, with a gush of affection ; "Andrée is the best of daughters."

The marshal thought for a moment that his old friend was about to weep. Admiring deeply this display of paternal sensibility, he exclaimed :

"The heart ! alas, my dear friend ! You alone can judge of the tenderness of which mademoiselle's heart is capable. Were I only five-and-twenty years of age, I would lay my life and my fortune at her feet !"

Andrée did not yet know how to receive coolly the full fire of a courtier's homage. She could only murmur some almost inaudible words.

"Mademoiselle," continued he, "the king requests you will accept a slight testimony of his satisfaction, and he has charged the baron, your father, to transmit it to you. What reply shall I make to his majesty from you ? "

" Sir," replied Andrée, animated by no feeling but that respect which is due to a monarch from all his subjects, " assure his majesty of my deep gratitude ; tell him that he honors me too highly by deigning to think of me, and that I am not worthy the attention of so powerful a monarch."

Richelieu seemed in raptures at this reply, which Andrée pronounced with a firm voice, and without hesitation. He took her hand, kissed it respectfully, and devouring her with his eyes :

" A royal hand," said he, " a fairy foot—mind, purity, resolution !—ah ! baron, what a treasure ! It is not a daughter whom you have—it is a queen ! "

With these words he retired, leaving Taverney alone with Andrée, his heart swelling with pride and hope.

Whoever had seen this advocate of antiquated theories, this skeptic, this scoffer, inhaling with delight the air of favoritism in its most disreputable channel, would have said that God had blinded at the same moment both his intellect and heart. Taverney alone might have replied, with reference to this change :

" It is not I who have changed—it is the times."

He remained then seated beside Andrée, and could not help feeling somewhat embarrassed ; for the young girl with her air of unconquerable serenity, and her clear, limpid, unfathomable look, seemed as if she would penetrate his most secret thoughts.

" Did not Monsieur de Richelieu, sir, say that his majesty had intrusted you with a testimony of his satisfaction ? May I ask what it is ? "

" Ah ! " thought Taverney, " she is curious—so much the better ! I could not have expected it. So much the better ! "

He drew the casket, which the marshal had given him the evening before, slowly from his pocket, just as a kind papa produces a paper of sweetmeats or a toy, which the children have devoured with their eyes before their hands can reach them.

" Here it is." said he.

" Ah ! jewels ! " said Andrée.

" Are they to your taste ? "

It was a set of pearls of great value. Twelve immense diamonds connected together the rows of pearls, while a diamond clasp, earrings, and a tiara of the same precious material, made the present worth at least thirty thousand crowns.

" Good heavens, father ! " exclaimed Andrée.

" Well ? "

" It is too handsome. The king has made some mistake. I should be ashamed to wear that. I have no dress suitable to the splendor of these diamonds."

" Oh, complain of it, I beg ! " said Taverney, ironically.

" You do not understand me, sir. I regret that I cannot wear these jewels, because they are too beautiful."

" The king, who gives the casket, mademoiselle, is generous enough to add the dresses."

" But, sir, this is goodness on the king's part——"

" Do you not think I have deserved it by my services ? "

" Ah, pardon me, sir ; that is true," said Andrée, drooping her head, but not quite convinced.

After a moment's reflection, she closed the casket.

" I shall not wear these diamonds," said she.

" And why not ? " said Taverney, uneasily.

" Because, my dear father, you and my brother are in want of necessaries, and this superfluity offends my eyes when I think of your embarrassments."

Taverney smiled and pressed her hand.

" Oh," said he, " do not think of that, my daughter. The king has done more for me than for you. We are in favor, my dear child. It would neither be respectful as a subject, nor grateful as a woman, to appear before his majesty without the present he has made you."

" I shall obey, sir."

" Yes, but you must obey as if it gave you pleasure to do so. These ornaments seem not to be to your taste."

" I am no judge of diamonds, sir."

" Learn, then, that the pearls alone are worth fifty thousand livres."

Andrée clasped her hands.

"Sir," said she, "it is most strange that his majesty should make me such a present ; reflect !"

"I do not understand you, mademoiselle," replied Taverney, dryly.

"If I wear these jewels, I assure you, sir, every one will be greatly surprised."

"Why ?" asked Taverney, in the same tone, and with a cold and imperious glance, which made Andrée lower her eyes.

"I feel a scruple."

"Mademoiselle, you must confess that it is strange one should entertain scruples, where even I, your father, feel none. Give me your young modest girls for seeing evil and finding it out, however closely hidden it is, and when none other had remarked it. None like maidenly and simple girls for making old grenadiers like myself blush."

Andrée hid her blushing face in her lovely white hands.

"Oh ! my brother," she murmured to herself, "why are you already so far from me ?"

Did Taverney hear these words, or did he guess their purport with that wonderful perspicacity which we know he possessed ? We cannot tell, but he immediately changed his tone, and, taking Andrée's hand in his :

"Come, my child," said he, "is not your father your friend ?"

A heavenly smile chased the shadow from Andrée's brow.

"Shall I not be here to love you—to advise you ? Are you not proud to contribute to my happiness and that of your brother ?"

"Oh, yes !" said Andrée.

The baron fixed a caressing look upon his daughter.

"Well !" said he, "you shall be, as Monsieur de Riche-lieu said just now, the Queen of Taverney. The king has distinguished you, and the dauphiness also," added he, hastily. "In your intimacy with these two august per-sonages, you will found our future fortunes by making them happy. The friend of the dauphiness, and—of the king ! What a glorious career ! You have superior talents and unrivaled beauty, a pure and healthy mind untainted by avarice and ambition. Oh ! my child, what a part you might play ! Do you remember the maiden who soothed the last moments of Charles VI. ? Her name is cherished in France. Do you remember Agnes Sorel, who restored the honor of the French crown ? All good Frenchmen respect her memory. Andrée, you will be the support of the old age of our glorious monarch. He will cherish you as his daughter, and you will reign in France by the divine right of beauty, courage, and fidelity ! ''

Andrée opened her eyes with astonishment. The baron resumed without giving her time to reflect :

'' With a single look you will drive away these wretched creatures who dishonor the throne ; your presence will purify the court. To your generous influence the nobility of the kingdom will owe the return of pure morals, politeness, and real gallantry. My daughter, you may be, you must be, the regenerating star of your country, and a crown of glory to your name. ''

'' But, '' said Andrée, all bewildered, '' what must I do to effect all this ? ''

The baron reflected for a moment.

'' Andrée, '' said he, '' I have often told you that in this world you must force men to be virtuous by making them love virtue. Sullen, melancholy, sermonizing virtue makes even those fly who wish most to approach her. Lend to your virtues all the allurements of coquetry—I had almost said of vice. It is an easy task for a talented and high-minded girl such as you are. Make yourself so lovely that the court shall talk only of you ; make yourself so agreeable to the king that he cannot do without you. Be so reserved and discreet toward all, except his majesty, that people will soon attribute to you all that power which you cannot fail ultimately to obtain. ''

'' I do not exactly understand your last advice, '' said Andrée.

'' Trust yourself to my guidance—you will fulfil my wishes without understanding them ; the best plane for such a wise and generous creature as you are. But, by the by, to enable you to put in practise my first counsel, I must furnish your purse. Take these hundred louis-d'ors and dress in the manner worthy of the rank to which you belong since his majesty has distinguished you."

Taverney gave the hundred louis to his daughter, kissed her hand, and left her.

He returned with rapid steps along the alley by which he had come, so much engrossed in his reflections that he did not perceive Nicole in eager conference with a nobleman at the extremity of the Bosquet des Amours.

CHAPTER L.

WHAT ALTHOTAS WANTED TO COMPLETE HIS ELIXIR.

THE day subsequent to this conversation, about four o'clock in the afternoon, Balsamo was seated in his cabinet in the Rue St. Claude, occupied in reading a letter which Fritz had just brought him. The letter was without signature. He turned it over and over in his hands.

"I know this writing," said he; "large, irregular, slightly tremulous, and full of faults in orthography."

And he read it once more. It ran as follows:

"MY LORD COUNT,—A person who consulted you some time before the fall of the late ministry, and who had consulted you a long time previously, will wait upon you to-day, in order to have another consultation. Will your numerous occupations permit you to grant this person a quarter of an hour between four and five this evening?"

After reading this for the second or third time, Balsamo fell back into his train of reflection.

"It is not worth while to consult Lorenza for such a trifle," said he; "besides, can I no longer guess myself? The writing is large—a sign of aristocracy; irregular and trembling—a sign of age; full of faults in orthography—

it must be a courtier. Ah ! stupid creature that I am ! it is the Duke de Richelieu ! Most certainly I shall have a half-hour at your service, my lord duke—an hour, did I say ?—a day ! Make my time your own. Are you not, without knowing it, one of my mysterious agents, one of my familiar demons ? Do we not both pursue the same task ? Do we not both shake the monarchy at the same time—you by making yourself its presiding genius, I by declaring myself its enemy ? Come then, duke, I am ready ! "

And Balsamo consulted his watch to see how long he must yet wait for the duke. At that moment a bell sounded in the cornice of the ceiling.

"What can be the matter ? " said Balsamo, starting ; " Lorenza calls me—she wishes to see me. Can anything unpleasant have happened to her ; or is it a return of those fits of passion which I have so often witnessed, and of which I have been at times the victim ? Yesterday she was thoughtful, gentle, resigned ; she was as I love to see her. Poor child ! I must go to her."

He arranged his dress, glanced at the mirror to see if his hair was not too much in disorder, and proceeded toward the stairs, after having replied to Lorenza's request by a ring similar to her own.

But, according to his invariable custom, Balsamo paused in the apartment adjoining that occupied by the young girl, and turning, with his arms crossed, toward the direction where he supposed her to be, he commanded her to sleep, with that powerful will which recognized no obstacles. Then, as if doubting his own power, or as if he thought it necessary to redouble his precautions, he looked into the apartment through an almost imperceptible crevice in the woodwork.

Lorenza was sleeping upon a couch, to which she had, no doubt, tottered under the influence of her master's will, and had sought a support for her sinking limbs. A painter could not have suggested a more poetic attitude. Panting and subdued beneath the power of the subtle fluid which Balsamo had poured upon her, Lorenza seemed like one of those beautiful Ariadnes of Vanloo, with heaving breasts and features expressive of fatigue or despair.

Balsamo entered by his usual passage, and stopped for a moment before her to contemplate her sleeping countenance. He then awoke her.

As she opened her eyes, a piercing glance escaped from between her half-closed lids; then, as if to collect her scattered thoughts, she smoothed back her long hair with her hands, dried her lips, moist with slumber, and seemed to reflect anxiously.

Balsamo looked at her with some anxiety. He had been long accustomed to the sudden transition from winning love to outbursts of anger and hatred; but this appearance, to which he was entirely unused—the calmness with which Lorenza on this occasion received him, instead of giving way to a burst of hatred—announced something more serious, perhaps, than he had yet witnessed.

Lorenza sat up on the couch, and fixing her deep soft eyes upon Balsamo, she said:

"Pray be good enough to take a seat beside me."

Balsamo started at the sound of her voice, expressing as it did such unusual mildness.

"Beside you!" said he. "You know, my Lorenza, that I have but one wish—to pass my life at your feet."

"Sir," replied Lorenza, in the same tone, "I pray you to be seated, although, indeed I have not much to say to you; but, short as it is, I shall say it better, I think, if you are seated."

"Now, as ever, my beloved Lorenza. I shall do as you wish."

And he took a chair near Lorenza, who was still seated upon the couch.

"Sir," said she, fixing her heavenly eyes upon Balsamo, "I have summoned you to request from you a favor."

"Oh, my Lorenza!" exclaimed Balsamo, more and more delighted, "anything you wish! speak—you shall have everything!"

"I wish for only one; but I warn you that I wish for this one most ardently."

" Speak, Lorenza, speak—should it cost my fortune, or half my life ! "

" It will cost you nothing, sir, but a moment of your time," replied the young girl.

Balsamo, enchanted with the turn the conversation was taking, was already tasking his fertile imagination to supply a list of those wishes which Lorenza was likely to form, and, above all, those which he could satisfy. "She will, perhaps," thought he, " ask for a servant and a companion. Well ! even this immense sacrifice—for it would compromise my secret and my friends—I will make for the poor child is in truth very unhappy in her solitude."

" Speak quickly, my Lorenza," said he aloud, with a smile full of love.

" Sir," said she, " you are aware that I am pining away with melancholy and weariness."

Balsamo sighed, and bent his head in token of assent.

" My youth," continued Lorenza, " is wasted ; my days are one long sigh—my nights a continual terror. I am growing old in solitude and anguish."

" Your life is what you have made it, Lorenza," said Balsamo ; " it is not my fault that this life which you have made so sad is not one to make a queen envious."

" Be it so. Therefore, it is I, you see, who have recourse to you in my distress."

" Thanks, Lorenza."

" You are a good Christian, you have sometimes told me, although——"

" Although you think me lost to heaven, you would say. I complete your thought, Lorenza."

" Suppose nothing, except what I tell you, sir ; and pray do not conjecture thus groundlessly."

" Proceed, then."

" Well, instead of leaving me plunged in this despair and wrath, grant me, since I am of no service to you——"

She stopped to glance at Balsamo, but he had regained his command over himself, and she only saw a cold look and contracted brow bent upon her.

She became animated as she met his almost threatening eye.

"Grant me," continued she—"not liberty—for I know that some mysterious secret, or rather your will, which seems all-powerful to me, condemns me to perpetual captivity—but at least to see human faces, to hear other voices than yours—permit me, in short, to go out, to walk, to take exercise."

"I had foreseen this request, Lorenza," said Balsamo, taking her hand; "and you know that long since your wish has been also my own."

"Well, then!" exclaimed Lorenza.

"But," resumed Balsamo, "you have yourself prevented it. Like a madman that I was—and every man who loves is such—I allowed you to penetrate into some of my secrets, both of science and politics. You know that Althotas has discovered the philosopher's stone, and seeks the elixir of life. You know that I and my companions conspire against the monarchies of this world. The first of these secrets would cause me to be burned as a sorcerer —the other would be sufficient to condemn me to be broken on the wheel for high treason. Besides, you have threatened me, Lorenza—you have told me that you would try every means to regain your liberty, and, this liberty once regained, that the first use you would make of it would be to denounce me to Monsieur Sartines. Did you not say so?"

"What can you expect? At times I lash myself to fury, and then I am half mad."

"Are you calm and sensible now, Lorenza? and can we converse quietly together?"

"I hope so."

"If I grant you the liberty you desire, shall I find in you a devoted and submissive wife—a faithful and gentle companion? You know, Lorenza, this is my most ardent wish."

The young girl was silent.

"In one word—will you love me?" asked Balsamo with a sigh.

"I am unwilling to promise what I cannot perform,"

said Lorenza ; " neither love nor hatred depends upon ourselves. I hope that God, in return for your good actions, will permit my hatred toward you to take flight, and love to return."

" Unfortunately, Lorenza, such a promise is not a sufficient guarantee that I may trust you. I require a positive, sacred oath, to break which would be a sacrilege—an oath which binds you in this world as in the next—which would bring with it your death in this world and your damnation in that which is to come."

Lorenza was silent.

" Will you take this oath ? "

Lorenza hid her face in her hands, and her breast heaved under the influence of contending emotions.

" Take this oath, Lorenza, as I shall dictate it, in the solemn terms in which I shall clothe it, and you shall be free."

" What must I swear, sir ? "

" Swear that you will never, under any pretext, betray what has come to your knowledge relative to the secrets of Althotas."

" Yes—I will swear it."

" Swear that you will never divulge what you know of our political meetings."

" I will swear that also."

" With the oath and in the form which I shall dictate ? "

" Yes. Is that all ? "

" No ; swear and this is the principal one, Lorenza ; for the other matters would only endanger my life, while upon the one I am about to name depends my entire happiness —swear that you will never, either at the instigation of another's will or in obedience to your own, leave me, Lorenza. Swear this and you are free."

The young girl started as if cold steel had pierced her heart.

" And in what form must the oath be taken ? "

" We will enter a church together, and communicate at the same altar. You will swear on the host never to betray anything relating to Althotas or my companions.

You will swear never to leave me. We will then divide the host in two, and each will take the half, you swearing before God that you will never betray me, and I that I will ever do my utmost to make you happy."

" No ! " said Lorenza ; " such an oath is a sacrilege."

" An oath, Lorenza, is never a sacrilege," replied Balsamo, sadly, " but when you make it with the intention of not keeping it."

" I will not take this oath," said Lorenza ; " I should fear to peril my soul."

" It is not—I repeat it—in taking an oath that you peril your soul—it is in breaking it."

" I cannot do it."

" Then learn patience, Lorenza," said Balsamo, without anger, but with the deepest sadness.

Lorenza's brow darkened like an overshadowed plain when a cloud passes between it and the sun.

" Ah ! you refuse ? " said she.

" Not so, Lorenza ; it is you who refuse."

A nervous movement indicated all the impatience the young girl felt at these words.

" Listen, Lorenza ! " said Balsamo. " This is what I will do for you, and believe me it is much."

" Speak ! " said the young girl, with a bitter smile. " Let me see how far your generosity will extend."

" God, chance, or fate—call it what you will—Lorenza, has united us in an indissoluble bond ; do not attempt to break this bond thus in life, for death alone can accomplish that."

" Proceed ; I know that," said Lorenza, impatiently.

" Well, in one week, Lorenza—whatever it may cost me, and however great the sacrifice I make—in eight days you shall have a companion."

" Where ? " asked she.

" Here."

" Here ! " she exclaimed—" behind these bars—behind these inexorable doors, these iron doors—a fellow-prisoner ! Oh, you cannot mean it, sir ; that is not what I ask."

" Lorenza, it is all that I can grant."

The young girl made a more vehement gesture of impatience.

"My sweetest girl," resumed Balsamo, mildly, "reflect a little; with a companion you will more easily support the weight of this necessary misfortune.

"You mistake, sir. Until now I have grieved only for myself, not for others. This trial only was wanting, and I see that you wish to make me undergo it. Yes, you will immure beside me a victim like myself; I shall see her grow thinner and paler, and pine away with grief even as I do. I shall see her dash herself, as I do, against these walls—that hateful door—which I examine twenty times each day to see where it opens to give you egress; and when my companion, your victim, has, like me, wounded her hands against the marble blocks in her endeavors to disjoin them; when, like me, she has worn out her eyelids with her tears; when she is dead, as I am, in soul and mind, and you have two corpses in place of one, you will say in your hateful benevolence 'These two young creatures amuse themselves—they keep each other company—they are happy!' Oh! no, no, no! a thousand times, no!"

And she passionately stamped her foot upon the ground, while Balsamo endeavored in vain to calm her.

"Come, Lorenza," said he, "I entreat you to show a little more mildness and calmness. Let us reason on the matter."

"He asks me to be calm—to be gentle—to reason! The executioner tells the victim whom he is torturing, to be gentle, and the innocent martyr to be calm!"

"Yes, Lorenza, I ask you to be gentle and calm, for your anger cannot change our destiny; it only imbitters it. Accept what I offer you, Lorenza; I will give you a companion who will hug her chains, since they have procured for her your friendship. You shall not see a sad and tearful face such as you fear, but smiles and gayety which will smooth your brow. Come, dearest Lorenza, accept what I offer, for I swear to you that I cannot offer you more."

"That means that you will place me near a hireling, to

whom you will say : ' I give you in charge a poor insane creature, who imagines herself ill and about to die ; soothe her, share her confinement, attend to her comforts, and I will recompense you when she is no more.'"

"Oh, Lorenza ! Lorenza !"

"No, that is not it ; I am mistaken," continued Lorenza, with bitter irony : "I guess badly. But what can you expect ? I am so ignorant, I know so little of the world. You will say to the woman : ' Watch over the madwoman, she is dangerous ; report all her actions, all her thoughts to me. Watch over her waking and sleeping.' And you will give her as much gold as she requires, for gold cost you nothing—you make it !"

"Lorenza, you wander ; in the name of Heaven, Lorenza, read my heart better ! In giving you a companion, my beloved, I compromise such mighty interests that you would tremble for me if you did not hate me. In giving you a companion, I endanger my safety, my liberty, my very life, and notwithstanding, I risk all to save you a little weariness."

"Weariness !" exclaimed Lorenza, with a wild and frantic laugh which made Balsamo shudder. "He calls it weariness !"

"Well ! suffering. Yes, you are right, Lorenza, they are poignant sufferings. I repeat, Lorenza, have patience ; a day will come when all your sufferings will cease—a day will come when you shall be free and happy."

"Will you permit me to retire to a convent and take the vows ? "

"To a convent ? "

"I will pray—first for you and then for myself. I shall be closely confined indeed, but I shall at least have a garden, air, space. I shall have a cemetery to walk in, and can seek beforehand among the tombs for the place of my repose. I shall have companions who grieve for their own sorrows and not for mine. Permit me to retire to a convent, and I will take any vows you wish. A convent, Balsamo ! I implore you on my knees to grant this request."

"Lorenza! Lorenza! we cannot part. Mark me well —we are indissolubly connected in this world! Ask for nothing which exceeds the limits of this house."

"Balsamo pronounced these last words in so calm and determined a tone, that Lorenza did not even repeat the request.

"Then you refuse me?" said she, dejectedly.

"I cannot grant it."

"Is what you say irrevocable?"

"It is."

"Well, I have something else then to ask," said she, with a smile.

"Oh, my good Lorenza! ever smile thus—only smile upon me, and you will compel me to do all you wish!"

"Oh, yes, I shall make you do all that I wish, provided I do everything that pleases you. Well, be it so; I will be as reasonable as possible."

"Speak, Lorenza, speak!"

"Just now you said, 'One day, Lorenza, your sufferings shall cease—one day you shall be free and happy.'"

"Oh, yes, I said so, and I swear before Heaven that I await that day as impatiently as yourself."

"Well, this day may arrive immediately, Balsamo," said the young Italian, with a caressing smile, which her husband had hitherto only seen in her sleep. "I am weary, very weary—you can understand my feelings; I am so young, and have already suffered so much! Well, my friend—for you say you are my friend—listen to me; grant me this happy day immediately."

"I hear you," said Balsamo, inexpressibly agitated.

"I end my appeal by the request I should have made at the commencement, Acharat."

The young girl shuddered.

"Speak, my beloved!"

"Well! I have often remarked, when you made experiments on some unfortunate animal, and when you told me that these experiments were necessary to the cause of humanity—I have often remarked that you possessed the secret of inflicting death, sometimes by a drop of poison, sometimes by an opened vein ; that this death was calm, rapid as lightning, and that these unfortunate and innocent creatures, condemned as I am to the miseries of captivity, were instantly liberated by death, the first blessing they had received since their birth. Well——"

She stopped and turned pale.

"Well, my Lorenza ?" repeated Balsamo.

"Well, what you sometimes do to those unfortunate animals for the interest of science, do now to me in the name of humanity. Do it for a friend, who will bless you with her whole heart, who will kiss your hand with the deepest gratitude, if you grant her what she asks. Do it, Balsamo, for me, who kneel here at your feet, who promise you with my last sigh more love and happiness than you caused me during my whole life !—for me, Balsamo, who promise you a frank and beaming smile as I quit this earth. By the soul of your mother ! by the sufferings of our blessed Lord ! by all that is holy and solemn and sacred in the world of the living and of the dead ! I implore you, kill me ! kill me !"

"Lorenza !" exclaimed Balsamo, taking her in his arms as she rose after uttering these last words—"Lorenza, you are delirious. Kill you ! You, my love !—my life !"

Lorenza disengaged herself by a violent effort from Balsamo's grasp, and fell on her knees.

"I will never rise," said she, "until you have granted my request. Kill me without a shock, without violence, without pain ; grant me this favor since you say you love me—send me to sleep as you have often done—only take away the awaking—it is despair !"

"Lorenza, my beloved !" said Balsamo. "Oh, God ! do you not see how you torture my heart ? What ! you are really so unhappy, then ? Come, my Lorenza, rise ; do not give way to despair. Alas ! do you hate me then so very much ?"

"I hate slavery, constraint, solitude ; and as you make me a slave, unhappy, and solitary—well, yes ! I hate you !"

"But I love you too dearly to see you die, Lorenza.

You shall not die, therefore ; I will effect the most diffi-cult cure I have yet undertaken, my Lorenza—I will make you love life."

"No, no, that is impossible ; you have made me long for death."

"Lorenza, for pity's sake !—I promise that soon——"

"Life or death !" exclaimed the young woman, becom-ing more and more excited. "This is the decisive day—will you give me life, that is to say, liberty ?—will you give me death, that is to say, repose ?"

"Life, my Lorenza, life !"

"Then that is liberty."

Balsamo was silent.

"If not, death—a gentle death—by a draught, a needle's point—death during sleep ! Repose ! repose ! repose !"

"Life and patience, Lorenza !"

Lorenza burst into a terrible laugh, and making a spring backward, drew from her bosom a knife, with a blade so fine and sharp that it glittered in her hand like a flash of lightning.

Balsamo uttered a cry, but it was too late. When he rushed forward and reached the hand, the weapon had already fulfilled its task, and had fallen on Lorenza's bleeding breast. Balsamo had been dazzled by the flash—he was blinded by the sight of blood.

In his turn he uttered a terrible cry, and seized Lorenza round the waist, meeting in midway her arm raised to deal a second blow, and receiving the weapon in his undefended hand. Lorenza with a mighty effort drew the weapon away, and the sharp blade glided through Balsamo's fingers. The blood streamed from his mutilated hand.

Then, instead of continuing the struggle, Balsamo ex-tended his bleeding hand toward the young woman, and said with a voice of irresistible command :

"Sleep, Lorenza, sleep !—I will it."

But on this occasion the irritation was such that the obedience was not as prompt as usual.

"No, no," murmured Lorenza, tottering and attempt-ing to strike again. "No, I will not sleep !"

"Sleep, I tell you !" said Balsamo, for the second time, advancing a step toward her—"sleep ! I command it !"

This time, the power of Balsamo's will was so great that all resistance was in vain. Lorenza heaved a sigh, let the knife fall from her hand, and sunk upon the cushions.

Her eyes still remained open, but their threatening glare died away, and finally they closed ; her stiffened neck drooped ; her head fell upon her shoulder like that of a wounded bird ; a nervous shudder passed through her frame—Lorenza was asleep.

Balsamo hastily opened her robe, and examined the wound, which seemed slight, although the blood flowed from it in abundance.

He then pressed the lion's eye, the spring started, and the back of the fireplace opened ; then, unfastening the counterpoise which made the trap-door of Althotas's chamber descend, he leaped upon it and mounted to the old man's laboratory.

"Ah ! it is you, Acharat," said the latter, who was still seated in his armchair, "you are aware that in a week I shall be a hundred years old. You are aware that before that time I must have the blood of a child or of an unmarried female."

But Balsamo heard him not. He hastened to the cupboard in which the magic balsams were kept, seized one of the vials of which he had often proved the efficacy, again mounted upon the trap, stamped his foot, and descended to the lower apartment.

Althotas rolled his armchair to the mouth of the trap with the intention of seizing him by his dress.

"Do you hear, wretch ?" said he ; "do you hear ? If in a week I have not a child or an unmarried woman to complete my elixir, I am a dead man !"

Balsamo turned ; the old man's eyes seemed to glare in the midst of his unearthly and motionless features, as if they alone were alive.

"Yes, yes," replied Balsamo ; "yes, be calm, you shall have what you want."

Then, letting go the spring, the trap mounted again, fitting like an ornament in the ceiling of the room.

After which he rushed into Lorenza's apartment, which he had just reached when Fritz's bell rang.

" Monsieur de Richelieu ! " muttered Balsamo ; "oh ! duke and peer as he is, he must wait."

CHAPTER LI.

M. DE RICHELIEU'S TWO DROPS OF WATER.

M. DE RICHELIEU left the house in the Rue St. Claude at half-past four. What his errand with Balsamo was will explain itself in the sequel.

M. de Taverney had dined with his daughter, as the dauphiness had given her leave to absent herself on this day in order that she might receive her father.

They were at dessert, when M. de Richelieu, ever the bearer of good news, made his appearance to announce to his friend that the king would not give merely a company to Philip, but a regiment. Taverney was exuberant in his expression of joy, and Andrée warmly thanked the marshal.

The conversation took a turn which may be easily imagined after what had passed ; Richelieu spoke of nothing but the king, Andrée of nothing but her brother, and Taverney of nothing but Andrée. The latter announced, in the course of conversation, that she was set at liberty from her attendance on the dauphiness ; that her royal highness was receiving a visit from two German princes, her relations ; and that in order to pass a few hours of liberty with them, which might remind her of the court of Vienna, Marie Antoinette had dismissed all her attend-ants, even her lady of honor, which had so deeply shocked Mme. de Noailles that she had gone to lay her grievances at the king's feet.

Taverney was, he said, delighted at this, since he had thus an opportunity of conversing with Andrée about many things relating to their fortune and name. This observation made Richelieu propose to retire, in order to leave the father and daughter quite alone ; but Mlle. de Taverney would not permit it, so he remained.

Richelieu was in a vein of moralizing ; he painted most eloquently the degradation into which the French nobility had fallen, forced as they were to submit to the ignominious yoke of these favorites of chance, these contraband queens, instead of the favorites of the olden times, who were almost as noble as their august lovers—women who reigned over the sovereign by their beauty and their love, and over his subjects by their birth, their strength of mind, and their loyal and pure patriotism.

Andrée was surprised at the close analogy between Richelieu's words and those she had heard from the Baron de Taverney a few days previously.

Richelieu then launched into a theory of virtue so spiritual, so pagan, so French, that Andrée was obliged to confess that she was not at all virtuous, according to M. de Richelieu's theories, and that true virtue, as the marshal understood it, was the virtue of Mme. Chateauroux, Mlle. de Lavillier, and Mme. Fousseuse.

From argument to argument, from proof to proof, Richelieu at last became so clear that Andrée no longer understood a word of what he said. On this footing the conversation continued until about seven o'clock in the evening, when the marshal rose, being obliged, as he said, to pay his court to the king at Versailles.

In passing through the apartment to take his hat, he met Nicole, who had always something to do wherever M. de Richelieu was.

" My girl," said he, tapping her on the shoulder, " you shall see me out. I want you to carry a bouquet which Madame de Noailles cut for me in her garden, and which she commissioned me to present to the Countess d'Egmont."

Nicole courtesied like the peasant girls in M. Rousseau's comic operas, whereupon the marshal took leave of father and daughter, exchanged a significant glance with Taverney, made a youthful bow to Andrée, and retired.

With the reader's permission, we will leave the baron and Andrée conversing about the fresh mark of favor conferred on Philip, and follow the marshal. By this means we shall know what was his errand at the Rue St. Claude, where he arrived at such a fearful moment.

Richelieu descended the stairs resting on Nicole's shoulder, and as soon as they were in the garden he stopped, and looking in her face, said :

" Ah, little one ! so we have a lover ? "

"I, my lord marshal ? " exclaimed Nicole, blushing crimson and retreating a step backward.

" Oh ! perhaps you are not called Nicole Legay ? "

" Yes, my lord marshal."

" Well, Nicole Legay has a lover."

" Oh, indeed ? "

" Yes, faith ; a certain well-looking rascal, whom she used to meet in the Rue Coq Heron, and who has followed her to Versailles."

" My lord duke, I swear——"

" A sort of exempt, called— Shall I tell you child, how Mademoiselle Legay's lover is called ? "

Nicole's last hope was that the marshal was ignorant of the name of the happy mortal.

" Oh, yes, my lord marshal ! tell me, since you have made a beginning."

" Who is called Monsieur de Beausire," repeated the marshal, " and who, in truth, does not belie his name."

Nicole clasped her hands with an affectation of prudery which did not in the least impose on Richelieu.

" It seems," said he, " we make appointments with him at Trianon. Peste ! in a royal château ! That is a serious matter. One may be discharged for these freaks, my sweet one ; and Monsieur de Sartines sends all young ladies who are discharged from the royal château to the Salpêtrière.

Nicole began to be uneasy.

" My lord," said she, " I swear to you that if Monsieur Beausire boasts of being my lover he is a fool and a villain, for indeed I am innocent."

"I shall not contradict you," said Richelieu.   "But have you made appointments with him or not ?"

"My lord duke, a rendezvous is no proof of——"

"Have you or have you not ?   Answer me."

"My lord——"

"You have.   Very well ; I do not blame you, my dear child.   Besides, I like pretty girls who display their charms, and I have always assisted them in so doing to the utmost of my power.   Only as your friend and protector I warn you."

"But have I been seen, then ?" asked Nicole.

"It seems so, since I am aware of it."

"My lord," said Nicole, resolutely, "I have not been seen ; it is impossible."

"As to that, I know nothing ; but the report is very prevalent, and must tend to fasten attention on your mistress.   Now you must be aware that being more the friend of the Taverneys than of the Legays, it is my duty to give the baron a hint."

"Oh, my lord !" exclaimed Nicole, terrified at the turn the conversation was taking, "you will ruin me.   Although innocent, I shall be discharged on the mere suspicion."

"In that case, my poor child, you shall be discharged at all events, for even now some evil-minded person or other, having taken offense at the rendezvous, innocent though they be, has informed Madame de Noailles of them."

"Madame de Noailles ! good heavens !"

"Yes ; you see the danger is urgent."

Nicole clasped her hands in despair.

"It is unfortunate, I am aware," said Richelieu ; "but what the deuce can you do ?"

"And you, who said just now you were my protector— you who have proven yourself to be such—can you no longer protect me ?" asked Nicole, with a wheedling cunning worthy of a woman of thirty.

"Yes, pardieu ! I can protect you."

"Well, my lord ?"

"Yes, but I will not."

"Oh ! my lord duke."

" Yes ; you are pretty, I know that, and your beautiful
eyes are telling me all sorts of things ; but I have lately
become rather blind, my poor Nicole, and I no longer understand the language of lovely eyes. Once I would
have offered you an asylum in my pavilion of Hanover,
but those days are over."

" Yet you once before received me there," said Nicole,
angrily.

" Ah ! that is ungrateful in you, Nicole, to reproach me
with having taken you there, when I did so to render you
a service ; for confess that without Monsieur Rafte's assistance, who made you a charming brunette, you would
never have entered Trianon, which, after all, perhaps,
would have been better than to be dismissed from it now.
But why the devil did you give a rendezvous to Monsieur
de Beausire, and at the very gate of the stables, too ? "

" So you know that also ? " said Nicole, who saw that
she must change her tactics, and place herself at the
marshal's discretion.

" Parbleu ! you see I know it ; and Madame de Noailles,
too. This very evening you have another appointment."

" That is true, my lord ; but on my faith I shall not go."

" Of course, you are warned ; but Monsieur de Beausire
is not warned, and he will be seized. Then, as he will not
like, of course, to be taken for a thief and be hanged, or
for a spy and be whipped, he will prefer to say—especially
as there is no disgrace in confessing it—' unhand me ! I
am the lover of the pretty Nicole.' "

" My lord duke, I will send to warn him."

" Impossible, my poor child ! By whom could you send ?
By him who betrayed you, perhaps ? "

" Alas ! that is true," said Nicole, feigning despair.

" What a becoming thing remorse is ! " exclaimed
Richelieu.

Nicole covered her face with her hands, taking care,
however, to leave space enough between her fingers to allow
her to observe every look and gesture of Richelieu.

" You are really adorable ! " said the duke, whom none
of these little tricks could escape ; " why am I not fifty

years younger ? No matter. Parbleu ! Nicole, I will bring you out of the scrape."

" Oh, my lord ! if you do that, my gratitude——"

" I don't want it, Nicole. On the contrary, I shall give you most disinterested assistance."

" Oh ! how good of you, my lord ; I thank you from the bottom of my heart."

" Do not thank me yet ; as yet you know nothing. Diable ! wait till you hear more."

" I will submit to anything, provided Mademoiselle Andrée does not dismiss me."

" Ah ! then you are very fond of Trianon ? "

" Very, my lord."

" Well, Nicole, in the very first place, get rid of this feeling."

" But why so, if I am not discovered, my lord ? "

" Whether you are discovered or not, you must leave Trianon."

" Oh ! why ? "

" I shall tell you : because if Madame de Noailles has found you out, no one, not even the king, could save you."

" Ah ! if I could only see the king."

" In the second place, even if you are not found out, I myself should be the means of dismissing you."

" You ? "

" Immediately."

" In truth, my lord marshal, I do not understand you."

" It is as I have had the honor of telling you."

" And that is your protection, is it ? "

" If you do not wish for it, there is yet time ; you have only to say the word, Nicole."

" Oh, yes ! my lord, on the contrary, I do wish for it."

" And I will grant it."

" Well ? "

" Well, this is what I will do for you. Hark ye ! "

" Speak, my lord."

" Instead of getting you discharged, and perhaps imprisoned, I will make you rich and free."

" Rich and free ? "

" Yes."

" And what must I do in order to be rich and free ? "

" Almost nothing."

" But what——"

" What I am about to tell you."

" Is it difficult ? "

" Mere child's play."

" Then," said Nicole, " there is something to do ? "

" Ah, dame ; you know the motto of this world of ours, Nicole—nothing for nothing."

"And that which I have to do, is it for myself, or for you ? "

The duke looked at Nicole.

" Tudieu ! " said he, " the little masker, how cunning she is ! "

" Well, finish, my lord duke."

" Well ! it is for yourself," replied he, boldly.

" Ah ! " said Nicole, who, perceiving that the marshal had need of her services, already feared him no longer, while her ingenious brain was busy endeavoring to discover the truth among the windings which, from habit, her companion always used ; " what shall I do for myself, my lord duke ? "

" This ; Monsieur de Beausire comes at half-past eleven, does he not ? "

" Yes, my lord marshal, that is his hour."

" It is now ten minutes past seven."

" That is also true."

" If I say the word he will be arrested."

" Yes, but you will not say it."

" No. You will go to him and tell him—but in the first place, Nicole, do you love this young man ? "

" Why, I have given him a rendezvous."

" That is no reason you may wish to marry him. Women take such strange caprices."

Nicole burst into a loud laugh.

" Marry him ! " said she. " Ha ! ha ! ha ! "

Richelieu was astounded ; he had not, even at court, met many women of this stamp.

"Well," said he, "so be it. You do not wish to marry him ; but in that case you love him. So much the better.

"Agreed ! I love Monsieur de Beausire. Let us take that for granted, my lord, and proceed."

"Peste ! what strides you make ! "

"Of course. You may readily imagine that I am anxious to know what remains for me to do."

"In the first place, since you love him, you must fly with him."

"Dame ! if you wish it particularly, I suppose I must."

"Oh ! I wish nothing about it—not so fast, little one."

Nicole saw that she was going too far, and that as yet she had neither the secret nor the money of her cunning opponent. She stopped, therefore, only to rise again afterward.

"My lord," said she, "I await your orders."

"Well, you must go to Monsieur de Beausire, and say to him : "We are discovered ; but I have a protector who will save you from St. Lazarus and me from Salpétrière. Let us fly.""

Nicole looked at Richelieu.

"Fly ?" repeated she.

Richelieu understood her cunning and expressive look.

"Parbleu !" said he, "of course I shall pay the expenses."

Nicole asked for no further explanation. It was plain that she must know all since she was to be paid.

The marshal saw what an important point Nicole had gained, and hastened to say all he had to say, just as a gambler is eager to pay when he has lost, in order to have the disagreeable task of paying over.

"Do you know what you are thinking of, Nicole ? " said he.

"Faith, no," replied the girl ; "but I suppose you, my lord marshal, who know so many things, can guess it."

"Nicole," he replied, "you were reflecting that if you

fled, your mistress might require you during the night, and not finding you, might give the alarm, which would expose you to the risk of being overtaken and seized."

"No," said Nicole, "I was not thinking of that, because, after all, my lord, I think I would prefer remaining here."

"But if Monsieur de Beausire is taken ?"

"Well, I cannot help it."

"But if he confess ?"

"Let him confess."

"Ah !" said Richelieu, beginning to be uneasy, "but in that case, you are lost."

"No ; for Mademoiselle Andrée is kindness itself, and as she loves me at heart, she will speak to the king for me ; so, even if Monsieur de Beausire is punished, I shall not share his punishment."

The marshal bit his lip.

"Nicole," said he, "I tell you you are a fool. Mademoiselle Andrée is not on such good terms with the king, and I will have you arrested immediately if you do not listen to me as I wish. Do you hear, you little viper ?"

"Oh, my lord ! my ears do not serve me so ill. I hear you, but I form my own conclusions."

"Good. Then you will go at once and arrange your plan of flight with Monsieur de Beausire."

"But how do you imagine, my lord marshal, that I shall expose myself to the risk of flight, when you tell me yourself that mademoiselle might awake, might ask for me, give the alarm, and a great deal more which I know not, but which you, my lord, who are a man of experience, must have foreseen ?"

Richelieu bit his lip again, but this time more deeply than before.

"Well, minion, if I have thought of these consequences, I have also thought of how to avoid them."

"And how will you manage to prevent mademoiselle from calling me ?"

"By preventing her awaking."

"Bah ! she awakes ten times during the night."

"Then she has the same malady that I have," said Richelieu, calmly.

"The same that you have?" said Nicole, laughing.

"Yes. I also awake ten times every night, only I have a remedy for this sleeplessness. She must use the same remedy, or if not, you will do it for her."

"What do you mean, my lord?"

"What does your mistress take in the evening before she goes to bed?"

"What does she take?"

"Yes; it is the fashion now to drink something in the evening. Some take orangeade or lemonade, others take eau-de-Melisse, others——"

"Mademoiselle drinks only a glass of pure water in the evening before going to bed; sometimes sweetened and flavored with orange-water, if her nerves are weak."

"Ah, excellent!" said Richelieu, "just as I do myself. My remedy will suit her admirably."

"How so?"

"I pour one drop of a certain liquid in my beverage and I then never wake all night."

Nicole tasked her brain to discover to what end the marshal's diplomacy tended.

"You do not answer," said he.

"I was just thinking that mademoiselle has not your cordial."

"I will give you some."

"Ah!" thought Nicole, seeing at last a ray of light through the darkness.

"You must put two drops of it into your mistress's glass—neither more nor less, remember—and she will sleep soundly, so that she will not call you, and consequently you will gain time."

"Oh! if that is all, it is very simple."

"You will give her the two drops?"

"Certainly."

"You promise me?"

"I presume it is for my own interest to do so; besides, I will lock the door so carefully——"

"By no means," said Richelieu, hastily. "That is exactly what you must not do; on the contrary, you must leave her room door open."

"Ah!" exclaimed Nicole, with suppressed joy. She now understood all. Richelieu saw it plainly.

"Is that all?" inquired she.

"Absolutely all. Now you may go and tell your exempt to pack up his trunks."

"Unfortunately, sir, it would be useless to tell him to fill his purse."

"You know that is my affair."

"Yes, I remember your lordship was kind enough to say——"

"Come, Nicole, how much do you want?"

"For what?"

"For pouring in the two drops of water."

"For that, nothing, my lord, since you assure me I do so for my own interest; it would not be just that you should pay me for attending to my own interest. But for leaving mademoiselle's door open—ah ' for that I warn you I must have a good round sum."

"At one word, how much?"

"I must have twenty thousand francs, my lord."

Richelieu started.

"Nicole," said he, with a sigh, "you will make some figure in the world."

"I ought to do so, my lord, for I begin to believe now that I shall attract attention. But with your twenty thousand francs we shall smooth difficulties."

"Go and warn Monsieur Beausire, Nicole; and when you return I will give you the money."

"My lord, Monsieur Beausire is very incredulous, and he will not believe what I tell him unless I can give him proofs."

Richelieu pulled out a handful of bank-notes from his pocket.

"Here is something on account," said he; "in this purse there are a hundred double louis."

"Your lordship will settle the account in full, and give

me the balance then, when I have spoken to Monsieur Beausire ? "

" No, pardieu ! I will settle it on the spot. You are a careful girl, Nicole ; it will bring you luck."

And Richelieu handed her the promised sum, partly in bank-notes and partly in louis d'ors and half-louis.

" There ! " said he, " is that right ? "

" I think so," said Nicole ; " and now, my lord, I want only the principal thing."

" The cordial ? "

" Yes ; of course your lordship has a bottle ? "

" I have my own, which I always carry about with me."
Nicole smiled.

" And then," said she, " Trianon is locked every night, and I have not a key."

" But I have one, as first gentleman of the chamber."

" Ah, indeed ? "

" Here it is."

" How fortunate all this is ! " said Nicole ; " it is one succession of miracles ! And now, my lord duke, adieu ! "

" How ! adieu ? "

" Certainly. I shall not see your lordship again, as I shall go as soon as mademoiselle is asleep."

" Quite right. Adieu, then, Nicole."

And Nicole, laughing in her sleeve, disappeared in the increasing darkness.

" I shall still succeed," said Richelieu. " But in truth, it would seem that I am getting old, and fortune is turning against me. I have been outwitted by this little one. But what matters it, if I return the blow ? "

CHAPTER LII.

THE FLIGHT.

NICOLE was a conscientious girl. She had received M. de Richelieu's money, and received it in advance, too, and she felt anxious to prove herself worthy of this confidence by earning her pay. She ran therefore as quickly as possible to the gate, where she arrived at forty minutes past seven, instead of half past.   Now, M. de Beausire, who, being accustomed to military discipline, was a punctual man, had been waiting there for ten minutes.   About ten minutes before, too, M. de Taverney had left his daughter, and Andrée was consequently alone.   Now, being alone, the young girl had closed the blinds.

Gilbert, as usual, was gazing eagerly at Andrée from his attic, but it would have been difficult to say if his eyes sparkled with love or hatred.   When the blinds were closed Gilbert could see nothing.   Consequently he looked in another direction, and while looking, he perceived M. de Beausire's plume, and recognized the exempt, who was walking up and down, whistling an air to kill time while he was waiting.

In about ten minutes, that is to say, at forty minutes past seven, Nicole made her appearance.   She exchanged a few words with M. Beausire, who made a gesture with his head as a sign that he understood her perfectly, and disappeared by the shady alley leading to the little Trianon. Nicole, light as a bird, returned in the direction she had come.

" Oh, ho ! " thought Gilbert.   " Monsieur the exempt and mademoiselle the femme de chambre have something to do or to say which they fear to have witnessed.   Very good ! "

Gilbert no longer felt any curiosity with respect to Nicole's movements, but actuated by the idea that the young girl was his natural enemy, he merely sought to collect a mass of proofs against her morality, with which proofs he might successfully repulse any attack, should she attempt one against him.   And as he knew the campaign might begin at any moment, like a prudent soldier he collected his munitions of war.

A rendezvous with a man in the very grounds of Trianon was one of the weapons which a cunning enemy such as Gilbert could not neglect, especially when it was imprudently placed under his very eyes.   Gilbert consequently wished to have the testimony of his ears as well

as that of his eyes, and to catch some fatally compromis-
ing phrases which would completely floor Nicole at the
first outset.   He quickly descended from his attic, therefore, hastened along the lobby, and gained the garden by
the chapel stairs.   Once in the garden he had nothing to
fear, for he knew all its hiding-places as a fox knows his
cover.   He glided beneath the linden-trees, then along the
espalier, until he reached a small thicket situated about
twenty paces from the spot where he calculated upon seeing Nicole.

As he had foreseen, Nicole was there.   Scarcely had he
installed himself in the thicket when a strange noise
reached his ears.   It was the chink of gold upon stone—
that metallic sound of which nothing, except the reality,
can give a correct idea.

Like a serpent Gilbert gilded along to a raised terrace
onttopped by a hedge of lilacs which at that season (early
in May) diffused their perfume around, and showered
down their flowers upon the passers who took the shady
alley on their way from the great to the little Trianon.

Having reached this retreat, Gilbert, whose eyes were
accustomed to pierce the darkness, saw Nicole emptying
the purse which M. de Richelieu had given her upon a
stone on the inner side of the gate and prudently placed
out of M. de Beausire's reach.

The large louis d'ors showered from it in bright confusion, while M. de Beausire, with sparkling eye and
trembling hand, looked at Nicole and her louis d'ors as if
he could not comprehend how the one should possess the
other.

Nicole spoke first.

"You have more than once, my dear Monsieur de
Beausire," said she, "proposed to elope with me."

"And to marry you!" exclaimed the enthusiastic
exempt.

"Oh, my dear sir! that is a matter of course; just
now, flight is the most important point.   Can we fly in
two hours?"

"In ten minutes, if you like."

"No ; I have something to do first, which will occupy me two hours."

"In two hours, as in ten minutes, I shall be at your orders, dearest."

"Very well. Take these fifty louis."

Nicole counted the fifty louis, and handed them through the gate to M. de Beausire, who, without counting them, stuffed them into his waistcoat pocket.

"And in an hour and a half," continued she, "be here with your carriage."

"But——" objected Beausire.

"Oh, if you do not wish, forget what has passed between us, and give me back my fifty louis."

"I do not shrink, dearest Nicole ; but I fear the result."

"For whom ?"

"For you."

"For me ?"

"Yes ; the fifty louis—once vanished, and vanished they will soon be—you will complain—you will regret Trianon—you will——"

"Oh ! how thoughtful you are, Monsieur de Beausire ! But fear nothing ? I am not one of those women who are easily made miserable. Have no scruples on that score ; when the fifty louis are gone, we shall see."

And she shook the purse which contained the other fifty ; Beausire's eyes were absolutely phosphorescent.

"I would charge through a blazing furnace for your sake !" exclaimed he.

"Oh ! content you—I shall not require so much from you, sir. Then it is agreed you will be here with the chaise in an hour and a half, and in two hours we shall fly ?"

"Agreed !" exclaimed Beausire, seizing Nicole's hand, and drawing it through the gate to kiss it.

"Hush !" said Nicole, "are you mad ?"

"No ; I am in love."

"Hum !" muttered Nicole.

"Do you not believe me, sweetheart ?"

"Yes, yes, I believe you.   Above all, be sure to have good horses."

" Oh, yes ! "

And they separated.

But a moment afterward, Beausire returned, quite alarmed.

" Hist ! " whispered he.

" Well, what is it ? " asked Nicole, already some distance off, and putting her hand to her mouth, so as to convey her voice further.

" And the gate ? " asked Beausire, " will you creep under it ? "

" How stupid he is ! " murmured Nicole, who at this moment was not ten paces distant from Gilbert.   Then she added, in a louder tone :   " I have the key."

Beausire uttered a prolonged " Oh ! " of admiration, and this time took to his heels for good and all.   Nicole hastened back with drooping head and nimble step to her mistress.

Gilbert, now left sole master of the field, put the following four questions to himself :

" Why does Nicole fly with Beausire, when she does not love him ?   How does Nicole come to possess such a large sum of money ?   Why has Nicole the key of the gate ?   Why does Nicole return to Andrée, when she might go at once ? "

Gilbert found an answer to the second question, but to the others he could find none.

Thus checked at the commencement, his natural curiosity and his acquired distrust were so much excited that he determined to remain in the cold, beneath the dew-covered trees, to await the end of this scene, of which he had witnessed the commencement.

Andrée had conveyed her father to the barriers of the Great Trianon, and was returning alone and pensive, when Nicole appeared, issuing from the alley leading to the famous gate, where she had been concerting her measures with M. de Beausire.

Nicole stopped on perceiving her mistress, and upon a

sign which Andrée made to her, she followed her to her apartment.

It was now about half-past eight in the evening. The night had closed in earlier than usual; for a huge cloud, sweeping from south to north, had overspread the whole sky, and all around, as far as the eye could reach over the lofty forest of Versailles, the gloomy shroud was gradually enveloping in its folds the stars a short time before sparkling in the azure dome. A light breeze swept along the ground, breathing warmly on the drooping flowers, which bent their heads, as if imploring Heaven to send them rain or dew.

The threatening aspect of the sky did not hasten Andrée's steps; on the contrary, melancholy and thoughtful, the young girl seemed to ascend each step leading to her room with regret, and she paused at every window as she passed to gaze at the sky, so much in harmony with her saddened mood, and thus to delay her return to her own little retreat.

Nicole, impatient, angry, fearing that some whim might detain her mistress beyond the usual hour, grumbled and muttered, as servants never fail to do when their masters are imprudent enough to satisfy their own caprices at the expense of those of their domestics.

At last, Andrée reached the door of her chamber, and sunk rather than seated herself upon a couch, gently ordering Nicole to leave the window, which looked upon the court, half open. Nicole obeyed; then, returning to her mistress with that affectionate air which the flatterer could so easily assume, she said:

"I fear mademoiselle feels ill this evening; her eyes are red and swollen, yet bright. I think that mademoiselle is in great need of repose."

"Do you think so?" asked Andrée, who had scarcely listened.

And she carelessly placed her feet upon a cushion of tapestry-work.

Nicole took this as an order to undress her mistress, and commenced to unfasten the ribbons and flowers of her head-dress—a species of edifice which the most skilful could not unbuild in less than a quarter of an hour. While she was thus employed, Andrée did not utter a word, and Nicole, thus left to follow her own wishes, hastened the business, without disturbing Andrée, whose preoccupation was so great that she permitted Nicole to pull out her hair with impunity.

When the night toilet was finished, Andrée gave her orders for the morrow. In the morning some books were to be fetched from Versailles which Philip had left there for his sister, and the tuner was to be ordered to attend to put the harpsichord in proper order.

Nicole replied that if she were not called during the night, she would rise early, and would have both these commissions executed before her young lady was awake.

"To-morrow also I will write to Philip," said Andrée, speaking to herself ; "that will console me a little."

"Come what will," thought Nicole, "I shall not carry the letter."

And at this reflection the girl, who was not quite lost yet, began to think, in saddened mood, that she was about for the first time to leave that excellent mistress, under whose care her mind and heart had been awakened. The thought of Andrée was linked in her mind with so many other recollections, that to touch it was to stir the whole chain which carried her back to the first days of infancy.

While these two young creatures, so different in their character and their condition, were thus reflecting beside each other, without any connection existing between their thoughts, time was rapidly flying, and Andrée's little time-piece, which was always in advance of the great clock of Trianon, struck nine.

Beausire would be at the appointed place, and Nicole had but half an hour to join her lover.

She finished her task as quickly as possible, not without uttering some sighs which Andrée did not even notice. She folded a night-shawl around her mistress, and as Andrée still sat immovable and her eyes fixed on the ceiling, she drew Richelieu's vial from her bosom, put two pieces of sugar into a goblet, added the water necessary to melt it, and without hesitation, and by the resolute force of her will, so strong in one so young, she poured two drops of the fluid from the vial into the water, which immediately became turbid, then changed to a slight opal tint, which soon died away.

"Mademoiselle," said Nicole, "your glass of water is prepared, your clothes are folded, the night-lamp is lighted. You know I must rise very early to-morrow morning ; may I go to bed now ?"

"Yes," replied Andrée, absently.

Nicole courtesied, heaved a last sigh, which, like the others, was unnoticed, and closed behind her the glass door leading to the anteroom. But instead of retiring into her little cell adjoining the corridor and lighted from Andrée's anteroom, she softly took to flight, leaving the door of the corridor ajar, so that Richelieu's instructions were scrupulously followed.

Then, not to arouse the attention of the neighbors, she descended the stairs on tiptoe, bounded down the outer steps, and ran quickly to join M. de Beausire at the gate.

Gilbert had not quitted his post. He had heard Nicole say that she would return in two hours, and he waited. But as it was now ten minutes past the hour, he began to fear that she would not return.

All at once he saw her running as if some one were pursuing her.

Nicole approached the gate, passed the key through the bars to Beausire, who opened it, rushed out, and the gate closed with a dull, grating noise. The key was then thrown among the grass in the ditch, near the spot where Gilbert was stationed. He heard it fall with a dead sound, and marked the place where it had dropped.

Nicole and Beausire in the meantime gained ground. Gilbert heard them move away, and soon he could distinguish, not the noise of a carriage, as Nicole had required, but the pawing of a horse, which, after some moments' delay—occupied doubtless by Nicole in recrimination, who had wished to depart, like a duchess, in her carriage—

changed to the clattering of his iron-shod feet on the pavement, and at last died away in the distance.

Gilbert breathed freely ; he was free, free from Nicole —that is to say, from his enemy.   Andrée was henceforth alone.

He took the contrary direction from the one Nicole was pursuing, and hurried toward the offices of Trianon.

CHAPTER LIII.

DOUBLE SIGHT.

WHEN Andrée was alone, she gradually recovered from the mental torpor into which she had fallen, and while Nicole was flying *en croupe* behind M. de Beausire, she knelt down and offered up a fervent prayer for Philip, the only being in the world she loved with a true and deep attachment ; and while she prayed, her trust in God assumed new strength and inspired her with fresh courage.

The prayers which Andrée offered were not composed of a succession of words strung one to the other ; they were a kind of heavenly ecstasy, during which her soul rose to her God and mingled with his spirit.

In these impassioned supplications of the mind, freed from earthly concerns, there was no alloy of self.   Andrée in some degree abandoned all thoughts of herself, like a shipwrecked mariner who has lost hope, and who prays only for his wife and children, soon to become orphans. This inward grief had sprung up in Andrée's bosom since her brother's departure, but it was not entirely without another cause.   Like her prayer, it was composed of two distinct elements, one of which was quite inexplicable to her.

It was, as it were, a presentiment, the perceptible approach of some impending misfortune.   It was a sensation resembling that of the shooting of a cicatrized wound. The acute pain is over, but the remembrance survives, and reminds the sufferer of the calamity, as the wound itself had previously done. She did not even attempt to explain her feelings to herself. Devoted, heart and soul, to Philip, she centered in her beloved brother every thought and every affection of her heart.

Then she rose, took a book from her modestly furnished library, placed the light within reach of her hand, and stretched herself on a couch. The book she had chosen, or, rather, upon which she had accidentally placed her hand, was a dictionary of botany. It may readily be imagined that this book was not calculated to absorb her attention, but rather to lull it to rest. Gradually, drowsiness weighed down her eyelids, and a filmy veil obscured her vision. For a moment the young girl struggled against sleep, twice or thrice she collected her scattered thoughts, which soon escaped again from her control ; then, raising her head to blow out the candle, she perceived the glass of water prepared by Nicole, stretched out her hand, and took the glass, stirred the sugar with the spoon, and, already half asleep, she approached the glass to her lips.

All at once, just as her lips were already touching the beverage, a strange emotion made her hand tremble, a moist and burning weight fell on her brow, and Andrée recognized with terror, by the current of the fluid which rushed through her nerves, that supernatural attack of mysterious sensations which had several times already triumphed over her strength and overpowered her mind. She had only time to place the glass upon the plate, when instantly, without a murmur, but with a sigh which escaped from her half-open lips, she lost the use of voice, sight, and reason, and seized with a death-like torpor, fell back as if struck by lightning upon her bed. But this sort of annihilation was but the momentary transition to another state of existence. For an instant she seemed perfectly lifeless, and her eyes closed in the slumber of death ; but all at once she rose, opened her eyes, which stared with a fearful fixity of gaze ; and, like a marble statue descending from its tomb, she once more stood upon the floor. There was no longer room for doubt. Andrée was sunk in that marvelous sleep which had several times already suspended her vital functions.

She crossed the chamber, opened the glass door, and entered the corridor, with the fixed and rigid attitude of breathing marble. She reached the stairs, descended step by step without hesitation and without haste, and emerged upon the portico. Just as Andrée placed her foot upon the topmost step to descend, Gilbert reached the lowest on his way to his attic. Seeing this white and solemn figure advancing as if to meet him, he recoiled before her, and, still retreating as she advanced, he concealed himself in a clump of shrubs. It was thus, he recollected, that he had already seen Andrée de Taverney at the Château de Taverney.

Andrée passed close by him, even touched him, but saw him not. The young man, thunder-struck, speechless with surprise, sunk to the ground on one knee. His limbs refused to support him—he was afraid.

Not knowing to what cause to attribute this strange excursion, he followed her with his eyes, but his reason was confounded, his blood beat impetuously against his temples, and he was in a state more closely bordering on madness than the coolness and circumspection necessary for an observer.

He remained, therefore, crouching on the grass among the leaves, watching as he had never ceased to do since this fatal attachment had entered his heart. All at once the mystery was explained; Andrée was neither mad nor bewildered, as he had for a moment supposed; Andrée was, with this sepulchral step, going to a rendezvous. A gleam of lightning now furrowed the sky, and by its blue and livid light Gilbert saw a man concealed beneath the somber avenue of linden-trees, and, notwithstanding the rapidity of the flash, he had recognized the pale face and disordered garments of the man, relieved against the dark background.

Andrée advanced toward this man, whose arm was extended as if to draw her toward him.

A sensation like the branding of a red-hot iron rushed

through Gilbert's heart ; he raised himself upon his knees to see more clearly. At that moment another flash of lightning illumined the sky.

Gilbert recognized Balsamo, covered with dust and perspiration—Balsamo, who, by some mysterious means, had succeeded in entering Trianon, and thus drew Andrée toward him as invincibly, as fatally, as the serpent fascinates its prey.

When two paces from him André stopped. Balsamo took her hand ; her whole frame shuddered.

" Do you see ? " he asked.

" Yes," replied Andrée ; " but in summoning me so suddenly you have nearly killed me."

" Pardon, pardon ! " replied Balsamo ; " but my brain reels—I am beside myself—I am nearly mad—I shall kill myself ! "

" You are indeed suffering," said Andrée, conscious of Balsamo's feelings by the contact of his hand.

" Yes, yes," replied Balsamo ; " I suffer, and I come to you for consolation. You alone can save me."

" Question me."

" Once more, do you see ? "

" Oh, perfectly ! "

" Will you follow me to my house ? Can you do so ? "

" I can, if you will conduct me there in thought."

" Come."

" Ah ! " said Andrée, " we are entering Paris ; we follow the boulevard ; we plunge into a street lighted by a single lamp."

" Yes, that is it. Enter, enter ! "

" We are in an antechamber. There's a staircase to the right, but you draw me toward the wall. The wall opens—steps appear——"

" Ascend ! " exclaimed Balsamo ; " that is our way."

" Ah ! we are in a sleeping-chamber ; there are lions, skins, arms—stay, the back of the fireplace opens."

" Pass through. Where are you ? "

" In a strange sort of room, without any outlet, and

the windows of which are barred. Oh! how disordered everything in the room appears!"

"But empty—it is empty, is it not?"

"Yes, empty."

"Can you see the person who inhabited it?"

"Yes, if you give me something which has touched her, which comes from her, or which belongs to her."

"Hold! there is some hair."

Andrée took the hair, and placed it on her heart.

"Oh! I recognize her!" said she. "I have already seen this woman. She was flying toward Paris."

"Yes, yes; you can tell me what she has been doing during the last two hours, and how she escaped?"

"Wait a moment; yes; she is reclining upon a sofa; her breast is half bared, and she has a wound on one side."

"Look, Andrée, look! do not lose sight of her."

"She was asleep—she awakes—she looks around—she takes a handkerchief and climbs upon a chair. She ties the handkerchief to the bars of the window—oh, God!"

"Is she really determined to die?"

"Oh, yes! she is resolute. But this sort of death terrifies her. She leaves the handkerchief tied to the bars— she descends—ah! poor woman."

"What?"

"Oh! how she weeps, how she suffers, and wrings her hands! She searches for a corner of the wall against which to dash her head!"

"Oh, my God! my God!" murmured Balsamo.

"She rushes toward the chimney-piece. It represents two marble lions; she will dash out her brains against the lions."

"What, then? Look, Andrée, look—it is my will!"

"She stops."

Balsamo breathed again.

"She looks——"

"What does she look at?" asked Balsamo.

"She has perceived some blood upon the lion's eye."

"Oh, heavens!"

"Yes, blood ; and yet she did not strike herself against it. Oh ! strange, the blood is not hers, it is yours."

"Mine ? " asked Balsamo, frantic with excitement.

"Yes, yours. You had cut your finger with a knife, with a poniard—and had touched the lion's eye with your bleeding hand. I see you."

"True, true. But how does she escape ? "

"Stay ; I see her examining the blood ; she reflects; then she places her finger where you had placed yours. Ah ! the lion's eye gives way—a spring acts—the chimney-board flies open."

"Oh, imprudent, wretched fool that I am ! I have betrayed myself ! "

Andrée was silent.

"And she leaves the room ? " asked Balsamo, "she escapes ? "

"Oh, you must forgive the poor woman—she was very miserable."

"Where is she ? whither does she fly ? Follow her, Andrée—it is my will."

"She stops for a moment in the chamber of furs and armor ; a cupboard is open, a casket, usually locked in this cupboard, is upon the table ; she recognizes the box ; she takes it."

"What does the box contain ? "

"Your papers, I think."

"Describe it."

"It is covered with blue velvet, and studded with brass nails, has clasps of silver, and a golden lock."

"Oh," exclaimed Balsamo, stamping with anger ; "it is she, then, who has taken the casket ? "

"Yes. She descends the stairs leading into the ante-room, opens the door, draws back the chain of the street door, and goes out."

"Is it late ? "

"It must be late, for it is dark."

"So much the better. She must have fled shortly be-fore my return, and I shall perhaps have time to overtake her. Follow her, Andrée, follow her ! "

" Once outside the house, she runs as if she were mad ;
she reaches the boulevard ; she hastens on without pausing."

" In which direction ? "

" Toward the Bastile."

" You see her yet ? "

" Yes ; she looks like a madwoman ; she jostles against
the passers-by ; she stops , she endeavors to discover where
she is : she inquires."

" What does she say ?   Listen, Andrée, listen ; in
Heaven's name, do not lose a syllable ! You said she inquired ? "

" Yes, from a man dressed in black. "

" What does she ask ? "

" She wishes to know the address of the lieutenant of
police."

" Oh ! then it was not a vain threat.   Does the person
give it her ? "

" Yes."

" What does she do ? "

" She retraces her steps, and turns down a winding
street.   She crosses a large square."

" The Place Royale ; it is the direct way.   Can you
read her intention ? "

" Follow her quickly ! Hasten ; she goes to betray
you ! If she arrives before you, and sees Monsieur de
Sartines, you are lost ! "

Balsamo uttered a terrible cry, plunged into the thicket,
rushed through a little door, which a shadowy apparition
opened and closed after him, and leaped with one bound
on his faithful Djerid who was pawing the ground at the
little gate.   Urged on at once by voice and spur, he darted
like an arrow toward Paris, and soon nothing was heard
but the clattering of his hoofs on the paved causeway.

As for Andrée, she remained standing there, cold, mute
and pale.   Then, as if Balsamo had borne away with him
life and strength, she tottered, drooped and fell.   Balsamo,
in his eagerness to follow Lorenza, had forgotten to
awaken her.

Andrée did not sink, as we have said, all at once, but gradually, in the manner we will attempt to describe.

Alone, abandoned, overpowered with that death-like coldness which succeeds any violent nervous shock, Andrée began to tremble and totter like one suffering from the commencement of an epileptic fit.

Gilbert had never moved—rigid, immovable, leaning forward, and devouring her with his gaze. But, as it may readily be imagined, Gilbert, entirely ignorant of magnetic phenomena, dreamed neither of sleep nor of suffered violence. He had heard nothing, or almost nothing, of her dialogue with Balsamo. But for the second time, at Trianon as at Taverney, Andrée had appeared to obey the summons of this man, who had acquired such a strange and terrible power over her. To Gilbert, therefore, everything resolved itself in this : Mlle. Andrée has, if not a lover, at least a man whom she loves, and to whom she grants a rendezvous at night.

The dialogue which had taken place between Andrée and Balsamo, although sustained in a low voice, had all the appearance of a quarrel. Balsamo, excited, flying, frantic, seemed like a lover in despair ; Andrée, left alone, mute and motionless, like the fair one he had abandoned.

It was at this moment that he saw the young girl totter, wring her hands, and sink slowly to the ground. Then she uttered twice or thrice a groan so deep that her oppressed heart seemed torn by the effort. She endeavored, or, rather, nature endeavored, to throw back the overpowering mass of fluid which, during the magnetic sleep, had endowed her with that double sight which we have seen, in the preceding chapter, produce such strange phenomena.

But nature was overpowered ; Andrée could not succeed in throwing off the remains of that mysterious will which Balsamo had forgotten to withdraw. She could not loose the marvelous, inexplicable ties which had bound her hand and foot ; and by dint of struggling, she fell into those convulsions which in the olden time the Pythoness suffered upon her tripod before the crowd of religious questioners who swarmed around the peristyle of the temple. Andrée lost her equilibrium, and uttering a heart-rending groan, fell to the ground as if she had been struck by the flash which at that moment furrowed the vault of heaven.

But she had not yet touched the earth when Gilbert, strong and agile as a panther, darted toward her, seized her in his arms, and, without being conscious that he carried a burden, bore her back into the chamber which she had left to obey Balsamo's summons, and in which the candle was yet burning beside the disarranged couch.

Gilbert found all the doors open as Andrée had left them. As he entered he stumbled against the sofa, and placed on it the cold and inanimate form of the young girl. The most pressing matter was to recall this beautiful statue to life. He looked round for the carafe, in order to sprinkle some drops of water in Andrée's face.

But just as his trembling hand was stretched forth to grasp the thin neck of the crystal ewer, it seemed to him that a firm but light step sounded on the stairs leading to Andrée's chamber.

It could not be Nicole, for Nicole had fled with M. de Beausire ; it could not be Balsamo, for Balsamo was spurring with lightning haste to Paris. It could, therefore, only be a stranger.

Gilbert, if discovered, was lost ; Andrée was to him like one of those princesses of Spain, whom a subject may not touch, even to save their life.

All these ideas rushed like a whirlwind through Gilbert's mind in less time than we can relate them. He could not calculate the exact distance of the footstep, which every moment approached still nearer, for the storm which raged without dulled every other sound ; but, gifted with extraordinary coolness and foresight, the young man felt that that was no place for him, and that the most important matter was to conceal himself from sight.

He hastily blew out the candle which illumined the apartment, and entered the closet which served as Nicole's sleeping-chamber. From this hiding-place he could see through the glass door into Andrée's apartment, and also into the antechamber.

In this antechamber a night-lamp was burning upon a little console-table. Gilbert had at first thought of extinguishing it as he had done the candle, but he had not time ; the step echoed upon the corridor, a repressed breathing was heard, the figure of a man appeared upon the threshold, glided timidly into the antechamber, and closed the door.

Gilbert had only time to hasten into Nicole's closet, and to draw the glass door after him.

He held his breath, pressed his face against the stained-glass panes, and listened eagerly.

The storm still howled wildly outside, large raindrops beat against the windows of Andrée's apartment and those of the corridor, where a casement, accidentally left open, creaked upon its hinges, and every now and then, dashed back by the wind which rushed into the corridor, struck noisily against its frame.

But the war of the elements, terrible as it was, produced no effect on Gilbert. His whole soul was concentrated in his gaze, which was riveted upon this man. He crossed the antechamber, passed not two paces distant from Gilbert, and unhesitatingly entered the principal apartment.

As he advanced, he jostled with his arm against the candle upon the table. The candle fell, and Gilbert heard the crystal socket break in falling on the marble table. Then the man called twice in a subdued voice :

" Nicole ! Nicole ! "

" What, Nicole ! " thought Gilbert, in his hiding-place. " Why does this man call Nicole instead of Andrée ? "

But as no voice replied to his, the man lifted the candle from the floor, and proceeded on tiptoe to light it at the night-lamp in the antechamber. It was then that Gilbert riveted his whole attention upon this strange nocturnal visitor ; he gazed as if his vision could have pierced the wall. All at once he trembled, and, even in his hiding-place, recoiled a step backward.

By the light of these two flames combined, Gilbert,

trembling and half dead with affright, recognized in this man who held the candle in his hands—the king !

Then all was explained—Nicole's flight, the money she had given Beausire, the door left open, the interviews between Richelieu and Taverney, and the whole of that dark and mysterious intrigue of which the young girl was the center.

He would have cried out, but fear—that unreflecting, capricious, irresistible feeling—the fear he felt for this man, whose name had still a charm—the King of France— tied Gilbert's tongue. He slipped stealthily from the closet, gained the antechamber, and fled as if the Avenger were behind him.

In the meantime, Louis entered the room, candle in hand, and perceived Andrée reclining on the couch, wrapped in a long muslin dressing-gown, her head drooping on her shoulder.

He murmured some words in a caressing voice, and putting his light upon the table, he knelt beside the young girl, and kissed her hand. It was icy cold. Alarmed, he started up, hastily put aside her dressing-gown, and placed his trembling hand upon her heart. Her heart was cold and motionless.

Just then a fearful peal of thunder made every article of furniture in the room shake, even to the couch before which Louis was standing. A livid and sulphurous flash of lightning threw so dazzling a light over Andrée's countenance, that Louis, alarmed at her paleness, her motionless, attitude, and her silence, started back, murmuring :

" This girl is surely dead ! "

At the came instant, the idea of having a corpse before him sent an icy chill through the king's veins. He seized the candle, held it close to Andrée's face, and hastily examined her features by the light of the trembling flame. Beholding her livid lips, her swollen and discolored eyes, her disheveled hair, her chest, which no breath stirred, he uttered a cry, let the light fall, staggered back, and reeled like a drunken man into the anteroom, against the walls of which he stumbled in his alarm.

Then his hasty step sounded upon the stairs, then on the gravel walks of the garden, and was soon lost in the howling storm which raged through the long alleys and shady groves of Trianon.

CHAPTER LIV.

THE WILL.

WE have seen Balsamo depart. Djerid bore him on with the speed of lightning, while the rider, pale with terror and impatience, bent forward over the flowing mane, breathing with half-opened lips the air which the crest of the noble steed cleft, as the rapid prow of the vessel cuts the waves.

Behind him, houses and trees disappeared like fantastic visions. He scarcely perceived, as he passed, the clumsy wagon groaning on its axle-tree, while its five huge horses started with affright at the approach of this living meteor which they could not imagine to belong to the same race as themselves.

Balsamo proceeded at this rate for a league, with whirling brain, sparkling eyes, and panting breath. Horse and rider had traversed Versailles in a few seconds. The startled inhabitants who happened to be in the streets had seen a long train of sparkles flash past them—nothing more. A second league was passed in like manner. Djerid had accomplished the distance in little more than a quarter of an hour, and yet this quarter of an hour had seemed to his rider a century. All at once a thought darted through his brain. He pulled up suddenly, throwing the noble courser back upon his haunches, while his fore feet plowed the ground.

Horse and rider breathed for a moment. Drawing a long breath, Balsamo raised his head. Then, wiping the perspiration from his forehead, while his nostrils dilated in the breeze of night, he murmured :

"Oh ! madman that you are, neither the rapidity of

your steed nor the ardor of your desire will ever equal the instantaneous effect of thunder or the rapidity of the electric flash, and yet it is that which you require to avert the danger impending over you. You require the rapid effect, the instantaneous, the all-powerful shock, which will paralyze the feet whose activity you fear, the tongue whose speech destroys you. You require, at this distance, the victorious sleep which restores to you the possession of the slave who has broken her chain. Oh! if she should ever again be in my power!"

And Balsamo ground his teeth, with a despairing gesture.

"Oh! you do well to wish, Balsamo, you do well to fly!" exclaimed he. "Lorenza has already arrived; she is about to speak—she has, perhaps, already spoken. Oh, wretched woman! no punishment can be terrible enough for you."

"Let me try," continued Balsamo, frowning, his eyes fixed, and his chin resting on his hand, "let me try. Either science is a dream or a fact—it is either impotent or powerful; let me try. 'Lorenza, Lorenza! it is my will that you sleep, wheresoever you may be. Lorenza, sleep—sleep; it is my will. I reckon upon your obedience.'

"Oh, no, no!" murmured he, despairingly; "no, I utter a falsehood; I do not believe—I dare not reckon upon it—and yet the will is all. Oh! I will it with my whole soul, with all the strength of my being! Cleave the air, my potent will; traverse all the current of opposing or indifferent wills; pass through walls in thy course like a bullet from a gun; follow her wherever she is. Go—strike—destroy! Lorenza! Lorenza! it is my will that you sleep. Be dumb at my command."

And for some moments he concentrated his thoughts upon this aim, imprinting it on his brain as if to lend it more speed in its flight toward Paris. Then, after this mysterious operation—to which, doubtless, all the divine atoms animated by God, the Master and Lord of all things, assisted—Balsamo, once more setting his teeth hard and clinching his hands, gave the reins to Djerid, but this

time without using either the knee or the spurs. It seemed
as if Balsamo wished to convince himself.

The noble steed paced gently onward in obedience to
the tacit permission of his master, placing his hoof gently
upon the pavement with that light and noiseless step peculiar to his race. During this brief interval, which, to
a superficial observer, would have seemed entirely lost,
Balsamo was arranging a complete plan of defense. He
concluded it just as Djerid entered the streets of Sèvres.
Arrived opposite the park-gates, he stopped and looked
round as if expecting some one. Almost immediately a
man emerged from beneath a carriage entrance and
advanced toward him.

"Is that you, Fritz?" asked Balsamo.

"Yes, master."

"Have you made inquiries?"

"Yes."

"Is Madame Dubarry in Paris or at Luciennes?"

"She is in Paris."

Balsamo raised his eyes to heaven with a triumphant
look.

"How did you come?"

"On Sultan."

"Where is he?"

"In the courtyard of this inn."

"Ready saddled?"

"Quite ready."

"Very well, be prepared to follow me."

Fritz hastened to bring out Sultan. He was a horse of
that strong, willing German race, who grumble a little at
forced marches, but who, nevertheless, go as long they have
breath in their lungs, on while there is a spur at their master's heel. Fritz returned to Balsamo, who was writing by
the light of a street lantern.

"Return to Paris," said he, "and manage by some
means to give this note to Madame Dubarry in person.
You have half an hour for this purpose. After which you
will return to the Rue St. Claude, where you will wait for
Madame Lorenza, who cannot fail to return soon. You

will let her pass without any observation and without
offering any opposition. Go, and remember, above all,
that in half an hour your commission must be executed."

"It is well," said Fritz, "it shall be done."

As he gave this confident reply to Balsamo, he attacked
Sultan with a whip and spur, and the good steed started
off, astonished at this unusual aggression, and neighing
piteously.

Balsamo, by degrees, resumed his composure, and took
the road to Paris, which he entered three-quarters of an
hour afterward, his features almost unruffled and his look
calm but pensive.

Balsamo was right.   However swift Djerid, the neighing
son of the desert, might be, his speed was powerless, and
thought alone could hope to overtake Lorenza in her
flight from prison.

From the Rue St. Claude she had gained the boulevard,
and, turning to the right, she soon saw the walls of the
Bastile rise before her.   But Lorenza, constantly a prisoner, was entirely ignorant of Paris.   Moreover, her first
aim was to escape from that accursed house in which she
saw only a dungeon ; vengeance was a secondary consideration.

She had just entered the Faubourg St. Antoine, hastening onward with bewildered steps, when she was accosted
by a young man who had been following her for some
moments with astonishment.

In fact, Lorenza, an Italian girl from the neighborhood
of Rome, having almost always lived a secluded life,
far from all knowledge of the fashions and customs
of the age, was dressed more like an Oriental than a Eu-
ropean lady ; that is, in flowing and sumptuous robes, very
unlike the charming dolls of that time, confined, like
wasps, in long tight waists, rustling with silk and muslin,
under which it was almost useless to seek a body, their
utmost ambition being to appear immaterial.

Lorenza had only adopted, from the French costume of
that period, the shoes with their two inch-high heels—
that strange-looking invention which stiffened the foot,

displayed the beauty of the ankle, and which rendered it impossible for the Arethusas of that rather mythological age to fly from the pursuit of their Alpheuses.

The Alpheus who pursued our Arethusa easily overtook her, therefore. He had seen her lovely ankles peeping from beneath her petticoats of satin and lace, her unpowdered hair, and her dark eyes sparkling with a strange fire from under a mantilla thrown over her head and neck, and he imagined he saw in Lorenza a lady disguised for a masquerade, or for a rendezvous, and proceeding on foot, for want of a coach, to some little house of the faubourg.

He approached her, therefore, and walking beside her hat in hand :

" Good heavens ! madame," said he, " you cannot go far in that costume, and with these shoes, which retard your progress. Will you accept my arm until we find a coach, and allow me the honor of accompanying you to your destination ? "

Lorenza turned her head abruptly, gazed with her dark, expressive eyes at the man who had thus made her an offer which to many ladies would have appeared an impertinent one, and stopping :

" Yes," said she, " most willingly."

The young man gallantly offered his arm.

" Whither are we going, madame ? " he asked.

" To the hotel of the lieutenant of police."

The young man started.

" To Monsieur de Sartines ? " he inquired.

" I do not know if his name be Monsieur de Sartines or not ; I wish to speak to whoever is lieutenant of police."

The young man began to reflect. A young and handsome woman, wandering alone in the streets of Paris, at eight o'clock in the evening, in a strange costume, holding a box under her arm, and inquiring for the hotel of the lieutenant of police, while she was going in the contrary direction, seemed suspicious.

" Ah, diable ! " said he, " the hotel of the lieutenant of police is not in this direction at all."

" Where is it, then ? "

" In the Faubourg St. Germain."

" And how must I go to the Faubourg St. Germain ? "

" This way, madame," replied the young man, calm, but always polite ; " and if you wish, we can take the first coach we meet——"

" Oh, yes, a coach ; you are right."

The young man conducted Lorenza back to the boulevard, and, having met a hackney-coach, he hailed it. The coachman answered his summons.

" Where to, madame ? " asked he.

" To the hotel of Monsieur de Sartines," said the young man.

And, with a last effort of politeness, or, rather, of astonishment, having opened the coach-door, he bowed to Lorenza, and, after assisting her to get in, he gazed after her departing form as we do in a dream or vision.

The coachman, full of respect for the dreadful name, gave his horses the whip, and drove rapidly in the direction indicated.

It was while Lorenza was thus crossing the Place Royale that Andrée, in her magnetic sleep, had seen and heard her, and denounced her to Balsamo. In twenty minutes Lorenza was at the door of the hotel.

" Must I wait for you, my fair lady ? " asked the coachman.

" Yes," replied Lorenza, mechanically.

And, stepping lightly from the coach, she disappeared beneath the portal of the splendid hotel.

CHAPTER LV.

THE HOTEL OF M. DE SARTINES.

THE moment Lorenza entered the courtyard she found herself surrounded by a crowd of soldiers and officers. She addressed the garde-française who stood nearest her, and begged him to conduct her to the lieutenant of police. The guardsman handed her over to the porter, who, seeing a beautiful stranger, richly dressed, and holding a magnificent coffer under her arm, thought that the visit might prove not to be an unimportant one, and preceded her up the grand staircase to an antechamber, where every comer could, after the sagacious scrutiny of the porter, be admitted to present an explanation, an accusation, or a request to M. de Sartines, at any hour of the day or night.

It is needless to say that the two first classes of visitors were more favorably received than the latter.

Lorenza, when questioned by the usher, only replied :

" Are you Monsieur de Sartines ? "

The usher was profoundly astonished that any one could mistake his black dress and steel chain for the embroidered coat and flowing wig of the lieutenant of police ; but as no lieutenant is ever angry at being called captain, as he marked the foreign accent of the lady, and as her firm and steady gaze was not that of a lunatic, he felt convinced that the fair visitor had something important in the coffer which she held so carefully and so securely under her arm.

But as M. de Sartines was a prudent and suspicious man, as traps had been laid for him with baits not less enticing than that of the beautiful Italian, there was good watch kept around him, and Lorenza had to undergo the investigation, the questioning, and the suspicions of half a dozen secretaries and valets. The result of all these questions and replies was, that M. de Sartines had not yet returned, and that Lorenza must wait.

Then the young woman sunk into a moody silence, and her eyes wandered over the bare walls of the vast antechamber.

At last the ringing of a bell was heard, a carriage rolled into the courtyard, and a second usher entered and announced to Lorenza that M. de Sartines was waiting for her.

Lorenza rose, and crossed two halls full of people with suspicious-looking faces, and dresses still more strange than her own. At last, she was introduced into a large cabinet of an octagon form, lighted by a number of wax-candles.

A man of from fifty to fifty-five years of age, enveloped in a dressing-gown, his head surmounted by a wig profusely powdered and curled, was seated at work before a lofty piece of furniture, the upper part of which, somewhat resembling in form a cupboard, was closed with two doors of looking-glass, in which the person seated could, without moving, see any one who entered the room, and could examine their features before they had time to compose them in harmony with his own.

The lower part of this article of furniture formed a secretaire. A number of rosewood drawers composed the front, each of which closed by the combination of some letter of the alphabet. M. de Sartines kept in them his papers, and the ciphers which no one in his lifetime could read, since the drawers opened for him alone, and which none could have deciphered after his death, unless in some drawer, still more secret than the others, he had found the key to the cipher.

This secretaire, or, rather, this cupboard, contained behind the glasses of the upper part twelve drawers also closed by an invisible mechanism. This piece of furniture, constructed expressly by the regent to contain his chemical or political secrets, had been given by that prince to Dubois, and left by Dubois to M. Dombreval, lieutenant of police. It was from this latter that M. de Sartines had inherited the press and the secret. However, M. de Sartines had not consented to use it until after the death of the donor, and even then he had had all the arrangements of the locks altered.

This piece of furniture had some reputation in the world, and shut too closely, people said, for M. de Sartines only to keep his wigs in it.

The grumblers, and their name was legion at this period, said that if it were possible to read through the panels of this secretaire, there would most certainly have been discovered, in one of its drawers, the famous treaty by virtue of which Louis XV. speculated in grain, through the intervention of his devoted agent, M. de Sartines.

The lieutenant of police, therefore, saw reflected in the

glass the pale, serious face of Lorenza, as she advanced toward him with the coffer still beneath her arm. In the center of the apartment the young girl stopped. Her costume, her figure, and the strangeness of her proceedings struck the lieutenant.

"Who are you?" asked he, without turning round, but looking at her in the glass. "What do you want with me?"

"Am I in the presence of Monsieur de Sartines, lieutenant of police?" replied Lorenza.

"Yes," replied he, abruptly.

"Who will assure me of that?"

M. de Sartines turned round.

"Will it be a proof that I am the man you seek," said he, "if I send you to prison?"

Lorenza made no reply. She merely looked around the room with that indescribable dignity peculiar to the women of Italy, and seemed to seek the chair which M. de Sartines did not offer her.

He was vanquished by this look, for M. the Count d' Alby de Sartines was a remarkably well-bred man.

"Be seated," said he, sharply.

Lorenza drew a chair forward and sat down.

"Speak quickly," said the magistrate. "Come, let me know what you want."

"Sir," said Lorenza, "I come to place myself under your protection."

M. de Sartines looked at her with the sarcastic look peculiar to him.

"Ah, ah!" said he.

"Sir," continued Lorenza, "I have been carried off from my family, and have, by a false marriage, fallen into the power of a man who for the last three years has oppressed me and made my life miserable."

M. de Sartines looked with admiration upon this noble countenance, and felt touched and charmed by this voice, so soft that it seemed like a strain of music.

"From what country do you come?" he asked.

"I am a Roman."

"What is your name ?"

"Lorenza."

"Lorenza what ?"

"Lorenza Feliciani."

"I do not know that family.   Are you a demoiselle ?"

Demoiselle at this period meant a lady of quality. In our days a lady thinks herself noble enough when she is married, and only wishes thenceforth to be called madame.

"I am a demoiselle," replied Lorenza.

"Well, what do you demand ?"

"I demand justice against this man who has stolen and incarcerated me."

"This is no affair of mine," said the lieutenant of police.   "Are you his wife ?"

"He says so, at least."

"How—says ?"

"Yes ; but I do not know anything of it, as the marriage was contracted while I slept.

"Peste ! you sleep soundly."

"What do you say ?"

"I say that it is not in my province.   Apply to a procureur and commence an action ; I do not like to meddle in family matters."

Upon which M. de Sartines waved his hand with a gesture which meant "Be gone !"   Lorenza did not move.

"Well ?" asked M. de Sartines, astonished.

"I have not done yet," said she ; and if I come to you, you must understand that it is not to complain of a trifling matter, but to revenge myself.   I have told you that the women of my country revenge themselves, but never complain."

"That is another affair," said M. de Sartines ; "but speak quickly, fair lady, for my time is precious."

"I told you that I came to you to ask for your protection ; shall I have it ?"

"Protection against whom ?"

"Against the man upon whom I wish to revenge myself."

"Is he powerful ?"

"More powerful than a king."

"Come, explain, my dear madame. Why should I protect you against a man who is, in your opinion, more powerful than a king, an act which is perhaps a crime? If you wish to be revenged on this man, revenge yourself. That is nothing to me; only if you commit a crime, I shall have to arrest you, after which we shall see—that is the routine."

"No, sir," said Lorenza; "no, you will not have me arrested, for my vengeance is of the greatest utility to you, to the king, to France. I shall revenge myself by revealing this man's secrets."

"Oh, ho! he has secrets?" said M. de Sartines, beginning to feel interested in spite of himself.

"Mighty secrets, sir."

"Of what kind?"

"Political ones."

"Mention them."

"But in that case, will you protect me?"

"What sort of protection do you require?" said the magistrate with a cold smile, "gold or affection?"

"I only ask permission, sir, to retire to a convent and to live there concealed and unknown. I ask that this convent may become my tomb, but that this tomb may never be violated by any one in the world."

"Ah!" said the magistrate, "that is not a very exacting demand. You shall have the convent. Speak."

"Then I have your word, sir?"

"I think I said so."

"Then," said Lorenza, "take this coffer; it contains mysteries which will make you tremble for the safety of the king and his dominions."

"Then, you know these mysteries?"

"Only partially; but I know they exist."

"And that they are important?"

"That they are terrible."

"Political secrets, you say?"

"Have you never heard that there existed a secret society?"

" Ah ! the freemasons ? "

" The invisibles."

" Yes, but I do not believe it."

" When you have opened this coffer you will believe."

" Ah !" said M. de Sartines, eagerly, " let me see."

And he took the coffer from Lorenza's hands. But suddenly, after a moment's reflection, he placed it upon the desk.

" No," said he, with an air of suspicion ; " open the coffer yourself."

" But I have not the key."

" How ! you have not the key ? You bring me a coffer which contains the safety of a kingdom, and you forget the key ? "

" Is it so very difficult, then, to open a lock ? "

" No, not when one knows it." Then, after a moment's pause, he added : " We have in this place keys for all kinds of locks ; you shall have a bunch (and he looked fixedly at Lorenza), and you shall open it yourself."

" Give it me," said Lorenza, without the slightest hesitation.

M. de Sartines held out a bunch of little keys of all kinds to the young girl. She took them. M. de Sartines touched her hand—it was cold as marble.

" But why," said he, " did you not bring the key of the coffer ? "

" Because the master of the coffer never lets it out of his possession ? "

" And who is the master of the coffer—this man who is more powerful than a king ? "

" What he is, no one can say. The Almighty alone knows how long he has lived ; the deeds he accomplishes none see but God."

" But his name—his name ? "

" I have known him change it ten times."

" Well, that by which you generally address him ? "

" Acharat."

" And he lives——"

" Rue St ——"

Suddenly Lorenza started, shuddered, and let the coffer. which she held in one hand, and the keys which she held in the other, fall to the ground. She made an effort to reply, her lips were distorted convulsively ; she raised her hands to her throat, as if the words she was about to utter had suffocated her ; then, tossing her trembling arms aloft, she fell her whole length upon the carpet of the study, unable to utter a single word.

" Poor girl ! " murmured M. de Sartines, " what the deuce is the matter with her ? She is really very pretty. Ah ! there is some jealousy at work in this project of revenge.

He rang the bell hastily, and in the meantime raised the young girl in his arms, who, with staring eyes and motionless lips, seemed already dead, and disconnected with this lower world. Two valets entered.

" Carry this young lady carefully into the adjoining apartment," said he ; " endeavor to revive her, but above all, use no violence. Go ! "

The valets obeyed and carried Lorenza out.

CHAPTER LVI.

THE COFFER.

WHEN he was alone, M. de Sartines turned the coffer round and round, with the air of a man who can appreciate the value of a discovery. Then he stretched out his hands and picked up the bundle of keys which had fallen from Lorenza's hands.

He tried them all ; none would fit.

He took several similar bunches from his drawer.

These bunches contained keys of all dimensions ; keys of all sorts of articles, coffers included ; common keys and microscopic keys, M. de Sartines might be said to possess a pattern of every key known.

He tried twenty, fifty, a hundred ; not one would even turn round The magistrate concluded, therefore, that the lock was only a feigned one, and that, consequently, his keys were only counterfeit keys.

He then took a small chisel and a little hammer from the same drawer, and with his white hand, buried in an ample frill of Mechlin lace, he burst open the lock, the faithful guardian of the coffer.

A bundle of papers appeared, instead of the destructive machine he had feared to find there, or instead of poisons which should diffuse a fatal odor around, and deprive France of its most useful magistrate.

The first words which met the magistrate's eye were the following, written in a handwriting which was evidently feigned :

"Master, it is time to abandon the name of Balsamo."

There was no signature, but merely the three letters, L. P. D.

"Ha !" said he, twitching the curls of his wig, "if I do not know the writing, I think I know the name. Balsamo—let me see—I must search the B's."

He opened one of his twenty-four drawers, and took from it a list, arranged in alphabetical order, written in a fine handwriting full of abbreviations, and containing three or four hundred names, preceded, followed, and accompanied by flaming notes.

"Oh, ho !" said he, "there is a long article on this Balsamo."

And he read the whole page with unequivocal signs of dissatisfaction. Then he replaced the list in the drawer, and continued the examination of the coffer.

He had not proceeded far till his brow assumed a darker hue, and soon he came to a note full of names and ciphers.

This paper seemed important ; it was much worn at the edges, and filled with pencil-marks. M. de Sartines rang the bell ; a servant appeared.

"The assistance of the chancery clerk," said he, "immediately. Let him come through the reception-rooms from the office to save time."

The valet retired. Two minutes afterward, a clerk with a pen in his hand, his hat under one arm, a large register under the other, and wearing sleeves of black serge over his coat-sleeves, appeared on the threshold of the study. M. de Sartines perceived his entrance in the mirror before him, and handed him the paper over his shoulder.

" Decipher this," said he.

" Yes, my lord," replied the clerk.

This decipherer of riddles was a little thin man, with pinched lips, eyebrows contracted by study, pale features, and head pointed both at top and bottom, a narrow chin, a receding forehead, projecting cheek bones, hollow and dull eyes, which often sparkled with intelligence.

M. de Sartines called him La Fouine.

" Sit down," said the magistrate to him, on seeing him rather embarrassed by his note-book, his code of ciphers, his paper and his pen.

La Fouine modestly took his seat upon the corner of a stool, approached his knees together, and began to write upon them, turning over his dictionary and searching his memory with an impassible countenance. In five minutes he had written :

§

" An order to assemble three thousand brothers in Paris.

§

" An order to form three circles and six lodges.

§

" An order to form a guard for the grand Copht, and, to contrive four dwellings for him, one in a royal household.

§

" An order to place five hundred thousand francs at his disposal for a police.

§

" An order to enroll the flower of literature and philosophy moving in the first Parisian circles.

§

" An order to hire or to gain over the magistracy, and particularly to make sure of the lieutenant of police, by corruption, violence, or cunning."

Here La Fouine stopped for a moment ; not that the poor man was reflecting, he took care not to do that, it would have been a crime, but because his page was filled, and the ink yet wet, so he was obliged to wait for its drying before he could proceed.

M. de Sartines, becoming impatient, snatched the paper from his hands and read it.

At the last paragraph, such an expression of fear was painted on his face that he turned a deeper pale at seeing himself change color in the mirror of his cupboard.

He did not return the paper to his clerk, but handed him a fresh sheet. The clerk once more commenced to write in proportion as he deciphered, which he did with a facility terrifying for all writers in cipher.

This time M. de Sartines read over his shoulder :

§

" To drop the name of Balsamo, which is already too well known in Paris, and to take that of the Count de Fe——"

A large blot of ink concealed the rest of the word.

While M. de Sartines was endeavoring to make out the last syllable, which would complete the name, a bell was rung outside, and a valet entering, announced :

" The Count de Fenix."

M. de Sartines uttered a cry, and at the risk of demolishing the harmonious edifice of his wig, he clasped his hands above his head, and hastened to dismiss his clerk by a secret door.

Then resuming his place before the desk, he said to the valet :

" Introduce him."

A few seconds afterward, M. de Sartines perceived in his glass the marked profile of the count, which he had already seen at court, on the day of Mme. Dubarry's presentation.

Balsamo entered without any hesitation whatever.

M. de Sartines rose, bowed coldly to the count, and, crossing one leg over the other, he seated himself ceremoniously in his armchair.

At the first glance the magistrate had divined the cause and the aim of this visit.

At the first glance also Balsamo had perceived the opened box, half emptied upon M. de Sartines' desk. His look, however hasty, at the coffer, did not escape the lieutenant of the police.

" To what chance do I owe the honor of your presence, my lord count ? " asked M. de Sartines.

" Sir," replied Balsamo, with a most affable smile, " I have had the honor of being presented to all the sovereigns, ministers, and ambassadors of Europe, but I have not found any one to present me to you ; I have, therefore, come to introduce myself."

" In truth, sir," replied the lieutenant of police, " you arrive most opportunely, for I feel convinced that had you not come of yourself, I should have had the honor of sending for you."

" Ah, indeed ! " said Balsamo. " What a coincidence ! "

M. de Sartines inclined his head with a sarcastic smile.

" Shall I be so fortunate as to be of any use to you ? " asked Balsamo.

And these words were uttered without a shadow of emotion or of uneasiness clouding his smiling features.

" You have traveled much, my lord count ? " asked th lieutenant of the police.

" A great deal, sir."

" Ah ! "

" You wish for some geographical information, perhaps ? A man of your capacity does not confine his observations to France alone, he surveys Europe—the world."

" Geographical is not exactly the word, count. Moral would be more correct."

"Have no scruples, I beg ; one is as welcome as the other. I am wholly at your service."

"Well, count, picture to yourself that I am in search of a most dangerous man—a man who, on my word, is a complete atheist."

"Oh !"

"A conspirator."

"Oh !"

"A forger."

"Oh !"

"A debauchee, a false coiner, a quack, a charlatan, the chief of a society—a man whose history I have in my books, in this box that you see here—everywhere, indeed."

"Ah ! yes, I comprehend," said Balsamo ; "you have the history, but not the man."

"No."

"Diable ! The latter seems to me the most important point."

"Of course ; but you shall see we are not far from having him. Certainly Proteus had not more forms, nor Jupiter more names, than this mysterious traveler. Acharat in Egypt—Balsamo in Italy—Somini in Sardinia —the Marquis Danna in Malta—the Marquis Bellegrini in Corsica—and lastly, the Count de —— ? "

"Count de —— ? " added Balsamo.

"The last name I could not decipher perfectly, sir. But I am sure you will be able to assist me, will you not ? For there is no doubt you must have met this man during your travels in each of the countries I have just now named."

"Enlighten me a little, I entreat," said Balsamo, quietly.

"Ah ! I understand ; you wish for a description of his person, do you not, count ? "

"Yes, sir, if you please."

"Well," said M. de Sartines, fixing a glance which he intended to be inquisitorial upon Balsamo, "he is a man of your age, of your size, of your figure. He is sometimes a great lord, scattering money on all sides—sometimes a charlatan, searching into the secrets of nature—sometimes a gloomy member of some mysterious brotherhood which meets by night, and swears ' Death to kings and the overthrow of all thrones. ' "

" Oh ! " said Balsamo, " that is very vague."

" How vague ? "

" If you knew how many men I have seen who resemble this description."

" Indeed ! "

" Of course ; and you must be a little more precise if you wish me to assist you. In the first place, do you know in which country he prefers to live ? "

" He dwells in all."

" But at present, for instance ? "

" At present he is in France."

" And what is his errand in France ? "

" He directs an immense conspiracy."

" Ah ! that is, indeed, some clue ; and if you know what conspiracy he directs you probably hold the thread by which to catch your man."

" I am just of your opinion."

" Well, if you think so, why, in that case, do you ask my advice ? It is useless."

" Ah ! but I am not yet decided."

" On what point ? "

" Whether I shall arrest him or not."

" I do not understand the *not*, Monsieur Lieutenant of Police, for if he conspires——"

" Yes ; but if he is partially defended by some name or some title."

" Ah, I understand. But what name, what title ? You must tell me that before I can assist you in your search, sir."

" Why, sir, I have told you that I know the name under which he conceals himself, but——"

" But you do not know the one which he openly uses—is that it ? "

" Yes, otherwise——"

" Otherwise you would arrest him ¿

" Instantly."

" Well, my dear Monsieur de Sartines, it is very fortunate, as you said just now, that I arrived at this moment,
for I will do you the service you require."

" You ? "

" Yes."

" You will tell me his name ? "

" Yes."

" His public name ? "

" Yes."

" Then you know him ? "

" Perfectly well."

" And what is his name ? " asked M. de Sartines, expecting some falsehood.

" The Count de Fenix."

" What, the name by which you were announced ? "

" The same."

" Your name ? "

" My name."

" Then, this Acharat, this Somini, this Marquis Danna,
this Marquis Pellegrini, this Joseph Balsamo, is you ? "

" Yes," said Balsamo, quietly—" is myself."

It was a minute before M. de Sartines could recover
from the vertigo which this frank avowal caused him.

" You see, I had guessed as much," said he.   " I knew
you.   I knew that Joseph Balsamo and the Count de
Fenix were the same."

" Ah ! " said Balsamo, " you are a great minister—I
confess it."

" And you most imprudent," said the magistrate, advancing toward the bell.

" Imprudent—why ? "

" Because I am going to have you arrested."

" What say you ? " replied Balsamo, stepping between
the magistrate and the bell.   " You are going to arrest
me ? "

" Pardieu ! what can you do to prevent me, may I
ask ? "

" You ask me ? "

" Yes."

" My dear lieutenant of police, I will blow your brains out."

And Balsamo drew from his pocket a charming little pistol, mounted in silver gilt, which, from its appearance, might have been chased by Benvenuto Cellini, and calmly leveled it at the forehead of M. de Sartines, who turned pale and sunk into an armchair."

" There," said Balsamo, drawing another chair close to that occupied by the lieutenant of police, and sitting down ; "now that we are comfortably seated, we can chat a little."

CHAPTER LVII.

CONVERSATION.

M. DE SARTINES took a moment or two to recover from his rather severe alarm. He had seen the threatening muzzle of the pistol presented before his very eye ; he had even felt the cold metal of the barrel upon his forehead. At last he recovered.

"Sir," said he, "you have an advantage over me. Knowing what sort of a man I had to deal with, I did not take the precautions usually adopted against common malefactors."

"Oh, sir," replied Balsamo, "now you are getting angry, and use injurious expressions. Do you not see how unjust you are ? I come to do you service."

M. de Sartines moved uneasily.

" Yes, sir, to serve you," resumed Balsamo, " and therefore you misunderstand my intentions ; you speak to me of conspirators at the very time when I come to denounce a conspiracy to you."

But Balsamo talked in vain. M. de Sartines did not at that moment pay any great attention to the words of his dangerous visitor, and the word conspiracy, which on other occasions would have been sufficient to make him bound from his seat, scarcely caused him to prick up his ears.

"Since you know so well who I am, sir, you are aware of my mission in France. Sent by his majesty the Great Frederick, I am more or less secretly the ambassador of his Prussian majesty. Now, by ambassador is understood an inquirer ; in my quality of inquirer I am ignorant of nothing that happens, and a subject upon which I am particularly well-informed is the monopoly of grain."

However unpretendingly Balsamo uttered these last words, they nevertheless produced more effect upon the lieutenant of police than all the others, for they made him attentive. He slowly raised his head.

"What is this affair about corn ?" said he, affecting as much assurance as Balsamo himself had displayed at the commencement of the interview. "Be good enough, in your turn, to instruct me, sir."

"Willingly, sir," said Balsamo. "This is the whole matter——"

"I am all attention."

"Oh, you do not need to tell me that. Some very clever speculators have persuaded his majesty the King of France that he ought to construct granaries for his people in case of scarcity. These granaries therefore have been constructed. While they were doing it, they thought it as well to make them large. Nothing was spared, neither stone nor brick, and they were made very large."

"Well ?"

"Well, they had then to be filled. Empty granaries were useless, therefore they were filled."

"Well, sir," said M. de Sartines, not seeing very clearly as yet what Balsamo was driving at.

"Well, you may readily conceive that to fill these very large granaries, a great quantity of grain was required. Is that not evident ?"

"Yes."

"To continue, then. A large quantity of grain withdrawn from circulation is one way of starving the people ; for, mark this : any amount taken from the circulation is equivalent to a failure in the production. A thousand · sacks of corn more in the granary are a thousand sacks of corn less in the market-place. If you only multiply these thousand sacks by ten, the corn will rise considerably."

M. de Sartines was seized with an irritating cough. Balsamo paused, and waited quietly till the cough was gone.

"You see, then," continued he, as soon as the lieutenant of police would permit him, "you see that the speculator in these granaries is enriched by the amount of the rise in value. Is that clear to you?"

"Perfectly clear, sir," said M. de Sartines; "but, as far as I can understand, it seems that you have the presumption to denounce to me a conspiracy or a crime of which his majesty is the author."

"Exactly," said Balsamo, "you understand me perfectly."

"That is a bold step, sir; and I confess that I am rather curious to see how his majesty will take your accusation; I fear much the result will be precisely the same that I proposed to myself on looking over the papers in this box before your arrival. Take care, sir, your destination in either case will be the Bastile."

"Ah! now you do not understand me at all."

"How so?"

"Good heavens! how incorrect an opinion you form of me, and how deeply you wrong me, sir, in taking me for a fool! What! you imagine I intend to attack the king —I, an ambassador, an inquirer? Why, that would be the work of a simpleton! Listen to the end, pray."

M. de Sartines bowed.

"The persons who have discovered this conspiracy against the French people—(forgive me for taking up your valuable time, sir, but you will see directly that it is not lost)—they who have discovered this conspiracy against the French people are economists—laborious and minute men, who, by their careful investigation of this underhand game, have discovered that the king does not play alone. They know well that his majesty keeps an exact register of the rate of corn in the different markets; they know that his majesty rubs his hands with glee when the rise has produced him eight or ten thousand crowns ; but they know also that beside his majesty there stands a man whose position facilitates the sales, a man who naturally, thanks to certain functions (he is a functionary, you must know), superintends the purchases, the arrivals, the packing—a man, in short, who manages for the king. Now, these economists—these microscopic observers, as I call them—will not attack the king, for of course they are not mad, but they will attack, my dear sir, the man, the functionary, the agent who thus haggles for his majesty."

M. de Sartines endeavored in vain to restore the equilibrium of his wig.

"Now," continued Balsamo, "I am coming to the point. Just as you, who have a police, knew that I was the Count de Fenix, so I know that you are Monsieur de Sartines."

"Well, what then ? " said the embarrassed magistrate.

"Yes, I am Monsieur de Sartines. What a discovery ! "

" Ah ! but cannot you understand that this Monsieur de Sartines is precisely the man of the price list, of the underhand dealings, of the stowing away—he who, either with or without the king's cognizance, traffics with the food of twenty-seven millions of French people, whom his office requires him to feed on the best possible terms. Now, just imagine the effect of such a discovery. You are not much beloved by the people ; the king is not a very considerate man. As soon as the cries of the famishing millions demand your head, the king—to avert all suspicion of connivance with you, if there is connivance or if there no connivance, to do justice—will cause you to be hung upon a gibbet, like Enguerrand de Marigny. Do you recollect Enguerrand ? "

" Imperfectly," said M. de Sartines, turning very pale ; "and it is a proof of very bad taste, I think, sir, to talk of gibbets to a man of my rank."

" Oh ! if I alluded to it," replied Balsamo, "it was because I think I see poor Enguerrand still before me. I assure you he was a perfect gentleman, from Normandy, of a very ancient family and a noble descent. He was chamberlain of France, captain of the Louvre, comptroller of finance and of buildings ; he was Count of Longueville, which county is more considerable than yours of Alby. Well, sir, I saw him hung upon the gallows of Montfaucon, which he had himself constructed. Thank God, it was not a crime to have said to him before the catastrophe, ' Enguerrand, my dear Enguerrand, take care—you are dipping into the finances to an extent that Charles of Valois will never pardon.' He would not listen to me, sir, and unfortunately he perished. Alas ! if you knew how many prefects of police I have seen, from Pontius Pilate down to Monsieur Bertin de Belille, Count de Bourdeilhes, Lord of Brantôme, your predecessor, who first introduced the lantern and prohibited the scales."

" M. de Sartines rose, and endeavored in vain to conceal the agitation which preyed upon him.

" Well," said he, " you can accuse me if you like. Of what importance is the testimony of a man such as you, who has no influence or connections ? "

" Take care, sir," said Balsamo ; " frequently those who seem to have no connections are connected far and wide ; and when I shall write the history of these corn speculations to my correspondent, Frederick, who you know is a philosopher—when Frederick shall hasten to communicate the affair, with his comments upon it, to Monsieur Arouet de Voltaire—when the latter, with his pen, whose reputation at least I hope you know, shall have metamorphosed it into a little comic tale in the style of ' L'homme aux quarante Ecus' —when Monsieur d'Alembert, that excellent geometrician, shall have calculated that the corn withdrawn from the public consumption by you might have fed a hundred millions of men for two or three years—when Helvetius shall have shown that the price of this corn, converted into crowns of six livres and piled up, would touch the moon, or into bank-notes, fastened together, would reach to St. Petersburg—when this calculation shall have inspired Monsieur de la Harpe to write a bad drama, Diderot a family conversation, and Monsieur Jean Jacques Rousseau, of Geneva, who has a tolerably sharp bite when he chooses, a terrible paraphrase of this conversation, with his own commentaries—when Monsieur Baron de Beaumarchais—may Heaven preserve you from treading on his toes !—shall have written a memoir, Monsieur Grimm a little letter, Monsieur de Holbach a thundering attack, Monsieur de Marmontel an amiable moral tale in which he will kill you by defending you badly—when you shall be spoken of in the Café de la Regence, the Palais Royal, at Oudinet's, at the king's dancers' (kept up, as you know, by Monsieur Nicolet)—ah ! Count d'Alby, you will be in a much worse case than poor Enguerrand de Marigny (whom you would not hear me mention) when he stood under the gallows for he asserted his innocence, and that with so much earnestness, that, on my word of honor, I believed him when he told me so."

At these words, M. de Sartines, no longer paying any heed to decorum, took off his wig and wiped his bald pate, which was bathed in perspiration.

"Well," said he, " so be it.   But all that will not prevent me in the least.   Ruin me if you can ; you have your proofs, I have mine.   Keep your secret, I shall keep the coffer."

" Oh, sir," said Balsamo, " that is another error into which I am surprised that a man of your talents should fall ; this coffer——"

" Well, what of it ? "

" You will not keep."

" Oh !" exclaimed M. de Sartines, with a sarcastic smile, " true ; I had forgotten that the Count de Fenix is a gentleman of the highway, who rifles travelers with the strong hand.   I forgot your pistol, because you have replaced it in your pocket.   Excuse me, my lord ambassador ! "

" But, good heavens ! why speak of pistols, Monsieur de Sartines ?   You surely do not believe that I mean to carry off the coffer by main force ; that when on the stairs I may hear your bell ring, and your voice cry, ' Stop thief !' Oh, no !   When I say that you will not keep this coffer, I mean that you will restore it to me willingly and without constraint."

" What, I ! " exclaimed the magistrate, placing his clenched hand upon the disputed object with so much weight that he nearly broke it.

" Yes, you."

" Oh ! very well, sir, mock away ; but as to taking this coffer, I tell you you shall only have it with my life.   And have I not risked my life a thousand times ?   Do I not owe it, to the last drop, to the service of his majesty ?   Kill me—you can do so ; but the noise will summon my avengers, and I shall have voice enough left to convict you of all your crimes.   Ah, give you back this coffer ! " added he, with a bitter smile, " all hell should not wrest it from me ! "

" And, therefore, I shall not employ the intervention of the subterranean powers.   I shall be satisfied with that of the person who is just now knocking at the gate of your courtyard."

And, in fact, just at that moment, three blows, struck with an air of command, were heard outside.

" And whose carriage," continued Balsamo, " is just now entering the court."

" It seems, then, that it is some friend of yours who is coming to honor me with a visit ? "

" As you say—a friend of mine."

" And I shall hand this coffer to him ? "

" Yes, my dear Monsieur de Sartines, you will give it to him."

The lieutenant of police had not finished his gesture of lofty disdain when a valet opened the door hastily, and announced that Mme. Dubarry wished for an interview.

M. de Sartines started, and looked in stupefied amazement at Balsamo, who required all his self-command to avoid laughing in the face of the honorable magistrate.

Close behind the valet appeared a lady who seemed to have no need of permission to enter.   It was the beautiful countess, whose flowing and perfumed skirts gently rustled as they brushed past the doorway of the cabinet.

" You, madame, you ! " exclaimed M. de Sartines, who, in the instinct of terror, had seized the open coffer in both hands, and clasped it to his breast.

" Good day, Sartines," said the countess, with her gayest smile ; then, turning to Balsamo, " good day, dear count," added she ; and she gave her hand to the latter, who familiarly bent over the white fingers, and pressed his lips where the royal lips had so often rested.

In this movement Balsamo managed to whisper a few words aside to the countess, which Sartines could not hear.

"Ah ! precisely," exclaimed the countess ; "there is my coffer."

" Your coffer ! " stammered M. de Sartines.

" Of course, my coffer—oh ! you have opened it, I see— you do not observe much ceremony."

" But, madame——"

" Oh, it is delightful ! The idea occurred to me at once that some one had stolen this coffer, and then I said to myself : ' I must go to Sartines ; he will find it for me.' You did not wait till I asked you ; you found it beforehand —a thousand thanks ! "

" And as you see," said Balsamo, " monsieur has even opened it."

" Yes, really ! who could have thought of it. It is dubious conduct of you, Sartines."

" Madame, notwithstanding all the respect I have for you," said the lieutenant of police, " I fear that you are imposed upon."

" Imposed, sir ! " said Balsamo ; " do you perchance mean that word for me ? "

" I know what I know," replied M. de Sartines.

" And I know nothing," whispered Mme. Dubarry, in a low voice to Balsamo. " Come, tell me what is the matter, my dear count ! You have claimed the fulfilment of the promise I made you, to grant the first favor you should ask. I keep my word like a woman of honor, and here I am. Tell me what must I do for you."

" Madame," replied Balsamo, aloud, " you confided the

care of this coffer and everything it contains to me, a few days ago."

"Of course," answered Mme. Dubarry, replying by a look to the count's appealing glance.

"Of course!" exclaimed M. de Sartines, "you say of course, madame?"

"Yes; madame pronounced the words loud enough for you to hear them, I should think."

"A box which contains perhaps ten conspiracies!"

"Ah! Monsieur de Sartines, you are aware that that word is rather an unfortunate one for you; do not repeat it. Madame asks for her box again; give it her—that is all."

"Do you ask me for it, madame?" said M. de Sartines, trembling with anger.

"Yes, my dear magistrate."

"But learn, at least——"

Balsamo looked at the countess.

"You can tell me nothing I do not know," said Mme. Dubarry; "give me the coffer; you may believe I did not come for nothing?"

"But in the name of Heaven, madame—in the name of his majesty's safety——"

Balsamo made an impatient gesture.

"The coffer, sir!" said the countess, abruptly; "the coffer—yes or no! Reflect well before you refuse."

"As you please, madame!" said M. de Sartines, humbly.

And he handed the coffer, into which Balsamo had already replaced all the papers scattered over the desk, to the countess.

Mme. Dubarry turned toward the latter with a charming smile.

"Count," said she, "will you carry this coffer to my carriage for me, and give me your hand through all these antechambers thronged with villainous-looking faces which I do not like to confront alone? Thanks, Sartines."

And Balsamo was already advancing toward the door with his protectress, when he saw M. de Sartines moving toward the bell.

"Countess," said Balsamo, stopping his enemy with a look, "be good enough to tell Monsieur de Sartines, who is quite enraged with me for having claimed this box—be good enough to tell him how much grieved you would be if any misfortune were to happen to me through the agency of the lieutenant of police, and how displeased you would be with him."

The countess smiled on Balsamo.

"You hear what the count says, my dear Sartines ?—well ! it is the simple truth.   The count is an excellent friend of mine, and I should be dreadfully angry with you if you displeased him in any way whatsoever.   Adieu, Sartines !"   And placing her hand in Balsamo's, who carried the coffer, Mme. Dubarry left the study of the lieutenant of police.

M de. Sartines saw them depart without displaying that fury which Balsamo expected him to manifest.

"Go !" said the conquered magistrate ; "go—you have the box, but I have the woman !"

And to compensate himself for his disappointment, he rang loud enough to break all the bells in the house.

CHAPTER LVIII.

SARTINES BEGINS TO THINK BALSAMO A SORCERER.

AT the violent ringing of M. de Sartines' bell an usher entered.

"Well !" asked the magistrate ; "this woman ?"

"What woman, my lord ?"

"The woman who fainted here just now, and whom I confided to your care."

"My lord, she is quite well," replied the usher.

"Very good ; bring her to me."

"Where shall I find her, my lord ?"

"What do you mean ?   In that room, of course."

"But she is not there, my lord."

"Not there.   Then where is she ?"

"I do not know."

"She is gone ?"

"Yes."

"Alone ?"

"Yes."

"But she could not stand."

"My lord, it is true that for some moments she remained in a swoon ; but five minutes after the Count de Fenix entered my lord's study, she awoke from this strange fit, which neither essence nor salts affected in the least. Then she opened her eyes, rose, and breathed, seemingly with an air of satisfaction."

"Well, what, then ?"

"She proceeded toward the door ; and, as my lord had not ordered that she should not be detained, she was allowed to depart.

"Gone !" cried M. de Sartines. "Ah ! wretch that you are ! I shall send you all to rot at Bicêtre ! Quick, quick ! send me my head-clerk !"

The usher retired hastily to obey the order he had received.

"The wretch is a sorcerer !" muttered the unfortunate magistrate. "I am a lieutenant of police to the king, but he is lieutenant of police to the devil !"

The reader has, no doubt, understood what M. de Sartines could not explain to himself. Immediately after the incident of the pistol, and while the lieutenant of the police was endeavoring to regain his equanimity, Balsamo, profiting by the momentary respite, had turned successively to the four cardinal points, quite sure of finding Lorenza in one of them, and had ordered her to rise and go out, and to return, by the way she had come, to the Rue St. Claude.

The moment this wish had been formed in Balsamo's mind, a magnetic current was established between him and the young woman, and the latter, obeying the order she had received by intuition, rose and retired, without any one opposing her departure.

M. de Sartines that same evening took to his bed, and

caused himself to be bled. The revulsion had been too strong for him to bear with impunity ; and the doctor assured him that a quarter of an hour more would have brought on an attack of apoplexy.

Meanwhile, Balsamo had accompanied the countess to her carriage, and had attempted to take his leave of her, but she was not a woman to let him go thus, without knowing, or at least without endeavoring to discover the solution of the strange event which had taken place before her. She begged the count to enter her carriage. The count obeyed, and a groom led Djerid behind.

" You see now, count," said she, " whether I am true or not, and whether, when I have called a man my friend, I spoke with the lips merely, or my heart. I was just setting out for Luciennes, where the king had said he would pay me a visit to-morrow morning ; but your letter arrived, and I left everything for you. Many would have been frightened at the words conspiracies and conspirators which Monsieur de Sartines threw in your teeth ; but I looked at your countenance before I acted and did as you wished me."

" Madame," replied Balsamo, " you have amply repaid the slight service I was able to render you ; but with me nothing is lost—you will find that I can be grateful. Do not imagine, however, that I am a criminal—a conspirator, as Monsieur de Sartines said. That worthy magistrate had received, from some person who betrayed me, this coffer, containing some chemical and hermetical secrets—which I shall share with you, that you may preserve your immortal, your splendid beauty, and your dazzling youth. Now, seeing the ciphers of my recipe, this excellent Monsieur de Sartines called the chancery clerk to assist him, who in order not to be found wanting, interpreted them after his own fashion. I think I have already told you, madame, that the profession is not yet entirely freed from the dangers which were attendant on it in the Middle Ages. Only young and intelligent minds like yours favor it. In short, madame, you have saved me from a great embarrassment I thank you for it, and shall prove my gratitude."

" But what would he have done with you if I had not come to your assistance ? "

" To annoy King Frederick, whom his majesty hates, he would have imprisoned me in Vincennes or the Bastile. I should have escaped from it, I know—thanks to my recipe for melting stone with a breath—but I should have lost my coffer, which contains, as I have had the honor of telling you, many curious and invaluable secrets, wrested by a lucky chance from eternal darkness."

" Ah, count ! you at once delight and reassure me. Then you promise me a philter to make me young again ? "

" Yes."

" And when will you give it me ? "

" Oh ! you need be in no hurry. You may ask for it twenty years hence, beautiful countess. In the meantime, I think you do not wish to become quite a child again."

" You are, in truth, a charming man. One question more, and I will let you go, for you seem in haste."

" Speak, countess."

" You said that some one had betrayed you. Is it a man or a woman ? "

" A woman."

" Ah ! ah ! count ! love affairs."

" Alas ! yes ; prompted by an almost frantic jealousy, which has produced the pleasant effect you have seen. It is a woman who, not daring to stab me with a knife, because she knows I cannot be killed, wanted to imprison and ruin me."

"What ! ruin you ? "

" She endeavored to do so, at least."

" Count, I will stop here," said the countess, laughing. " Is it the liquid silver which courses through your veins that gives you that immortality which makes people betray you instead of killing you ? Shall I set you down here, or drive you to your own house ? Come, choose ! "

" No, madame, I cannot allow you to inconvenience yourself on my account. I have my horse, Djerid."

" Ah ! that wonderful animal which, it is said, outstrips the wind ? "

" He seems to please you, madame."

" He is, in truth, a magnificent steed."

" Allow me to offer him to you, on the condition that you alone ride him."

" Oh ! no, thank you. I do not ride on horseback ; or, at least, I am a very timid horsewoman. I am as much obliged to you, however, as if I accepted your offer. Adieu ! my dear count ; do not forget my philter in ten years."

" I said twenty."

" Count, you know the proverb : ' a bird in the hand,' and if you could even give it me in five years—there's no knowing what may happen."

" Whenever you please, countess ; are you not aware that I am entirely at your command ? "

" Only one word more, count."

" I am all attention, madame."

" It proves that I have great confidence in you to speak of it."

Balsamo, who had already alighted from the carriage, suppressed his impatience, and approached the countess.

" It is reported everywhere," continued Mme. Dubarry, " that the king is rather taken with this little Taverney."

" Ah ! madame," said Balsamo, " is it possible ? "

" A very great partiality, it is said. You must tell me if it is true. Count, do not deceive me ; I beseech you to treat me as a friend. Tell me the truth, count."

" Madame," replied Balsamo, " I will do more ; I will promise you that Mademoiselle Andrée shall never be anything to the king."

" And why not ? " cried Mme. Dubarry.

" Because I will it so," said Balsamo.

" Oh ! " said Mme. Dubarry, incredulously.

" You doubt ? "

" Is it not allowed ? "

" Never doubt the truths of science, madame. You have believed me when I said yes ; believe me when I say no."

" But, in short, have you the means——"

" Well ? "

"Means capable of annihilating the king's will, or conquering his whims?"

Balsamo smiled.

"I create sympathies," said he.

"Yes, I know that."

"You believe it, even?"

"I believe it."

"Well, I can create aversions also, and if needful, impossibilities. Therefore, countess, make your mind easy—I am on the watch."

Balsamo uttered all these fragments of sentences with an absence of mind which Mme. Dubarry would not have taken as she did for inspiration, had she known the feverish anxiety which Balsamo felt to be with Lorenza as quickly as possible.

"Well, count," said she, "assuredly you are not only my prophet of happiness, but also my guardian angel. Count, mark my words: defend me and I will defend you. Alliance! union!"

"Agreed, madame," replied Balsamo, kissing the countess's hand.

Then closing the door of the carriage, which the countess had stopped upon the Champs-Elysées, he mounted his horse, who neighed joyously, and was soon lost to view in the shadows of night.

"To Luciennes!" said the countess, consoled.

This time Balsamo whispered softly, and gently pressed his knees against Djerid's sides, who started off at a gallop.

Five minutes afterward he was in the vestibule of the Rue St. Claude, looking at Fritz.

"Well?" asked he, anxiously.

"Yes, master," replied the domestic, who was accustomed to read his looks.

"She has returned?"

"She is upstairs."

"In which room?"

"In the chamber of furs."

"In what state is she?"

"Oh! very much exhausted. She ran so quickly that,

although I saw her coming, for I was watching for her, I had scarcely time to hasten to meet her."

" Indeed ! "

" Oh ! I was quite alarmed. She swept on like a tempest ; rushed upstairs without taking breath ; and when she entered the room, she fell upon the large black lion's skin. You will find her there."

Balsamo hastily ascended, and found Lorenza where Fritz had said. She was struggling in vain against the first convulsions of a nervous crisis. The fluid had weighed upon her too long already, and forced her to violent efforts. She was in pain, and groaned deeply ; it seemed as if a mountain weighed upon her breast, and that she endeavored with both hands to remove it.

Balsamo looked at her with an eye sparkling with anger, and, taking her in his arms, he carried her into her apartment, the mysterious door of which closed behind him.

CHAPTER LIX.

THE ELIXIR OF LIFE.

BALSAMO had just entered Lorenza's apartment, and was preparing to awake her and overwhelm her with all the reproaches which his gloomy anger prompted, fully determined to punish her according to the dictates of that anger, when a triple knock upon the ceiling announced that Althotas had watched for his return and wished to speak to him.

Nevertheless, Balsamo waited ; he was hoping either that he had been mistaken or that the signal had been accidental, when the impatient old man repeated his blows. Balsamo therefore—fearing, no doubt, to see him descend, as he had already done before, or that Lorenza, awakened by an influence opposed to his own, might acquire the knowledge of some other particulars no less dangerous for him than his political secrets—Balsamo, therefore, after having, if we may so express it, charged Lorenza with a fresh stratum of the electric fluid, left the room to rejoin Althotas.

It was high time ; the trap-door was already half-way from the ceiling. Althotas had left his wheeled armchair, and was seen squatting down upon the movable part of the ceiling which rose and fell. He saw Balsamo leave Lorenza's room.

Squatting down thus, the old man was at once hideous and terrible to behold.

His white face, in those parts which still seemed as if they belonged to a living being, was purple with the violence of his rage. His meager and bony hands, like those of a human skeleton, trembled and shook ; his hollow eyes seemed to vacillate in their deep caverns ; and, in a language unknown even to his disciple, he was loading him with the most violent invectives.

Having left his armchair to touch the spring, he seemed to live and move only by the aid of his long arms, lean and angular as those of a spider ; and issuing, as we have said, from his chamber, inaccessible to all but Balsamo, he was about to descend to the lower apartment. To induce this feeble old man, indolent as he was, to leave his armchair (that cleverly constructed machine which spared him all fatigue) , and consent to perform one of the actions of common life—to induce him to undergo the care and fatigue of such a change in his usual habits, it must have required no ordinary excitement thus to withdraw him from the ideal life in which he existed, and plunge him into the everyday world.

Balsamo, taken as it were in the fact, seemed at first astonished, then uneasy.

" Ah !" exclaimed Althotas, " there you are, you good-for-nothing—you ingrate ! There you are, coward who desert your master ! "

Balsamo called all his patience to his aid, as he invariably did when he spoke to the old man.

" But," replied he, quietly, " I think, my friend, you have only just called me."

" Your friend ? " exclaimed Althotas ; " your friend ?

you vile human creature ! You dare to speak the language of your equals to me ! I have been a friend to you—more than a friend—a father, a father who has educated, instructed, and enriched you. But you, my friend ? Oh, no ! for you abandon me—you assassinate me ! "

" Come, master, you disturb your bile ; you irritate your blood ; you will make yourself ill."

" Ill ? absurdity ! Have I ever been ill, except when you made me a sharer, in spite of myself, in some of the miseries of your impure human-kind ? Ill ! have you forgotten that it is I who heal others ? "

" Well, master," replied Balsamo, coldly, " I am here. Let us not lose time in vain."

" Yes, I advise you to remind me of that. Time ! time ! which you oblige me to economize—me, for whom this element, circumscribed to all the world, should be endless, unlimited ! Yes, my time flies—yes, my time is lost—my time, like the time of other people, falls minute by minute, into the gulf of eternity, when for me it ought to be eternity itself ! "

" Come, master ! " said Balsamo, with unalterable patience, lowering the trap to the ground as he spoke, placing himself upon it, and causing it to rise again to its place in the room ; " come, what is it you want ? You say I starve you, but are you not in your forty days of regimen ? "

" Yes, yes, doubtless ; the work of regeneration commenced thirty-two days ago."

" Then, tell me of what do you complain ? I see two or three bottles of rain-water, the only kind you drink, still remaining."

" Of course ; but do you imagine I am a silk-worm, that I can complete the grand work of renovation of youth and of transformation alone ? Do you imagine that, powerless as I am, I can compose alone the elixir of life ? Or think you, that reclined on my side, and enervated by cooling drinks, my sole nourishment, I could have presence of mind enough, when left to my own resources and without your assistance, to complete the minute work of my regeneration, in which, as you, unfortunate wretch, well know, I must be aided and supported by a friend ? "

" I am here, master—I am here. Answer me, now," said Balsamo, replacing the old man in his chair almost in spite of himself, as he would have done a hideous infant ; " answer me—you have not been in want of distilled water, for, as I said before, there are three bottles still remaining. This water, as you know, was all collected in the month of May ; there are your biscuits of barley and of sesamum, and I myself administered to you the white drops you prescribed."

" Yes, but the elixir ! The elixir is not yet made ! You do not remember it, for you were not there—it was your father, your father, who was far more faithful than you are—but at the last fiftieth I had the elixir ready a month beforehand. I had my retreat on Mount Ararat. A Jew provided me with a Christian child, still at its mother's breast, for its weight in gold ; I bled it according to the rule ; I took the last three drops of its arterial blood, and in an hour my elixir, which only wanted this ingredient, was composed. Therefore, my first regeneration succeeded wonderfully well. My hair and teeth fell out during the convulsions which succeeded the absorption of that wondrous elixir, but they grew again—the latter badly enough, I know, because I neglected the precaution of letting the elixir flow into my throat through a golden conduit. But my hair and my nails grew again in this second youth, and I began again to live as if I were only fifteen. Now I am old again—I am bordering on the extreme limit—and, if the elixir is not ready, if it is not safely inclosed in this bottle, if I do not bestow all possible care upon this work, the science of a century will be annihilated with me, and the admirable, the sublime secret I possess will be lost for man, who, in me and through me, approaches the divinity ! Oh ! if I fail—if I am mistaken, if I miss it, Acharat—it will be your fault ; and take care, for my anger will be terrible—terrible ! "

As he uttered these last words, a livid glare shot from

his dying eyeballs, and the old man fell into a brief convulsion, which ended in a violent fit of coughing.

Balsamo instantly lavished the most eager attention on him, and the old man recovered. His complexion had become deathlike, instead of pale. This feeble attack had weakened his strength so much that one would have thought he was dying.

" Come, master," said Balsamo, " tell me plainly what you want."

" What do I want ? " said he, looking fixedly at Balsamo.

" Yes."

" What I want is this——"

" Speak ; I hear you, and I will obey, if what you ask is possible."

" Possible ! possible ! " muttered the old man, contemptuously. " You know that everything is possible."

" Yes, with time and science."

" Science I have, and I am on the point of conquering time. My dose has succeeded. My strength has almost entirely left me. The white drops have caused the expulsion of all the remaining portion of my former nature. Youth, like the sap of the trees in May, rises under the old bark, and buds, so to speak, through the old wood. You may remark, Acharat, that the symptoms are excellent ; my voice is weak, my sight is three quarters gone ; sometimes I feel my mind wander ; I have become insensible to the transition from heat to cold. I must therefore hasten to finish my elixir in order that, on the appointed term of my second fifty years, I may at once pass from a hundred to twenty. The ingredients for the elixir are all made, the conduit is ready ; I want nothing but the three drops of blood I told you of."

Balsamo made a gesture of repugnance.

" Very well," said Althotas ; let us abandon the child, since it is so difficult, and since you prefer to shut yourself up the whole day with your mistress to seeking it for me."

" You know, master, that Lorenza is not my mistress," replied Balsamo.

"Oh! oh! oh!" exclaimed Althotas; "you say that! You think to impose on me as on the masses; you would make me believe in an immaculate creature, and yet you are a man!"

"I swear to you, master, that Lorenza is as pure as an angel! I swear to you that love, earthly felicity, domestic happiness—I have sacrificed all to my project. For I also have my regenerating work; only, instead of applying it to myself alone, I shall apply it to all the world."

"Fool! poor fool!" cried Althotas; "I verily believe he is going to speak to me of his cataclysms of flesh-worms, his revolutions of ant-hills, when I speak to him of life and eternal youth!"

"Which can only be acquired at the price of a fearful crime—and besides——"

"You doubt, I see you doubt—miserable wretch!"

"No, master; but since you give up the child, tell me, what do you want?"

"I must have the first unmarried woman you meet. A woman is the best—I have discovered that, on account of the affinity of the sexes. Find me that, and quickly, for I have only eight days longer."

"Very well, master, I will see—I will search."

Another lightning flash, more terrible than the first, sparkled in the old man's eyes.

"You will see! you will search!" he cried. "Oh! is that your reply? I expected it, and I don't know why I am surprised. And since when, thou worm of the earth! was the creature entitled to speak thus to its master? Ah! you see me powerless, disabled, supplicating, and you are fool enough to think me at your mercy! Yes or no, Acharat? And answer me without embarrassment or falsehood, for I can see and read your heart; for I can judge you, and shall punish you."

"Master," replied Balsamo, "take care; your anger will do you an injury."

"Answer me—answer!"

"I can only say the truth to my master; I will see if I can procure what you desire, without injuring ourselves.

I will endeavor to find a man who will sell you what you want ; but I will not take the crime upon myself. This is all I can say."

" You are very fastidious ! " said Althotas, with a bitter smile.

" It is so, master," said Balsamo.

Althotas made so violent an effort, that with the help of his two arms resting on the arms of the chair he raised himself to his feet.

" Yes or no ? " said he.

" Master, yes, if I find it ; no, if I do not."

" Then you will expose me to death, wretch ? you will economize three drops of blood of an insignificant, worthless creature such as I require, and let a perfect creature such as I am fall into the eternal gulf ! Listen, Acharat ! " said the old man, with a smile fearful to behold, " I no longer ask you for anything ; I ask absolutely nothing. I shall wait, but if you do not obey, I must serve myself ; if you desert me, I must help myself ! You have heard me—have you not ? Now go ! "

Balsamo, without replying to this threat, prepared everything the old man might want. He placed the drinks and the food within his reach, and performed all the services a watchful servant would perform for his master, a devoted son for his father ; then, absorbed by a thought very different from that which tormented Althotas, he lowered the trap to descend, without remarking that the old man followed with a sardonic and ominous grin.

Althotas was still grinning like an evil genius when Balsamo stood before the still sleeping Lorenza.

CHAPTER XIII.

THE STRUGGLE.

Balsamo stood before her, his heart swelling with mournful thoughts, for the violent ones had vanished.

The scene which had just taken place between himself and Althotas had led him to reflect on the nothingness of all human affairs, and had chased anger from his heart. He remembered the practise of the Greek philosopher who repeated the entire alphabet before listening to the voice of that black divinity, the counselor of Achilles.

After a moment of mute and cold contemplation before the couch on which Lorenza was lying :

"I am sad," said he to himself; "but resolved, and I can look my situation fair in the face. Lorenza hates me ; Lorenza has threatened to betray me. My secret is no longer my own ; I have given it into the woman's power, and she casts it to the winds. I am like the fox who has withdrawn from the steel trap only the bone of his leg, but who has left behind his flesh and his skin, so that the huntsmen can say on the morrow, ' The fox has been taken here ; I shall know him again, living or dead.'

" And this dreadful misfortune which Althotas cannot comprehend, and which therefore I have not even mentioned to him—this misfortune which destroys all my hopes in this country—and consequently in this world, of which France is the soul, I owe to the creature sleeping before me—to this beautiful statue with her entreating smile. To this tempting angel I owe dishonor and ruin, and shall owe to her captivity, exile, and death.

" Therefore," continued he, becoming more animated, " the sum of evil has exceeded that of good, and Lorenza is dangerous. Oh, serpent ! with thy graceful folds which nevertheless strangle, with thy golden throat which is nevertheless full of venom—sleep on, for when thou awakest I shall be obliged to kill thee ! "

And with a gloomy smile Balsamo slowly approached the young woman, whose languid eyes were turned toward him as he approached, as the sunflower and volubilis open to the first rays of the rising sun.

"Oh!" said Balsamo, "and yet I must forever close those eyes which now beam so tenderly on me, those beautiful eyes which are filled with lightning when they no longer sparkle with love."

Lorenza smiled sweetly, and smiling, she displayed the double row of her pearly teeth.

"But if I kill her who hates me," said Balsamo, wringing his hands, "I shall also kill her who loves me."

And his heart was filled with the deepest grief, strangely mingled with a vague desire.

"No, no," murmured he; "I have sworn in vain; I have threatened in vain; no, I shall never have the courage to kill her. She shall live, but she shall live without being awakened. She shall live in this factitious life, which is happiness for her, while the other is despair. Would that I could make her happy. What matters to me the rest—she shall only have one existence, the one I create; the one during which she loves me, that which she lives at this moment."

And he returned Lorenza's tender look by a look as tender as her own, placing his hand as he did so gently on her head. Lorenza, who seemed to read Balsamo's thoughts as if they were an open book, gave a long sigh, rose gradually with the graceful languor of sleep, and placed her two white arms upon Balsamo's shoulders, who felt her perfumed breath upon his cheek.

"Oh, no, no!" exclaimed Balsamo, passing his hand over his burning forehead and his dazzled eyes: "no, this intoxicating life will make me mad; and, with this siren, glory, power, immortality will all vanish from my thoughts. No, no; she must awake, I must do it."

"Oh!" continued he, "if I awake her, the struggle will begin again. If I awake her, she will kill herself, or she will kill me, or force me to destroy her. Oh! what an abyss!

"Yes, this woman's destiny is written ; it stands before
me in letters of fire—love ! death !—Lorenza, Lorenza !
thou art doomed to love and to die ! Lorenza, Lorenza !
I hold thy life and thy love in my hands !"

Instead of a reply, the enchantress rose, advanced toward Balsamo, fell at his feet, and gazed into his eyes with
a tender smile. Then she took one of his hands and
placed it on her heart.

"Death !" said she, in a low voice, which whispered
from her lips, brilliant as coral when it issues from the
caverns of the deep ; "death, but love !"

"Oh !" said Balsamo, "it is too much. I have struggled as long as a human being could struggle. Demon,
or angel of futurity, whichever thou art ! thou must be
content. I have long enough sacrificed all the generous
passions in my heart to egotism and pride. Oh ! no, no.
I have no right thus to rebel against the only human feeling which still remains lurking in my heart. I love this
woman, I love her, and this passionate love injures her
more than the most terrible hatred could do. This love
kills her. Oh, coward ! oh, ferocious fool that I am ! I
cannot even compromise with my desires. What ! when
I breathe my last sigh ; when I prepare to appear before
God—I, the deceiver, the false prophet—when I throw off
my mantle of hypocrisy and artifice before the Sovereign
Judge—shall I have not one generous action to confess,
not the recollection of a single happiness to console me in
the midst of my eternal sufferings ?

"Oh ! no, no, Lorenza ; I know that in loving thee I
lose the future ; I know that my revealing angel will wing
its flight to heaven if I thus change your entire existence
and overturn the natural laws of your being. But, Lorenza, you wish it, do you not ?"

"My beloved !" she sighed.

"Then you accept the factitious instead of the real life?"

"I ask for it on my knees—I pray for it—I implore it.
This life is love and happiness."

"And will it suffice for you when you are my wife, for
I love you passionately ?"

"Oh ! I know it; I can read your heart."

"You will never regret your wings, poor dove; for know that you will never again roam through radiant space for me to seek the ray of light Jehovah once deigned to bestow upon his prophets. When I would know the future, when I would command men, alas ! alas ! the voice will not reply. I have had in thee the beloved woman and the helping spirit; I shall only have one of the two now, and yet——"

"Ah ! you doubt, you doubt," cried Lorenza, "I see doubt like a dark stain upon your heart."

"You will always love me, Lorenza ? "

"Always ! always ! "

Balsamo passed his hand over his forehead.

"Well, it shall be so," said he.

And raising Lorenza, he folded her in his arms and pressed a kiss upon her head—a seal of his promise to love and cherish her till death.

CHAPTER LXI.

LOVE.

FOR Balsamo another life had commenced, a life hitherto unknown in his active, troubled, multiplied existence. For three days that had been for him no more anger, no more apprehension, no more jealousy; for three days he had not heard the subject of politics, conspirators, or conspiracies, as much as whispered. By Lorenza's side, and he had not left her for an instant, he had forgotten the whole world. This strange, inexplicable love, which, as it were, soared above humanity, this intoxicating and mysterious attachment, this love of a shadow, for he could not conceal from himself that with a word he could change his gentle bride into an implacable enemy—this love snatched from hatred, thanks to an inexplicable caprice of nature or of science, plunged Balsamo into happiness which bordered on madness.

More than once, during these three days, rousing him-

self from the opiate torpor of love, Balsamo looked at his
ever-smiling, ever-ecstatic companion—for from thenceforth, in the existence he had created for her, she reposed
from her factitious life in a sort of ecstasy equally factitious—and when he saw her calm, gentle, happy, when she
called him by the most affectionate names, and dreamed
aloud her mysterious love, he more than once asked himself if some ruthless demon had not inspired Lorenza with
the idea of deceiving him with a falsehood in order to lull
his vigilance, and when it was lulled, to escape and only
appear again as the Avenging Euemnides.

In such moments Balsamo doubted of the truth of a
science received by tradition from antiquity, but of which
he had no evidence but examples. But soon the ever-
springing fountain of her affection reassured him.

"If Lorenza was feigning," argued he with himself,
"if she intended to fly from him, she would seek opportunities for sending me away, she would invent excuses
for occasional solitude ; but, far from that, her gentle
voice ever whispers, stay ! "

Then Balsamo's confidence in himself and in science
returned. Why indeed should the magic secret to which
alone he owed his power have become all at once and without any transition a chimera, fit only to throw to the winds
as a vanished recollection, as the smoke of an extinguished
fire ? Never with relation to him had Lorenza been more
lucid, more clear-sighted. All the thoughts which sprung
up in his mind, all the feelings which made his heart
bound, were instantly reproduced in hers. It remained
to be seen if this lucidity were not sympathy ; if, beyond
himself and the young girl, beyond the circle which their
love had traced, and which their love illuminated with its
light—the eyes of her soul, so clear-sighted before this
new era of continued sleep, could yet pierce the surrounding darkness.

Balsamo dared not make the decisive trial ; he hoped
still, and this hope was the resplendent crown of his happiness.

Sometimes Lorenza said to him with gentle melancholy :

" Acharat, you think of another than me, of a northern woman, with fair hair and blue eyes. Acharat! Acharat! this woman always moves beside me in your thoughts."

Balsamo looked tenderly at Lorenza.

" You see that in me ?" said he.

" Oh ! yes, as clearly as I read the surface of a mirror."

" Then you know it is not love which makes me think of that woman, replied Balsamo ; " read in my heart, dearest Lorenza ! "

" No," replied she, bending her head ; " no, I know it well. But yet your thoughts are divided between us two, as in the days when Lorenza Feliciani tormented you— the naughty Lorenza, who sleeps, and whom you will not again awake."

" No, my love, no," exclaimed Balsamo ; " I think only of thee, at least with the heart. Have I not forgotten all, neglected everything—study, politics, work—since our happiness ? "

" And you are wrong," said Lorenza, " for I could help you in your work."

" How ? "

" Yes ; did you not once spend whole hours in your laboratory ? "

" Certainly. But I renounce all these vain endeavors. They would be so many hours taken from my life—for during that time I should not see you."

" And why should I not follow you in your labors as in your love ? Why should I not make you powerful as I make you happy ? "

" Because my Lorenza, it is true, is beautiful ; but she has not studied. God gives beauty and love, but study alone gives science."

" The soul knows everything."

" Then you can really see with the eyes of your soul ? "

" Yes."

" And you can guide me in the grand search after the philosopher's stone ? "

" I think so."

" Come, then."

And Balsamo, encircling her waist with his arm, led her into his laboratory. The gigantic furnace, which no one had replenished for four days, was extinguished, and the crucibles had grown cold upon their chafing-dishes.

Lorenza looked around on all these strange instruments —the last combination of expiring alchemy—without surprise. She seemed to know the purpose which each was intended to fulfil.

"You are attempting to make gold," said she, smiling.

"Yes."

"All these crucibles contain preparations in different stages of progress ?"

"All stopped—all lost ; but I do not regret it."

"You are right, for your gold would never be anything but colored mercury ; you can render it solid, perhaps, but you cannot transform it."

"But gold can be made ?"

"No."

"And yet Daniel of Transylvania sold the receipt for the transmutation of metals to Cosmo I. for twenty thousand ducats."

"Daniel of Transylvaina deceived Cosmo I."

"And yet the Saxon Payken, who was condemned to death by Charles II., ransomed his life by changing a leaden ingot into a golden one, from which forty ducats were coined, besides, taking as much from the ingot as made a medal which was struck in honor of the clever alchemist."

"The clever alchemist was nothing but a clever juggler. He merely substituted the golden ingot for the leaden one ; nothing more. Your surest way of making gold, Acharat, is to melt into ingots, as you do already, the riches which your slaves bring you from the four quarters of the world."

Balsamo remained pensive.

"Then the transmutation of metals is impossible ?" said he.

"Impossible."

"And the diamond—is it, too, impossible to create ?"

"Oh ! the diamond is another matter," said Lorenza.

"The diamond can be made, then ?"

"Yes ; for, to make the diamond, you have not to trans-
mute one body into another.   To make the diamond is
merely to attempt the simple modification of a known
element."

"Then you know the element of which the diamond is
formed ?"

"To be sure ; the diamond is pure carbon crystallized."

Balsamo was almost stunned ; a dazzling, unexpected,
unheard-of light flashed before his eyes.   He covered
them with both hands, as if the flame had blinded him.

"Oh, bountiful Creator !" said he, "you give me too
much—some danger threatens me !   What precious ring
must I throw into the sea to appease the jealousy of my
fate !   Enough, Lorenza, for to-day."

"Am I not yours ? order, command me."

"Yes, you are mine ; come, come."

And he drew her out of the laboratory, crossed the
chamber of furs, and without paying any attention to a
light creaking noise he heard overhead, he once more entered the barred room with Lorenza.

"So you are pleased with your Lorenza, my beloved
Balsamo ?"

"Oh !" exclaimed he.

"What did you fear, then ?   Speak—tell me all."

Balsamo clasped his hands and looked at Lorenza with
an expression of such terror that a spectator ignorant of
what was passing in his heart would have been totally at a
loss to account for it.

"Oh !" murmured he, "and I was near killing this
angel—I was near expiring of despair before resolving the
problem of being at once powerful and happy !   I forgot
that the limits of the possible always exceed the horizon
traced by the present state of science and that the
majority of truths which have become facts have always
in their infancy been looked upon as dreams.   I thought
I knew everything, and I knew nothing !"

The young Italian smiled divinely.

" Lorenza ! Lorenza ! " continued Balsamo, " the mysterious design of the Creator is then accomplished, which
makes woman to be born of the substance of the man, and
which commands them to have only one heart in common ! Eve is revived for me—an Eve who will not have
a thought that is not mine, and whose life hangs by the
thread which I hold. It is too much, my God ! for a
creature to possess ! I sink under the weight of thy
gift ! "

And he fell upon his knees, gazing with adoration upon
the gentle beauty, who smiled on him as no earthly creature can smile.

" Oh, no ! " he continued, " no, you shall never leave
me more ! I shall live in all safety under your look, which
can pierce into the future. You will assist me in those
laborious researches which you alone, as you have said,
can complete, and which one word from you will render
easy and successful. You will point me out, since I cannot make gold—gold being a homogeneous substance, a
primitive element—you will point me out in what corner
of the world the Creator has concealed it ; you will tell
me where the rich treasures lie which have been swallowed
up in the vast depths of the ocean. With your eyes I
shall see the pearl grow in the veined shell, and man's
thoughts spring up under their gross earthly covering.
With your ears I shall hear the dull sound of the worm
beneath the ground, and the footsteps of my enemy as he
approaches ! "

And Lorenza still smiled upon him ; and as she smiled
she replied to his words by affectionate caresses.

" And yet," whispered she, as if she could see each
thought which whirled through his restless brain, " and
yet you doubt still, Acharat, as you have said, if I can
cross the circle of our love—you doubt if I can see into
the distance ; but you console yourself by thinking that
if I cannot see, she can."

" She ! who ? "

" The fair-haired beauty. Shall I tell you her name ? "

" Yes."

" Stay—Andrée."

" Ah, yes ! You can read my thoughts. Yet a last expiring fear still troubles me. Can you still see through space, though material obstacles intervene ? "

" Try me."

" Give me your hand, Lorenza. "

The young girl passionately seized Balsamo's hand.

" Can you follow me ? "

" Anywhere."

" Come."

And Balsamo, leaving in thought the Rue St. Claude, drew Lorenza's thoughts along with him.

" Where are we ? " asked he.

" We are upon a hill," replied the young Italian.

" Yes, you are right," said Balsamo, trembling with delight ; " but what do you see ? "

" Before me—to the right or to the left ? "

" Before you."

" I see a long alley with a wood on one side, a town on the other, and a river which separates them, and loses itself in the horizon, after flowing under the walls of a large château."

" That is right, Lorenza. The forest is that of Vesinet ; the town St. Germain ; the château is the Château de Maisons. Let us enter the pavilion behind us. What do you see there ? "

" Ah ! in the first place, in the antechamber, a little negro fantastically dressed, and employed in eating sugar-plums."

" Yes, Zamore ; proceed, proceed ! "

" An empty salon, splendidly furnished. The spaces above the doors painted with goddesses and cupids."

" The salon is empty, you say ? "

" Yes."

" Let us go still further."

" Ah ! we are in a splendid boudoir, lined with blue satin embroidered with flowers of natural colors."

" Is that empty also ? "

" No ; a lady is reclining upon a sofa."

"What lady ? Do you not remember to have seen her before ? "

"Yes ; it is the Countess Dubarry."

"Right, Lorenza ! I shall go frantic with delight. What does the lady do ? "

"She is thinking of you, Balsamo."

"Of me ? "

"Yes."

"Then you can read her thoughts ? "

"Yes ; for I repeat, she is thinking of you."

"For what purpose ? "

"You have made her a promise."

"Yes."

"You promised her that water of beauty which Venus, to revenge herself on Sappho, gave to Phaon."

"Yes, yes ! you are right again ! And what does she do while thinking ? "

"She comes to a decision."

"What decision ? "

"She reaches out her hand toward the bell ; she rings ; another young lady enters."

"Dark or light-haired ? "

"Dark."

"Tall or short ? "

"Little."

"Her sister. Listen to what she says to her."

"She orders the horses to be put to her carriage."

"Where does she wish to go ? "

"To come here."

"Are you sure ? "

"She is giving the order. Stay—she is obeyed. I see the horses and the carriage. In two hours she will be here."

Balsamo fell upon his knees.

"Oh ! " exclaimed he, "if in two hours she should really be here, I shall have nothing left to ask for on earth ! "

"My poor Balsamo ! then you still feared ? "

"Yes, yes ! "

"And why did you fear ? Love, which completes the material existence, increases also our mental powers. Love, like every generous emotion, brings us nearer to God, and all wisdom comes from God.

"Lorenza ! Lorenza ! you will drive me mad with joy."

Balsamo now only waited for another proof to be completely happy. This proof was the arrival of Mme. Dubarry.

The two hours of suspense were short. All measures of time had completely ceased for Balsamo.

Suddenly the young girl started and took Balsamo's hand.

"You are doubting yet," said she, " or you wish to know where she is at this moment."

"Yes," said Balsamo, " you are right."

"Well," replied Lorenza, " she is thundering along the boulevards at the full speed of her horses ; she approaches ; she turns into the Rue St. Claude ; she stops before the door and knocks."

The apartment in which they were, was so retired and quiet, that the noise of the iron knocker could not penetrate its recesses. But Balsamo, raised upon one knee, was anxiously listening.

At this moment two knocks, struck by Fritz, made him bound to his feet, for the reader will remember that two knocks were the signal of an important visit.

"Oh !" said he, " then it is true !"

"Go and convince yourself, Balsamo ; but return quickly."

Balsamo advanced toward the fireplace.

"Let me accompany you," said Lorenza, " as far as the door of the staircase."

"Come !"

And they both passed together into the chamber of furs.

"You will not leave this room ?"

"No ; I will await you here. Oh ! do not fear ; you know the Lorenza who loves you is not the Lorenza whom you fear. Besides——" She stopped and smiled.

" What ? " asked Balsamo.

" Can you not read in my soul as I read yours ? "

" Alas ! no."

" Besides, you can command me to sleep until you return. Command me to remain immovable upon this sofa, and I shall sleep and be motionless."

" Well, my Lorenza, it shall be so. Sleep and await my return here."

Lorenza, already struggling with sleep, fell back upon the sofa, murmuring :

" You will return soon, my Balsamo, will you not ? "

Balsamo waved his hand. Lorenza was already asleep. But, so beautiful, so pure—with her long flowing hair, the feverish glow upon her cheeks, her half-opened and swimming eyes—so little like a mortal, that Balsamo turned again, took her hand and kissed it, but dared not kiss her lips.

Two knocks were heard a second time. The lady was becoming impatient, or Fritz feared that his master had not heard him. Balsamo hastened to the door, but as he closed it behind him, he fancied he heard a second creaking noise like the former one. He opened the door again, looked round, and saw nothing but Lorenza sleeping, and her breast heaving beneath the magnetic sleep.

Balsamo closed the door and hastened toward the salon, without uneasiness, without fear, without foreboding—all heaven in his heart. But he was mistaken ; it was not sleep alone which oppressed Lorenza's bosom and made her breathe so heavily. It was a kind of dream which seemed to belong to the lethargy in which she was plunged —a lethargy which nearly resembled death.

Lorenza dreamed, and in the hideous mirror of her gloomy dreams she fancied she saw through the darkness which commenced to close around her, the oaken ceiling open, and something like a large circular platform descend slowly with a regular, slow, measured movement, accompanied by a disagreeable hissing noise. It seemed to her as if she breathed with difficulty, as if she were almost suffocated by the pressure of this moving circle.

It seemed to her as if upon this moving trap something moved—some misshapen being like Caliban in the "Tempest"—a monster with a human face—an old man whose eyes and arms alone were living, and who looked at her with his frightful eyes, and stretched his fleshless arms toward her.

And she—she, poor child—she writhed in vain without power to escape, without dreaming of the danger which threatened her. She felt nothing but the grasp of two living flesh-hooks seizing upon her white dress, lifting her from her sofa and placing her upon the trap, which reascended slowly toward the ceiling, with the grating noise of iron scraping against iron, and amid a hideous mocking laugh from the monster with the human face who was raising her aloft without shock and without pain.

CHAPTER LXII.

THE PHILTER.

As Lorenza had foretold, it was Mme. Dubarry who had just knocked at the gate.

The beautiful countess had been ushered into the salon. While awaiting Balsamo's arrival, she was looking over that curious Book of Death engraved at Mayence, the plates of which, designed with marvelous skill, show death presiding over all the acts of man's life, waiting for him at the door of the ballroom after he had pressed the hand of the woman he loves, dragging him to the bottom of the water in which he is bathing, or hiding in the barrel of a gun he carries to the chase. Mme. Dubarry was at the plate which represents a beautiful woman daubing her face with rouge and looking at herself in the glass, when Balsamo opened the door and bowed to her, with the smile of happiness still beaming upon his face.

"Excuse me, madame, for having made you wait; but I had not well calculated the distance, or was ignorant of the speed of your horses. I thought you still at the Place Louis XV."

" What do you mean ? " asked the countess. " You knew I was coming, then ? "

" Yes, madame ; it is about two hours ago since I saw you in your boudoir lined with blue satin, giving orders for your horses to be put to the carriage."

" And you say I was in my blue satin boudoir ? "

" Embroidered with flowers colored after nature. Yes, countess, you were reclining upon a sofa ; a pleasing thought passed through your mind ; you said to yourself : ' I will go and visit the Count de Fenix,' then you rang the bell."

" And who entered ? "

" Your sister, countess—am I right ? You requested her to transmit your orders, which were instantly executed."

" Truly, count, you are a sorcerer. You really alarm me."

" Oh ! have no fear, countess ; my sorcery is very harmless."

" And you saw that I was thinking of you ? "

" Yes ; and even that you thought of me with benevolent intentions."

" Ah ! you are right, my dear count ; I have the best possible intentions towards you, but confess that you deserve more than intentions—you, who are so kind and so useful, and who seemed destined to play in my life the part of tutor, which is the most difficult part I know."

" In truth, madame, you make me very happy. Then I have been of use to you ? "

" What ! you are a sorcerer, and cannot guess ? "

" Allow me, at least, the merit of being modest."

" As you please, my dear count ; then I will first speak of what I have done for you."

" I cannot permit it, madame ; on the contrary, speak of yourself, I beseech you."

" Well, my dear count, in the first place give me that talisman which renders one invisible ; for on my journey here, rapid as it was, I fancied I recognized one of Monsieur de Richelieu's grays."

" And this gray ? "

" Followed my carriage, carrying on his back a courier."

" What do you think of this circumstance, and for what purpose could the duke have caused you to be followed ? "

" With the intention of playing me some scurvy trick. Modest as you are, my dear Count de Fenix, you must be aware that nature has gifted you with personal advantages enough to make a king jealous of my visits to you or of yours to me."

" Monsieur de Richelieu cannot be dangerous to you in any way, madame," replied Balsamo.

" But he was so, my dear count ; he was dangerous before this last event."

Balsamo comprehended that there was a secret concealed beneath the words which Lorenza had not yet revealed to him. He did not therefore venture on the unknown ground, and replied merely by a smile.

" He was, indeed," repeated the countess ; " and I was nearly falling a victim to a most skilfully constructed plot—a plot in which you also had some share, count."

" I engaged in a plot against you ? Never, madame ! "

" Was it not you who gave the Duke de Richelieu the philter ? "

" What philter ? "

" A draught which causes the most ardent love."

" No, madame ; Monsieur de Richelieu composes those draughts himself, for he has long known the recipe ; I merely gave him a simple narcotic."

" Ah ! indeed ? "

" Upon my honor ! "

" And on what day did Monsieur de Richelieu ask for this narcotic ? Remember the date, count ; it is of importance."

" Madame, it was last Saturday—the day previous to that on which I had the honor of sending you, through Fritz, the note requesting you to meet me at Monsieur de Sartines'."

"The eve of that day!" exclaimed the countess. "The eve of the day on which the king was seen going to the little Trianon? Oh! now everything is explained."

"Then, if all is explained, you see I only gave the narcotic."

"Yes, the narcotic saved us all."

This time Balsamo waited; he was profoundly ignorant of the subject.

"I am delighted, madame," replied he, "to have been useful to you, even unintentionally."

"Oh! you are always kindness itself. But you can do more for me than you have ever yet done. Oh! doctor! I have been very ill, poetically speaking, and even now I can scarcely yet believe in my recovery."

"Madame," said Balsamo, "the doctor, since there is a doctor in the case, always requires the details of the illness he is to cure. Will you give me the exact particulars of what you have experienced?—and, if possible, do not forget a single symptom."

"Nothing can be more simple, my dear doctor, or dear sorcerer—whichever you prefer. The eve of the day on which this narcotic was used, his majesty refused to accompany me to Luciennes. He remained like a deceiver, as he is, at Trianon, pretending fatigue, and yet, as I have since learned, he supped at Trianon with the Duke de Richelieu and the Baron de Taverney."

"Ha!"

"Now you understand. At supper the love-draught was given to the king."

"Well, what happened?"

"Oh! that is difficult to discover. The king was seen going in the direction of the offices of Trianon, and all I can tell you is, that his majesty returned to Trianon through a fearful storm, pale, trembling, and feverish—almost on the verge of delirium."

"And you think," said Balsamo, smiling, "that it was not the storm alone which alarmed his majesty?"

"No, for the valet heard him cry several times: 'Dead, dead, dead!'"

" Oh ! " said Balsamo.

" It was the narcotic," continued Mme. Dubarry.
" Nothing alarms the king so much as death, and next to
death its semblance. He had found Mademoiselle de Taverney sleeping a strange sleep, and must have thought her
dead."

" Yes, yes; dead indeed," said Balsamo, who remembered having fled without awakening Andrée ; " dead or
at least presenting all the appearance of death. Yes, yes
—it must be so. Well, madame, and what then ? "

" No one knows what happened during the night. The
king, on his return, was attacked by a violent fever and a
nervous trembling, which did not leave him until the
morning, when it occurred to the dauphiness to open the
shutters and show his majesty a lovely morning, with the
sun shining upon merry faces. Then all these unknown
visions disappeared with the night, which had produced
them. At noon the king was better, took some broth,
and ate a partridge's wing ; and in the evening——"

" And in the evening ? " repeated Balsamo.

" In the evening," continued Mme. Dubarry, " his
majesty, who no doubt would not stay at Trianon after his
fright, came to see me at Luciennes."

The triumphant countenance and graceful but roguish
look of the countess reassured Balsamo as to the power the
favorite yet exercised over the king.

" Then you are satisfied with me, madame ? " inquired
he.

" Delighted, count ! and when you spoke of impossibilities you could create, you told the exact truth."

And in token of thanks she gave him her soft, white,
perfumed hand, which was not fresh as Lorenza's, but
almost as beautiful.

" And now, count, let us speak of yourself."

Balsamo bowed like a man ready to listen.

" If you have preserved me from a great danger," continued Mme. Dubarry, " I think I have also saved you from
no inconsiderable peril."

" Me⌡ " said Balsamo, concealing his emotion. " I do

not require that to feel grateful to you ; but yet, be good enough to inform me in what——"

" Yes. The coffer question——"

" Well, madame ? "

" Contained a multitude of secret ciphers, which Monsieur de Sartines caused all his clerks to translate. All signed their several translations, executed apart, and all gave the same result. In consequence of this, Monsieur, de Sartines arrived at Versailles this morning while I was there, bringing with him all these translations and the dictionary of diplomatic ciphers."

" Ha ! and what did the king say ? "

" The king seemed surprised at first, then alarmed. His majesty easily listens to those who speak to him of danger. Since the stab of Damien's penknife, there are two words which are ever eagerly hearkened to by Louis XV. ; they are : ' Take care ! ' "

" Then Monsieur de Sartines accused me of plotting ? "

" At first Monsieur de Sartines endeavored to make me leave the room ; but I refused, declaring that as no one was more attached to his majesty than myself, no one had a right to make me leave him when danger was in question. Monsieur de Sartines insisted, but I resisted, and the king, looking at me in a manner I know well, said :

" ' Let her remain, Sartines ; I can refuse her nothing to-day.'

" Then you understand, count, that as I was present, Monsieur de Sartines, remembering our adieu, so clearly expressed, feared to displease me by attacking you. He therefore spoke of the evil designs of the King of Prussia toward France ; of the disposition prevalent to facilitate the march of rebellion by supernatural means. In a word, he accused a great many people, proving always by the papers he held that these persons were guilty."

" Guilty of what ? "

" Of what ! Count, dare I disclose secrets of state ? "

" Which are our secrets, madame. Oh ! you risk nothing. I think it is my interest not to speak."

" Yes, count, I know that Monsieur de Sartines wished to prove that a numerous and powerful sect, composed of bold, skilful, resolute agents, were silently undermining the repect due to the king, by spreading certain reports concerning his majesty."

" What rumors ? "

" Saying, for instance, that his majesty was accused of starving his people."

" To which the king replied——"

" As the king always replied, by a joke."

Balsamo breathed again.

" And what was the joke ? " he asked.

" ' Since I am accused of starving the people,' said he, ' there is only one reply to make to the accusation—let us feed them.'

" ' How so, sire ? ' said Monsieur de Sartines.

" ' I will take the charge of feeding all those who spread this report and moreover, will give them safe lodging in my château of the Bastile.' "

A slight shudder passed through Balsamo's limbs, but he retained his smiling countenance.

" What followed ? " asked he.

" Then the king seemed to consult me by a smile. ' Sire,' said I, ' I can never believe that those little black characters which Monsieur de Sartines has brought to you mean that you are a bad king.'

" Then the lieutenant of the police exclaimed loudly.

" ' Any more,' I added, ' than they prove that our clerks can read.' "

" And what did the king say, countess ? " asked Balsamo.

" That I might be right, but that Monsieur de Sartines was not wrong."

" Well, and then ? "

" Then a great many lettres-de-cachet were made out, and I saw that Monsieur de Sartines tried to slip among them one for you. But I stood firm, and arrested him by a single word.

" ' Sir,' I said, aloud, and before the king, ' arrest all

Paris, if you like—that is your business, but you had better reflect a little before you lay a finger on one of my friends —if not——'

" ' Oh, ho ! ' said the king, ' she is getting angry ; take care, Sartines.'

" ' But, sire, the interest of the kingdom——'

" ' Oh ! you are not a Tully,' said I, crimson with rage, ' and I am not a Gabrielle.'

" ' Madame, they intend to assassinate the king, as Henri IV. was assassinated.'

" For the first time the king turned pale, trembled, and put his hand on his head.

" I feared I was vanquished.

" ' Sire,' said I, ' you must let Monsieur de Sartines have his own way ; for his clerks have, no doubt, read in these ciphers that I also am conspiring against you.'

" And I left the room.

"But, dame ! my dear count, the king preferred my company to that of Monsieur de Sartines, and ran after me.

" ' Ah ! for pity's sake, my dear countess,' said he, ' pray do not get angry.'

" ' Then send away that horrid man, sire ; he smells of dungeons.'

" ' Go, Sartines—be off with you ! ' said the king, shrugging his shoulders.

" ' And, for the future, I forbid you not only to visit me, but even to bow to me,' added I.

" At this blow our magistrate became alarmed ; he approached me, and humbly kissed my hand.

" ' Well,' said he, ' so be it ; let us speak no more of it, fair lady, but you will ruin the state. Since you absolutely insist upon it, your protégé shall be respected by my agents.' "

Balsamo seemed plunged in a deep reverie.

" Well," said the countess, " so you do not even thank me for having saved you from the pleasure of lodgings in the Bastile, which, perhaps, might have been unjust, but assuredly no less disagreeable on that account."

Balsamo made no reply. He drew a small vial, filled with a fluid red as blood, from his pocket.

"Hold, madame!" said he; "for the liberty you have procured for me, I give you twenty years of additional youth."

The countess slipped the vial into her bosom, and took her leave joyous and triumphant.

Balsamo still remained thinking.

"They might perhaps have been saved," said he, "but for the coquetry of a woman. This courtezan's little foot dashes them down into the depths of the abyss. Decidedly, God is with us!"

CHAPTER LXIII.

BLOOD.

THE door had no sooner closed upon Mme. Dubarry than Balsamo ascended the secret staircase and entered the chamber of furs. This conversation with the countess had been long, and his impatience had two causes.

The first was the desire to see Lorenza; the second, the fear that she might be fatigued; for in the new life he had given her there was no room for weariness of mind; she might be fatigued, inasmuch as she might pass, as she sometimes did, from the magnetic sleep to ecstasy; and to this ecstatic state always succeeded those nervous crises which prostrated Lorenza's strength, if the intervention of the restoring fluid did not restore the necessary equilibrium between the various functions of her being.

Balsamo, therefore, having entered and closed the door, immediately glanced at the couch where he had left Lorenza.

She was no longer there.

Only the fine shawl of cashmere embroidered with golden flowers, which had enveloped her like a scarf, was still lying upon the cushions, as an evidence that she had been in the room, and had been reclining on them.

Balsamo stood motionless, gazing at the empty sofa.

Perhaps Lorenza had felt herself incommoded by a strange odor which seemed to have filled the room since he left it ; perhaps, by a mechanical movement, she had usurped some of the functions of actual life, and instinctively changed her place.

Balsamo's first idea was that Lorenza had returned to the laboratory, whither she had accompanied him a short time previously.

He entered the laboratory.   At the first glance it seemed empty ; but in the shadow of the gigantic furnace, or behind the Oriental tapestry, a woman could easily conceal herself.

He raised the tapestry, therefore—he made the circuit of the furnace—nowhere could he discover even a trace of Lorenza.

There remained only the young girl's chamber, to which she had, no doubt, returned ; for this chamber was a prison to her only in her waking state.

He hastened to the chamber and found the secret door closed.   This was no proof that Lorenza had not entered. Nothing was more probable, in fact, than that Lorenza, in her lucid sleep, had remembered the mechanism, and remembering it, had obeyed the hallucination of a dream barely effaced from her mind.   Balsamo pressed the spring.

The chamber was empty like the laboratory ; it did not appear as if Lorenza had even entered it.

Then a heartrending thought—a thought which, it will be remembered, had already stung his heart—chased away all the suppositions, all the hopes of the happy lover.

Lorenza had been playing a part ; she must have feigned to sleep in order to banish all distrust, all uneasiness, all watchfulness from her husband's mind ; and at the first opportunity had fled again, this time with surer precautions, warned as she had been by a first, or rather by two former experiences.

At this idea Balsamo started up and rang for Fritz.

Then as Fritz, to his impatient mind, seemed to delay, he hastened to meet him and found him on the secret staircase.

"The signora ?" said he.

' Well, master ?" said Fritz, seeing by Balsamo's agitation that something extraordinary had taken place.

"Have you seen her ?"

"No, master."

"She has not gone ?"

"From where ?"

"From this house, to be sure !"

"No one has left the house but the countess, behind whom I have just closed the gate."

Balsamo rushed up the stairs again like a madman. Then he fancied that the giddy young creature, so different in her sleep from what she was when waking, had concealed herself in a moment of childish playfulness ; that from the corner where she was hid she was now reading his heart, and amusing herself by terrifying him, in order to reassure him afterward. Then he recommenced a minute search.

Not a nook was omitted, not a cupboard forgotten, not a screen left in its proper place. There was something in this search of Balsamo's like the frantic efforts of a man blinded by passion, alternating with the feeble and tottering gait of a drunkard. He could then only stretch out his arms and cry, " Lorenza ! Lorenza !" hoping that the adored creature would rush forth suddenly and throw herself into his arms with an exclamation of joy.

But silence alone, a gloomy and uninterrupted silence, replied to his extravagant thoughts and mad appeals.

In running wildly about, dashing aside the furniture, shouting to the naked walls, calling Lorenza, staring without seeing any object or forming a single coherent thought, Balsamo passed three minutes, that is to say, three centuries, of agony.

He recovered by degrees from this half-insane hallucination, dipped his hand in a vase of iced water, moistened his temples, and pressing one hand in the other, as if to force himself to be cool, he chased back, by his iron will, the blood which was beating wildly against his brain, with that fatal, incessant, monotonous movement which indicates life when there is merely motion and silence, but which is a sign of death or madness when it becomes tumultuous and perceptible.

"Come," said he, "let me reason : Lorenza is not here ; no more false pretenses with myself ; Lorenza is not here, she must be gone. Yes, gone, quite gone ! "

And he looked around once more, and once more shouted her name.

"Gone !" continued he ; "in vain Fritz asserts that he has not seen her. She is gone—gone !

"Two cases present themselves :

"Either he has not seen Lorenza, and after all, that is possible, for a man is liable to error, or he has seen her, and has been bribed by her.

"Fritz bribed !

"Why not ? In vain does his past fidelity plead against this supposition. If Lorenza, if love, if science—could so deeply deceive and lie, why should the frail nature of a fallible human being not deceive also ?

"Oh ! I will know all, I will know all ! Is there not Mademoiselle de Taverney left ? Yes, through Andrée I shall know if Fritz has betrayed me, if Lorenza is false ; and this time—oh ! this time, as love has proved false, as science has proved an error, as fidelity has become a snare —oh ! this time Balsamo will punish without pity, without sparing, like a strong man who revenges himself, who chases pity from his heart, and keeps only pride.

"Let me see : the first step is to leave this as quickly as possible, not to let Fritz suspect anything, and to fly to Trianon."

And Balsamo, seizing his hat, which had rolled on the ground, rushed toward the door.

But all at once he stopped.

"Oh !" said he, "before anything else (my God ! poor old man, I had forgotten him), I must see Althotas. During my delirium, during the spasm of forced and unnatural love, I have neglected the unfortunate old man, I have been ungrateful and inhuman ! "

And with the feverishness which now animated all his

movements, Balsamo approached the spring which put in motion the trap in the ceiling, and the movable scaffold quickly descended.

Balsamo placed himself upon it, and, aided by the counterpoise, mounted again—still overwhelmed by the anguish of his mind and heart, and without thinking of anything but Lorenza. Scarcely had he attained the level of the floor when the voice of Althotas struck upon his ear and roused him from his gloomy reverie.

But to Balsamo's great astonishment, the old man's first words were not reproaches, as he had expected · he was received with an outburst of simple and natural gayety.

The pupil looked with an astonished gaze upon his master.

The old man was reclining upon his spring chair. He breathed noisily and with delight, as if at each inspiration he added a day to his life ; his eyes, full of a gloomy fire, but the expression of which was enlivened by a smile upon his lips, were fixed eagerly upon his visitor.

Balsamo summoned up all his strength, and collected his ideas, in order to conceal his grief from his master, who had so little indulgence for human weaknesses.

During this moment of reflection, Balsamo felt a strange oppression weigh upon his breast. No doubt the air was vitiated by being too constantly breathed, for a heavy, dull, close, nauseous odor, like the one he had already felt below, but there in a slighter degree, floated in the air, and like the vapors which rise from lakes and marshes, in autumn at sunrise and sunset, had taken a shape and rested on the windows.

In this dense and acrid atmosphere, Balsamo's heart throbbed, his head felt confused, a vertigo seized upon him, and he felt that respiration and strength were fast failing him.

"Master," said he, seeking some object on which to support himself, and endeavoring to dilate his lungs, "master, you cannot live here ; there is no air."

"You think so ?"

"Oh !"

"Nevertheless, I breathe very well in it!" replied Althotas, gayly, "and I live, as you see."

"Master, master!" replied Balsamo, growing more and more giddy, "let me open a window; see! it rises from the floor like an exhalation of blood."

"Of blood! ah! you think so? Of blood?" cried Althotas, bursting into a laugh.

"Oh! yes; yes, I feel the miasma which is exhaled from a newly killed body. I could weigh it, so heavily does it press upon my brain and heart."

"That is it," said Althotas, with his sardonic laugh; "that is it. I also perceive it. You have a tender heart and a weak brain, Acharat."

"Master," said Balsamo, pointing with his finger at the old man, "master, you have blood upon your hands; master, there is blood upon this table; there is blood everywhere, even in your eyes, which shine like two torches; master, the smell which I breathe, and which makes me giddy, which is suffocating me, is the smell of blood!"

"Well, what then?" said Althotas, quickly; "is this the first time in your life that you have smelled it?"

"No."

"Have you never seen me make experiments? Have you never made any yourself?"

"But human blood!" said Balsamo, pressing his hand upon his burning forehead.

"Ah! you have a subtle sense of smell," said Althotas. "Well, I did not think human blood could be distinguished from that of any other animal."

"Human blood!" muttered Balsamo.

And as he reeled backward, and felt for some projecting point to support him, he perceived with horror a vast copper basin, the shining sides of which reflected the purple color of the freshly spilled blood.

The enormous vase was half filled.

Balsamo started back terrified.

"Oh, this blood!" exclaimed he; "whence comes this blood?"

Althotas made no reply, but his watchful glance lost

none of the feverish fluctuations and wild terror of Balsamo. Suddenly the latter uttered a fearful groan.

Then, stooping like some wild beast darting upon its prey, he rushed to a corner of the room, and picked up from the floor a silken ribbon embroidered with silver, to which was hanging a long tress of black hair.

After this wild, mournful, terrible cry, a death-like silence reigned for a moment in the old man's apartment. Balsamo slowly raised the ribbon, shuddered as he examined the tresses, which a golden pin fastened to the silk at one end, while, cut off sharply at the other, they seemed like a fringe, the extremity of which had been dipped in a wave of blood, the red and sparkling drops of which were still apparent on the margin.

In proportion as Balsamo raised his hand, it trembled still more.

"Whence does this come?" murmured he, in a hollow voice, loud enough, however, for another to hear and reply to his question.

"That?" asked Althotas.

"Yes, that."

"Well! it is a silken ribbon tying some hair."

"But the hair—in what is it steeped?"

"You can see—in blood."

"In what blood?"

"Parbleu! in the blood I wanted for my elixir—in the blood which you refused me, and which, therefore, I was forced to procure for myself."

"But this hair, these tresses, this ribbon—from whom did you take them? This is not a child's hair."

"And who told you it was a child I had killed?" asked Althotas, quietly.

"Did you not want the blood of a child for your elixir?" said Balsamo. "Did you not tell me so?"

"Or of an unmarried female, Acharat—or of an unmarried female."

Vnd Althotas stretched his long bony hand from the chair, and took a vial, the contents of which he tasted with delight.

Then, in his most natural tone, and with his most affectionate smile :

" I have to thank you, Acharat," said he ; " you were wise and far-sighted in placing that woman beneath my trap, almost within reach of my hand. Humanity has no cause for complaint. The law has nothing to lay hold upon. He ! he ! it was not you who gave me the young creature without whom I should have perished ! No ! I took her. He ! he ! thanks, my dear pupil ! thanks, my dear Acharat ! "

And he once more put the vial to his lips.

Balsamo let fall the tress of hair which he held ; a dreadful light flashed across his mind.

Opposite to him was the old man's table—a large marble slab always heaped with plants, books, and vials. This table was covered with a long cloth of white damask with dark flowers, on which the lamp of Althotas shed a reddish light, and which displayed an ominous outline which Balsamo had not before remarked.

He seized a corner of the cloth and hastily pulled it away.

But instantly his hair stood on end—his gaping mouth could not utter the horrible cry which almost suffocated him.

Under this shroud he had perceived Lorenza's corpse stretched upon this table, her face livid and yet smiling, and her head hanging backward as if dragged down by the weight of her long hair.

A large wound gaped underneath the collar-bone, from which not a single drop of blood escaped. Her hands were rigid, and her eyes closed beneath their purple eyelids.

" Yes, blood ! the last three drops of an unmarried woman's blood, that is what I wanted," said the old man, putting the vial to his lips for the third time.

" Wretch ! " thundered Balsamo, whose cry of despair at last burst from each pore, " die, then ! for she was my wife—my wedded wife ! You have murdered her in vain ! Die in your sin ! "

The eyes of Althotas quivered at these words, as if an electric shock had made them dance in their orbits ; his pupils were fearfully dilated, his toothless gums chattered, the vial fell from his hand upon the floor, and broke into a thousand pieces, while he—stupefied, annihilated, struck at once in heart and brain—fell back heavily upon his chair.

Balsamo bent with a sob over Lorenza's body, and pressing his lips to her blood-stained hair, sunk senseless on the ground.

CHAPTER LXIV.

DESPAIR.

THE Hours, those mysterious sisters who cleave the air hand in hand with a flight so slow for the wretched, so rapid for the happy, paused in their onward motion folding their heavy wings over this chamber loaded with sighs and groans.

Death on one side, agony on the other, and between them despair—grievous as agony, deep as death.

Balsamo had not uttered a word since the terrible cry which had been wrung from his breast.

Since the terrible revelation which had cast down the ferocious joy of Althotas, Balsamo had not moved.

As for the hideous old man, thus violently thrown back into life, such as God grants it to man, he seemed as much bewildered in this new element as the bird struck by a leaden bullet and fallen from the skies into a lake on whose surface it flutters, unable to employ its wings.

The horror expressed in his pale and agonized features revealed the immeasurable extent of his disappointment.

In fact, Althotas no longer even took the trouble to think, since he had seen the goal at which his spirit aimed, and which it thought firm as a rock, vanish like empty vapor.

His deep and silent despair seemed almost like insensibility. To a mind unaccustomed to measure his, it might have seemed an indication of reflection ; to Balsamo's, who, ever who, did not even look upon him, it marked the death-agony of power, of reason, and of life.

Althotas never took his eyes from the broken vial, the image of the nothingness of his hopes. One would have said he counted the thousand scattered fragments, which, in falling, had diminished his life by so many days. One would have said he wished to drink in with his look the precious fluid which was spilled upon the floor, and which, for a moment, he had believed to be immortality.

At times, also, as if the grief of this disenchantment was too poignant, the old man raised his dull eyes to Balsamo, then from Balsamo his glance wandered to Lorenza's corpse.

He resembled, at these moments, one of those savage animals which the huntsman finds in the morning caught in the trap by the leg, and which he stirs for a long time with his foot without making them turn their heads, but who, when he pricks them with his hunting-knife, or with the bayonet of his fowling-piece, obliquely raise their bloodshot eyes, throwing on him a look of hatred, vengeance, reproach, and surprise.

"Is it possible," said this look, so expressive even in its agony, "is it credible that so many misfortunes, so many shocks, should overwhelm me, caused by such an insignificant being as the man I see kneeling there a few yards from me, at the feet of such a vulgar object as that dead woman ? Is it not a reversion of nature, an overturning of science, a cataclysm of reason, that the gross student should have deceived the skilful master ? Is it not monstrous that the grain of sand should have arrested the wheel of the superb chariot, so rapid in its almost unlimited power, in its immortal flight ? "

As for Balsamo—stunned, heart-broken, without voice or motion, almost without life—no human thought had yet dawned amid the dark vapors of his brain.

Lorenza ! his Lorenza ! His wife, his idol, doubly precious to him as his revealing angel and his love—Lorenza, his delight and his glory, the present and the future, his strength and faith—Lorenza, all he loved, all he wished for, all he desired in this world—Lorenza was lost to him forever.

He did not weep, he did not groan, he did not even sigh.

He was scarcely surprised at the dreadful misfortune which had befallen him. He was like one of those poor wretches whom an inundation surprises in their bed, in the midst of darkness. They dream that the water gains upon them, they awake, they open their eyes and see a roaring billow breaking over their head, while they have not even time to utter a cry in their passage from life to death.

During three hours Balsamo felt himself buried in the deepest abyss of the tomb. In his overwhelming grief, he looked upon what had happened to him as one of the dark dreams which torment the dead in the eternal silent night of the sepulcher.

For him there no longer existed Althotas, and with him all hatred and revenge had vanished. For him there no longer existed Lorenza, and with her all life, all love had fled. All was sleep, night, nothingness! Thus the hours glided past, gloomily, silently, heavily, in this chamber where the blood congealed and the lifeless form grew rigid.

Suddenly amid the death-like silence a bell sounded thrice.

Fritz, doubtless, was aware that his master was with Althotas, for the bell sounded in the room itself.

But although it sounded three times with an insolently strange noise, the sound died away in space.

Balsamo did not raise his head.

In a few moments, the same tinkling, only louder this time, sounded again ; but, like the first, it could not arouse Balsamo from his torpor.

Then at a measured interval, but not so far from the second as it had been from the first, the angry bell a third time made the room resound with multiplied echoes of its wailing and impatient sounds.

Balsamo did not start, but slowly raised his head and interrogated the empty space before him with the cold solemnity of a corpse rising from the tomb.

The bell never ceased ringing.

At last his increasing energy awoke him to partial consciousness.

The unfortunate husband took his hand from the hand of the corpse. All the heat had left his body without passing into his lifeless bride's.

" Some important news or some great danger," muttered Balsamo to himself. " May it prove a great danger ! "

And he rose to his feet.

" But why should I reply to this summons ? " continued he, aloud, without heeding the gloomy sound of his words echoing beneath the somber vault of this funereal chamber ; " can anything in this world henceforth interest or alarm me ? "

Then, as if in reply, the bell struck its iron tongue so rudely against its brazen sides, that the clapper broke and fell upon a glass retort, which flew in pieces with a metallic sound, and scattered the fragments upon the floor.

Balsamo resisted no longer ; besides, it was important that none, not even Fritz, should come to seek him where he was.

He walked, therefore, with steady step to the spring, pressed it, and placed himself upon the trap, which descended slowly and deposited him in the chamber of furs.

As he passed the sofa, he brushed against the scarf which had fallen from Lorenza's shoulders when the pitiless old man, impassible as death itself, had carried her off in his arms.

This contact, more living seemingly than Lorenza herself, sent an icy shudder through Balsamo's veins. He took the scarf and kissed it, using it to stifle the cries which burst from his heaving breast.

Then he proceeded to open the door of the staircase.

On the topmost step stood Fritz, all pale and breathless, holding a torch in one hand, and in the other the cord of the bell, which, in his terror and impatience, he continued to pull convulsively. On seeing his master, he uttered a cry of satisfaction, followed by one of surprise and fear. But Balsamo, ignorant of the cause of this double cry, replied only by a mute interrogation.

Fritz did not speak, but he ventured—he, usually so respectful—to take his master's hand, and lead him to the large Venetian mirror that ornamented the mantelpiece, at the back of which was the passage into Lorenza's apartment.

" Oh, look ! your excellency," said he, showing him his own image in the glass.

Balsamo shuddered. Then a smile—one of those deathly smiles which spring from infinite and incurable grief,—flitted over his lips. He had understood the cause of Fritz's alarm.

Balsamo had grown twenty years older in an hour. There was no more brightness in his eyes, no more color in his cheeks ; an expression of dullness and stupefaction overspread his features ; a bloody foam fringed his lips ; a large spot of blood stained the whiteness of his cambric shirt.

Balsamo looked at himself in the glass for a moment without being able to recognize himself, then he determinedly fixed his eyes upon the strange person reflected in the mirror.

" Yes, Fritz," said he, " you are right."

Then remarking the anxious look of his faithful servant :

" But why did you call me ? " inquired he.

" Oh, master ! for them."

" For them ? "

" Yes."

" Whom do you mean by them ? "

" Excellency," whispered Fritz, putting his mouth close to his master's ear, " the *five masters.*"

Balsamo shuddered.

" All ? " asked he.

" Yes, all."

" And they are here ? "

" Here."

" Alone ? "

" No ; each has an armed servant waiting in the court-yard."

" They came together ? "

" Yes, master, together, and they were getting impatient, that is why I rang so many times and so violently."

Balsamo, without even concealing the spot of blood beneath the folds of his frill, without attempting to repair the disorder of his dress, began to descend the stairs, after having asked Fritz if his guests had installed themselves in the salon or in the large study.

" In the salon, excellency," replied Fritz, following his master.

Then, at the foot of the stairs, venturing to stop Balsamo, he asked :

" Has your excellency no orders to give me ? "

" None, Fritz."

" Excellency——" stammered Fritz.

" Well ? " asked Balsamo, with infinite gentleness.

" Will your excellency go unarmed ? "

" Unarmed ? Yes."

" Even without your sword ? "

" And why should I take my sword, Fritz ? "

" I do not know," said the faithful servant, casting down his eyes, " but I thought—I believed—I feared——"

" It is well, Fritz—you may go."

Fritz moved away a few steps in obedience to the order he had received, but returned.

" Did you not hear ? " asked Balsamo.

" Excellency, I merely wished to tell you that your double-barreled pistols are in the ebony case upon the gilt stand."

" Go, I tell you ! " replied Balsamo.

And he entered the salon.

CHAPTER LXV.

THE JUDGMENT.

FRITZ was quite right; Balsamo's guests had not entered the Rue St. Claude with a pacific display nor with a benevolent exterior.

Five horsemen escorted the traveling carriage in which the masters had come; five men, with a haughty and somber mien, armed to the teeth, had closed the outer gate and were guarding it while appearing to await their masters' return.

A coachman and two footmen on the carriage-seat concealed under their overcoats each a small hanger and a musket. It had much more the air of a warlike expedition than a peaceful visit, these people's appearance in the Rue St. Claude.

It was for this reason that the nocturnal invasion of these terrible men, the forcible taking possession of the hotel, had inspired the German with an unspeakable terror. He had at first attempted to refuse entrance to the whole party when he had seen the escort through the wicket, and had suspected them to be armed; but the all-powerful signals they had used—that irresistible testimony of the right of the newcomers—had left him no option. Scarcely were they master of the place, than the strangers, like skilful generals, posted themselves at each outlet of the house, taking no pains to dissemble their hostile intentions.

The pretended valets in the courtyard and in the passages, the pretended masters in the saloon, seemed to Fritz to bode no good; therefore he had broken the bell.

Balsamo, without displaying any astonishment, without making any preparation, entered the room, which Fritz had lighted up in honor of these, as it was his duty to do toward all guests who visited the house.

His five visitors were seated upon chairs around the room, but not one rose when he appeared.

He, as master of the house, having looked at them, bowed politely ; then only did they rise and gravely return his salute.

Balsamo took a chair in front of them, without noticing or seeming to notice the strange order of their position. In fact, the five armchairs formed a semicircle like to those of the ancient tribunals, with a president supported by two assessors, and with Balsamo's chair placed in front of that of the president, and occupying the place accorded to the accused in a council or pretorium.

Balsamo did not speak first, as in other circumstances he would have done ; he looked around without seeing any object clearly—still affected by a kind of painful drowsiness, which had remained after the shock.

"It seems, brother, that you have understood our errand," said the president, or rather he who occupied the center seat ; "yet you delayed to come, and we were already deliberating if we should send to see you."

"I do not understand your errand," said Balsamo, calmly.

"I should not have imagined so, from seeing you take the position and attitude of an accused before us."

"An accused ?" stammered Balsamo, vacantly, shrugging his shoulders. "I do not understand you."

"We will soon make you understand us. Not a difficult task, if I may believe your pale cheeks, your vacant eyes, and trembling voice. One would think you did not hear."

"Oh, yes, I hear," replied Balsamo, shaking his head, as if to banish the thoughts which oppressed it.

"Do you remember, brother," continued the president, "that in its last communication, the superior committee warned you against a treasonable attempt meditated by one of the great ones of the order ?"

"Perhaps so—yes—I do not deny it."

"You reply as a disordered and troubled conscience might be expected to do ; but rouse yourself—be not cast down—reply with that clearness and precision which your terrible position requires. Reply to my questions with the certainty that we are open to conviction, for we have neither

prejudice nor hatred in this matter. We are the law ; it
does not pronounce a verdict until the evidence is heard."

Balsamo made no reply.

"I repeat it, Balsamo, and my warning once given, let
it be to you like the warning which combatants give to each
other before commencing their struggle. I will attack you
with just but powerful weapons ; defend yourself ! "

The assistants, seeing Balsamo's indifference and imper-
turbable demeanor, looked at one another with astonishment, and then again turned their eyes upon the president.

" You have heard me, Balsamo, have you not ? " repeated
the latter.

Balsamo made a sign of the head in the affirmative.

" Like a well-meaning and loyal brother, I have warned
you, and given you a hint of the aim of my questionings.
You are warned, guard yourself ; I am about to commence
again.

" After this announcement," continued the president,
" the association appointed five of its members to watch in
Paris the proceedings of a man who was pointed out to us
as a traitor.   Now, our revelations are not subject to error.
We gather them, as you yourself know, either from devoted
agents, from the aspect of events, or from infallible symptoms and signs among the mysterious combinations which
nature has as yet revealed to us alone.   Now one of us had a
vision respecting you ; we know that he has never been
deceived ; we were upon our guard, and watched you."

Balsamo listened without giving the least sign of
impatience or even of intelligence.   The president continued :

" It was not an easy task to watch a man such as you.
You enter everywhere ; your mission is to have a footing
wherever your enemies have a residence or any power whatever.   You have at your disposal all your natural resources
—which are immense—and which the association intrusts
to you to make its cause triumphant.   For a long time we
hovered in a sea of doubt when we saw enemies visit you,
such as Richelieu, a Dubarry, a Rohan.   Moreover, at the
last assembly in the Rue Plastriere you made a long speech

full of clever paradoxes, which led us to imagine that you were playing a part in flattering and associating with this incorrigible race, which it is our duty to exterminate from the face of the earth. For a long time we respected the mystery of your behavior, hoping for a happy result ; but at last the illusion was dispelled."

Balsamo never stirred, and his features were fixed and motionless, insomuch that the president became impatient.

" Three days ago," said he, " five lettres-de-cachet were issued. They had been demanded from the king by Monsieur de Sartines ; they were filled as soon as signed, and the same day were presented to five of our principal agents, our most faithful and devoted brothers residing in Paris. All five were arrested ; two were taken to the Bastille, where they are kept in the most profound secrecy ; two are at Vincennes, in the oubliette ; one in the most noisome cell in Bicêtre. Did you know this circumstance ? "

" No," said Balsamo.

" That is strange after what we know of your relations with the lofty ones of the kingdom. But there is something stranger still."

Balsamo listened.

" To enable Monsieur Sartines to arrest these five faithful friends he must have had the only paper which contains the names of the victims in his possession. This paper was sent to you by the Supreme Council in 1769, and to you it was assigned to receive the new members and immediately invest them with the rank which the Supreme Council assigned them."

Balsamo expressed by a gesture that he did not recollect the circumstance.

" I shall assist your memory. The five persons in question were represented by five Arabic characters ; and these characters, in the paper you received, corresponded with the names and initials of the new brothers."

" Be it so," said Balsamo.

" You acknowledge it ? "

" I acknowledge whatever you please."

The president looked at his assessors, as if to order them to take a note of this confession.

"Well," continued he, "on this paper—the only one, remember, which could have compromised the brothers—there was a sixth name. Do you remember it?"

Balsamo made no reply.

"The name was—the Count de Fenix."

"Agreed," said Balsamo.

"Then why—if the name of the five brothers figured in five lettres-de-cachet—why was yours respected, caressed, and favorably received at court and in the antechambers of ministers? If our brothers merited prison, you merited it also. What have you to reply?"

"Nothing."

"Ah! I can guess by your objection. You may say that the police had by private means discovered the names of the obscure brethren, but that it was obliged to respect yours as an ambassador and a powerful man. You may even say that they did not suspect this name."

"I shall say nothing."

"Your pride outlives your honor. These names the police could only have discovered by reading the confidential note which the Supreme Council had sent you; and this is the way it was seen. You kept it in a coffer. Is that true?"

"It is."

"One day a woman left your house carrying the coffer under her arm. She was seen by our agents and followed to the hotel of the lieutenant of police in the Faubourg St. Germain. We might have arrested the evil at it source; for if we had stopped the woman and taken the coffer from her, everything would have been safe and sure. But we obeyed the rules of our constitution, which command us to respect the secret means by which some members serve the cause, even when these means have the appearance of treason or imprudence."

Balsamo seemed to approve of this assertion, but with a gesture so little marked that had it not been for his previous immobility it would have been unnoticed.

"This woman reached the lieutenant of police," said the president; "she gave him the coffer; and all was discovered. Is this true?"

"Perfectly true."

The president rose.

"Who was this woman?" he exclaimed; "beautiful, impassioned, devotedly attached to you body and soul, tenderly loved by you—as spiritual, as subtle—as cunning as one of the angels of darkness who assist men to commit evil! Lorenza Feliciani is the woman, Balsamo!"

Balsamo uttered a groan of despair.

"You are convicted," said the president.

"Have it so," replied Balsamo.

"I have not yet finished. A quarter of an hour after she had entered the hotel of the lieutenant of police, you arrived. She had sown the treason—you came to reap the reward. The obedient servant had taken upon herself the perpetration of the crime—you came to add the finishing stroke to the infamous work. Lorenza departed alone. You renounced her, doubtless, and would not compromise yourself by accompanying her; you left triumphantly along with Madame Dubarry, summoned there to receive from your own lips the information you sold her. You entered her carriage, as the boatman entered the boat with the sinner, Mary the Egyptian. You left behind the papers which ruined us with Monsieur de Sartines, but you brought away the coffer which might have ruined you with us. Fortunately we saw you—God's light is with us when we need it most."

Balsamo bowed without speaking.

"I now conclude," added the president. "Two criminals have been pointed out to the order: a woman, your accomplice, who may be innocent perhaps, but who, in point of fact, has injured our cause by revealing one of our secrets; and you, the master, the great Copht, the enlightened mind, who have had the cowardice to shelter yourself behind this woman, that your treason may be less clearly seen."

Balsamo raised his head, and fixed a look upon the commissioners, burning with all the rage which had smoldered in his breast since the commencement of the interrogation.

" Why do you accuse this woman ? " asked he.

" Ah ! we know that you will endeavor to defend her ; we know that you love her almost to idolatry. That you prefer her to everything in the world. We know that she is your treasure of science, of happiness, and of fortune, we know that she is more precious to you than all the world beside."

" You know all this ? " said Balsamo.

" Yes, we know it ; and we shall punish you through her more than through yourself."

" Finish ! "

The president rose.

" This is the sentence :

" Joseph Balsamo is a traitor—he has broken his oath ; but his knowledge is immense, and he is useful to the order. Balsamo must live for the cause he has betrayed. He belongs to his brothers, though he has cast them off."

" Ha ! " said Balsamo, gloomily, almost savagely.

" A perpetual prison will protect the association against any renewal of his treachery, at the same time that it will permit the brothers to gather the knowledge from him which it has a right to expect from all its members.

" As to Lorenza Feliciani, a terrible punishment——"

" Hold ! " said Balsamo, with perfect calmness in his voice, " you forget that I did not defend myself—the accused must be heard in his own justification. A word, a single proof, will suffice ; wait one moment and I will bring you the proof I have promised."

The commissaries seemed to deliberate for a moment.

" Ah ! you fear lest I should kill myself," said Balsamo, with a bitter smile. " If that had been my wish, it would have been already done. There is that in this ring which would kill you all five times over had I opened it. You fear I should escape ; let me be guarded if you wish it."

" Go ! " said the president.

Balsamo disappeared for about a moment. Then he was heard heavily descending the staircase. He entered bearing the cold, rigid, and discolored body of Lorenza upon his shoulder, her white hand hanging to the ground.

"Here is the woman I adored, who was my treasure, my only happiness, my life—the woman who, as you say, has betrayed you—here, take her ! God did not wait for you to punish, gentlemen !"

And with a movement quick as lightning, he let the corpse glide from his arms, and sent it rolling on the carpet to the feet of the judges, whom her cold hair and the dead and motionless hands touched, to their great horror, while by the light of the lamps they saw the wide gash gaping in the neck white as a swan's.

"Now pronounce the sentence !" added Balsamo.

The horrified judges uttered a cry, and, seized with maddening terror, fled in indescribable confusion. Soon their horses were heard neighing and trampling in the courtyard ; the outer gate grated on its hinges ; and then silence, the solemn silence of the tomb, returned to seat itself beside despair and death.

CHAPTER LXVI.

DOOM.

WHILE the terrible scene which we have just described was taking place between Balsamo and the five masters, nothing apparently had changed in the rest of the house. The old man had seen Balsamo enter his apartment and bear away Lorenza's corpse, and this new demonstration had recalled him to what was passing around him.

But when he saw Balsamo take up the dead body and descend with it into the lower rooms, he fancied it was the last and eternal adieu of this man whose heart he had broken, and fear descended on his soul with an overwhelming force, which, for him who had done all to avoid death, doubled the horror of the grave.

Not knowing for what purpose Balsamo left him, nor whither he was going, he began to call out :

"Acharat! Acharat!"

It was the name his pupil had borne in childhood, and he hoped it would have retained its influence over the man.

But Balsamo continued to descend.   Having touched the ground, he even forgot to make the trap reascend, and disappeared in the corridor.

"Ah!" cried Althotas, "see what man is—a blind, ungrateful animal! Return, Acharat, return! Ah! you prefer the ridiculous object called a woman to the perfection of humanity which I represent! You prefer a fragment of life to immortality!

"But no!" he exclaimed, after a moment's pause, "the wretch has deceived his master—he has betrayed my confidence like a vile robber—he feared that I should live because I surpass him so much in science—he wanted to inherit the laborious work I had nearly concluded--he laid a trap for me, his master and benefactor! Oh, Acharat!"

And gradually the old man's anger was aroused, his cheeks were dyed with a hectic tinge, his half-closed eyes seemed to glow with the gloomy brightness of those phosphorescent lights which sacrilegious children place in the cavities of a human skull.   Then he cried:

"Return, Acharat! return! look to yourself! You know that I have conjurations which evoke fire and raise up supernatural spirits! I have evoked Satan—him whom the magi called Phegor, in the mountains of Gad—and Satan was forced to leave his bottomless pit and appear before me! I have conferred with the seven angels who ministered to God's anger upon the same mountain where Moses received the ten commandments! By my will alone I have kindled the great tripod with its seven flames which Trajan stole from the Jews! Take care, Acharat, take care!"

But there was no reply.

Then his brain became more and more clouded.

"Do you not see, wretch, "said he, in a choking voice, "that death is about to seize me as it would the meanest mortal! Listen, Acharat! you may return; I will do you no harm ; return, I renounce the fire ; you need not fear the evil spirit, nor the seven avenging angels. I renounce vengeance, and yet I could strike you with such terror that you would become an idiot and cold as marble, for I can stop the circulation of the blood. Come back, then, Acharat ; I will do you no harm, but, on the contrary, I can do you much good. Acharat, instead of abandoning me, watch over my life, and you shall have all my treasures and all my secrets. Let me live, Acharat, that I may teach them to you. See ! see !"

And with gleaming eyes and trembling fingers he pointed to the numerous objects, papers, and rolls scattered through the vast apartments. Then he waited, collecting all his fast-failing faculties to listen.

"Ah ! you come not !" he cried ; " you think I shall die thus, and by this murder—for you are murdering me —everything will belong to you. Madman ! were you even capable of reading the manuscripts which I alone am able to decipher—were the spirit even to grant you my wisdom for a lifetime of one, two, or three centuries to make use of the materials I have gathered—you shall not inherit them ! No—no—a thousand times no ! Return, Acharat—return for a moment, were it only to behold the ruin of this whole house ; were it only to contemplate the beautiful spectacle I am preparing you ! Acharat ! Acharat ! Acharat !"

There was no answer, for Balsamo was during this time replying to the accusation of the five masters by showing them the mutilated body of Lorenza. The cries of the deserted old man grew louder and louder, despair redoubled his strength, and his hoarse yellings, reverberating in the long corridors, spread terror afar, like the roaring of a tiger who has broken his chain or forced the bars of his cage.

"Ah, you do not come !" shrieked Althotas ; " you despise me—you calculate upon my weakness. Well, you shall see ! Fire ! Fire ! Fire !"

He articulated these cries with such vehemence, that Balsamo, now freed from his terrified visitors, was roused

by them from the depth of his despair.   He took Lorenza's
corpse in his arms, reascended the staircase, laid the dead
body upon the sofa, where two hours previously it had reposed in sleep, and mounting upon the trap, he suddenly
appeared before Althotas.

"Ah ! at last !" cried the old man, with savage joy.
"You were afraid ! you saw I could revenge myself, and
you came.   You did well to come, for in another moment
I should have set this chamber on fire."

Balsamo looked at him, shrugged his shoulders slightly,
but did not deign to reply."

'I am athirst !" cried Althotas ; " I am athirst ! give
me drink, Acharat ! "

Balsamo made no reply.   He did not move ; he looked
at the dying man as if he would not lose an atom of his
agony.

"Do you hear me ? " howled Althotas, "do you hear
me ? "

The same silence, the same immobility on the part of
the gloomy spectator.

"Do you hear me, Acharat ? " vociferated the old man,
almost tearing his throat in his efforts to give emphasis to
this last burst of rage ; "water, give me water ! "

Althotas's features were rapidly decomposing.

There was no longer fire in his looks, but only an unearthly glare ; the blood no longer coursed beneath his
sunken and cadaverous cheek, motion and life were almost
dead within him.   His long, sinewy arms in which he had
carried Lorenza like a child, were raised, but inert and
powerless as the membranes of a polypus.   His fury had
worn out the feeble spark which despair had for a moment revived in him.

"Ah !" said he, "ah ! you think I do not die quickly
enough !   You mean to make me die of thirst !   You gloat
over my treasures and my manuscripts with longing eyes !
Ah ! you think you have them already ! wait—wait ! "

And with an expiring effort, Althotas took a small bottle from beneath the cushions of the armchair, and un-
corked it.   At the contact with the air, a liquid flame

burst from the glass vessel, and Althotas, like some potent magician, shook this flame around him.

Instantly the manuscripts piled round the old man's armchair, the books scattered over the room, the rolls of paper disinterred with so much trouble from the pyramids of Cheops and the subterranean depths of Herculaneum, took fire with the rapidity of gunpowder. A sheet of flame overspread the marble slab, and seemed to Balsamo's eyes like one of those flaming circles of hell of which Dante sings.

Althotas, no doubt, expected that Balsamo would rush amid the flames to save this valuable inheritance which the old man was annihilating along with himself ; but he was mistaken. Balsamo did not stir, but stood calm and isolated upon the trap-door, so that the fire could not reach him.

The flames wrapped Althotas in their embrace, but instead of terrifying him, it seemed as if the old man found himself once more in his proper element, and that, like the salamanders sculptured on our ancient castles, the fire caressed instead of consuming him.

Balsamo still stood gazing at him. The fire had reached the woodwork and completely surrounded the old man; it roared around the feet of the massive oaken chair on which he was seated ; and, what was most strange, though it was already consuming the lower part of his body, he did not seem to feel it.

On the contrary, at the contact with the seemingly purifying element, the dying man's muscles seemed gradually to distend, and an indescribable serenity overspread his features like a mask. Isolated from his body at this last hour, the old prophet, on his car of fire, seemed ready to wing his way aloft. The mind, all powerful in its last moments, forgot its attendant matter, and, sure of having nothing more to expect below, it stretched ardently upward to those higher spheres to which the fire seemed to bear it.

At this instant Althotas's eyes, which at the first reflection of the flames seemed to have been re-endowed with life, gazed vaguely and abstractedly at some point in space which was neither heaven nor earth. They looked as if they would pierce the horizon, calm and resigned, analyzing all sensation, listening to all pain, while, with his last breath on earth, the old magician muttered in a hollow voice his adieus to power, to life, and hope.

"Ah!" said he, "I die without regret; I have possessed everything on earth, and have known all; I have had all power which is granted to a human creature; I had almost reached immortality!"

Balsamo uttered a sardonic laugh whose gloomy echo arrested the old man's attention. Through the flames which surrounded him as with a veil he cast a look of savage majesty upon his pupil.

"You are right," said he; "one thing I had not fore-seen—God!"

Then, as if this mighty word had uprooted his whole soul, Althotas fell back upon his chair. He had given up to God the last breath which he had hoped to wrest from Him.

Balsamo heaved a sigh, and without endeavoring to save anything from the precious pile upon which this second Zoroaster had stretched himself to die, he again descended to Lorenza, and touched the spring of the trap which readjusted itself in the ceiling, veiling from his sight the immense furnace which roared like the crater of a volcano.

During the whole night the fire roared above Balsamo's head like a whirlwind, without his making an effort either to extinguish it or to fly. Stretched beside Lorenza's body he was insensible to all danger; but contrary to his expectations, when the fire had devoured all, and laid bare the vaulted walls of stone, annihilating all the valuable contents, it extinguished itself, and Balsamo heard its last howlings, which like those of Althotas, gradually died away in plaints and sighs.

*   *   *   *   *   *   *

[After the spirit-stirring scenes just narrated, in which the principal personages of the tale vanish from the stage, we have thought it better to hurry over the succeeding chapters, in which the book is brought to an end, merely giving the reader the following succinct account of their contents, as the effect of them when read at full length has been on ourselves, and we doubt not would be in the public, to detract from and weaken the interest which was wound up to so high a pitch by the preceding portion of the narrative.—EDITOR.]

From the death-like lethargy into which Andrée had been plunged by Balsamo's neglect to arouse her from the magnetic sleep, she at length recovered, but so utterly prostrate, both in mind and body, as to be wholly unfit for the performance of her duties at court. She therefore asked for and obtained from the dauphiness permission to retire into a convent, and the kindness of her royal mistress procured for her admission among the Carmelite Sisters of St. Denis, presided over by Mme. Louise of France, whom we have already met in these pages.

This, it may readily be imagined, gave a death-blow to the unrighteous hopes of the Baron de Taverney, her father, and to the noble aspirations of her brother Philip. Frowned upon by the king, and the scoff of the sycophantic courtiers, among the foremost of whom was his old friend, the Duke de Richelieu, Taverney—after a stormy interview with his son, whom he disowned and cast off to seek his fortunes where he best might—slunk back, despair and every evil passion boiling within his breast, to his patrimonial den, where, it is to be presumed, he found amid his misfortunes such consolation from his exalted philosophy as it was well calculated to afford.

Philip, heartbroken by his sister's sufferings and the malicious whispers of the corrupt court, decided upon sailing for America, at that time the land of promise for ardent admirers and followers of liberty. His example was imitated by Gilbert, who had now also nothing to detain him in France, where his high-flown and romantic hopes were forever blasted, and they both took shipping in the same vessel from Havre.

Of Balsamo little more is said, and that little does not

enlighten us as to his future fate. Weakened both in bodily health and in his influence over the secret brotherhood, he vegetated rather than lived in his mansion of the Rue St. Claude, to reappear, it is presumed, amid the stormy scenes of the French Revolution.

Having thus given a rapid *résumé* of the intermediate events, we come at once to the

EPILOGUE.

THE NINTH OF MAY.

On the ninth of May, 1774, at eight o'clock in the evening, Versailles presented a most curious and interesting spectacle.

From the first day of the month the king, Louis XV., attacked with a malady, the serious nature of which his physicians at first dared not confess to him, kept his couch, and now began anxiously to consult the countenances of those who surrounded him, to discover in them some reflection of the truth or some ray of hope.

The physician Bordeu had pronounced the king suffering from an attack of smallpox of the most malignant nature, and the physician La Martinière, who had agreed with his colleague as to the nature of the king's complaint, gave it as his opinion that his majesty should be informed of the real state of the case, "in order that, both spiritually and temporarily, as a king and as a Christian, he should take measures for his own safety and that of his kingdom."

"His most Christian majesty," said he, "should have extreme unction administered to him."

La Martinière represented the party of the dauphin—the opposition. Bordeu asserted that the bare mention of the serious nature of the disease would kill the king, and said that for his part he would not be a party to such regicide.

Bordeu represented Mme. Dubarry's party.

In fact, to call in the aid of the Church to the king was

to expel the favorite. When religion enters at one door, it is full time for Satan to make his exit by the other.

In the meantime, during all these intestine divisions of the faculty, of the royal family, and of the different parties of the court, the disease took quiet possession of the aged, corrupt, and worn-out frame of the king, and set up such a strong position that neither remedies nor prescriptions could dislodge it.

From the first symptoms of the attack, Louis beheld his couch surrounded by his two daughters, the favorite, and the courtiers whom he especially delighted to honor. They still laughed and stood firm by one another.

All at once the austere and ominous countenance of Mme. Louise of France appeared at Versailles. She had quitted her cell to give to her father, in her turn, the care and consolation he so much required.

She entered, pale and stern as a statue of Fate. She was no longer a daughter to a father, a sister to her fellow-sisters ; she rather resembled those ancient prophetesses who in the evil day of adversity poured in the startled ears of kings the boding cry, " Woe ! Woe ! Woe ! "

She fell upon Versailles like a thunder-shock at the very hour when it was Mme. Dubarry's custom to visit the king, who kissed her white hand and pressed them like some healing medicament to his aching brow and burning cheeks.

At her sight all fled. The sisters, trembling, sought refuge in a neighboring apartment. Mme. Dubarry bent the knee and hastened to those which she occupied ; the privileged courtiers retreated in disorder to the antechambers ; the two physicians alone remained standing by the fireside.

" My daughter ! " murmured the king, opening his eyes, heavy with pain and fever.

" Yes, sire," said the princess, "your daughter."

" And you come——"

" To remind you of God."

The king raised himself in an upright posture, and attempted to smile.

"For you have forgotten God," resumed Mme. Louise.
"I!"

"And I wish to recall Him to your thoughts."

"My daughter! I am not so near death, I trust, that
your exhortations need be so very urgent. My illness is
very slight—a slow fever attended with some inflammation."

"Your malady, sire," interrupted the princess, "is
that which, according to etiquette, should summon around
your majesty's couch all the great prelates of the kingdom. When a member of the royal family is attacked
with the smallpox, the rites of the Church should be administered without loss of time."

"Madame!" exclaimed the king, greatly agitated, and
becoming deathly pale, "what is that you say?"

"Madame!" broke in the terrified physicians.

"I repeat," continued the princess, "that your majesty
is attacked with the smallpox."

The king uttered a cry.

"The physicians did not tell me so," replied he.

"They had not the courage. But I look forward to
another kingdom for your majesty than the kingdom of
France. Draw near to God, sire, and solemnly review
your past life."

"The smallpox!" muttered Louis; "a fatal disease!
Bordeu! La Martinière! can it be true?"

The two practitioners hung their heads.

"Then I am lost!" said the king, more and more terrified.

"All diseases can be cured, sire," said Bordeu, taking
the initiative, "especially when the patient preserves his
composure of mind."

"God gives peace to the mind and health to the body,"
replied the princess.

"Madame!" said Bordeu, boldly, although in a low
voice, "you are killing the king!"

The princess deigned no reply. She approached the
sick monarch, and taking his hand, which she covered
with kisses:

" Break with the past, sire," said she, "and give an example to your people. No one warned you ; you ran the risk of perishing eternally. Promise solemnly to live a Christian life if you are spared—die like a Christian if God calls you hence ! "

As she concluded, she imprinted a second kiss on the royal hand, and with a slow step took her way through the antechambers. There she let her long black veil fall over her face, descended the staircase with a grave and majestic air, and entered her carriage, leaving behind her a stupefaction and terror which cannot be described.

The king could not rouse his spirits except by dint of questioning his physicians, who replied in terms of courtly flattery.

" I do not wish," said he, " that the scene of Metz with the Duchess de Chateauroux should be re-enacted here. Send for Madame d'Aiguillon and request her to take Madame Dubarry with her to Rueil."

This order was equivalent to an expulsion. Bordeu attempted to remonstrate, but the king ordered him to be silent. Bordeu, moreover, saw his colleague ready to report all that passed to the dauphin, and, well aware what would be the issue of the king's malady, he did not persist, but quitting the royal chamber, he proceeded to acquaint Mme. Dubarry with the blow which had just fallen on her fortunes.

The countess, terrified at the ominous and insulting expression which she saw already pictured on every face around her, hastened to withdraw. In an hour she was without the walls of Versailles, seated beside the Duchess d'Aiguillon, who, like a trustworthy and grateful friend, was taking the disgraced favorite to her château of Rueil, which had descended to her from the great Richelieu.

Bordeu, on his side, shut the door of the king's chamber against all the royal family, under pretext of contagion. Louis' apartment was thenceforward walled up ; no one might enter but Religion and Death.

The king had the last rites of the Church administered to him that same day, and this news soon spread through

Paris, where the disgrace of the favorite was already known, and circulated from mouth to mouth.

All the court hastened to pay their respects to the dauphin, who closed his doors and refused to see any one.

But the following day the king was better, and sent the Duke d'Aiguillon to carry his compliments to Mme. Dubarry. This day was the ninth of May, 1774.

The court deserted the pavilion occupied by the dauphin, and flocked in such crowds to Rueil, where the favorite was residing, that since the banishment of M. de Choiseul to Chanteloup such a string of carriages had never been witnessed.

Things were in this position, therefore : would the king live and Mme. Dubarry still remain queen ? or, would the king die, and Mme. Dubarry sink to the condition of an infamous and execrable courtesan ?

This was why Versailles, on the evening of the ninth of May, in the year 1774, presented such a curious and interesting spectacle.

On the Place d'Armes, before the palace, several groups had formed in front of the railing, who, with sympathetic air, seemed most anxious to hear the news.

They were citizens of Versailles or Paris, and every now and then, with all the politeness imaginable, they questioned the gardes-du-corps, who were pacing slowly up and down the Court of Honor with their hands behind their backs, respecting the king's health.

Gradually these groups dispersed. The inhabitants of Paris took their seats in the pataches or stage-coaches to return peaceably to their own homes, while those of Versailles, sure of having the earliest news from the fountainhead, also retired to their several dwellings.

No one was to be seen in the streets but the patrols of the watch, who performed their duty a little more quietly than usual, and that gigantic world called the Palace of Versailles became by degrees shrouded in darkness and silence, like that greater world which contained it.

At the angle of the street bordered with trees which extends in front of the palace, a man advanced in years

was seated on a stone bench overshadowed by the already
leafy boughs of the horse-chestnuts, with his expressive
and poetic features turned toward the château, leaning
with both hands on his cane, and supporting his chin on
his hands.

He was, nevertheless, an old man, bent by age and ill
health, but his eye still sparkled with something of its
youthful fire, and his thoughts glowed even more brightly
than his eyes.

He was absorbed in melancholy contemplation, and did
not perceive a second personage, who, after peeping curi-
ously through the iron railing, and questioning the gardes-
du-corps, crossed the esplanade in a diagonal direction,
and advanced straight toward the bench with the intention of seating himself upon it.

This personage was a young man with projecting cheek-
bones, low forehead, aquiline nose, slightly bent to one
side, and a sardonic smile.   While advancing toward the
stone bench he chuckled sneeringly, although alone,
seeming to reply by this manifestation to some secret
thought.

When within three paces of the bench, he perceived the
old man and paused, scanning him with his oblique and
stealthy glance, although evidently fearing to let his
purpose be seen.

" You are enjoying the fresh air, I presume, sir. ? "
said he, approaching him with an abrupt movement.

The old man raised his head.

" Ha ! " exclaimed the newcomer, " it is my illustrious
master ! "

" And you are my young practitioner ? " said the old
man.

" Will you permit me to take a seat beside you, sir ? "

" Most willingly."   And the old man made room on the
bench beside him.

" It appears that the king is doing better ? " said the
young man ; " the people rejoice."   And he burst a second
time into his sneering laugh.

The old man made no reply.

"The whole day long carriages have been rolling from Paris to Rueil, and from Rueil to Versailles. The Countess Dubarry will marry the king as soon as his health is re-established !" And he burst into a louder laugh than before.

Again the old man made no reply.

"Pardon me, if I laugh at fate," continued the young man, with a gesture of nervous impatience, "but every good Frenchman, look you, loves his king, and my king is better to-day."

"Do not jest thus on such a subject, sir," said the old man, gently. "The death of a man is always a misfortune for some one, and the death of a king is frequently a great misfortune for all."

"Even the death of Louis XV. ?" interrupted the young man, in a tone of irony. "Oh, my dear master, a distinguished philosopher like you, to sustain such a proposition ! I know all the energy and skill of your paradoxes, but I cannot compliment you on this one."

The old man shook his head.

"And, besides," added the newcomer, "why think of the king's death ? Who speaks of such an event ? The king has the smallpox. Well, we all know that complaint ; the king has beside him Bordeu and La Martinière, who are skilful men. Oh ! I will wager a trifle, my dear master, that Louis, the well-beloved, will escape his turn. Only this time the French people do not suffocate themselves in churches, putting up vows for him, as on the occasion of his former illness. Mark me ! everything grows antiquated and is abandoned."

"Silence !" said the old man, shuddering ; "silence ! for I tell you you are speaking of a man over whom at this moment the destroying angel of God hovers."

His young companion, surprised at this strange language, looked at the speaker, whose eyes had never quitted the façade of the château.

"Then you have more positive intelligence ?" inquired he.

"Look !" said the old man, pointing with his finger to

one of the windows of the palace, "what do you behold yonder?"

"A window lighted up; is that what you mean?"

"Yes; but lighted in what manner?"

"By a wax candle placed in a little lantern."

"Precisely."

"Well?"

"Well, young man, do you know what the flames of that wax-light represent?"

"No, sir."

"It represents the life of the king."

The young man looked more fixedly at his aged companion, as if to be certain that he was in his perfect senses.

"A friend of mine, Monsieur de Jussieu," continued the old man, "has placed that wax-light there, which will burn as long as the king is alive."

"It is a signal, then?"

"A signal which Louis XV.'s successor devours with his eyes from behind some neighboring curtain. The signal, which shall warn the ambitious of the dawn of a new reign, informs a poor philosopher like myself of the instant when the breath of the Almighty sweeps away at the same moment an age and a human existence."

The young man shuddered in his turn, and moved closer to his companion.

"Oh!" said the aged philosopher, "mark well this night, young man. Behold what clouds and tempests it bears in its murky bosom. The morning which will succeed it I shall witness, no doubt, for I am not old enough to abandon hope of seeing the morrow; but a reign will commence on that morrow which you will see to its close, and which contains mysteries which I cannot hope to be a spectator of. It is not, therefore, without interest that I watch yonder trembling flame, whose signification I have just explained to you."

"True, my master," murmured the young man, "most true."

"Louis XIV. reigned seventy-three years," continued the old man; "how many will Louis XVI. reign?"

"Ah !" exclaimed the younger of the two, pointing to the window, which had just become shrouded in darkness.

"The king is dead," said the old man, rising, with a sort of terror. And both kept silence for some minutes.

Suddenly a chariot, drawn by eight fiery horses, started at full gallop from the courtyard of the palace. Two outriders preceded it, each holding a torch in his hand.

In the chariot were the dauphin, Marie Antoinette, and Mme. Elizabeth, the sister of the king. The flames of the torches threw a gloomy light on their pale features. The carriage passed close to the two men, within ten paces of the bench from which they had risen.

"Long live King Louis XVI. ! Long live the queen !" shouted the young man, in a loud, harsh voice, as if he meant to insult this new-born majesty instead of saluting it.

The dauphin bowed, the queen showed her face at the window, sad and severe. The carriage dashed by and disappeared.

"My dear Monsieur Rousseau," said the younger of the two spectators, "there is our friend, Mademoiselle Dubarry, a widow."

"To-morrow she will be exiled," said his aged companion. "Adieu ! Monsieur Marat."

THE END.

CPSIA information can be obtained at www.ICGtesting.com
Printed in the USA
BVOW08s1852301213

340519BV00001B/1/A